TREVANIAN

"is primarily interested in giving the reader a good time, and he resoundingly succeeds."

The New York Times Book Review

TREVANIAN

"one hell of a pleasure to read."

The Washington Post

TREVANIAN

"has both wit and intelligence ... something for everybody."

The New York Times

TREVANIAN

"an authentic storyteller."

USA Today

THE EIGER SANCTION

Trevanian

BALLANTINE BOOKS • NEW YORK

Library of Congress Catalog Card Number: 72-84293

ISBN 0-345-31737-8

This edition published by arrangement with
Crown Publishers, Inc.

Printed in Canada

First Ballantine Books Edition: September 1984

MONTREAL:
May 16

Earlier that night, rain had fallen on Boulevard St. Laurent, and there were still triangular pools on the uneven sidewalk. The rain had passed, but it remained cool enough to justify CII operative Wormwood's light tan raincoat. His taste ran more to trench coats, but he dared not wear one, knowing his fellow agents would scoff. Wormwood compromised by turning the collar of his raincoat up and plunging his hands deep into his pockets. One of these hands was clenched around a piece of bubble gum he had received only twenty minutes before from an evil-smelling gnome on the forbidding grounds of Ste. Justine hospital. The gnome had stepped out suddenly from the bushes, giving Wormwood a dreadful start, which he had tried to convert into a gesture of Oriental defense. The image of feline alertness might have been more effective if he had not had the misfortune to back into a rosebush.

Wormwood's step was crisp along the emptying street. He felt uplifted by a sense—not of greatness, to be sure—but of *adequacy*. For once he had not muddled the job. His reflection rippled along a dark shopwindow, and he was not displeased with what he saw. The confident glance and determined stride more than compensated for the sloping shoulders and balding head. Wormwood twisted his palms outward to correct his shoulder slump because someone once told him that the best way to achieve manly posture was to walk with the palms forward. It was most uncomfortable, and it made him walk rather like a penguin, but he did it whenever he thought of it.

He was painfully reminded of his recent encounter with the rosebush, but he discovered that he could relieve his discomfort by nipping the seam of his pants between thumb and forefinger and tugging it away from his buttocks. And this he did from time to time, ignoring the open curiosity of passersby.

He was content. "It's got to be a matter of confidence," he told himself. "I knew I could pull this off, and I pulled it off!" He treasured a theory that one attracted bad luck by anticipating it, and the results of his last several assignments seemed to lend support to the concept. In general, theories did not hold up for Wormwood. To his problem of balding, he had applied the principle of Keep It Short and You'll Keep It Long, and he always wore a crew cut that made him appear less significant than necessary, but his hair continued to fall. For a while, he had clung to the theory that early balding indicated uncommon virility, but personal experience eventually forced him to abandon this hypothesis.

"This time I'm home free, and no screw-up. Six o'clock tomorrow morning I'll be back in the States!"

His fist tightened down on the bubble gum. He could not afford another failure. The men at home base were already referring to him as the "one-man Bay of Pigs."

As he turned left into Lessage Lane, the street seemed empty of sound and people. He took note of this. By the time he had turned south again on St. Dominique, it was so silent that the sound of his footfalls seemed to clip back at him from the facades of unlit, dreary brick buildings. The silence did not disturb him; he whistled as a matter of choice.

"This think-positive bit really scores," he thought jazzily. "Winners win, and that's a fact." Then his round boyish face contracted into concern as he wondered if it was also true that losers lose. He tried to remember his college logic course. "No," he decided at length, "that doesn't necessarily follow. Losers don't always lose. But winners always win!" He felt better for having thought it out.

He was only one block from his third-rate hotel. He could see the damaged sign H TEL in vertical red neon down the street.

"Almost home free."

He recalled CII Training Center instructions always to approach your destination from the opposite side of the street, so he crossed over. He had never fully understood the reason for this rule, beyond simple sneakiness, but it would no more occur to him to demand an explanation than it would to disobey.

St. Dominique's wrought iron streetlamps had not yet fallen prey to urban uglification in the form of lip-blacking mercury lamps, so Wormwood was able to amuse himself by watching his shadow slip out from beneath his feet and grow long before him, until the next lamp assumed domination and projected his shadow, ever shortening, behind him. He was looking over his shoulder, admiring this photic phenomenon, when he ran into the lamppost. Upon recovery, he glanced angrily up and down the street, mentally daring anyone to have seen.

Someone had seen, but Wormwood did not know this, so he glared at the offending lamppost, straightened his shoulders by twisting his palms forward, and crossed to his hotel.

The hall was reassuringly redolent of that medley of mildew, Lysol, and urine characteristic of rundown hotels. According to subsequent reports, Wormwood must have entered the hotel between 11:55 and 11:57. Whatever the exact time, we may be sure he checked it, delighting as always in the luminosity of his watch's dial. He had heard that the phosphorescent material used on watch dials could cause skin cancer, but he felt that he made up for the risk by not smoking. He had developed the habit of checking the time whenever he found himself in a dark place. Otherwise, what was the use of having a watch with a luminous dial? It was probably the time he spent considering this that made the difference between 11:55 and 11:57.

As he climbed the dimly lit staircase with its damp, scrofulous carpet, he reminded himself that "winners win." His spirits sank, however, when he heard the sound of coughing from the room next to his. It was a racking, gagging, disease-laden cough that went on in spasms throughout the night. He had never seen the old man next door, but he hated the cough that kept him awake.

Standing outside his door, he took the bubble gum from his pocket and examined it. "Probably microfilm. And it's probably between the gum and the paper. Where the funnies usually are."

His key turned the slack lock. As he closed the door behind himself, he breathed with relief. "There's no getting around it," he admitted. "Winners— "

But the thought choked in mid-conception. He was not alone in the room.

With a reaction the Training Center would have applauded, he popped the bubble gum, wrapper and all, into his mouth and swallowed it just as the back of his skull was crushed in. The pain was very sharp indeed, but the sound was more terrible. It was akin to biting into crisp celery with your hands over your ears—but more intimate.

He heard the sound of the second blow quite clearly—a liquid crunch—but oddly it did not hurt.

Then something did hurt. He could not see, but he knew they were cutting open his throat. The image of

8

it made him shudder, and he hoped he wouldn't be sick. Then they began on his stomach. Something cold rippled in and out of his stomach. The old man next door coughed and gagged. Wormwood's mind chased the thought that had been arrested by his first fright.

"Winners win," he thought, then he died.

NEW YORK:
June 2

". . . and, if nothing else, this semester should have taught you that there is no significant relationship between art and society—despite the ambitious pronunciamentos of the popular mass-culturists and mass-psychologists who are driven to spiteful inclusions when faced by important fields beyond their ken. The very concepts of 'society' and 'art' are mutually foreign, even antagonistic. The regulations and limitations of . . ."

Dr. Jonathan Hemlock, Professor of Art, spun out his closing lecture to the mass class in Art and Society —a course he abhorred to teach, but one which was the bread and butter of his department. His lecture style was broadly ironic, even insulting, but he was vastly popular with the students, each of whom imagined his neighbor was writhing under Dr. Hemlock's superior disdain. They interpreted his cold acidity as an attractive bitterness in the face of the unfeeling bourgeois world, an epitome of that *Weltschmerz* so precious to the melodramatic soul of the undergraduate.

Hemlock's popularity with students had several unrelated bases. For one, at thirty-seven he was the youngest full professor in the Art faculty. The students assumed therefore that he was a liberal. He was not a liberal, nor was he a conservative, a Tory,

11

a wet, an isolationist or a Fabian. He was interested only in art, and he was indifferent to and bored by such things as politics, student freedom, the war on poverty, the plight of the Negro, war in Indochina, and ecology. But he could not escape his reputation as a "student's professor." For example, when he met classes after an interruption caused by a student revolt, he openly ridiculed the administration for lacking the ability and courage to crush so petty a demonstration. The students read this as a criticism of the establishment, and they admired him more than ever.

". . . after all, there are only Art and non-Art. There are no such things as Black Art, Social Art, Young Art, Pop Art, Mass Art. These are merely fictional rubrics designed to grace, through classification, the crap of inferior daubers who . . ."

Male students who had read of Hemlock's international exploits as a mountain climber were impressed by the image of scholar/athlete, despite the fact that he had not climbed for several years. And young ladies were attracted by his arctic aloofness, which they assumed concealed a passionate and mysterious nature. But he was far from the physical idiom of the romantic type. Slim and of average height, only his precise and wiry movements and his veiled green-gray eyes recommended him to their sexual fantasies.

As one might suspect, Hemlock's popularity did not extend to the faculty. They resented his academic reputation, his refusal to serve on committees, his indifference to their projects and proposals, and his much-publicized student charisma, which term they always inflected so as to make it sound like the opposite of scholarly integrity. His major protection against their snide bile was the rumor that he was independently wealthy and lived in a mansion on Long Island. Typical academic liberals, the faculty were stunned and awkward in the face of wealth, even rumored wealth. There was no way for them to disprove or substantiate these rumors because none of them had ever been invited to his home, nor were they likely to be.

". . . the appreciation of art cannot be learned. It requires special gifts—gifts which you naturally assume you possess because you have been brought up on the belief that you were created equal. What you don't realize is that this only means you are equal to one another . . ."

Speaking automatically, Hemlock allowed his eye to wander over the front row of his amphitheatre classroom. As usual, it was filled with smiling, nodding, mindless girls, their skirts hitched too high and their knees unconsciously apart. It occurred to him that, with their up-turned little smiles and round, empty eyes, they looked like a row of umlaut U's. He never had anything to do with the female students: students, virgins, and drunks he held to be off limits. Opportunities were rife, and he was not enfeebled by free-floating morality; but he was a sporting man, and he ranked the making of these dazzled imbeciles with shining deer and dynamiting fish at the base of the dam.

As always, the bell coincided with the last word of his lecture, so he wrapped up the course by wishing the students a peaceful summer unsullied by creative thought. They applauded, as they always did on last day, and he left quickly.

As he turned the corner of the hall, he encountered a miniskirted co-ed with long black hair and eyes made up like a ballerina's. With excited catches of breath, she told him how much she had enjoyed the course and how she felt closer to Art than ever before.

"How nice."

13

"The problem I have, Dr. Hemlock, is that I have to keep a B average, or I lose my scholarship."

He fished in his pocket for his office keys.

"And I'm afraid I'm not going to do well enough in your final. I mean—I have gained a great *feeling* for Art—but you can't always put feelings down on paper." She looked up at him, gathered her courage, and tried hard to make her eyes terribly meaningful. "So, if there's anything I can do to get a better grade —I mean, I'd be willing to do anything at all. Really."

Hemlock spoke gravely. "You've considered all the implications of that offer?"

She nodded and swallowed, her eyes shining with anticipation.

He lowered his voice confidentially. "Do you have anything planned for tonight?"

She cleared her throat and said no, she didn't.

Hemlock nodded. "Do you live alone?"

"My roommate's gone for the week."

"Good. Then I suggest you break out the books and study your ass off. That's the surest way I know to ensure your grade."

"But . . ."

"Yes?"

She crumpled. "Thank you."

"A pleasure."

She walked slowly down the hall as Hemlock entered his office, humming to himself. He liked the way he had done that. But his euphoria was transient. On his desk he found notes he had written to himself, reminders of bills soon due and past due. University rumors of private wealth were baseless; the truth was that Hemlock spent each year a little more than three times his income from teaching, books, and commissions for appraisal and evaluation. Most of his money—about forty thousand a year—he earned by moonlighting. Jonathan Hemlock worked for the

Search and Sanction Division of CII. He was an assassin.

The telephone buzzed, and he pressed down the flashing button and lifted the receiver. "Yes?"

"Hemlock? Can you talk?" The voice belonged to Clement Pope, Mr. Dragon's first assistant. It was impossible to miss the strained, hushed tone. Pope loved playing spy.

"What can I do for you, Pope?"

"Mr. Dragon wants to see you."

"I assumed as much."

"Can you get over here in twenty minutes?"

"No." Actually, twenty minutes was ample time, but Jonathan loathed the personnel of Search and Sanction. "What about tomorrow?"

"This is top drawer. He wants to see you *now*."

"In an hour, then."

"Look, pal, if I were you I'd get my ass over here as soon as—" but Jonathan had hung up.

For the next half hour Jonathan puttered around his office. When he was sure he would arrive at Dragon's in something over the predicted hour, he called a taxi and left the campus.

As the grimy, ancient elevator tugged him to the top floor of a nondescript Third Avenue office building, Jonathan automatically noted the familiar details: the scaly gray paint on the walls, the annual inspection stamps slapped haphazardly over one another, the Otis recommendation for load limit, twice scratched out and reduced in deference to the aging machinery. He anticipated everything he would see for the next hour, and the anticipation made him uneasy.

The elevator stopped and swayed slackly while the doors clattered open. He stepped out on the top floor of offices, turned left, and pushed open the heavy NO ADMITTANCE fire door leading to a stairwell. Sitting on the dank cement stairs, his tool-box beside him, was a huge Negro workman in coveralls. Jonathan nodded and stepped past him up the steps. One flight up, the stairs came to an end, and he pressed out through another fire door to what had been the loft of the building before CII had installed a suite of offices there. The smell of hospital, so sharply remembered, filled the hallway where an overblown cleaning woman slowly swung a mop back and forth over the same spot. On a bench to one side of a door bearing: "Yurasis Dragon: Consulting Service," sat a beefy man in a business suit, his briefcase in his lap. The man rose to face Jonathan, who resented being touched by these people. All of them, the Negro worker, the cleaning woman, the businessman, were CII guards; and the toolbox, the mop handle, and the briefcase all contained weapons.

Jonathan stood with his legs apart, his hands against the wall, embarrassed and annoyed with himself for being embarrassed, while the businessman's professional hands frisked part of his body and clothing.

"This is new," the businessman said, taking a pen from Jonathan's pocket. "You usually carry one of French make—dark green and gold."

"I lost it."

"I see. Does this have ink in it?"

"It's a pen."

"I'm sorry. I'll either have to keep it for you until you come out, or I can check it out. If I check it out, you'll lose the ink."

"Why don't you just keep it for me."

The businessman stepped aside and allowed Jonathan to enter the office.

"You are eighteen minutes late, Hemlock," Mrs. Cerberus accused as soon as he had closed the door behind him.

"Thereabouts." Jonathan was assailed by the overwhelming hospital smell of the glistening outer office. Mrs. Cerberus was squat and muscular in her starched white nurse's uniform, her coarse gray hair cropped short, her cold eyes pinched into slits by pouches of fat, her sandpaper skin appearing to have been scrubbed daily with sal soda and a currycomb, her thin upper lip aggressively mustachioed.

"You're looking inviting today, Mrs. Cerberus."

"Mr. Dragon does not like to be kept waiting," she snarled.

"Who among us really does?"

"Are you healthy?" she asked without solicitude.

"Reasonably."

"No cold? No known contact with infection?"

"Just the usual lot: pellagra, syphilis, elephantiasis."

She glared at him. "All right, go in." She pressed a button that unlocked the door behind her, then returned to the papers on her desk, not dealing with Jonathan further.

He stepped into the interlock chamber; the door clanged shut behind him; and he stood in the dim red light Mr. Dragon provided as a mezzo-phase from the glittering white of the outer office to the total dark of his own. Jonathan knew he would adapt to the dark more quickly if he closed his eyes. At the same time, he slipped out of his suit coat. The temperature in the interlock and in Mr. Dragon's office was maintained at a constant 87°. The slightest chill, the briefest contact with cold or flu virus would incapacitate Mr. Dragon for months. He had almost no natural resistance to disease.

The door to Mr. Dragon's office clicked and swung open automatically when the cooler air Jonathan had introduced into the interlock had been heated to 87°.

"Come in, Hemlock," Mr. Dragon's metallic voice invited from the darkness beyond.

Jonathan put out his hands and felt his way forward toward a large leather chair he knew to be opposite Mr. Dragon's desk.

"A little to the left, Hemlock."

As he sat, he could dimly make out the sleeve of his white shirt. His eyes were slowly becoming accustomed to the dark.

"Now then. How have you been these past months?"

"Rhetorical."

Dragon laughed his three dry, precise ha's. "True enough. We have been keeping a protective eye on you. I am informed that there is a painting on the black market that has taken your fancy."

"Yes. A Pissarro."

"And so you need money. Ten thousand dollars, if I am not misinformed. A bit dear for personal titillation."

"The painting is priceless."

"Nothing is priceless, Hemlock. The price of this painting will be the life of a man in Montreal. I have never understood your fascination with canvas and crusted pigment. You must instruct me one day."

"It's not a thing you can learn."

"Either you have it or you haven't, eh?"

"You either got it or you ain't."

Dragon sighed. "I guess one has to be born to the idiom." No accent, only a certain exactitude of diction betrayed Dragon's foreign birth. "Still, I must not deride your passion for collecting paintings. Without it, you would need money less often, and we would be deprived of your services." Very slowly, like a photograph in the bottom of a developing tray, the image of Mr. Dragon began to emerge through the dark as Jonathan's eyes dilated. He anticipated the revulsion he would experience.

"Don't let me waste too much of your time, Mr. Dragon."

"Meaning: let's get to the matter at hand." There was disappointment in Dragon's voice. He had taken a perverse liking to Jonathan and would have enjoyed chatting with someone from outside the closed world of international assassination. "Very well, then. One of our men—code call: Wormwood—was killed in Montreal. There were two assailants. Search Division has located one of them. You will sanction this man."

Jonathan smiled at the cryptic jargon of CII, in which "demote maximally" meant purge by killing, "biographic leverage" meant blackmail, "wet work" meant killing, and "sanction" meant counterassassination. His eyes adjusted to the dark, and Dragon's face become dimly visible. The hair was white as silk thread, and kinky, like a sheep's. The features, floating in the retreating gloom, were arid alabaster. Dragon was one of nature's rarest genealogical phenomena: a total albino. This accounted for his sensitivity to light; his eyes and eyelids lacked protective pigment. He had also been born without the ability to produce white corpuscles in sufficient quantity. As a result, he had to be insulated from contact with people who might carry disease. It was also necessary that his blood be totally replaced by massive transfusions each six months. For the half century of his life, Dragon had lived in the dark, without people, and on the blood of others. This existence had not failed to affect his personality.

Jonathan looked at the face, awaiting the emergence of the most disgusting feature. "You say Search has located only *one* of the targets?"

"They are working on the second one. It is my hope that they will have identified him by the time you arrive in Montreal."

"I won't take them both. You know that." Jonathan had made a moral bargain with himself to work for CII only when it was fiscally necessary. He had to be on his guard against sanction assignments being forced on him at other times.

"It may be necessary that you take both assignments, Hemlock."

"Forget it." Jonathan felt his hands grip the arms of his chair. Dragon's eyes were becoming visible. Totally without coloration, they were rabbit pink in the iris and blood red in the pupil. Jonathan glanced away in involuntary disgust.

Dragon was hurt. "Well, well, we shall talk about the second sanction when the time comes."

Dragon smiled thinly. "People seldom come to me with good news."

"This sanction is going to cost you twenty thousand."

"Twice your usual fee? Really, Hemlock!"

"I need ten thousand for the Pissarro. And ten for my house."

"I am not interested in your domestic economy. You need twenty thousand dollars. We normally pay ten thousand for a sanction. There are two sanctions involved here. It seems to work out well."

"I told you I don't intend to do both jobs. I want twenty thousand for one."

"And I am telling you that twenty thousand is more more than the job is worth."

"Send someone else then!" For an instant, Jonathan's voice lost its flat calm.

Dragon was instantly uneasy. Sanction personnel were particularly prone to emotional pressures from their work and dangers, and he was always alert for signs of what he called "tension rot." In the past year, there had been some indications in Jonathan. "Be reasonable, Hemlock. We have no one else available just now. There has been some . . . attrition . . . in the Division."

Jonathan smiled. "I see." After a short silence, "But if you have no one else, you really have no choice. Twenty thousand."

"You are completely without conscience, Hemlock."

"But then, we always knew that." He was alluding to the results of psychological tests taken while serving with Army Intelligence during the Korean War. After re-testing to confirm the unique pattern of response, the chief army psychologist had summarized his findings in singularly unscientific prose:

. . . Considering that his childhood was marked by extreme poverty and violence (three juvenile convictions for assault, each precipitated by his being tormented by other youngsters who resented his extraordinary intelligence and the praise it received from his teachers), and considering the humiliations he underwent at the hands of indifferent relatives after the death of his mother (there is no father of record), certain of his antisocial, antagonistic, annoyingly superior behaviors are understandable, even predictable.

One pattern stands out saliently. The subject has extremely rigid views on the subject of friendship. There is, for him, no greater morality than loyalty, no greater sin than disloyalty. No punishment would be adequate to the task of repaying the person who took advantage of his friendship. And he holds that others are equally bound to his personal code. An educated guess would suggest that his pattern emerges as an overcompensation for feelings of having been abandoned by his parents.

There is a personality warp, unique to my experience and to that of my associates, that impels us to caution those responsibile for the subject. The man lacks normal guilt feelings. He is totally without the nerve of conscience. We have failed to discover any vestige of negative response to sin,

21

crime, sex, or violence. This is not to imply that he is unstable. On the contrary he is, if anything, too stable—too controlled. Abnormally so.

Perhaps he will be viewed as ideal for the purposes of Army Intelligence, but I must report that the subject is, in my view, a personality somehow incomplete. And socially very dangerous.

"So you refuse to take the two sanctions, Hemlock, and you insist on twenty thousand for just one."

"Correct."

For a moment the pink-and-red eyes rested thoughtfully on Jonathan as Dragon rolled a pencil between his palms. Then he laughed his three dry, precise ha's. "All right. You win for now."

Jonathan rose. "I assume I make contact with Search in Montreal?"

"Yes. Search Section Hapleleaf is headed by a Miss Felicity Arce—I assume that is how it is pronounced. She will give you all instructions."

Jonathan slipped on his coat.

"About this second assassin, Hemlock. When Search has located him—"

"I won't need money for another six months."

"But what if *we* should need *you?*"

Jonathan did not answer. He opened the door to the interlock, and Dragon winced at the dim red light.

Blinking back the brilliance of the outer office, Jonathan asked Mrs. Cerberus for the address of Search Section Mapleleaf.

"Here." She thrust a small white card before his eyes and gave him only five seconds to memorize it before replacing it in her file. "Your contact will be Miss Felicity Arce."

"So that really is how it's pronounced. My, my."

LONG ISLAND:
June 2

Now on CII expense account, Jonathan took a cab all the way from Dragon's office to his home on the north shore of Long Island.

A sense of peace and protection descended on him as he closed behind him the heavy oaken door to the vestibule, which he had left unaltered when he converted the church into a dwelling. He passed up through a winding, Gothic-arched stair to the choir loft, now partitioned into a vast bedroom overlooking the body of the house, and a bathroom twenty feet square, in the center of which was a deep Roman pool he used as a bath. While four faucets roared hot water into the pool, filling the room with steam, he undressed, carefully brushed and folded his clothes, and packed his suitcase for Montreal. Then he lowered himself gingerly into the very hot water. He floated about, never allowing himself to think about Montreal. He was without conscience, but he was not without fear. These sanction assignments were accomplished, as difficult mountain climbs once had been, on the highhoned edge of nerve. The luxury of this Roman bath—which had absorbed the profits from a sanction—was more than a sybaritic reaction to the privations of his childhood, it was a necessary adjunct to his uncommon trade.

Dressed in a Japanese robe, he descended from the

choir loft and entered through heavy double doors
the body of his house. The church had been laid out
in classic cruciform, and he had left all the nave as
open living space. One arm of the transept had been
converted to a greenhouse garden, its stained glass
replaced by clear, and a stone pool with a fountain
set in the midst of tropical foliage. The other arm of
the cross was lined with bookshelves and did service
as a library.

He padded barefoot through the stone-floored,
high-vaulted nave. The light from clerestories above
was adequate to his taste for dim cool interiors and
vast unseen space. At night, a switch could be thrown
to illuminate the stained glass from without, sketch-
ing collages of color on the walls. He was particularly
fond of the effect when it rained and the colored light
danced and rippled along the walls.

He opened the gate and mounted two steps to his
bar, where he made himself a martini and sipped
with relish as he rested his elbows back on the bar
and surveyed his house with contented pride.

After a time, he had an urge to be with his paintings, so he descended a curving stone stairwell to the
basement chamber where he kept them. He had
labored evenings for half a year putting in the floor
and walling the room with panels from a Renaissance
Italian palace that had served interim duty in the
grand hall of an oil baron's North Shore mansion.
He locked the door behind him and turned on the
lights. Along the walls leaped out the color of Monet,
Cézanne, Utrillo, Van Gogh, Manet, Seurat, Degas,
Renoir, and Cassatt. He moved around the room
slowly, greeting each of his beloved Impressionists,
loving each for its particular charm and power, and
remembering in each instance the difficulty—often
danger—he had encountered in acquiring it.

The room contained little furniture for its size: a
comfortable divan of no period, a leather pouf with

strap handles so he could drag it along to sit before one picture or another, an open Franklin stove with a supply of dry cedar logs in an Italian chest beside it, and a Bartolomeo Cristofore pianoforte which he played with great precision, if little soul. On the floor was a 1914 Kashan—the only truly perfect oriental. And in a corner, not far from the Franklin stove, was a small desk where he did most of his work. Above the desk and oddly out of keeping with the decor were a dozen photographs attached haphazardly to the wall. They were candid shots of mountain episodes capturing climbers with awkward or boyishly clowning expressions—brave men who could not face a lens without embarrassment which they hid by ludicrous antics. Most of the photographs were of Jonathan and his lifelong climbing companion, Big Ben Bowman, who, before his accident, had bagged most of the major peaks of the world with characteristic lack of finesse. Ben simply battered them down with brute strength and unconquerable will. They had made an odd but effective team: Jonathan the wily tactician, and Big Ben the mountain-busting animal.

Only one of the photographs was of a lowland man. In memory of his sole friendship with a member of the international espionage clique, Jonathan kept a photo in which the late Henri Baq grinned wryly at the camera. Henri Baq, whose death Jonathan would one day avenge.

He sat at his desk and finished the martini. Then he took a small packet from the drawer and filled the bowl of an ornate hookah which he set up on the rug before his Cassatt. He hunched on the leather pouf and smoked, stroking the surface of the canvas with liberated eyes. Then, from nowhere, as it did from time to time, the thought strayed into his mind that he owed his whole style of life—academics, art, his house—to poor Miss Ophel.

Poor Miss Ophel. Sere, fluttering, fragile spinster. Miss Ophel of the sandpaper crotch. He had always thought of her that way, although he had had the good sense to play it shy and grateful when she had visited him in the juvenile home. Miss Ophel lived alone in a monument to Victorian poor taste on the outskirts of Albany. She was the last of the family that had founded its fortune on fertilizer brought down the Erie Canal. But there would be no more Ophels. Such modest maternity as she possessed was squandered on cats and birds and puppies with saccharine nicknames. One day it occurred to her that social work might be diverting—as well as being *useful.* But she lacked the temperament for visiting slums that stank of urine and for patting children's heads that well might have had nits, so she asked her lawyer to keep an eye out for a needy case that had some refinement about it. And the lawyer found Jonathan.

Jonathan was in a detention home at the time, paying for attempting to decrease the surplus population of North Pearl Street by two bantering Irish boys who had assumed that, because Jonathan astounded the teachers of P.S. 5 with his knowledge and celerity of mind, he must be a queer. Jonathan was the smaller boy, but he struck while the others were still saying "Oh, yeah?" and he had not overlooked the ballistic advantage of an eighteen-inch lead pipe he had spied lying in the alley. Bystanders had intervened and saved the Irish boys to banter again, but they would never be handsome men.

When Miss Ophel visited Jonathan she found him to be mild and polite, well informed, and oddly attractive with his gentle eyes and delicate face, and definitely *worthy.* And when she discovered that he was as homeless as her puppies and birds, the thing was settled. Just after his fourteenth birthday, Jonathan took up residence in the Ophel home and, after a series of intelligence and aptitude tests, he faced a parade of tutors who groomed him for university.

Each summer, to broaden his education, she took him to Europe where he discovered a natural aptitude for languages and, most importantly to him, a love for the Alps and for climbing. On the evening of his sixteenth birthday there was a little party, just the two of them and champagne and petits fours. Miss Ophel got a little tipsy, and a little tearful over her empty life, and very affectionate toward Jonathan. She hugged him and kissed him with her dusty lips. Then she hugged him tighter.

By the next morning, she had made up a cute little nickname for it, and almost every evening thereafter she would coyly ask him to do it to her.

The next year, after a battery of tests, Jonathan entered Harvard at the age of seventeen. Shortly before his graduation at nineteen, Miss Ophel died peacefully in her sleep. On the surprisingly small residue of her estate, Jonathan continued his education and took occasional summer trips to Switzerland, where he began to establish his reputation as a climber.

He had taken his undergraduate degree in comparative linguistics cashing in on his logical bent and native gift for language. He might have gone on in that field, but for one of those coincidences that form our lives in spite of our plans.

As a caprice, he took a summer job assisting a professor of Art in the cataloging of artistic orts left over from the confiscation of Nazi troves after the war. The *gratin* of these re-thefts had gone to an American newspaper baron, and the leavings had been given to the university as a sop to the national conscience—a healthy organ that had recently rebounded from the rape of Hiroshima with no apparent damage.

In the course of the cataloging, Jonathan listed one

small oil as "unknown," although the packing slip had assigned it to a minor Italian Renaissance painter. The professor had chided him for the mistake, but Jonathan said it was no error.

"How can you be so sure?" the professor asked, amused.

Jonathan was surprised at the question. He was young and still assumed that teachers knew their fields. "Well, it's obvious. We saw a painting by the same man last week. And this was not painted by the same hand. Just look at it."

The professor was uncomfortable. "How do you know that?"

"Just look at it! Of course, it's possible that the other one was mislabeled. I have no way to know."

An investigation was undertaken, and it developed that Jonathan was correct. One of the paintings had been done by a student of the minor master. The fact had been recorded and had been general knowledge for three hundred years, but it had slipped through the sieve of Art History's memory.

The authorship of a relatively unimportant painting was of less interest to the professor than Jonathan's uncanny ability to detect it. Not even Jonathan could explain the process by which, once he had studied the work of a man, he could recognize any other painting by the same hand. The steps were instant and instinctive, but absolutely sure. He always had trouble with Rubens and his painting factory, and he had to treat Van Gogh as two separate personalities—one before the breakdown and stay at St. Rémy, one after—but in the main his judgments were irrefutable, and before long he became indispensable to major museums and serious collectors.

After schooling, he took a post teaching in New York, and he began publishing. The articles rolled off, and the women rolled through his Twelfth Street apartment, and the months rolled by in a pleasant and pointless existence. Then, one week after his first book came off the press, his friends and fellow citizens decided he was particularly well suited to blocking bullets in Korea.

As it turned out, he was not often called upon to block bullets, and the few that came his way were dispatched by fellow Americans. Because he was intelligent, he was put into Army Intelligence: Sphinx Division. For four wasted years, he defended his nation from the aggressions of the leftist imperialism by uncovering attempts of enterprising American soldiers to flesh out their incomes by sharing Army wealth with the black markets of Japan and Germany. His work required that he travel, and he managed to squander a laudable amount of government time and money on climbing mountains and on collecting data to keep his academic reputation shiny with articles.

After the nation had handily taught the North Koreans their lesson, Jonathan was released to civilian activities, and he took up more or less where he had left off. His life was pleasant and directionless. Teaching was easy and automatic; articles seldom needed and never received the benefit of a second draft; and his social life consisted of lazing about his apartment and making the women he happened to meet, if the seduction could be accomplished with limited effort, as usually it could. But this good life was slowly undermined by the growth of his passion for collecting paintings. His Sphinx work in Europe had brought into his hands a half dozen stolen Impressionists. These first acquisitions kindled in him the unquenchable fire of the collector. Viewing and appreciating were not enough—he had to possess. Channels to underground and black market paintings were open to him through Sphinx contacts, and his unequaled eye prevented him from being cheated. But his income was insufficient to his needs.

For the first time in his life, money became important to him. And at that very juncture, another major need for money appeared. He discovered a magnificent abandoned church on Long Island that he instantly recognized as the ideal home for himself and his paintings.

His pressing need for money, his Sphinx training, and his peculiar psychological makeup, devoid of any sense of guilt—these things combined to make him ripe for Mr. Dragon.

Jonathan sat for a while, deciding where he would hang his Pissarro when he purchased it from the pay for the Montreal sanction. Then he rose lazily, cleaned and put away the hookah, sat at his pianoforte and played a little Handel, then he went to bed.

MONTREAL:
June 5

The high rise apartment complex was typical of middle-class democratic architecture. All of the dwellers could get a glimpse of La Fontaine Park, but none could see it well, and some only after acrobatic excesses from their cramped, cantilevered balconies. The lobby door was a heavy glass panel that hinged eight inches from the edge; there was red commercial wall-to-wall carpet, plastic ferns, a padded self-service elevator, and meaningless escutcheons scattered along the walls.

Jonathan stood in a sterile hallway, awaiting response to the buzzer and glancing with distaste at an embossed Swiss print of a Cézanne designed to lend luxury to the corridor. The door opened and he turned around.

She was physically competent, even lush; but she was hardly gift wrapped. In her tailored suit of tweed, she seemed wrapped for mailing. Thick blond bangs, cheekbones wide, lips full, bust resisting the constriction of the suit jacket, flat stomach, narrow waist, full hips, long legs, tapered ankles. She wore shoes, but he assumed her toes were adequate as well.

"Miss . . .?" he raised his eyebrows to force her to fill in the name because he was still unwilling to rely on the pronunciation.

"Felicity Arce," she said, holding out her hand

hospitably. "Do come in. I've looked forward to meeting you, Hemlock. You're well thought of in the trade, you know."

She stepped aside and he entered. The apartment was consonant with the building: expensive anticlass. When they shook hands, he noticed that her forearm glistened with an abundance of soft golden hair. He knew that to be a good sign.

"Sherry?" she offered.

"Not at this time of night."

"Whiskey?"

"Please."

"Scotch or bourbon."

"Do you have Laphroaig?"

"I'm afraid not."

"Then it doesn't matter."

"Why don't you sit down while I pour it." She walked away to a built-in bar of antiqued white under which lurked a suspicion of pine. Her movements were strong, but sufficiently liquid about the waist. He sat at one end of a sectional divan and turned toward the other, so that it would be downright impolite of her to sit anywhere else. "You know," he commented, "this apartment is monumentally ugly. But my guess is that you are going to be very good."

"Very good?" she asked over her shoulder, pouring whiskey generously.

"When we make love. A little more water, please."

"Like so?"

"Close enough."

She smiled and shook her head as she returned with the drink. "We have other things to do than make love, Hemlock." But she sat on the divan as he directed her to with a wave of his hand.

He sipped. "We have time for both. But of course it's up to you. Think about it for a while. And meanwhile, tell me what I have to know about this sanction."

Miss Arce looked up at the ceiling and closed her eyes for a second, collecting her thoughts. "The man they killed was code call: Wormwood—not much of a record."

"What was he doing in Canada?"

"I have no idea. Something for CII home base. It's really none of our business anyway."

"No, I suppose not." Jonathan held out his hand and she took it with a slight greeting pressure of the fingers. "Go on."

"Well, Wormwood was hit in a small hotel on Casgrain Avenue—hm-m-m, that's nice. Do you know that part of town?"

"No." He continued stroking the inside of her wrist.

"Fortunately, CII home base was covering him with a backup man. He was in the next room, and he overheard the hit. As soon as the two assassins left, he went into Wormwood's room and made a standard strip of the body. Then he contacted Search and Sanction immediately. Mr. Dragon got me right on it."

Jonathan kissed her gently. "You're telling me that this backup man just sat next door and let this Wormwood get it?"

"Another whiskey?"

"No, thank you." He stood up and drew her after him. Where is it? Through there?"

"The bedroom? Yes." She followed. "You must know how they work, Hemlock. The backup man's assignment is to observe and report, not to interfere. Anyway, it seems they were testing a new device."

"Oh? What kind of device? I'm sorry, dear. These little hooks always confuse me."

"Here, I'll do it. They've always had a problem covering the movements and sound of the backup man when they stake him out in the next room. Now

33

they've hit on the idea of having him *make* noise, rather than trying to keep him quiet—"

"Good God! Do you keep these sheets in the refrigerator?"

"That's silk for you. What they're experimenting with is a tape recording of the sound of an old man's coughing—playing it day and night, advertising the presence of someone in the next room, but someone no one would imagine is an agent. Oh! I'm very sensitive there. It tickles now, but it won't later. Isn't that clever?"

"The coughing old man? Oh, yes, clever."

"Well, as soon as Mr. Dragon sent me the B-3611 form I got to work. It was pretty easy. The outside is particularly good for me."

"Yes, I sensed that."

"It seems this Wormwood wasn't a total incompetent. He wounded one of the two men. The backup agent saw them leave the hotel, and even from the window he could tell that one of them was limping. The other one—the one who wasn't hurt—must have been panicked. He ran—Oh, that is beautiful!—He ran into a lamppost across from the hotel. When he stopped to recover, the backup man recognized him. The rest was—agh! Agha!—the rest was easy."

"What's the mark's name?"

"Kruger. Garcia Kruger. A very bad type."

"You're kidding about the name."

"I never kid about names. Oh-a-ar! Graggah!"

"What do you mean, he's a bad type?"

"The way he got Wormwood. He—Oh, God! He . . . He . . ."

"Press down with the soles of your feet!"

"All right. Wormwood swallowed a pellet he was carrying. Kruger went after it with a knife. Throat and stomach. Oh! Adagrah! Oh, yes . . . yes . . ."

"Read much Joyce?"

She forced words out through a tight jaw, small

squeaks of air escaping from her contracted throat. "No, Agh! Why do you ask?"

"Nothing important. What about the other man?"

"The one who limped? Don't know yet. Not a professional, we're sure of that."

"How do you know he's not a professional?"

"He got sick while Kruger was working on Wormwood. Threw up on the floor. Ogha? Ogah? Arah-ahagh-ga-gahg!" She arched her strong back and lifted him off the bed. He joined her in release.

For a time there were soft caresses and gentle pelvic adjustments.

"You know, Hemlock," her voice was soft, relaxed, and a little graveled from effort. "You really have magnificent eyes. They're rather tragicomic eyes."

He expected this. They always talked about his eyes afterwards.

Some time later, he sat on the edge of the tub, holding up a rubber sac in an unsuccessful attempt to allow water to seek its own level. Part of his charm lay in these little attentions.

"I've been thinking about your gun, Hemlock."

"What about it?"

"The information sent up by Mr. Dragon indicated you used a large caliber."

"True. I have to. I'm not much of a shot. Finished?"

"Uh-huh."

They dressed and had another whiskey in the sterile living room. In detail, Miss Arce went over the daily habits and routine of Garcia Kruger, answering questions raised by Jonathan. She ended with: "It's all in the tout we amassed. You should study it, then destroy it. And here's your gun." She gave him a bulky brown package. "Will I see you again?"

"Would that be wise?"

"I suppose not. May I tell you something? Just as I—well, at the top—can you imagine what ran through my mind?"

"No."

"I remembered that you were a killer."

"And that bothered you?"

"Oh, no! Quite the contrary. Isn't that odd?"

"It's rather common, actually." He collected the tout and the gun and walked to the door. She followed him, anticipating a final kiss, insensitive to his postcoitus frost.

"Thank you," she said softly, "for the advice about pushing down with the feet. It certainly helps."

"I like to leave people a little richer for having known me."

She held out her hand and he took it. "You really have magnificent eyes, Hemlock. I'm very glad you came."

"Good of you to have me."

In the hall, as he waited for the elevator, he felt pleased about the evening. It had been simple, uncomplicated, and temporarily satisfying: like urination. And that was the way he preferred his lovemaking to be.

In general, his sex life was no more heroic than, say, the daydreams of the average bachelor. But romantic activity tended to peak when he was on sanction assignments. For one thing, opportunities abounded at such times. For another, his sexual appetite was whetted by the danger he faced, perhaps a microcosmic instance of that perverse force of nature that inflates birthrates during wartime.

Once in bed, he was really very good. His mechanical competence was not a matter of plumbing, in which respect he differed little from the mass of men. Nor, as we have seen, was it a result of wooing and careful preparation. It was, instead, a function of his remarkable staying powers and his rich experience.

Of the experience, it suffices to say that his control was seldom betrayed by the tickle of curiosity. After Ankara, and Osaka, and Naples, there were no postures, no ballistic nuances foreign to him. And there were only two kinds of women with whom he had never had experience: Australian Abos and Eskimos. And neither of these ethnic gaps was he eager to fill, for reasons of olfactory sensitivity.

But the more significant contribution to his epic endurance was tactile. Jonathan felt nothing when he made love. That is to say, he had never experienced that local physical ecstasy we associate with climax. To be sure, his biological factory produced semen regularly, and an overabundance disturbed him, interfered with his sleep, distracted him from work. So he knew great relief at the moment of discharge. But his relief was a termination of discomfort, not an achievement of pleasure.

So he was more to be pitied for the basis of his remarkable control than he was to be envied for the competence it granted him.

MONTREAL:
June 9

He finished his smoke then flushed the contents of his ashtray down the toilet. He sat fully clothed on his bed and did a calming unit, breathing deeply and regularly, softening in turn every muscle in his body, his fingertips pressed lightly together and his concentration focused on his crossed thumbs. The dim of his hotel room was lacerated by lances of sunlight through the partially closed blinds. Motes of dust hovered in the shafts of light.

He had passed the morning rehearsing Garcia Kruger's daily routine for a final time before he destroyed the Search tout. Then he had visited two art galleries, strolling with deliberate step, pressing his metabolic rate down to prepare himself for the task before him.

When his body and mind were completely ready, he rose slowly from bed and opened the top drawer of a chest to take out a brown bag folded over at the top like a lunch bag, but containing the silenced revolver Miss Arce had given him. He slipped an identical bag, empty and folded flat, into his coat pocket, then he left his room.

Kruger's office was on a narrow, dirty street just off St. Jacques, near the Bonaventure Freight Station. "Cuban Import and Export—Garcia Kruger."

An ostentatious name for a company that received and sent no shipments, and a ludicrous name for the man, the product of some random sperm a German sailor had left for safekeeping in the womb of a Latin lady. Just in front of the building some children were playing *cache-cache* among the stoops. In fleeing from a pursuer, a ragged gamin with a hungry face and aerodynamic ears bumped into Jonathan, who held onto him to keep him from falling. The boy was surpised and embarrassed, so he scowled to conceal his discomfort.

"I'm afraid you've had it, kid," Jonathan said in French. "Running into a Protestant citizen is an act of FLQ terrorism. What's your name?"

The boy read game-playing in Jonathan's mock-tough voice, and he went along with it. "Jacques," he said, with the broad *au* diphthong of Quebec horsetalk.

Jonathan mimed a notebook in the palm of his hand. "J-a-c-q-u-e-s. Right! If it happens again, I'll turn you over to Elliot."

After an instant of indecision, the boy grinned at Jonathan and ran off to continue his play.

Garcia Kruger shared a second floor with a dentist and a dance instructor. The lower halves of their windows were painted over with advertisements. Just inside the entrance, Jonathan found the cardboard box he had instructed Miss Arce to have left for him. He carried it up the worn wooden stairs, the loose strips of cross-hatched metal squeaking under his foot. The corridor was cool and silent after the brilliant, cacophonous street. Both the dentist and the dance instructor had gone home for the day, but Jonathan knew from the tout that he would find Kruger in.

His knock was answered by, "Who's there?" from an irritated voice within.

"I'm looking for Dr. Fouchet," Jonathan said in

a valid imitation of the smiling/stupid voice of a salesman.

The door opened a few inches and Kruger looked out over a latch chain. He was tall, cadaverous and balding, with a day's growth on his cheeks and dots of white mucus in the corners of his eyes. His shirt was crumpled blue and white stripe, wet in irregular crescents under the arms. And on his forehead there there was a scabbed-over bruise, doubtless from his contact with the lamppost.

Jonathan looked awkward and incompetent with the cardboard box in his arms and the brown paper bag balanced on top and held under his chin. "Hi. I'm Ed Benson? Arlington Supplies?"

Kruger told him the dentist was gone for the day, and started to close the door. Jonathan quickly explained that he had promised to bring Dr. Fouchet a sample of their new dental floss, but he had been delayed ". . . and not by business either," he added, winking.

Kruger leered knowingly, and from his teeth it was evident that he was only casually acquainted with the dentist. But his tone was not civil. "I told you he was out."

Jonathan shrugged. "Well, if he's out, he's out." He started to turn away. Then, as though an idea had struck him, "Say! I could leave the sample with you, sir. And you could give it to Dr. Fouchet in the morning." He produced his most disarming smile. "It would sure get my ass out of the sling."

Grudgingly, Kruger said he would take it. Jonathan started to hand him the box, but the latch chain was in the way. Kruger closed the door with an angry snap, undid the chain, and opened it again. As Jonthan entered, he babbled about how hot it was on the street, but how it wasn't so much the heat as the humidity that got you down. Kruger grunted and turned away to look out the window, leaving Jonathan to put the box down wherever he could in the littered office.

Thunt! The sound of a silenced thirty-eight firing through a paper bag.

Kruger was spun around and slammed into the corner between two windows on which "Cuban Imports" was written backward. He stared at Jonathan with total astonishment.

Jonathan watched him narrowly, expecting a movement toward him.

Kruger lifted his hands, palms up, with a touching gesture of "Why?"

Jonathan considered firing again.

For two terribly long seconds, Kruger remained there, as though nailed to the wall.

Jonathan began to smart with discomfort. "Oh, come on!"

And Kruger slid slowly down the wall as death dimmed his eyes and set them in an infinity focus, the repulsive white dots of mucus still visible. Never having met Kruger before today, and not having any apparent motive, Jonathan had no fear of identification. He folded up the ruptured bag and placed it and the gun inside the fresh bag he had brought along.

People never carry guns in brown paper bags.

Outside in the glare of the street, the children still played around the stoops. Little Jacques saw Jonathan emerge from Kruger's building, and he waved from across the street. Jonathan made a gun with his finger and shot at the boy, who threw up his hands and fell to the pavement in a histrionic facsimile of anguish. They both laughed.

MONTREAL/NEW YORK/LONG ISLAND: June 10

While he waited for the plane to taxi off, Jonathan laid out his briefcase and papers on the seat beside him and began taking notes for the long-overdue article on "Toulouse-Lautrec: A Social Conscience." He had promised it to the editors of an art journal with a liberal bent. He could spread out in comfort because it was his practice, when on CII expense account, to purchase two adjacent seats to insulate himself against unwanted conversation. On this occasion, the extravagance may have been unnecessary, as the first-class compartment was nearly empty.

His line of thought was severed by the paternal and plebeian voice of the pilot assuring him that he knew where they were going and at what altitude they would fly. His interest in the Lautrec article was too fragile to survive the interruption, so he began glancing through a book he had promised to review. It was a study of *Tilman-Riemanschneider: The Man and His Times.* Jonathan was acquainted with the author and he knew the book would be a compromise between academic and general readerships—an alternation between the turgid and the cute. Nevertheless, he intended to give it a handsome review in obedience to his theory that the surest way to maintain position at the top of the field was to advance and support men of clearly inferior capacities.

He sensed the brush of her perfume, a spicy but light fragrance that he recalls to this day, suddenly and when he least wants to.

"Both of these seats are yours?" she asked.

He nodded without looking up from his work. To his great disappointment, he had caught a glimpse of a uniform out of the tail of his eye, and he rejected her, realizing that stewardesses, like nurses, were something a man made do with in strange towns when there was not time to seek women.

"Veblen had a phrase for that." Her voice was like a flow of warm honey.

Surprised by erudition in a stewardess, he closed the book on his lap and looked up into the calm, amused eyes. Soft brown with harlequin flecks of gold. "The phrase would apply equally to Mimi in the last act."

She laughed lightly: strong white teeth and slightly petulant lips. Then she checked his name off a list on a clipboard, and walked aft to deal with other passengers. With unabashed curiosity, he examined her taut bottom with its characteristic African shape that lifts black women to so convenient an angle. Then he sighed and shook his head. He returned to the Riemanschneider study, but his eyes moved over the pages without the words getting to his brain. Later he took notes; then he dozed.

"Shit?" she asked, her lips close to his ear.

He woke and turned his head to look up at her. "Pardon me?" The movement brought her bust to within three inches of his nose, but he kept his eyes on hers.

She laughed—again the harlequin flecks of gold in the brown eyes—and sat back on the armrest.

"You *did* begin this conversation by saying 'shit,' didn't you? he asked.

"No. I didn't say it. I asked it."

"Does that go along with coffee, tea, and milk?"

"Only on our competitors' lines. I was reading over your shoulder, and I saw the word 'shit' with two exclamation points on your notepad. So I asked."

"Ah. It was a comment on the content of this book I'm reviewing."

"A study of scatology?"

"No. A shoddy piece of research obfuscated by crepuscular logic and involute style."

She grinned. "I can stand crepuscular logic, but involute style really makes my ass tired."

Jonathan enjoyed the raised oriental corners of her eyes in which a hint of derision lurked. "I refuse to believe you're a stewardess."

"As in: What's a girl like you doing in . . .? Actually, I'm not a stewardess at all. I'm a high-jacker in drag."

"That's reassuring. What's your name?"

"Jemima."

"Stop it."

"I'm not putting you on. That's really my name. Jemima Brown. My mother was hooked on ethnic lore."

"Have it your way. So long as we both admit that it's clearly too much for a black girl to have a name like that."

"I don't know. People don't forget you if your name is Jemima." She adjusted her perch on the arm-rest, and the skirt slipped up.

Jonathan concentrated on not noticing. "I doubt that men would forget you easily if your name was Fred."

"Goodness me, Dr. Hemlock! Are you the kind of man who tries to pick up stewardesses?"

"Not normally, but I'm coming around to it. How did you know my name?"

She became serious and confidential. "It's this mystic thing I have with names. A gift of sorts. I look at a person carefully. Then I concentrate. Then I check the passenger list. And *voilà!* The name just comes to me."

"All right. What do people call you when they're not hooked on ethnic lore?"

"Jem. Only they spell it like the jewel kind of gem." A soft gong caused her to look up. "We're coming in. You'll have to fasten your safety belt." Then she moved aft to deal with the less interesting passengers.

He would have liked to ask her out to dinner or something. But the moment had been lost, and there is no social sin like poor timing. So he sighed and turned his attention to the tilted and toylike picture of New York beyond the window.

He saw Jemima briefly in JFK terminal. While he was hailing a taxi, she passed with two other stewardesses, the three walking quickly and in step, and he remembered his general dislike of the ilk. It would not be accurate to say that he put her out of his mind during the long drive home to the North Shore, but he was able to tuck her away into a defocused corner of his consciousness. It was oddly comforting to know she existed out there—like having a little something keeping warm on the back of the stove.

Jonathan soaked in the steaming water of his Roman bath, the tension of the past few days slowly dissolving, the cords of his neck unknotting, the tightness behind his eyes and in his jaw muscles melting reluctantly. But the knot of fear remained in his stomach.

A martini at his bar; a pipe in the basement gallery;

and he found himself rummaging around in the kitchen for something to eat. His search was rewarded with some Danish biscuits, a jar of peanut butter, a small tin of kimchee, and a split of champagne. This gastronomic holocaust he carried to the wing of the transept he had converted into a greenhouse garden, and there he sat beside the plashing pool, lulled by the sound of the water and the brush of warm sunlight.

Little drops of perspiration tingled on his back as he began to doze, the vast peace of his house flowing over him.

Then suddenly he snapped up—an image of surprised eyes with white dots of mucus had chased him out of a dream. He was nauseated.

Getting too old for this, he complained. How did I ever get into it?

Three weeks after the discovery of the abandoned church had added to his need for money, he had found himself in Brussels attending a convention and squandering Ford Foundation money. Late one wet and blustery night, a CII agent dropped into his hotel room and, after beating about the bush, asked him to do a service for his country. Recovering from a good laugh, Jonathan asked for a fuller explanation. The task was fairly simple for a man with Sphinx training: they wanted him to slip an envelope into the briefcase of an Italian delegate to the convention. It is difficult to say why he agreed to the thing. He was bored, to be sure, and the hint of fiscal return came at a time when he had just located his first Monet. But there was also the fact that the Italian had recently had the effrontery to suggest that he knew almost as much about the Impressionists as Jonathan.

At all events, he did the thing. He never knew what was in the envelope, but he later heard that the

Italian had been picked up by agents of his own government and imprisoned for conspiracy.

When he returned to New York, he found an envelope waiting for him with two thousand dollars in it. For expenses, the note had said.

In the ensuing months, he performed three similar messenger jobs for CII and received the same liberal pay. He was able to buy one painting and several sketches, but the church was still beyond his means. He feared that someone else would buy his home—he already thought of it as his. The danger of this was really rather remote. Most of the Long Island religious groups were abandoning traditional churches in favor of A-frame redwood boxes more suited to their use of God.

The climax of this work—a testing period, he discovered later—came in Paris where he was passing the Christmas vacation advising a Texas museum on purchases—attempting to convince them that small paintings could be as valuable as big ones. CII set up an assignment, a simple matter of introducing damaging material into the notebooks of a French government official. Unfortunately, the mark walked in while Jonathan was at work. The ensuing battle went badly at first. As the pair grappled and wrestled around the room, Jonathan was distracted by his attempt to protect a Limoges shepherdess of rare beauty which was in constant danger of being knocked from its fragile table. Twice he released his hold on the Frenchman to catch it as it toppled, and twice his adversary took the opportunity to belabor his back and shoulders with his walking stick. For many minutes the struggle continued. Then suddenly the Frenchman had the statuette in his hand and he hurled it at Jonathan. With shock and fury at the wanton destruction of a thing of beauty, Jonathan saw it shatter against a marble fireplace. He roared with rage and drove the heel of his hand into the rib cage just below the heart. Death was instantaneous.

Later that night Jonathan sat near the window of a café on the Place St. Georges, watching snow swirl around scuttling passersby. He was surprised to recognize that the only thing he felt about the episode —other than the bruises—was a deep regret over the Limoges shepherdess. But one thing he decided irrevocably: he would never again work for CII.

Late one afternoon ,shortly after the beginning of the second semester, he was interrupted in his office work by a visit from Clement Pope. His dislike for this officious flunkey was immediate and enduring.

After Pope had cautiously closed the office door, checked into the cubicle reserved for Jonathan's assistants, and glanced out the windows to the snow-dappled campus, he said meaningfully, "I'm from CII. SS Division."

Jonathan scarcely glanced up from his papers. "I'm sorry, Mr. Pope. Working for you people no longer amuses me."

"SS stands for Search and Sanction. You've heard of us?"

"No."

Pope was pleased. "Our security is the tightest. That's why nobody has heard of us."

"I'm sure your reputation is deserved. Now, I'm busy."

"You don't have to worry about that Frog, buddy-boy. Our people in Paris covered it up." He sat on the edge of the desk and paged through the first papers he found there.

Jonathan's stomach tightened. "Get out of here."

Pope laughed. "You really expect me to walk out that door, pal?"

Jonathan judged the distance betwen them. "Either the door or the window. And we're four stories up." His gentle, disarming smile came on automatically.

"Listen, pal—"

"And get your ass off my desk."

"Look, buddy—"

"And don't call me 'buddy' or 'pal.'"

"Man, if I weren't under orders . . ." Pope flexed his shoulders and considered the situation for a second, then he rose from the desk. "Mr. Dragon wants to talk to you." Then, to save face, he added, "And right now!"

Jonathan walked to the corner of his office and drew himself a cup of coffee from the urn. "Who is this Mr. Dragon?"

"My superior."

"That doesn't narrow the field much, does it."

"He wants to talk to you."

"So you said." Jonathan set the cup down. "All right. I'll make an appointment for him."

"To come here? That's funny!"

"Is it?"

"Yeah." Pope frowned and made a decision. "Here, read this, pal." He drew an envelope from his coat pocket and handed it to Jonathan.

Dear Dr. Hemlock:

If you are reading this, my man has already failed to persuade you by sheer force of personality. And I am not suprised. Naturally, I should have come to see you in person, but I don't get about well, and I am most pressed for time.

I have a proposition for you that will demand very little of your time and which can net you upwards of thirty thousand dollars per annum, tax free. I believe a stipend like this would allow you to purchase the church on Long Island you have been yearning for, and it might even permit you to add to your illegal collection of paintings.

Obviously, I am attempting to impress you with my knowledge of your life and secrets, and I do so hope I have succeeded.

If you are interested, please accompany Mr. Pope to my office where you shall meet . . .

Your Obedient Servant,
Yurasis Dragon

Jonathan finished the letter and replaced it thoughtfully in its envelope.

"Well?" Pope asked. "What do you say, pal?"

Jonathan smiled at him as he rose and crossed the room. Pope was smiling in return when the backhand slap knocked him off balance.

"I told you not to call me 'pal.' Dr. Hemlock will do just fine."

Tears of anger and smart stood in Pope's eyes, but he controlled himself. "Are you coming with me?"

Jonathan tossed the letter onto his desk. "Yes, I think I shall."

Before they left, Pope took the letter and put it in his pocket. "Mr. Dragon's name appears on paper nowhere in the United States," he explained. "Matter of fact, I don't remember him writing a letter to anyone before."

"So?"

"That ought to impress you."

"Evidently I impress Mr. Dragon."

Jonathan groaned and woke up. The sunlight had gone, and the greenhouse garden was filled with a gray, inhospitable light. He rose and stretched the stiffness out of his back. Evening was bringing leaden skies from the ocean. Outside, the chartreuse undersides of leaves glowed dimly in the still air. The forevoice of thunder predicted a heavy rain.

He padded into the kitchen. He always looked forward to rain, and he prepared to receive it. When, some minutes later, the storm rolled over the church, he was enthroned in a huge padded chair, a heavy book in his lap and a pot of chocolate on the table beside him. Beyond the pool of light in which he read, dim patterns of yellow, red, and green rippled over the walls as the rain coursed down the stained glass windows. Occasionally, the forms within the room brightened and danced to flashes of lightning. Hard-bodied rain rattled on the lead roof; and wind screamed around corners.

For the first time, he went through the ritual of the ancient elevator in the Third Avenue office building, of the disguised guards outside Dragon's office, of the ugly and hygienic Miss Cerberus, of the dim red light and superheated interlock chamber.

His eyes slowly irised open, discovering misty forms. And for the first time Dragon's bloodred eyes emerged to shock and sicken him.

"You find my appearance disturbing, Hemlock?" Dragon asked in his atonic, cupric voice. "Personally, I've come to terms with it. The affliction is most rare —something of a distinction. Genetic indispositions like these indicate some rather special circumstances of breeding. I fancy the Hapsburgs took a similar pride in their hemophilia." The dry skin around Dragon's eyes crinkled up in a smile, and he laughed his three arid ha's.

The parched, metallic voice, the unreal surroundings, and the steady gaze of those scarlet eyes made Jonathan want this interview to end. "Do you have anything against coming to the point?"

"I don't mean to draw this chat out unduly, but I have so little opportunity to chat with men of intelligence."

"Yes, I met your Mr. Pope."

"He is loyal and obedient."

"What else can he be?"

Dragon was silent for a moment. "Well, to work. We have made a bid on an abandoned Gothic church on Long Island. You know the one I mean. It is our intention to have it torn down and to convert the grounds into a training area for our personnel. How do you feel about that, Hemlock?"

"Go on."

"If you join us, we shall withdraw our bid, and you will receive a sufficient advance in salary to make a down payment. But before I go on, tell me something. What was your reaction to killing that French fellow who broke the statuette?"

In truth, Jonathan had not even thought about the affair since the morning after it happened. He told Dragon this.

"Grand. Just grand. That confirms the Sphinx psychological report on you. No feelings of guilt whatsoever! You are to be envied."

"How did you know about the statuette?"

"We took telephoto motion pictures from the top of a nearby building."

"Your cameraman just happened to be up there."

Dragon laughed his three dry ha's. "Surely you don't imagine the Frenchman walked in on you by coincidence?"

"I could have been killed."

"True. And that would have been regrettable. But we had to know how you reacted under pressure before we felt free to make this handsome offer."

"What exactly do you want me to do?"

"We call it 'sanctioning.' "

"What do other people call it?"

"Assassination." Dragon was disappointed when the word dropped without rippling Jonathan's exterior. "Actually, Hemlock, it's not so vicious as it sounds to the virgin ear. We kill only those who have killed CII agents in the performance of their duties. Our retribution is the only defense the poor fellows have. Allow me to give you some background on our organization while you are making up your mind to join us. Search and Sanction . . ."

CII came into being after the Second World War as an anode organization for collecting the many bureaus, agencies, divisions and cells engaged in intelligence and espionage during that conflict. There is no evidence that these groups contributed to the outcome of the war, but it has been claimed that they interfered less than did their German counterparts, principally because they were less efficient and their errors were, therefore, less telling.

The government realized the inadvisability of dumping onto the civilian population the social misfits and psychological mutants that collect in the paramilitary slime of spy and counterspy, but something had to be done with the one hundred and two organizations that had flourished like fungus. The Communists were clearly devoted to the game of steal-the-papers-and-photograph-something; so, with a kind of ambitious me-too-ism, our elected representatives brought into being the bulky administrative golem of the CII.

The news media refer to CII as "Central Intelligence Institute." This is a result of creative back-thinking. Actually, CII is not a set of initials; it is a number, the Roman reading of the 102 smaller organizations out of which the department was formed.

Within two years, CII had become a political fact of alarming proportions. Their networks spread within and without the nation, and the information they collected concerning the sexual peculiarities and financial machinations of many of our major political figures made the organization totally untouchable and autonomous. It became the practice of CII to inform the President after the fact.

Within four years, CII had made our espionage system the laughingstock of Europe, had aggravated the image of the American abroad, had brought us to the brink of war on three occasions, and had amassed so vast a collection of trivial and private information that two computer systems had to be housed in their underground headquarters in Washington—one to retrieve fragments of data, the second to operate the first.

A bureaucratic malignancy out of control, the organization continued to grow in power and personnel. Then the expansion unexpectedly tapered off and stopped. CII computers informed its leaders of a remarkable fact: its losses of personnel abroad were just breaking even with its ambitious recruiting operations at home. A team of analysts from Information Limited was brought in to study the astonishing attrition. They discovered that 36 percent of the losses were due to defection; 27 percent were caused by mishandling of punched computer cards (which losses they advised CII to accept because it was easier to write the men off than to reorganize Payroll and Personnel Division); 4 percent of the losses were attributed to inadequate training in the handling of explosives; and 2 percent were simply "lost"—victims of European railroad schedules.

The remaining 31 percent had been assassinated. Loss through assassination presented very special problems. Because CII men worked in foreign countries without invitation, and often to the detriment of the established governments, they had no recourse to official protection. Organization men to the core, the CII heads decided that another Division must be established to combat the problem. They relied on their computers to find the ideal man to head the new arm, and the card that survived the final sorting bore the name: Yurasis Dragon. In order to bring Mr. Dragon to the United States, it was necessary to absolve him of accusations lodged at the War Crimes Tribunal concerning certain genocidal peccadillos, but CII considered him worth the effort.

The new division was called Search and Sanction —or the SS. The in-house slang name, Sweat Shop, is based on the initials and a back formation corruption of "wet shop," in which "wet work"—killing—is the primary function. The Search Division handled the task of discovering those responsible for the assassination of a CII agent. Sanction Division punished the offenders with death.

It was typical of Dragon's sense of the dramatic that the personnel of Sanction all carried code names based on poisons. "Wormwood" had been a Sanction courier. And there was a beautiful Eurasian woman who always made love to the target (of either sex) before killing. Her code name was Belladonna. Dragon never assigned Jonathan a code name. He considered it providential that he already bore a name appropriate to a scholar: Hemlock, the poison of Socrates.

Dragon gave a glossed and romantic version of these facts to Jonathan. "Are you with us, Hemlock?"

"If I refuse?"

"I wouldn't have brought you here had I considered that likely. If you refuse, the church you have set your heart on will be demolished, and your personal freedom will be in jeopardy."

"How so?"

"We know about the paintings you have collected. And duty would demand that we report their existence, unless, of course, doing so would deprive us of a trusted and useful associate." The carmine eyes flickered under cotton puff eyebrows. "Are you with us?"

Jonathan experienced a plunging vertigo as he nodded over the book in his lap. He caught his breath and blinked down at the unremembered page. The chocolate had cooled and a tan skin had formed over it. The thunder and wind had passed over, leaving only the regular, soporific rattle of rain against the stained glass window. He rose, turned off the reading light, and walked with the certainty of custom through the dark nave. Still weary after a day of lazing, he rested for a time in his vast sixteenth-century bed, looking out past the rail of the choir loft to the dimly rippling colored windows, letting his aural attention stray, tuning in and and out the sound of the rain.

The Montreal tension was still a knot in his stomach. The first layers of sleep closed over him gently, only to be harshly dissipated when he jolted upright in fear. He tried to hold any image before his mind to cover the white dots of mucus. And he found himself concentrating on harlequin flecks in warm brown eyes.

Suddenly he was awake and sick. He had passively fought it all day, but he could no longer. After vomiting, he lay quite nude on the cold tiles of his bathroom floor for more than an hour, putting his mind back together.

Then he returned to bed, and to the image of the harlequin flecks.

LONG ISLAND:
June 11

Jonathan's rise to consciousness was neither crisp nor lucid. He came up through turgid layers of discomfort. Dream remnants were mixed with intruding reality. In either the reality or the dream, someone was trying to take his jewels from him—family jewels, they were. No. No, Gems.

His groin tingled. He brought the room into focus through defensive slits. "Oh, no!" he croaked. "What the hell are you doing, Cherry?"

"Good morning, Jonathan," she said cheerily. "Did that tickle?"

He groaned and turned over on his stomach.

Cherry, dressed only in her tennis shorts, slipped under the sheet with him, her lips touching his ear. "Nibble, nibble, nibble," she said, and did.

"Go away," he muffled into his pillow. "If you don't leave me alone, I'll . . ." He could think of no appropriate punishment, so he groaned.

"What will you do?" she asked brightly. "Rape me? You know, I've been thinking about rape a lot lately. It's not a good thing because it doesn't give the couple a chance to communicate on an interhuman level. But it has one advantage over masturbation. It isn't so lonely. You know what I mean? Well, if you're bent on raping me, I guess I'll have to take it

59

like a woman." And she spun over and threw her arms and legs out, like St. Andrew crucified.

"Oh, for Christ's sake, Cherry! I ought to spank your ass."

She was instantly up on one elbow, speaking with serious concern. "I never suspected you were a sadist, Jonathan. But I guess it's the duty of a woman in love to satisfy the sexual peculiarities of her man."

"You're not a woman in love. You're a woman in heat. But all right! You win! I'm getting up. Why don't you go down and make me a cup of coffee."

"It's right there beside you, impetuous lover. I made it before I came up." There was a tray with a coffee pot and two cups on the bedside table. She arranged his pillows as he pulled himself to a sitting position, then she poured out his coffee and passed him the cup, which he had to struggle to balance when she climbed back into bed and sat beside him, their shoulders and hips touching, her leg over his. Jonathan sensed that the major league sex play was over for the moment, but she was still nude to the navel and her bikini tan gave her white breasts the advantage of contrast against the soft copper of the rest of her.

"Hey, Jonathan?" she said earnestly, as she looked into the bottom of her coffee cup, "let me ask you something. It's true, isn't it, that the early morning would be about the best time for me to get at you. It's true, isn't it, that men often wake up with erections."

"That usually means they have to piss," he growled into his cup.

She digested this bit of information in silence. "Nature is wasteful," she commented sadly. Then her spirits bounced back. "But never mind! Sooner or later, I'll catch you at an unguarded moment. Then *bam!*"

"Bam?"

"Not very onomatopoetic, I guess."

"Let's hope not."

She was withdrawn for a moment, then she turned to him and asked, "It isn't *me,* is it? I mean, if I weren't a virgin you'd take me, wouldn't you?"

He locked his fingers behind his head and stretched all the way to his pointed toes. "Certainly. In an instant. Bam."

"Because," she pursued, "I'm really fairly pretty, and I'm filthy rich, and my bod's not bad." She paused for a complimentary comment. "Hey! We were talking about my bod!" Again she paused. "Well, at least my breasts are nice, aren't they?"

He did not look over. "Certainly. They're great."

"Now cut it out! *Look* at them. They're a little small by current standards, but they're firm and cute, don't you think?"

He cradled one in his palm and inspected it with professional myopia. "Very fine," he vouched. "And two in number, which is especially reassuring."

"Then why don't you break down and make love to me?"

"Because you are self-consciously cute. Furthermore, you are a virgin. I could forgive the cuteness on the assumption that you'll outgrow it. But the virginity—never. Now why don't you put your blouse back on."

"No-o. I don't think so. Who knows? You might suddenly get a normal impulse and—ta-da!"

"Ta-da?"

"It's better than bam. Here, let me give you more coffee." She refilled his cup then carried her own to the edge of the loft, where she leaned against the railing, looking out over the nave musingly.

Cherry was Jonathan's nearest neighbor, occupying with her domestic staff a rambling mansion a quarter of a mile down the road. They shared the cost of maintaining the artificial sand beach that connected their properties. Her late father, the corporation lawyer James Mathew Pitt, had bought the estate shortly before his death, and Cherry enjoyed managing the property. During trips, Jonathan entrusted her with the care of his home and the payment of his local bills. Of necessity, she had a key, and she drifted in and out to use his library and to borrow champagne for her parties. He never attended these parties, not caring to meet the liberated young people of her circle. Needless to say, Cherry knew nothing about him, save that he was a teacher and art critic and that, so far as she knew, he was independently well off. She had never been invited to descend into the private gallery in the basement.

Little by little, their sex play had developed into a pattern of epic enticements and stoic refusals, the whole thing based on their mutual understanding that it was Jonathan's role to fend her off. She would have been at a loss, had he ever failed to do so. The battle was never totally without charm because it was fought with humor on both sides. And there was the spice of distant possibility to keep a tang in their relationship.

After a longish silence, Cherry spoke without turning to him. "Do you realize that I am the only twenty-four-year-old virgin on Long Island—discounting paraplegics and some nuns? And it's all your fault. You owe it to mankind to get me started."

Jonathan swung out of bed. "Avoiding virgins is not only a matter of ethics with me. It's also a matter of mechanics. Virgins are hard on older men."

"O.K. Punish yourself. Deny yourself the delights of the flesh. See if I care." She followed him into the bathroom where she had to raise her voice to be heard over the roar of water into his Roman pool. "I really do care, you know. After all, *someone's* got to get me started."

He called from the toilet beyond. "Someone's got

to collect the garbage too. But not me." He punctuated with a flush.

"Nice analogy!"

He returned to the bathroom and lowered himself into the hot water. "Why don't you get dressed and go make us a little breakfast."

"I want to be your lover, not your wife." But she returned reluctantly to the bedroom.

"And put your shirt on before you go down," he called after her. "You might meet Mr. Monk down there." Mr. Monk was the groundsman.

"I wonder if *he'd* be willing to relieve me of this disgraceful chastity?"

"Not on what I pay him," Jonathan mumbled to himself.

"I assume you want your eggs raw," she called as she left.

After breakfast, she wandered about in the greenhouse garden while he brought the morning mail into the library, where he intended to do a touch of work. He was surprised and disturbed not to find the usual blue envelope from CII containing his cash payment. By routine, it was always placed by hand in his mailbox during the night after his return from a sanction. He was sure this was no oversight. Dragon was up to something. But there was nothing he could do but wait, so he went over his accounts and discovered that, after he had spent the ten thousand for the new Pissarro and paid his groundsman in advance for the summer, he would have very little left. There would be no lavish living this season, but he would get by. His major concern was that he had promised the underground art dealer in Brooklyn that he would have the money today. He decided to telephone and persuade him to hold the painting for an extra day.

". . . so when *can* you pick it up, Jonathan?" the

dealer asked, his voice crisp with the overarticulated consonants of the Near East.

"Tomorrow, I imagine. Or the next day."

"Make it the next day. Tomorrow I take the family to Jones Beach. And you will have the twelve thousand we agreed on?"

"I will have the *ten* thousand we agreed on."

"It was only ten?" the dealer asked, his voice laden with grief.

"It was only ten."

"Jonathan, what am I doing? I am allowing my friendship for you to threaten the future of my children. But—a deal is a deal. I am philosophic. I can lose with grace. But make sure you bring the money before noon. It is dangerous for me to keep the item here. And also, I have another prospective buyer."

"You're lying, of course."

"I don't lie. I steal. There is another buyer. For twelve thousand. He contacted me today. So, if you don't want to lose the painting, be prompt. You understand?"

"I understand."

"Good. So! How is the family?"

"I'm not married. We go through this every time. You always ask me how the family is, and I always remind you that I am not married."

"Well, I am a forgetful man. Remember how I forgot it was only ten thousand? But seriously, you should get a family. Without children to work for, what is life? Answer me that."

"I'll see you in two days."

"I look forward to it. Be punctual, Jonathan. There is another buyer."

"So you told me."

For several minutes after he hung up, Jonathan sat gloomily at his desk, his spirits dampened by fear of losing the Pissarro. He wondered uneasily what was in Dragon's oblique mind.

"Feel like banging balls?" Cherry called from across the nave.

There was nothing to be gained by moping, so he agreed. The storm had rinsed the sky clear of clouds and the day was brilliant with sunlight. They played tennis for an hour, then they cut their thirsts with splits of champagne. She imitated his sacrilegious habit of drinking the wine from the bottle, like beer. Later they cooled off with a short swim. Cherry swam in her tennis togs, and when she came out, her shorts were nearly transparent.

"I feel like an Italian starlet," she remarked, looking down at the dark écu outline through her wet shorts.

"So do I," he said, dropping down on the hot sand.

They small-talked while she let handfuls of sand seep from her fist onto his back. She mentioned that she was going to spend the weekend on the Point with some of her friends. She invited him to come along. He refused; her too-young and too-liberal friends bored him with their nomadic affections and catatonic minds.

A cool wind scudded down the beach, an omen that there would be rain again before evening, and Cherry, after proposing without much hope that Jonathan take her into the warmth of his bed, went home.

On his way back to the church, Jonathan caught sight of Mr. Monk, his groundsman. For a moment he considered backtracking to avoid encounter, but embarrassed at being cowed by an employee, he walked bravely onward. Mr. Monk was the best gardener on the Island, but he was not much sought after. Thoroughly paranoiac, he had developed a theory that grass, flowers, and shrubs were his personal enemies, out to get him by means as diabolic as they were devious. It was his practice to rip up weeds, trim hedges, or cut grass with sadistic glee and retributive energy, all the while heaping scatalogical abuse on the offending flora. As though to spite him, gardens and grounds flourished under his hand, and this he viewed as a calculated insult, and his hatred flowed the more freely.

He was growling to himself as he punished the edge of a flower bed with a spade when Jonathan approached diffidently. "How are things going, Mr. Monk?" he asked tentatively.

"What! Oh, it's you, Dr. Hemlock. Rotten! That's how things are going! These shitty flowers want nothing but water! Water, water, water! A bunch of turd-eating lushes, they are. Water heads! Say, what kind of swimming suit was that neighbor lady wearing? I could see right through to her boobs. A little cross-eyed, they were. You take a look at this spade! Near bent in half! That's how they make them these days! Not worth a tiny pinch of coon shit! I remember the time when a spade . . ."

Jonathan mumbled apologetically that everything looked fine, and he sneaked off toward his house.

Once under the cool and reassuring expanse of the vaulted nave, he discovered he was hungry. He compiled a lunch of macadamia nuts, Polish sausage, an apple, and a split of champagne. Then he smoked a pipe and relaxed, purposely not harkening for the ring of his telephone. Dragon would contact him when he was ready. Best just to wait for him.

To distract his thoughts, he went down to the gallery and passed some time with his paintings. When he had taken as much from them as he could just then, he sat at his desk and worked desultorily on the overdue Lautrec article, but it was no good. His mind returned to Dragon's intentions, and to the threatened Pissarro. Without putting it into words, he had known for some time that he could not continue working for CII. Conscience, of course, played no part in his growing disaffection. The only pangs he ever felt over killing a member of the scabby sub-culture of espionage were resentments at being brought into contact with them. Perhaps it was weariness. Tension, maybe. If only there were a way to support his lifestyle, his home, and his paintings without association with the Dragons and the Popes and the Melloughs . . .

Miles Mellough. His jaw set at the thought of the name. For nearly two years he had been waiting patiently for fate to give him a chance at Miles. He must not leave the cover of CII until that debt was attended to.

He had permitted very few people to penetrate his armor of cool distance. To those who had, he was fiercely loyal, and he insisted that his friends participate in his rigid views of friendship and loyalty. But in the course of his life, only four men had gotten close enough to merit his friendship, and to run the concomitant risk of his wrath. There was Big Ben Bowman, whom he had not seen for three years, but with whom he used to climb mountains and drink beer. And there was Henri Baq, a French espionage agent who had had the gift of finding laughter in everything, and whose gut had been cut open two years ago. And there was Miles Mellough, who had been responsible for Baq's death after having been Henri and Jonathan's closest friend.

The fourth had been The Greek, who had betrayed Jonathan during a sanction job. Only luck, and a desperate four-mile swim through a night sea had saved Jonathan's life. Of course, Jonathan should have been worldly enough to realize that any man who trusts a Cyprian Greek deserves a Trojan fate, but this did not prevent him from biding his time until he ran across him in Ankara. The Greek was not aware that Jonathan knew who had sold him out—

perhaps, being Greek, he had even forgotten the incident—so he accepted the gift of his favorite arrack without hesitation. The bottle had been doctored with Datura. The old Turk who did the job used the ancient method of burning the Datura seeds and catching the smoke in an earthen jar into which the arrack was then poured.

The Greek is now, and will always be, in an asylum, where he sits huddled in a corner, rocking back and forth, humming a single note endlessly.

The score with The Greek settled, only Miles Mellough's debt was still outstanding. Jonathan was sure that one day he would happen upon Miles.

The jangle of the telephone jarred him from his morbid stream of free association.

"Hemlock? Reports are in from Montreal. Good job, pal." Clement Pope's brassy, insurance salesman voice was enough to make Jonathan testy.

"My money wasn't in the mailbox this morning, Pope."

"Well, how about that?"

Jonathan took a deep breath to control himself. "Let me talk to Dragon."

"Talk to me. I can handle it."

"I'm not going to waste time with a flunkey. Get Dragon to the phone."

"Maybe if I came out there and we had a good chat . . . ?" Pope was taunting. He knew that Jonathan could not afford to be seen in his company. With Dragon's necessary seclusion, Pope had become the public face of SS Division. Being seen with him was tantamount to having a "Support CII" sticker on your automobile.

"If you want the money, pal, you'd better cooperate. Dragon won't talk to you over the phone, but he will see you."

"When?"

"Right now. He wants you to take a train in as soon as possible."

"All right. But remind him that I am depending on that money."

"I'm just sure he knows that, buddy-o." Pope hung up.

Someday, Jonathan promised himself, I'll be alone in a room with that bastard for just ten minutes . . .

Upon reconsideration, he settled for five.

NEW YORK:
June 11

You're looking especially attractive this afternoon, Mrs. Cerberus."

She did not bother to look up. "Scrub your hands in the sink over there. Use the green soap."

"This is new." Jonathan crossed to the hospital sink with its surgeon's elbow lever instead of the conventional twist tap.

"That elevator is filthy," she said, her voice as scaly as her complexion. "And Mr. Dragon is in a weakened condition. He's near the end of a phase." This meant that he would soon receive his semiannual total replacement transfusion.

"Do you intend to donate?" Jonathan asked, rubbing his hands dry under a jet of hot air.

"We are not the same blood type."

"Do I detect a note of regret?"

"Mr. Dragon's blood type is very rare," she said with evident pride.

"In humans at any rate. May I go in now?"

She fixed a diagnostic glare on him. "Any colds? Flu? Digestive disorder?"

"Only a mild pain in the ass, and that's a recent development."

Mrs. Cerberus pressed the buzzer on her desk, and she waved him into the interlock without further comment.

The usual dim red light was not on, but the rising heat was as stifling as ever. The door to Dragon's office clicked open. "Come in, Hemlock." Dragon's metallic voice had a weak flutter in it. "Please forgive the absence of the red light. I am more than usually fragile, and even that dim light is painful to me."

Jonathan groped forward for the back of the leather chair. "Where is my money?"

"That's my Hemlock. Directly to the point. No time wasted with the conversational amenities. The slums have left their mark."

"I need the money."

"True. Without it you will be unable to meet your house payments—to say nothing of purchasing that Pissarro you covet. By the way, I hear there is another bidder on the painting. Pity if you lost it."

"You intend to hold out on me?"

"Permit me an academic question, Hemlock. What would you do if I were to withhold payment?"

"Light these." Jonathan slipped his fingers into his shirt pocket.

"What have you there?" There was no worry in Dragon's voice. He knew how thoroughly his men searched everyone who entered.

"A book of matches. Do you have some idea of the pain it's going to cause you when I strike them one by one?"

Dragon's thin fingers flew automatically to his eyes, but he knew that his colorless skin would afford little protection. With forced bravado he said, "Very good, Hemlock. You confirm my confidence in you. In future, my men will have to search for matches as well."

"My payment?"

"There. On the desk. Actually, I intended to give you the money all the time. I kept it only to assure your coming here to listen to my proposition." He laughed his three arid ha's. "That was a good one with the matches!" The laugh changed into a weak, wheezing cough, and for a time he could not speak. "Sorry. I'm not really well."

"To put you at ease," Jonathan said, slipping the chubby envelope of bills into his coat pocket, "I should tell you that I don't have any matches. I never smoke in public."

"Of course! I had forgotten." There was real praise in his voice. "Very good indeed. Forgive me if I have seemed overly aggressive. I am ill just now, and that makes me tetchy."

Jonathan smiled at the uncommon word. Occasionally Dragon's alien English was betrayed by just such sounds: odd word choices, overpronunciations, mishandlings of idiom. "What's this all about, Dragon?"

"I have an assignment you must take."

"I thought we talked about that. You know I never take jobs unless I need the money. Why don't you use one of your other Sanction people?"

The pink-and-red eyes emerged. "I would if it were possible. Your reluctance is a nuisance. But this assignment requires an experienced mountain climber and, as you might imagine, men of such talents do not abound within our department."

"I haven't climbed for more than three years."

"We have considered that. There is time to bring you back into condition."

"Why do you need a climber?"

"I could discuss details only if you were willing to cooperate on the assignment."

"In which case, forget it."

"I have a further inducement for you, Hemlock."

"Oh?"

"One of our former employees—an erstwhile friend of yours, I believe—is involved in the affair." Dragon paused for effect. "Miles Mellough."

73

After a moment, Jonathan said, "Miles is none of your business. I'll take care of him in my own way."

"You are a rigid man, Hemlock. I hope you don't break when you are forced to bend."

"Forced how."

"Oh, something will occur to me." There was a heavy flutter in his voice and he pressed his hand against his chest to relieve the pain. "On your way out, would you ask Mrs. Cerberus to come to me, there's a good fellow?"

Jonathan pressed back into the shallow entrance to Dragon's office building, trying to avoid the rain which fell in plump drops that exploded into a haze on the sidewalk. The liquid roar eclipsed the city's babble. An empty taxi came slowly up the street, and Jonathan jumped out to take his place in a line of supplicants who waved and shouted as the cab cruised majestically by, the driver whistling contentedly to himself, doubtless contemplating some intriguing problem of Russian grammar. Jonathan returned to the shelter of his meager cave and looked out glumly on the scene. Streetlights came on, their automatized devices duped into believing it was evening by the darkening storm. Another taxi appeared and Jonathan, knowing better, nevertheless stepped forward to the curb on the outside chance that this driver was not independently wealthy and had some mild interest in profit. Then he saw that the taxi was occupied. As he turned back, the driver sounded his horn. Jonathan stood still, puzzled and getting wetter. The driver beckoned him over. Jonathan pointed at his chest with a foolish "me?" expression on his face. The back door opened and Jemima called out, "Are you going to get in, or do you like it out there?"

Jonathan jumped in, and the cab turned out into traffic, disdainfully ignoring trumpeted protests from the car abreast that was forced into the oncoming stream.

"I don't mean to drip on you," Jonathan said, "but you really do look lovely. Where did you come from? Did I mention you look lovely?" He was boyishly glad to see her again. It seemed that he had thought of her often. But probably not, he decided. Why should he?

"I saw you step out," she explained, "and you looked so funny that I took pity on you."

"Ah. You fell for an ancient ploy. I always try to look funny when I'm drowning in the rain. You never know when some passing stewardess will take pity on you."

The cabby turned and looked over the back of the seat with classic indifference to competing traffic. "That'll be double fare you know, buddy."

Jonathan told him that was just fine.

"Because we ain't supposed to pick up two fares in the rain like that." He deigned to glance briefly at the oncoming traffic.

Jonathan said he would take care of it.

"Hell, everybody and his brother would be picking up the whole damned city if we didn't charge double fare. You know that for yourself."

Jonathan leaned forward and smiled at the driver politely in the rearview mirror. "Why don't we divide up the labor here? You drive, and we'll talk." Then he asked Jemima, "How do you manage to look so calm and lovely when you're starving to death?"

"Am I starving to death?" The harlequin flecks of gold danced with amusement in her warm brown eyes.

"Certainly, you are. Its a wonder you haven't noticed it."

"I take it you're inviting me out to dinner."

"I am that. Yes."

She looked at him quizzically. "Now, you know

that when I picked you up in the rain, I didn't pick you up in all the possible senses of that phrase, don't you?"

"Good Lord, we hardly know each other! What are you suggesting? How about dinner?"

She considered it a moment, tempted. Then, "No-o, I think not."

"If you hadn't said no, what would your second choice have been?"

"Steak, red wine, and a small tangy salad."

"Done." Jonathan leaned forward and told the driver to turn south to an address on Fourteenth Street.

"How about making up your mind, buddy?"

"Drive."

When the taxi pulled up in front of the restaurant, Jemima touched Jonathan's sleeve. "I saved you from melting. You are going to buy me a dinner. And that's it, right? After dinner everybody goes home. Each to his own home. OK?"

He took her hand and looked earnestly into her eyes. "Gem, you have very fragile faith in your fellowman." He squeezed the hand. "Tell me about it? Who was he—the man who hurt you so?"

She laughed, and the cab driver asked if they were going to get out or not. As Jemima dashed into the restaurant, Jonathan paid the cabby and told him he had been a real brick. Rain and traffic obscured the last word, so the driver stared at Jonathan for a moment, but he decided it was wiser to drive off in a wheel-squealing miff.

The restaurant was simple and expensive, designed for eating, not for gazing at the decor. Partly because he felt festive, and partly to impress Jemima, Jonathan ordered a bottle of Lafite.

"May I suggest 1959?" the wine steward asked, with the rhetorical assumption that his guidance was impeccable.

"We're not French," Jonathan said, not taking his eyes from Jemima.

"Sir?" The arch of the eyebrow had that blend of huff and martyrdom characteristic of upper echelon servants.

"We're not French. Prenubile wines hold no fascination for us. Bring a '53 if you have it, or a '55 if not."

As the steward departed, Jemima asked, "Is this Lafite something special?"

"You don't know?"

"No."

Jonathan signaled the steward to return. "Forget the Lafite. Bring us an Haut-Brion instead."

Assuming the change was a fiscal reconsideration, the steward made an elaborate production of scratching the Lafite off his pad and scribbling down the Haut-Brion.

"Why did you do that?" Jemima asked.

"Thrift, Miss Brown. Lafite is too expensive to waste."

"How do you know, I might have enjoyed it."

"Oh, you'd have enjoyed it all right. But you wouldn't have appreciated it."

Jemima looked at him narrowly. "You know? I have this feeling you're not a nice person."

"Niceness is an overrated quality. Being nice is how a man pays his way into the party if he hasn't the guts to be tough or the class to be brilliant."

"May I quote you?"

"Oh, you probably will."

"Ah-h—Johnson to Boswell?"

"James Abbott McNeill Whistler to Wilde. But not a bad guess."

"A gentleman would have pretended I was right. I was right about your not being a nice person."

"I'll try to make up for it by being other things. Witty, or poetic perhaps. Or even terribly interested in you, which, by the way, I am." His eyes twinkled.

"You're putting me on."

"I admit it. It's all a facade. I just pretend to be urbane as an armor for my vulnerable hypersensitivity."

"Now I'm getting a put-on within the put-on."

"How do you like being on Flugle Street?"

"Help."

Jonathan laughed and let the con lie where it was.

Jemima sighed and shook her head. "Man, you're really a social buzz saw, aren't you. I like to put people on myself by skipping logical steps in the conversation until they're dizzy. But that sort of thing isn't even in your league, is it?"

"I don't know that you could call it a league. After all, there's only one team and one player."

"Here we go again."

"Let's take time out for dinner."

The salad was crisp, the steaks huge and perfect, and they washed them down with the Haut-Brion. Throughout the meal they chatted lightly, allowing the topic to pivot on a word or a sudden thought, ranging from art to politics to childhood embarrassments to social issues, clinging to a subject only so long as there was amusement in it. They shared a sense of the ridiculous and took neither themselves nor the great names in art and politics too seriously. Often it was unnecessary to finish a sentence—the other predicting the thrust and nodding agreement or laughing. And sometimes they shared brief, relaxed silences, neither feeling a need to keep up conversation as a defense against communication. They sat next to a window. The rain alternately rattled and relented. They made ludicrous guesses about the professions and destinations of the passersby. Without recognizing it, Jonathan was dealing with Gem as though she were a man—an old friend. He drifted with the stream of conversation honestly, forgetting the pre-bed banter that usually constituted the basis of his small talk with women.

"A college teacher?" Gem asked incredulously. "Don't tell me that, Jonathan. You're undermining my stereotypes."

"How about you as a stewardess? How did that ever happen?"

"Oh, I don't know. Came out of college after changing majors every year and tried to find a job as a Renaissance Woman, but there wasn't a heading like that in the want ads. And traveling around seemed like a possible thing to do. It also struck me as kind of fun to be the first black stewardess on the line—I was their public relations *Negress*." She pronounced the word prissily, ridiculing those who would use it. "How about you? How did you happen to become a college teacher?"

"Oh, I came out of college and tried to find a job as a Renaissance Man, but . . ."

"All right. Forget it."

In the course of the chat, Jonathan discovered that she would be in New York for a three-day layover, and that pleased him. They drifted into another easy silence.

"What's funny?" she asked in response to his slight smile.

"Nothing," he said. "Me."

"Synonyms?"

"I just . . ." He smiled gently at her over the table. "It just occurred to me that I am not bothering to be clever with you. I usually make it a point to be clever."

"How about all that Flugle Street business?"

"Hustler talk. Dazzle talk. But I don't think I'd care to dazzle you."

She nodded and looked out the window, giving her attention to the random scatter of light where the rain danced on the puddles. After a while, she said, "That's nice."

He knew what she meant. "Yes, it's nice. But it's a little disconcerting."

She nodded again. And they both knew she meant that it was a little disconcerting for her, too.

A series of non-sequitur pivots brought them to the subject of houses, and Jonathan waxed enthusiastic about his own. For half an hour he described details to her, trying hard to make her see them. She listened actively, letting him know through small movements of her eyes and head that she understood and shared. When he stopped suddenly, realizing that he had been talking steadily and probably boorishly, she said, "It must be nice to feel that way about a house. And it's safe too, of course."

"Safe?"

"A house can't lean on you emotionally. Can't burden you by loving you back. You know what I mean."

He knew exactly, and he experienced a negative twinge at her emotional acumen. It occurred to him that he would enjoy having her at his home—passing a day sitting around and chatting. He told her so.

"It sounds like fun. But we couldn't go now. That wouldn't be good. I pick you up in a cab, we have dinner, then we run off to your house. Technically speaking, that would constitute a 'quicky.' It doesn't sound like our sort of thing."

He agreed that it was not their sort of thing. "We could make some sort of pact. I imagine we're capable of not making love for a day or two."

"You'd cheat."

"Probably."

"And if you didn't, I would."

"I'm glad to hear that."

The restaurant was closing, and their waiter had already made many polite intrusions with offers of unwanted service. Jonathan tipped rather too much, paying for the splendid time he had had, rather than for the service, which he had not noticed.

They decided to walk back to her hotel because it was not too far, and because the streets were empty and cool after the rain. They strolled, sharing swatches of talk and longer periods of silence. Her hand was in the bend of his arm, and she drew his attention to little things she noticed with a slight press of her fingers, which he acknowledged with a gentle return flex.

Surprisingly quickly they found themselves at her hotel. In the lobby they shook hands, then she said, "It is all right if I come out on the train tomorrow morning? You can meet me at the station, and we'll take a look at this church of yours."

"I think that would be . . . just fine."

"Good night, Jonathan."

"Good night."

He walked to the train station, noticing along the way that the city seemed less ugly than usual. Probably the rain.

LONG ISLAND:
June 12

He padded across the expanse of his choir loft bedroom, concentrating on his coffee cup, but spilling some into the saucer anyway. It was a large, two-handled *café au lait* mug, and for several minutes he leaned against the rail, taking long resuscitating draughts and looking down with pride and pleasure upon the nave where low-angle morning sun pierced the dim space with lances of variegated light. He was only at peace when he had his home around him, like armor. His thoughts strayed back and forth between pleasant anticipation of Jemima and vague discomfort over the tone of his last meeting with Dragon.

Later, down in the gallery, he screwed up his courage and tried again to work on the Lautrec article. He penciled a few notes, then the lead broke. That was it. Fate. He might have plowed on, wading through uninspired, mealy prose—but not if it entailed resharpening his pencil. It wasn't his fault that the pencil had broken.

On his desk top lay the blue pay envelope from Dragon, chubby with tenscore one-hundred-dollar bills. He picked it up and looked around for a safe place to put it. His eye caught none, so he dropped it back on the desk. For a man who went to such extremes to make money, Jonathan had none of the instincts of the miser. Money had no attraction for him. Goods, comforts, and possessions were another matter. It delighted him to remember that by tomorrow afternoon he would own the pointillist Pissarro. He looked around the walls, deciding where to hang it, and his eye fell on the Cézanne that Henri Baq had stolen for him in Budapest as a birthday present. Memories of Henri came to him: the curiously warped Basque wit . . . their laughter when they described close calls to each other . . . that staggering drunk in Arles when they had played at bullfighting with their jackets and the angry traffic. And he recalled the day Henri died, trying to hold his guts in with his hands, seeking a witty punch line to go out on, and not being able to come up with one.

Jonathan snapped his head to clear the images out, but no good. He sat at the pianoforte and chorded aimlessly. They had been a team—he and Henri and Miles Mellough. Miles worked for Search, Jonathan for Sanction, and Henri for the French counterpart of CII. They had performed assignments competently and quickly, and they always found time to sit around in bars, talking about art and sex and . . . whatever.

Then Miles set up Henri's death.

Jonathan slipped into a bit of Handel. Dragon had said that Miles was involved somehow in this sanction he was trying to force on Jonathan. For almost two years, Jonathan had anticipated the day when he could face Miles again.

Don't think about it. Jemima is coming.

He left the chamber, locking the door behind him, and strolled over the grounds to while away the slow-moving time before her arrival. The breeze was fresh, and the leaves of the plane trees lining the drive scintillated in the sun. Overhead, the sky was taut blue, but on the northern horizon over the water hovered a tight bundle of cloud that promised a fresh storm that night. Jonathan loved storms.

He wandered through the formal English garden

with its newly clipped box hedges enclosing an involute maze. From the depths of the labyrinth he could hear the angry click! click! click! of Mr. Monk's trimming shears.

"Argh! There!" Click! "That'll teach you, you simpleminded shrub!" Click! Click! "OK, wise ass twig! Stick it out, and I'll cut it off for you! Like that!" Click!

Jonathan tried to locate the sound within the maze so he might avoid an encounter with Mr. Monk. Stealthily, he moved down the alley, rolling the pressure underfoot to reduce the sound.

"You got something against them other branches?" Mr. Monk's voice was honey sweet. "Oh-h-h, you don't like their company. Well, I understand. You're just some kind of loner, keepin' away from the bunch like that." Then suddenly he roared, "Pride! That's your trouble! And I got a cure for pride!" Click! "There!"

Jonathan squatted beside the wall of hedge, not daring to move, uncertain of the direction of Mr. Monk's voice. There was a long silence. Then he began to picture himself, cringing at the thought of meeting his groundsman. He smiled, shook his head, and stood up.

"What you doin', Dr. Hemlock?" Mr. Monk asked from directly behind him.

"Oh! Well! Hello." Jonathan frowned and dug his toe into the turf. "This—ah—this grass here, Mr. Monk. I've been examining it. Looks funny to me. Don't you think so?"

Mr. Monk had not noticed, but he was always willing to believe the worst of growing things. "Funny in what way, Dr. Hemlock?"

"Well, it's . . . greener than usual. Greener than it ought to be. You know what I mean."

Mr. Monk examined the area near the shrubbery, then compared it with nearby grass. "Is that right?"

His eyes grew round with rage as he turned on the offending patch.

Jonathan walked down the alley with determined casualness and turned at the first corner. As he paced more quickly to the house, he heard Mr. Monk's voice from within the labyrinth.

"You stupid weeds! Always screwing up! If you ain't brown and scruffy, you're too green! Well, this'll fix you!" Snip!

Jonathan drove along the tree-lined road to the station. The train would probably be late, in the Long Island tradition, but he could not run the risk of keeping Jemima waiting. His automobile was a vintage Avanti—a car consonant with his hedonistic lifestyle. It was in poor condition because he drove it hard and gave it little attention, but its line and grace appealed to him. When it finally broke down for good, he intended to use it as a planter on his front lawn.

He parked close to the platform, his bumper touching the gray, weathered planking. The warming sun liberated a smell of creosote from the wood. Because it was Sunday, the platform and the parking area were deserted. He leaned back in the seat and waited drowsily. He would never consider standing on a train platform to wait because . . .

. . . Henri Baq had bought his on the cement arrival dock of the Gare St. Lazare. Jonathan often thought of the steamy clangor of that vast steel-domed station. And of the monstrous grinning clown.

Henri had been off guard. An assignment had just ended, and he was going on his first vacation without his wife and children. Jonathan had promised to see him off, but he had been delayed in the tangle of traffic in the Place de L'Europe.

He caught sight of Henri, and they waved over the

heads of the crowd. It must have been just then that the assailant slipped the knife into Henri's stomach. The dispatcher's voice boomed its undecipherable drone into the hiss of steam and rattle of baggage wagons. By the time Jonathan pushed his way through the throng, Henri was leaning against a huge poster for the Winter Circus.

"*Qu'as-tu?*" Jonathan asked.

Henri's drooping Basque eyes were infinitely sad. He clutched the front of his jacket with one hand, the fist pressed against his stomach. He smiled foolishly and shook his head with an I-don't-believe-it expression, then the smile contorted into a grin of pain, and he slid to a sitting posture, his feet straight out before him like a child's.

When Jonathan stood up after feeling Henri's throat for pulse, he came face to face with the insane grin of the clown on the poster.

Marie Baq had not wept. She thanked Jonathan for coming to tell her, and she gathered the children together in another room for a talk. When they came back, their eyes were red and puffy, but none of them was still crying. The eldest boy—also Henri—assumed his role and asked Jonathan if he would care for an apéritif. He accepted, and later he took them across the street to a café for supper. The youngest, who did not really understand what had happened, ate with excellent appetite, but no one else did. And once the eldest girl made a snorting noise as the dike of her control broke, and she ran to the ladies' room.

Jonathan sat up that night over coffee with Marie. They talked of practical and fiscal matters across the kitchen table covered with oilcloth from which daydreaming children had picked flecks of plastic. Then for a long time there was nothing to talk about. Close to dawn she pushed herself out of the chair with a sigh so deep it whimpered. "One must continue to live, Jonathan. For the little ones. Come. Come to bed with me."

There is nothing so life-embracing as lovemaking. Potential suicides almost never do. Jonathan lived with the Baqs for two weeks, and each night Marie used him like medicine. One evening she said calmly, "You should go now, Jonathan. I don't think I need you anymore. And if we continued after I ceased to need you, that would be a different thing."

He nodded.

When the youngest son heard that Jonathan was going away he was disappointed. He had intended to ask Jonathan to take him to the Winter Circus.

Several weeks later, Jonathan learned that Miles Mellough had set up the assassination. Because Miles left CII at the same time, Jonathan had never been sure which side had ordered the sanction.

"Nice job of meeting the train," Jemima said looking in the window from the off-driver side.

He started. "I'm sorry. I didn't notice it come in." He realized how thin that sounded, considering the desolate platform.

As they drove toward his place, she trailed her hand out the window, cupping the wind aerodynamically, as children do. He thought she looked smart and fresh in her white linen dress with its high mandarin collar. She sat deep in the seat, either completely relaxed or totally indifferent.

"Are those the only clothes you brought?" he asked, turning his head toward her, but keeping his eyes on the road.

"Yes, sure. I'll bet you were expecting some night things discreetly carried in a brown paper bag."

"The bag could have been any color. I wouldn't have cared." He braked and turned into a side road, then backed onto the highway again.

"You forgot something?"

"No. We're going back to the village. To buy you some clothes."

"You don't like these?"

"They're fine. But they're not much for working in."

"Working?"

"Certainly. You thought this was a vacation?"

"What kind of work?" she asked warily.

"I thought you might enjoy helping me paint a boat."

"I'm being had."

Jonathan nodded thoughtfully.

They stopped at the only shop in the village open on Sundays, a spurious Cape Cod structure decorated with fishing nets and glass balls calculated to delight weekend tourists from the city. The proprietor was no taciturn Down Easter; he was an intense man in his mid-forties, tending slightly to weight, wearing a tight-fitting Edwardian suit and a flowing pearl gray ascot. When he spoke, he thrust his lower jaw forward and relished the nasal vowels with deliberate sincerity.

While Jemima was in the back of the store picking out some shorts, a shirt, and a pair of canvas shoes, Jonathan selected other things, accepting the proprietors' estimate of size. The advice was not given graciously; there was a tone of peevish disappointment. "Oh, about a ten, I guess," the proprietor said, then compressed his lips and averted his eyes. "Of course, it will change when she's had a few children. Her kind always does." His eyebrows were in constant motion, each independent of the other.

Jonathan and Gem had driven a distance when she said, "That's the first time I've been a victim of prejudice on those grounds."

"I've known and admired a lot of women," Jonathan said in an accurate imitation of the proprietor's voice. "Some of my best friends are women . . ."

89

"But you wouldn't want your brother to marry one, right?"

"Well, you know what happens to land values if a woman moves into the neighborhood."

The shadows of trees lining the road rippled in regular cadence over the hood, and sunlight flickered stroboscopically in the corners of their eyes.

She squeezed one of the packages. "Hey, what's this?"

"I'm sorry, but they didn't have any brown paper bags."

She paused a second. "I see."

The car turned into the drive and came around a line of plane trees screening the church from view. He opened the door and let her precede him into the house. She stopped in the midst of the nave and turned around, taking the total in. "This isn't a house, Jonathan. It's a movie set."

He stepped around from his side of the boat to see how she was coming along. With her nose only ten inches from the wood and her tongue between her teeth with concentration, she was daubing at an area about a foot square that constituted the extent of her progress.

"You got the spot," he said, "but you've missed the boat."

"Hush up. Get around and paint your own side."

"All done."

She humphed. "Slapdash careless work, I imagine."

"Any chance of your finishing before winter sets in?"

"Don't worry about me, man. I'm the goal-oriented type. I'll keep at this until it's done. Nothing could lure me away from the dignity of honest labor."

"I was going to suggest lunch."

"Sold." She dropped the brush into the can of thinner and wiped her hands with a rag.

After bathing and changing clothes, she joined him at the bar for a prelunch martini.

"That's some bathtub you've got."

"It pleases me."

They drove across the island to take lunch at The Better 'Ole: seafood and champagne. The place was nearly empty, and it was cool with shadow. They chatted about how it was when they were children, and about Chicago jazz versus San Francisco, and Underground films, and how they both liked chilled melon balls for dessert.

They lay side by side on the warm sand under a sky no longer brittle blue, but bleaching steadily with a high haze that preceded the wall of heavy gray cloud pressing inevitably from the north. They had changed back into work clothes, but had not returned to work.

"That's enough sun and sand for me, sir," Jemima said eventually, and she pushed herself to a sitting position. "And I don't feel much like getting stormed on, so I'm going up and stroll around in the house. OK?"

He hummed drowsy acquiescence.

"Is it all right if I make a phone call? I have to tell the airline where I am."

He did not open his eyes, fearful of damaging the half-doze he was treasuring. "Don't talk more than three minutes," he said, barely moving his mouth.

She kissed him gently on his relaxed lips.

"OK," he said. "But no more than four minutes."

When he returned to the house it was late afternoon and the cloud pack was unbroken from horizon to horizon. He found Jemima lounging in the library, looking through a portfolio of Hokusai prints. He looked over her shoulder for a time, then drifted up to his bar. "It's getting cold. Care for some sherry?" His voice bounced through the nave.

"Sounds fine. I don't like your bar, though."

"Oh?"

She followed him as far as the altar rail. "It's too much nose-thumbing, if you know what I mean."

"As in, 'Oh, grow up'?"

"Yes. As in that." She accepted the chalice of wine and sat on the rail sipping it. He watched her with proprietary pleasure.

"Oh, by the way!" She stopped drinking suddenly. "Do you know that there's a madman on your grounds?"

"Is that so?"

"Yes. I met him on my way up here. He was snarling and digging a hole that looked terribly like a grave."

Jonathan frowned. "I can't imagine who that could be."

"And he was mumbling to himself."

"Was he?"

"Yes. Real vulgar stuff."

He shook his head. "I'll have to look into it."

She did the salad while he broiled steaks. The fruit had been chilling since they got home, and the purple grapes mauved over with a haze of frost when they met the humid air of the garden where places had been set at a wrought iron table, despite the probability of rain. He opened a bottle of Pichon-Longue-ville-Baron, and they ate while the onset of night smoothly transferred the source of light from the treetops of the flickering hurricane lamps on the table. The flicker stopped, the air grew dense and unmoving, and occasional flashes along the storm line glittered to the north. They watched the scudding sky grow darker while little breaths of cool wind leading the storm reanimated the lamps and fluttered the black-and-silver foliage around them. For long afterwards, Jonathan was to remember the meteor trail of Jemima's glowing cigarette when she lifted it to smoke.

He spoke out of a longish silence. "Come with me. I want to show you something."

She followed him back into the house. "There's a certain spookiness about this, you know," she said as he got the key from the back of the kitchen drawer and led her down the half-turn stone steps. "Into the catacombs? Probably a lime pit in the cellar. What do I really know about you? Maybe I should drop bits of bread so I can find my way back out."

Jonathan turned on the lights and stepped aside. She walked past him, drawn in by the paintings that radiated from the walls. "Oh, my! Oh, Jonathan!"

He sat at his desk chair, watching her as she moved from canvas to canvas with an uneven pulsing flow, attracted by the next painting, unwilling to leave the last. She made little humming sounds of pleasure and admiration, rather as a contented child does when eating breakfast alone.

Her eyes full, she sat on the carved piano bench and looked down at the Kashan for some time. "You're a singular man, Jonathan Hemlock."

He nodded.

"All this just for you. This megalomaniac house; these . . ." she made a sweeping gesture with her hand and eyes. "You keep all this to yourself."

"I'm a singularly selfish man. Like some champagne?"

"No."

She looked down and shook her head sadly. "All this matters to you a great deal. Even more than Mr. Dragon led me to believe."

"Yes, it matters, but . . ."

. . . For some minutes they said nothing. She did not look up, and he, after the first shocked glance, tried to calm his confusion and anger by forcing his eye to roam over the paintings.

Finally he sighed and pushed himself out of the chair. "Well, lady, I'd better be getting you to the depot. Last train for the city . . ." His voice trailed off.

She followed him obediently up the stone steps. While they had been in the gallery, the storm had broken violently above without their hearing it. Now they climbed up through layers of quickening, muffled sound—the metallic rattle of rain on glass, the fluting and flap of wind, the thick, distant rumblings of thunder.

In the kitchen she asked, "Do we have time for that glass of champagne you offered me?"

He protected his hurt by the dry freeze of politeness. "Certainly. In the library?"

He knew she was distressed, and he wielded his artificial social charm like a bludgeon, chatting lightly about the paucity of transportation to his corner of Long Island, and of the particular difficulties the rain imposed. They sat facing each other in heavy leather chairs while the rain rattled horizontally against the stained glass, and the walls and floor rippled with reds and greens and blues. Jemima cut into the flow of anticommunicative chat.

"I guess I shouldn't have just dropped it on you like that, Jonathan."

"Oh? How should you have dropped it, Jemima?"

"I couldn't let it go on—I mean, I couldn't let *us* go on without your knowing. And I couldn't think of a more gentle way to tell you."

"You might have hit me with a brick," he suggested. Then he laughed. "I must have been dazzled.

94

You're a real dazzler. I should have recognized the anti-chance of coincidence. You on the plane from Montreal. You just happened to pass by Dragon's office in that taxi. How was it supposed to work, Jemima? Were you supposed to bring me to a white heat of desire, then deny your body unless I agreed to do this sanction for Dragon? Or were you going to whisper insidious persuasions into my ear as I lay in the euphoria of postcoitus vulnerability."

"Nothing so cool. I was told to steal your payment for the last assignment."

"That's certainly direct."

"I saw it lying on your desk downstairs. Mr. Dragon says you need the money badly."

"He's right. Why you? Why not one of his other flunkeys?"

"He thought I would be able to get close to you quickly."

"I see. How long have you worked for Dragon?"

"I don't really work for him. I'm CII, but I'm not Search and Sanction. They chose someone out of your department to avoid recognition."

"Very sensible. What do you do?"

"I'm a courier. The stewardess front is good for that."

He nodded. "Have you had many assignments like this? Using your body to get at someone?"

She considered, then rejected the easy lie. "A couple."

He was silent for a moment. Then he laughed. "Aren't we the pair? A selfish killer and a patriotic whore. We should mate just to see what the offspring would be. I have nothing against selfish whores, but patriotic killers are the worst kind."

"Jonathan." She leaned forward, suddenly angry. "Do you have any idea how important this assignment Mr. Dragon wants you to take is?"

He regarded her with bland silence; he had no intention of making anything easier.

"I know he didn't give you the details. He couldn't unless he was sure you would take the job. But if you knew what is at stake, you would cooperate."

"I doubt that."

"I wish I could tell you. But my instructions—"

"I understand."

After a pause, she said, "I tried to get out of it."

"Oh? Did you?"

"This afternoon, while we were lying on the beach, I realized what a rotten thing it would be to do, now that we were . . ."

"Now that we were what?" He arched his eyebrows in cool curiosity.

Her eyes winced. "Anyway, I left you and came up here to call Dragon and ask him to let me out."

"I assume he refused."

"He couldn't speak to me. He was undergoing a transfusion or something. But his man refused—whatshisname."

"Pope." He finished his wine and placed the glass on a table deliberately. "It's a little hard for me to buy, you know. You've been on this thing for some time—since Montreal. And you seem convinced that I ought to take this assignment—"

"You *must*, Jonathan!"

". . . and despite all that, you expect me to believe that one gentle afternoon has changed your mind. I can't help feeling you're making the mistake of trying to con a con."

"I haven't changed my mind. It's only that I didn't want to do the thing myself. And you know perfectly well that this has been more than just a gentle afternoon."

He looked at her, his eyes moving from one of hers to the other. Then he nodded, "Yes, it's been more than that."

"For me, it wasn't just this afternoon. I've spent days going over your records—which, by the way, are embarrassingly complete. I know what your boyhood was like. I know how CII roped you into your job in the first place. I know about the killing of your friend in France. And even before this assignment, I'd seen you on educational television." She grinned. "Lecturing about art in your superior, sassy way. Oh, I was ninety percent hooked before I met you. Then, down in your room—I was really pleased when you invited me down there. I couldn't help babbling. I knew from the files that you never bring anyone there. Anyway, down in the room, with you sitting there so happy, and all those beautiful paintings, and that blue envelope with your money sitting so unprotected on your desk . . . I had to tell you that's all."

"You have anything else to say?"

"No."

"You don't want to talk about shoes, or ships, or sealing wax?"

"No."

"In that case," he crossed to her and drew her out of the chair by her hands. "I'll race you up the stairs."

"You're on."

A rain-shimmered shaft of light lay across her eyes, revealing at surprising moments the harlequin flecks of gold. He lowered his forehead to hers, closed his eyes, and hummed a raspy note of satisfaction and pleasure. Then he drew back so he could see her better. "I'm going to tell you something," he said, "and you mustn't laugh."

"Tell me."

"You have the most beautiful eyes."

She looked up at him with eternal feminine calm. "That's very sweet. Why should I laugh?"

"Someday I'll tell you." He kissed her gently. "On second thought, I probably won't tell you. But that warning about laughing still goes."

"Why?"

"Because if you laugh, you'll lose me."

The image amused her, so she laughed, and she lost him.

"I warned you, right? Although it really doesn't matter, for all the good I was doing you."

"Don't talk about it."

He laughed in his turn. "You know something? This is going to come at you as a big surprise. Endurance is my forte. I'm not conning. That's normally what I have to recommend me. Endurance. How's that for yaks?"

"We have all kinds of time. At least you didn't reach for a cigarette."

He rolled over onto his back and spoke quietly into the common dark above them. "All things taken into consideration, Nature's really a capricious bitch. I've never cared much about the women I was with— I usually don't feel much of anything. And so I'm a paragon of control. And they do very well indeed. But with you—when I cared and it mattered, and *because* I cared and it mattered—I suddenly became the fastest gun in the east. Like I said, Nature's a bitch."

Gem turned to him. "Hey, what is all this? You're talking like it was afterwards. And here all the time I've been hoping it was between times."

He swung out of bed. "You're right! It's between times. You just wait there while I get us a resuscitating split of champagne."

"No, wait." She sat up in bed, her body outlined with silver backlight and splendid. "Come back here and let me talk to you."

He lay across the bottom of the bed and put his

cheek against her feet. "You sound serious and portentous and all."

"I am. It's about this job for Mr. Dragon—"

"Please, Gem."

"No. No, now just keep quiet for a second. It has to do with a biological device that the other side is working on. It's a very ugly thing. If they come up with it before we do . . . That could be terrible, Jonathan."

He hugged her feet to him. "Gem, it doesn't matter who's ahead in this kind of race. It's like two frightened boys dueling with hand grenades at three feet. It really doesn't matter who pulls the pin first."

"What does matter is that we aren't so likely to pull the pin!"

"If you're saying that the average shopkeeper in Seattle is a humane guy, that's perfectly true. But so is the average shopkeeper in Petropavlovsk. The fact is that the pin is in the hands of men like Dragon or, even worse, at the mercy of a short circuit in some underground computer."

"But, Jonathan—"

"I'm not going to take the job, Gem. I never do sanctions when I have enough money to get along. And I don't want to talk about it anymore. All right?"

She was silent. Then she made her decision. "All right."

Jonathan kissed her feet and stood up. "Now how about that champagne?"

Her voice arrested him at the top of the loft stairs. "Jonathan?"

"Madam?"

"Am I your first black?"

He turned back. "Does that matter?"

"Of course it matters. I know you're a collector of paintings, and I wondered . . ."

He sat on the edge of the bed. "I ought to smack your bottom."

"I'm sorry."

"You still want some champagne?"

She opened her arms and beckoned with her fingers. "Afterwards."

LONG ISLAND:
June 13

Jonathan simply opened his eyes, and he was awake. Calm and happy. For the first time in years there was no blurred and viscous interphase between sleeping and waking. He stretched luxuriously, arching his back and extending his limbs until every muscle danced with strain. He felt like shouting, like making a living noise. His leg touched a damp place on the sheet, and he smiled. Jemima was not in bed, but her place was still warm and her pillow was scented lightly with her perfume, and with the perfume of her.

Nude, he swung out of bed and leaned over the choir loft rail. The steep angle of the tinted shafts of sunlight across the nave indicated late morning. He called for Jemima, his voice booming back satisfactorily from the arches.

She appeared at the door to the vestry-kitchen. "You roared, sir?"

"Good morning!"

"Good morning." She wore the trim linen suit she had arrived in, and she seemed to glow white in the shadow. "I'll have coffee ready by the time you've bathed." And she disappeared through the vestry door.

He splashed about in the Roman bath and sang, loudly but not well. What would they do today? Go into the city? Or just loaf around? It did not matter.

101

He toweled himself down and put on a robe. It had been years since he had slept so late. It must be nearly—Jesus Christ! The Pissarro! He had promised the dealer he would pick it up by noon!

He sat on the edge of the bed, waiting impatiently for the phone on the other end of the line to be picked up.

"Hello? Yes?" The dealers' voice had the curving note of artificial interest.

"Jonathan Hemlock."

"Oh, yes. Where are you? Why are you calling?"

"I'm at my home."

"I don't understand, Jonathan. It is after eleven. How can you be here by noon?"

"I can't. Look, I want you to hold the painting for me a couple of hours. I'm on my way now."

"There is no need to rush. I cannot hold the painting. I told you I had another buyer. He is with me at this moment. It is tragic, but I warned you to be here on time. A deal is a deal."

"Give me one hour."

"My hands are tied."

"You said the other buyer had offered twelve thousand. I'll match it."

"If only I could, my good friend. But a deal is—"

"Name a price."

"I am sorry, Jonathan. The other buyer says he will top any price you make. But, since you have offered fifteen thousand, I will ask him." There was a mumble off-phone. "He says sixteen, Jonathan. What can I do?"

"Who is the other bidder?"

"Jonathan!" The voice was filled with righteous shock.

"I'll pay an extra thousand just to know."

"How can I tell you, Jonathan? I am bound by my ethics. And furthermore, he is right here in the same room with me."

"I see. All right, I'll give you a description. Just say yes if it fits. That's a thousand dollars for one syllable."

"At that rate, think what the Megilloth would bring."

"He's blond, crew-cut, chunky, small eyes—close set, face heavy and flat, probably wearing a sport jacket, his tie and socks will be in bad taste, he is probably wearing his hat in your home—"

"To a T, Jonathan. T as in thousand."

It was Clement Pope. "I know the man. He must have a top price. His employer would never trust him with unlimited funds. I offer eighteen thousand."

The dealer's voice was filled with respect. "You have that much in cash, Jonathan?"

"I have."

There was another prolonged and angry mumble off-phone. "Jonathan! I have wonderful news for you. He says he can top your offer, but he does not have the cash with him. It will be several hours before he can get it. Therefore, my good friend, if you are here by one o'clock with the nineteen thousand, the painting is yours along with my blessing."

"Nineteen thousand?"

"You have forgotten the fee for information?"

The painting would cost almost everything Jonathan had, and he would have to find some way to face his debts and Mr. Monk's wages. But at least he would have the Pissarro. "All right. I'll be there by one."

"Wonderful, Jonathan. My wife will have a glass of tea for you. So now tell me, how are you feeling? And how are the children?"

Jonathan repeated the terms of the arrangement so there would be no mistake, then he hung up.

For several minutes he sat on the edge of the bed, his eyes fixed in space, his hatred for Dragon and

Pope collecting into an adamantine lump. Then he caught the smell of coffee and remembered Jemima.

She was gone. And the blue envelope, chubby with its hundred-dollar bills, was gone with her.

In a brace of rapid telephone calls designed to salvage at least the painting, Jonathan discovered that Dragon, weak after his semiannual transfusion, would not speak to him, and that the art dealer, although sympathetic to his problem and solicitous of his family's health, was firm in his intent to sell the Pissarro to Pope as soon as the money was produced.

Jonathan sat alone down in the gallery, his gaze fixed on the space he had reserved for the Pissarro. Beside him on the desk was an untouched *café au lait* cup. And next to the cup was a note from Jemima:

Jonathan:

I tried to make you understand last night how important this assignment

Darling, I would give anything if

Yesterday and last night meant more to me than I can ever tell you, but there are things that

I had to guess. I hope you take sugar in your coffee.

Love (really)
Jemima

She had taken nothing but the money. He found the clothes he had bought neatly folded on the kitchen table. Even their dishes from last night's supper were washed and put away.

He sat. Hours passed. Above him, unseen in the empty nave, shafts of colored light and blocks of shadow swung imperceptibly on silent hinges, and evening came.

The bitterest part of his anger was turned inward.

He was ashamed at being so gullible. Her warmth and radiance had blinded him, a self-inflicted abacination.

In his mental list of those who had used friendship as a weapon against him, he inscribed Jemima's name under Miles Mellough's.

"The moving finger writes," he mused to himself, "and having writ, gestures."

He closed the door to the gallery and locked it— for the last time that summer.

NEW YORK:
June 14

"... the burdens of the flesh, eh, Hemlock?" Dragon's voice quivered fragilely. His body was thin and weightless under the black silk sheets; his brittle-boned head scarcely dented the ebony pillow upon which his ovine hair crumpled damply. Jonathan watched the long albescent hands flutter weakly at the hems of the turned-back bedding. A certain dim light was necessary to those who attended to his medical needs, and against the pain of this light, his eyes were covered with a thick, padded black mask.

Mrs. Cerberus bent over him, her lepidote face creased with concern as she withdrew a large needle from his hip. Dragon winced, but quickly converted the expression into a thin smile.

It was the first time Jonathan had been in the bedroom behind Dragon's office. The chamber was small and draped entirely in black, and the hospital stench was overpowering. Jonathan sat unmoving on a wooden bedside chair.

"They feed me intravenously for a few days after each transfusion. Sugar and salt solution. Not a gourmet's menu, you will agree." Dragon turned his head on the pillow, directing the black eyepads toward Jonathan. "I take it by your arctic silence that you are not overwhelmed by my stoicism and brave good humor?"

Jonathan did not respond.

With a wave so feeble that gravity tugged the hand down, Dragon dismissed Mrs. Cerberus, who brushed past Jonathan with a swish of starched clothes.

"I normally enjoy our chats, Hemlock. They have an exhilarating spice of dislike about them." He spoke in aspirate breaths, stopping midphrase when necessary, allowing his labored exhalation to group the words arbitrarily. "But in this condition I am not an adequate intellectual rival. So forgive me for coming directly to the point. Where is Miss Brown?"

"Oh? Is that really her name?"

"As it happens, yes. Where is she?"

"You're telling me you don't know?"

"She turned the money over to Mr. Pope yesterday. After which she quite disappeared. You'll forgive me if I suspect you."

"I don't know where she is. But I'm interested. If you find out, please tell me."

"I see. Remember, Hemlock, she is one of ours. And you are in an ideal position to know what happens to those who harm our people."

"Let's talk about the assignment."

"Nothing must happen to Miss Brown, Hemlock."

"Let's talk about the assignment."

"Very well." Dragon sighed, shuddering with the effort. "But I regret your loss of sportsmanship. How does the Americanism go? Win a few . . .?"

"Did you used to pull the wings off flies when you were young, Dragon?"

"Certainly not! Not flies."

Jonathan chose not to pursue the subject. "I assume the sanction has to do with the second man in Montreal. The one who was wounded in the struggle with whoeveritwas?"

"Agent Wormwood. Yes. At the time we sent you to Montreal, Search knew almost nothing about this second man. Since that time, they have been piecing together fragments of information—rumors, second sheets from note pads, statements from informers, swatches of taped telephone conversations—all the usual bits from which guilt is constructed. To be truthful, we still have less information than we have ever worked with before. But it is absolutely vital that the man be sanctioned. And quickly."

"Why? It wouldn't be the first time your people pulled a blank. What's so important about this man?"

Dragon's phosphorescent brow wrinkled as he balanced a problem for a moment, then he said, "Very well, I'll tell you. Perhaps then you will understand why we have behaved so harshly with you. And perhaps you will share our anxiety over this man." He paused, seeking a place to begin. "Tell me, Hemlock. From your Army Intelligence experience, how would you describe the ideal biological weapon?"

"Is this small talk?"

"Most pertinent."

Jonathan's voice took on the pendulum rhythm of recitation. "The disease should kill, but not quickly. The infected should require hospitalization and care, so that each case pulls one or two attendants out of action along with the victim. It should spread of itself by contact and contagion so that it will expand beyond the perimeters of the attack zone, carrying panic with it. And it must be something against which our own forces can be protected."

"Exactly. In short, Hemlock, certain virulent forms of bubonic would be ideal. Now, for years the other side has been working to develop a biological weapon based on bubonic. They have come a long way. They have perfected the delivery device; they have isolated a strain of virus with ideal characteristics; and they have injections that render their forces immune."

"I guess we'd better not piss them off."

Dragon winced with semantic pain. "Ah, the

slums. Never far from the surface with you, are they? Fortunately, our own people have not been idle. We have made considerable strides in similar directions."

"Defensively, of course."

"A retaliatory weapon."

"Certainly. After all, we wear the white hats."

"I'm afraid I do not understand."

"An Americanism."

"I see. Now, both sides have reached impasses. Our people lack the ability to immunize against the virus. The other side lacks a satisfactory culture medium that will keep the virus alive through the extremes of temperature and shock involved in intercontinental missile delivery. We are working on discovering their process of immunization, and they would like very much to know the composition of our culture medium."

"Have you considered direct barter?"

"Please don't feel called upon to lighten my illness with little jokes, Hemlock."

"How does all this fascinating business affect me?"

"CII was given the assignment of delaying the other side's progress."

"The task was entrusted to CII? The CII of the Cuban Invasion? The CII of the Gaza incident? The CII of the Spy Ships? It would seem our government enjoys playing Russian roulette with an automatic."

Dragon's voice was crisp. "In point of fact, Dr. Hemlock, we have gone a long way toward effectively negating their entire biological warfare program."

"And how was this wonder accomplished?"

"By allowing them to intercept our formula for the culture medium." There was a certain pride in Dragon's tone.

"But not the real one," Jonathan assumed.

"But not the real one."

"And they are so stupid that they will not discover this."

"It is not a matter of stupidity. The medium passes every laboratory test. When our people stumbled upon it—"

"Sounds like our people."

". . . *when our people* came upon the medium, they believed they had the answer to keeping the virus alive under all conditions. We gave it exhaustive tests. If we had not chanced to test it under combat conditions, we would never have discovered its flaw."

"Under combat conditions?"

"This is none of your affair." Dragon was angry at himself for the slip.

"It's about those white hats."

Dragon seemed to slump with fatigue, although he made no movement. He appeared to collapse from within, to become smaller in the chest and thinner in the face. He drew several shallow breaths, blowing each out through slack lips and puffing cheeks.

"So then, Hemlock," he continued after recovery, "you can understand our urgency."

"Frankly, I don't. If we're so far out ahead in this criminal competition . . ." he shrugged.

"We recently suffered a great setback. Three of our most important scientists have died within the last month."

"Assassination?"

"No-o." Dragon was palpably uncomfortable. "I told you that we had not yet developed an effective immunization, and . . . This is not a laughing matter, Hemlock!"

"I'm sorry." Jonathan wiped the tears from his eyes and attempted to control himself. "But the poetic justice . . ." He laughed afresh.

"You are easily moved to risibility." Dragon's voice was icy. "May I go on?"

Jonathan waved a permissive hand and chuckled again to himself.

"The method we used to allow the medium to fall

into enemy hands was not without brilliance. We had it transferred to one of our agents, this Wormwood, in Montreal."

"And you let the fact of the transfer leak to the other side."

"More subtle than that, Hemlock. We did everything in our power to prevent them from intercepting —with one exception. We used an incompetent agent for the job."

"You just pushed this ass out in the traffic and let them run over him?"

"Wormwood was a man of dangerously limited abilities. Sooner or later . . ." He made a gesture of inevitability. "At this point, you enter the picture. For our little ploy to be successful, the assassination of Wormwood had to be avenged just as though we were seriously chagrined at his loss. Indeed, considering the importance of the information, the other side would expect us to sanction with more than usual vigor. And we must not disappoint them. CII considers it vital to the national defense that we pursue and liquidate *both* of the men involved in the assassination. And—for certain reasons—you are the only man who can accomplish the second sanction." Dragon paused, his mathematical mind scanning over the conversation to judge if he had left any vital matter out. He decided he had not. "Do you understand now why we brought such uncommon pressure to bear on you?"

"Why am I the only man who can accomplish the sanction?"

"First. Do you accept this assignment?"

"I accept."

The cotton tuft eyebrows raised a fraction of an inch. "Just like that? No further aggression?"

"You'll pay for it."

"I expect to. But not too much, of course."

"We'll see. Tell me about the target."

Dragon paused to collect his strength. "Allow me to begin with the details of Wormwood's murder. There were two men involved. The active role was played by Garcia Kruger, now no longer with us. It was probably he who delivered the first blow; it was almost certainly he who cut open Wormwood's throat and stomach with a pocket knife to retrieve the pellet he had swallowed. The second man was evidently not prepared for violence on this level. He was sickened by the operation; he vomited on the floor. I tell you this to acquaint you with the kind of man you will be dealing with. From his actions in the room and after, Search estimates that he is not a professional from the other side. The chances are that he was involved in the business for the money—a motive you must be sympathetic with."

"What's my target's name?"

"We don't know."

"Where is he now?"

"We don't know."

With growing doubt, Jonathan asked, "You have a description, haven't you?"

"Only the vaguest, I'm afraid. The target is male, not a Canadian citizen, and he is evidently an accomplished mountain climber. We were able to put that much together from one letter delivered to his hotel several days after his departure."

"That's lovely. You want me to kill every climber who hasn't the good fortune to be Canadian."

"Not quite. Our man will be involved in a climb in the Alps this summer."

"That narrows it to maybe three or four thousand men."

"Fewer than that, Hemlock. We know which mountain he will attempt."

"Well?"

"The Eiger." Dragon waited for the effect.

After a pause filled with images of the most

terrifying moments in his climbing career, Jonathan asked with fatalistic assurance, "North Face, of course."

"That is correct." Dragon enjoyed the concern evident in Jonathan's voice. He knew of the two disastrous attempts Jonathan had made on that treacherous face, each of which had failed to claim his life by only the narrowest margin.

"If this man is taking a shot at the Eigerwand, the chances are good that my work will be done for me." Jonathan admired the target, whoever he was.

"I am not a pantheist, Hemlock. God is acknowledgedly on our side, but we are less sure of Nature. After all, you twice attempted the face, and yet you are alive." Dragon took pleasure in reminding him that: "Of course, both of your attempts were unsuccessful."

"I got back off the face alive both times. For Eigerwand, that's a kind of success." Jonathan turned back to business. "Tell me, how many teams are now training for a go at the North Face?"

"Two. One is an Italian team—"

"Forget that one. After the '57 affair, no sane man would go on the hill with an Italian team."

"So my researchers have informed me. The other attempt is scheduled for six weeks from now. The International Alpine Association is sponsoring a goodwill climb to be made by representative climbers from Germany, Austria, France, and the United States."

"I've read about it."

"The American representative was to have been a Mr. Lawrence Scott."

Jonathan laughed. "I know Scotty well; we've climbed together. You're insane if you imagine he had anything to do with the Montreal business."

"I am not insane. My disability is acroma, not acromania. We share your belief in Mr. Scott's innocence. Recall that I said he *was* to have been the American representative. Unfortunately, he had an automotive accident yesterday, and he will not climb for many years, if ever."

Jonathan recalled Scotty's free-swinging, ballet-cum-mathematics style. "You really are a shit, you know."

"Be that as it may, the American Alpine Association will contact you soon to replace Mr. Scott. There will be no objection from the international association. Your fame as a climber precedes you."

"The AAA wouldn't contact me. I haven't climbed for years. They know that. They know I'm not up to a go at the Eiger."

"Nevertheless, they will contact you. The State Department has brought certain pressure to bear on them. So, Hemlock," Dragon said with a tone of wrapping the business up, "your target is either the Frenchman, the German, or the Austrian. We have worked out a way to discover which one before the climb starts. But, to lend verisimilitude to your cover, you will train as though you were actually going to make the climb. And there is always the possibility that the sanction will be made on the face itself. By the way, an old friend of yours will be in Switzerland with you: Mr. Benjamin Bowman."

"Big Ben?" Despite the circumstances, the thought of drinking beer and joking with Big Ben again pleased Jonathan. "But Ben can't make that climb. He's too old for Eiger. So, for that matter, am I."

"The Alpine Association did not select him as a climber. He will be arranging equipment and transportation for the team and managing things. There's a term for it."

"Ground man."

"Ground man, then. We were rather hoping that Mr. Bowman knew about your work with us. Does he?"

"Certainly not."

"Pity. It might be useful to have a devoted associate with you, should it turn out that we cannot nominate the target for you before the climb begins. It might be wise for you to take him into your confidence."

Jonathan rejected the idea out of hand. With his simple and robust sense of ethics, Big Ben would never understand killing for profit. Risking one's life for sport was a different matter. That made excellent sense to Ben.

Dragon's mention that Jonathan would meet a former acquaintance flashed the image of Miles Mellough through his mind. He recalled Dragon's allusion to him during their last conversation. "What part does Mellough play in all this?"

"I assumed you would ask. Frankly, we are not sure. He arrived in Montreal two days before Wormwood's assassination, and he departed the day after. We both know Mr. Mellough too well to imagine a coincidence. It is my assumption that he acted as courier for the culture formula. Naturally, we did not interfere with him until he had passed on the information. Now that that's done, I have no objection to his falling victim to your epic sense of loyalty and honor —like that Greek fellow did. Indeed, we offer you Mr. Mellough as a kind of fringe benefit."

"Six weeks," Jonathan mused. "I'll have to work very hard at conditioning."

"That is your affair."

"Big Ben runs a training school in Arizona. I want to go there for a month."

"If you wish."

"At your expense."

Dragon's voice was heavy with the sarcasm he reserved for the mercenary instincts of his agents. "Naturally, Hemlock." He groped above him for a buzzer to summon Mrs. Cerberus. For his part, the conversation was ended. Jonathan observed his fumbling efforts without offering assistance. "Now that you know the background, Hemlock, you can appreciate why we need you—and only you—to undertake this sanction. You used to climb mountains, and there seem to be so many people of your acquaintance somehow involved in this matter. You appear to be tangled in the skein of fate."

Mrs. Cerberus entered with an officious rustle of crisp clothing. She brushed past Jonathan, knocking against his chair with her formidable hip. He wondered if this ghastly pair copulated. Who else would be available for Dragon? He looked at them and decided that, if they had offspring, they would produce something that could model for Hieronymus Bosch.

In dismissal Dragon said, "I will keep you informed to whatever extent I consider necessary."

"Doesn't it strike you that we have passed over the matter of payment?"

"Oh, of course. We intend to be particularly generous, considering the rigors of the assignment and the emotional difficulties concomitant to our little combat of wills. You will receive thirty thousand dollars upon completion of the sanction. Of course, the stolen twenty thousand dollars is on its way back to you. And as for the Pissarro, Miss Brown made it clear on the telephone the other day that she would not perform her task unless we promised to present it to you as a gift. And that we do. I am sure that is more than you expected."

"Frankly, it is more than I expected you to offer. But it's much less than I shall receive."

"Oh?" Mrs. Cerberus placed a restraining hand on Dragon's arm, solicitous of his blood pressure.

"Yes," Jonathan continued easily. "I shall receive the Pissarro right now, and a hundred thousand dollars when I finish the job. Plus expenses, of course."

"You recognize that this is outrageous."

"Yes. But I view it as retirement pay. This is the last assignment I am going to take for your people."

"That, of course, is your own decision. Unlike those on the other side, we have no desire to keep you after your affection for us had fled. But we do not intend to support you for life."

"A hundred thousand will only support me for four years."

"After which?"

"I'll think of something by then."

"I have no doubt of it. But a hundred thousand dollars is out of the question."

"Oh, no, it isn't. I have listened patiently while you described the pressing need for the sanction, and your need for me—and no one else—to handle it. You have no choice but to pay what I ask."

Dragon was pensive. "You are punishing us for Miss Brown. Is that it?"

Jonathan flashed angrily. "Just pay the money."

"I have been expecting your withdrawal from our organization for some time, Hemlock. Mr. Pope and I were discussing the possibility just this morning."

"That's another thing. If you want to keep Pope intact, keep him out of my way."

"You are striking to the right and left in your rage, aren't you." Dragon considered for a moment. "You have something more on your mind. You know perfectly well that I could promise the money now, then either fail to pay or get it back from you by some means."

"That will never happen again," Jonathan said coldly. "I shall receive the money now—a cashier's check sent to my bank with instructions that it will be paid to me on my appearance or your further instructions, not before seven weeks from now. If I fail to make the sanction, I'll probably be dead, and the check will go uncashed. If I make it, I take the money and retire. If I don't, you can instruct the bank to pay the money to you, on proof of my death."

Dragon pressed the thick pads against his eyes and searched the blackness for a flaw in Jonathan's case. Then his hands dropped to the black sheets. He laughed his three ha's. "Do you know, Hemlock? I think you have us." There was a mixture of wonder and admiration in his voice. "The check will be sent to your bank as you have directed; the painting will be in your home when you return."

"Good."

"I imagine this is the last time I shall have the pleasure of your company. I shall miss you, Hemlock."

"You always have Mrs. Cerberus here."

There was a flat sadness in the response. "True."

Jonathan rose to leave, but he was restrained by Dragon's last question. "You are quite sure that you had nothing to do with the disappearance of Miss Brown?"

"Quite sure. But I suspect she'll turn up sooner or later."

LONG ISLAND:
That Evening

Mauve and pewter skies at sunset; the leaden skin of the ocean undulated in low furrows, alive only at the thin froth edge that the tide had languidly carried up close to his feet.

He had sat on the hard sand of the lower beach for hours, since his return from the city. Feeling heavy and tired, he rose with a grunt and batted the sand from his trousers. He had not yet been in the house, having chosen instead, after a moment of indecision at the door, to roam the grounds.

In the vestibule he discovered a large rectangle wrapped in brown paper and tied with string. He assumed it was the Pissarro, but he did not bother to examine it; indeed, he did not even touch it. As a matter of principle, he had insisted on its return from Dragon, but he no longer had a taste for it.

The nave was cool and thick with shadow. He walked its length and mounted the steps to his bar. He splashed half a glass of Laphroaig into a tumbler and drank it off, then he refilled his glass and turned to face the nave, leaning his elbows on the bar.

A dim arc of light caught the tail of his eye—the firefly trail of a cigarette.

"Gem?"

Jonathan crossed rapidly to the dim female figure sitting in the greenhouse garden.

"What are you doing here?"

"Making myself available, as usual," Cherry answered. "It that for me?" She indicated the glass of Scotch.

"No. Go home." Jonathan sat in a wicker chair opposite her, not so displeased with the idea of company as he seemed, but feeling the sick adrenalin collapse of vast disappointment.

"I don't know what I'm going to do with you, Dr. Hemlock," Cherry rose to get the drink he had refused her. "You're always trying to butter me up," she said over her shoulder as she walked up to the bar. "I know what you're after with all that sweet talk about 'No! Go home.' You're just trying to get into my pants. Maybe the only way to get rid of you is to finally give in." She paused to allow him to respond. He did not. "Yeah, yeah, yeah," she continued, still covering her initial sting with a balm of words, "I guess that's the only way I'll get any peace. Hey! Is there such a thing as a Freudian pun?" Her next pause drew no response either. By now she had returned with her drink, and she slumped petulantly into her chair. "All right. How do you feel about the films of Marcel Carné? Do you believe the advantages of nonstick cooking with Teflon justify the expense of the space program? Or what are your views on the tactical problems of mass retreat should there ever be a war between the Italians and the Arabs?" Then she paused. "Who's Gem?"

"Go home."

"By which I infer she is a woman. She must be something else, considering how fast you got over here, from the bar just now."

Jonathan's voice was paternal. "Look, dear. I'm not up to it tonight."

"The evening sparkles with puns. Can I get you another drink?"

"Please."

"You don't want me to go home really," she said as she went again to the bar. "You're feeling bad, and you want to talk about it."

"You couldn't be more wrong."

"About your feeling bad?"

"About my wanting to talk about it."

"This Gem person must really have come at you. I hate her without even knowing her. Here." She gave him the tumbler. "I'm going to get you all liquored up, and I'm going to make you on the rebound." She produced her best imitation of a witch's cackle.

Jonathan was angry, therefore embarrassed. "For Christ's sake, I'm not on the rebound!"

"Liar, liar, your pants are on fire. Say, I'll bet they really are."

"Go home."

"Was she pretty good in bed?"

Jonathan's voice chilled instantly. "Now you'd better really go home."

Cherry was cowed. "I'm sorry, Jonathan. That was a stupid thing to say. But gee-golly, pal, how do you think it affects a girl's ego when she's been trying to make a man for ever and ever, then some other woman with an unlikely name just takes him—like that." She tried several times to snap her fingers, but produced no sound. "I never could do that."

Jonathan smiled in spite of himself. "Listen, dear. I'll be leaving tomorrow morning."

"For how long?"

"Most of the summer."

"Because of this girl?"

"No! I'm going to do a little climbing."

"You just happen to suddenly decide on that after you meet this woman, right?"

"She has nothing to do with it."

"I really have to doubt that. All right. When are you leaving?"

"Dawnish."

"Well, great! We have the whole night. What do you say, mister. Huh? Huh? What do you say? You going to set me loose before you go? Remember, it's going to be a long summer for us virgins."

"Will you look after the place while I'm away?"

"Gladly. Now, let's talk about return favors."

"Drink up and go home. I have to get some sleep."

Cherry nodded resignedly. "OK. That woman must really have come at you. I hate her."

"Me too," he said quietly.

"Oh, bullshit, Jonathan!"

"There's a new facet of your vocabulary."

"I think I'd better go home."

He walked her to the door and kissed her on the forehead. "I'll see you when I get back."

"Hey, what do you say to a mountain climber? You tell an actor to break a leg, but that sounds kind of ominous for a mountain climber."

"You say you hope it's a go."

"I hope it's a go."

"Thank you. Good night."

"Great. Thanks a lot for that 'good night.' I'll just cling to that all night long."

ARIZONA:
June 15

Standing between his suitcases at the grassy edge of a modest airfield, Jonathan watched the CII cabin jet from which he had just deplaned turn and, with a majestic conversion of power into pollution, taxi to the leeward end of the strip. The wave of heat behind its engine rippled the landscape; its atonic roar was painful.

From across the strip, a new but battered Land-Rover darted out between two corrugated metal hangars, skidded in a right-angle turn that sprayed dust over complaining mechanics, bounced with all four wheels off the ground over a mound of gravel, narrowly missed a Piper that was warming up, triggering a vigorous exchange of abuse between driver and pilot, then bore down on Jonathan with a maximum acceleration until, at the last possible moment, the four-wheel brakes were locked and the Rover screeched to a side-slipping stop, its bumper only inches from Jonathan's knee.

Big Ben Bowman was out before the Land-Rover stopped rocking. "Jon! Goddam my eyes, how are you?" He ripped one suitcase from Jonathan's grasp and tossed it into the back of the vehicle with scant concern for the contents. "I'll tell you one thing, ol' buddy. We're going to drink a bunch of beer before you get out of here. Hey!" His broad hairy paws closed down on Jonathan's upper arms, and after an awkward crushing hug, Jonathan was held out at arm's length for inspection. "You're looking good, ol' buddy. A little soft, maybe. But goddam my ass if it ain't good to see you! Wait till you see the ol' place. It's got . . ." The scream of the CII jet taxiing to take off eclipsed all sound, but Big Ben talked on insouciantly as he loaded Jonathan's second bag and grappled its owner into the Rover. Ben hopped around to jump in behind the wheel, slapped into gear, and they jumped off, bouncing over the drain ditch beside the field as they described a wide skidding turn. Jonathan gripped the seat and shouted as he caught sight of the CII jet roaring down on them from the left. Big Ben laughed and made a sharp cut to the right, and for a moment they raced parallel to the jet, under the shadow of its wing. "No chance!" Ben shouted over the combined din, and he turned left, passing so close behind the jet that Jonathan felt the hot, gritty blast of its engine.

"For Christ's sake, Ben!"

"Can't help it! Can't beat a jet!" Then he roared with laughter and jammed down on the gas pedal. They cut around the random scatter of airport buildings without using the designed roads, leaped the curbing to the main highway, and knifed through traffic with a U-turn that made brakes squeal and horns bleat angrily. Ben gestured classically to the offended drivers.

About a mile out of town they skidded off the highway onto a dirt road. "Just a piece down this way, ol' buddy," Ben shouted. "You remember?"

"About twenty miles, isn't it?"

"Yeah, about. Takes eighteen minutes, unless I'm in a hurry."

Jonathan gripped the "chicken bar" and said as casually as he could, "I don't see any special reason to hurry, Ben."

"You won't recognize the old place!"

"I hope I get a chance to see it."

"What?"

"Nothing!"

As they raced along, bouncing over chuckholes, Ben described some of the improvements he had made. Evidently the whole character of his climbing school had changed to some kind of resort ranch. He looked at Jonathan while he talked, only glancing at the road to make corrections when he felt the wheels go into the soft shoulder. Jonathan had forgotten Ben's crisis-style of driving. On a sheer face with nothing but rotten rock to cling to, there was no man he would rather have beside him, but in the driver's seat . . .

"Oh-oh! Hang on!"

They were suddenly in a cut-back turn and going too fast to make it. The Rover bounced over the shoulder, and the wheels on Jonathan's side dug into the soft sand. For an interminable moment they balanced on those wheels, then Ben whipped to the right, slamming the wheels back to the sand and beginning a fishtail skid. He steered into the skid and pressed down on the gas, converting the skid into a power slide that spun them back up onto the road. "God-dam my ass if I don't forget that turn every time!"

"Ben, I think I'd rather walk."

"OK, OK." He laughed and slowed down for a time, but by inevitable degrees their speed increased, and it was not long before Jonathan's hands were white-knuckled on the chicken bar again. He decided there was nothing to be gained by wearing himself out trying to guide the Land Rover by positive concentration, so he relaxed fatalistically and tried to empty his mind of thought.

Big Ben chuckled.

"What is it?" Jonathan asked.

"I was thinking about the Aconcagua. Remember what I did to that old bitch?"

"I remember."

They had met in the Alps. The gulf between their temperaments suggested that they would be an unlikely team, and neither had been pleased when they were thrown together because their partners were unavailable for climbs they had set their hearts on. So with formidable misgivings they decided to make the climbs together, and they treated each other with that politeness that substitutes for friendship. Slowly and reluctantly they discovered that their polar talents as climbers meshed to create a powerful team. Jonathan attacked a mountain like a mathematical problem, picking routes, evaluating supplies against energy, against time; Big Ben pounded the face into submission with his uncommon strength and indomitable will. Fanciful fellow climbers came to refer to them as The Rapier and The Mace, which nicknames caught the fancy of writers who contributed articles on their achievements to Alpine journals. Jonathan was particularly suited to rock work where the minute tactics of leverage and purchase fitted his intellectual style. Big Ben took over when they were on ice and snow where he would pant and bull through the drifts, breasting an upward path like an inevitable machine of fate.

In bivouac, their differences of personality again operated as a lubricant for the social friction these cramped and sometimes dangerous quarters induce. Ben was older by ten years, loquacious, loudly appreciative of humor. So divergent were their backgrounds and values that they were never in social competition. Even in the lodge after a victory they celebrated in their different ways with different people, and they rewarded themselves that night with different kinds of girls.

For six years they passed the climbing seasons together, bagging peaks: Walker, Dru, the Canadian Rockies. And their international reputations were in no way diminished by Jonathan's contributions to mountaineering publications in which their accomplishments were recorded with calculated phlegmatic understatement that eventually became the stylistic standard for such journals.

It was quite natural, therefore, that when a team of young Germans determined to assail Aconcagua, the highest peak in the Western Hemisphere, they contacted Jonathan and Ben to accompany them. Ben was particularly enthusiastic; it was his kind of climb, a grinding, man-eroding ascent requiring little in the way of surface tactics, but much in the way of endurance and supply strategy.

Jonathan's response was cooler. As was just, considering that they had conceived the plan, the Germans were to be the primary assault pair. Jonathan and Ben working in support and going after the peak only if something untoward happened to the Germans. It was fair that it should be so, but it was not Jonathan's way. Unlike Ben, who loved each step of a climb, Jonathan climbed for the victory. The great expense involved also dampened Jonathan's exuberance, as did the fact that his particular talents would be of secondary importance on a climb like this.

But Ben was not to be denied. Their financial problems he solved by selling the small ranch that was his livelihood; and in a long telephone call he persuaded Jonathan by admitting that, considering his age, this would probably be the last major climb he would ever make.

As it turned out, he was right.

From the sea, Aconcagua seems to rise up just behind Valparaiso, a regular and, from that distance, gentle cone. But getting there is half the hell. Its base is tucked in among a tangle of lower mountains, and the team spent a week alternating between the antithetical torments of miasmic jungle and dusty ravines as they followed the old Fitz-Gerald route to the foot.

There is in this world no more demoralizing climb than that vast heap of rotten rock and ice. It destroys men, not with the noble counterstrokes of an Eigerwand or a Nanga Parbat, but by eroding a man's nerve and body until he is a staggering, whimpering maniac. No single stretch of the hill is particularly difficult, or even interesting in the Alpine sense. It is no exaggeration to say that any athletic layman could handle any given thousand feet of it, if properly equipped and conditioned to the thin air. But Aconcagua rises thousands upon thousands of feet, and one climbs hour after hour up through shale and ragged rock, through moraine and crevassed glacier, day upon day, with no sense of accomplishment, with no feeling that the summit is nearing. And time and again, the flash storms that twist around the peaks pin the climbers down for who knows how long. Maybe forever. And still that pile of garbage left from the Creation goes on and upward.

Within three thousand feet of the summit, one of the Germans gave in, demoralized with mountain sickness and the bone-deep cold. "What's the use?" he asked. "It really doesn't matter." They all knew what he meant. So slight is the technical challenge of the Aconcagua that it is less a cachet to a climber's career than an avowal of the latent death wish that drives so many of them up.

But no bitch-kitty of a hill was going to stop Big Ben! And it was unthinkable that Jonathan could let him go it alone. It was decided that the Germans would stay where they were and try to improve the camp to receive the new summit team when they staggered back.

The next fifteen hundred feet cost Ben and Jonathan an entire day, and they lost half of their provisions in a near fall.

The next day they were pinned down by a flash storm. Saint Elmo's fire sparkled from the tips of their ice axes. With wooden fingers they clung to the edges of the strip of canvas that was their only protection from the screaming wind. The fabric bellied and flapped with pistol-shot reports; it twisted and contorted in their numb hands like a maddened wounded thing seeking vengeance.

With the coming of night, the storm passed, and they had to kick the canvas from hands that had lost the power to relax. Jonathan had had it. He told Ben they must go back the next morning.

Ben's teeth were clenched and tears of frustration flowed from the corners of his eyes and froze on the stubble of his beard. "Goddam it!" he sobbed. "Goddam this frigging hill!" Then his temper ruptured and he went after the mountain with his ice axe, beating it and tearing at it until the thin air and fatigue left him panting on the snow. Jonathan pulled him up and helped him back to their scant cover. By full dark they were dug in as comfortably as possible. The wind moaned, but the storm remained lurking in ambuscade, so they were able to get a little rest.

"You know what it is, ol' buddy?" Ben asked in the close dark. He was calm again, but his teeth were chattering with the cold, and that lent a frighteningly unstable sound to his voice. "I'm getting old, Jon. This has got to be my last hill. And goddam my ass if this old bitch is going to bust me. You know what I mean?"

Jonathan reached out in the dark and gripped his hand.

A quarter of an hour later Ben's voice was calm and flat. "We'll try tomorrow, right?"

"All right," Jonathan said. But he did not believe it.

The dawn brought ugly weather with it, and Jonathan surrendered his last feeble hope of making the summit. His concern now was getting down alive.

About noon, the weather healed up and they dug themselves out. Before Jonathan could phrase his reasons for turning back, Ben had started determinedly upward. There was nothing to do but follow.

Six hours later they were on the summit. Jonathan's memory of the last *étape* is foggy. Step after step, breaking through the wind crust and sinking up to the crotch in the unstable snow, they pressed blindly on, stumbling, slipping, reason reduced to concentration on the task of one more step.

But they were on the summit. They could not see a rope's length out into the swirling spindrift.

"Not even a goddamed view!" Ben complained. Then he fumbled with the drawstring of his plastic outer pants and dropped them away. After a struggle with his wool ski pants, he stood up free and expressed his contempt for the Aconcagua in ancient and eloquent style.

As they plunged and picked their way back down, eager to make time, but fearful of setting off an avalanche, Jonathan noticed that Ben was clumsy and unsteady.

"What's wrong?"

"Ain't got no feet down there, ol' buddy."

"How long since you felt them?"

"Couple of hours, I guess."

Jonathan dug a shallow shelter in the snow and fumbled Ben's boots off. The toes were white and hard as ivory. For a quarter of an hour Jonathan held the frigid feet against his bare chest inside his coat. Ben howled with vituperation as feeling returned to one foot, replacing numbness with surges of pain. But the other foot remained rigid and white, and Jonathan knew there was nothing to be gained by continuing first aid. But there was great danger of a fresh storm catching them in the open. They pushed on.

The Germans were magnificent. When the two came staggering into camp, they took Ben from Jonathan and all but carried him down. It was all Jonathan could do to stumble along behind, broken-winded and half snow-blind.

Ben looked uncomfortable and out of place sitting up against a pile of pillows in the Valparaiso hospital. By way of small talk, Jonathan accused him of malingering there because he was making the nurses every night.

"I wouldn't touch them with a barge pole, ol' buddy. Anyway who would take a man's toes when he ain't looking would take just about anything."

That was the last mention of the amputated toes. They both knew Big Ben would never make a major climb again.

They felt neither elation nor accomplishment as they watched the mountain slip into the sea beyond the stern of their ship. They did not feel proud of having made it, nor did the Germans feel shame for having failed. That is the way it is with that pile of fossilized shit.

Back in the States, Ben set about establishing his little school for climbing in a corner of Arizona where many kinds of natural face problems abound. So few people wanted the kind of advanced training he offered that Jonathan wondered how he kept his head above water. To be sure, he and twenty or so other skilled climbers made it a practice to patronize Ben's school, but that is just what it was—patronizing. The repeated struggles to force Ben to accept payment for lodging and training embarrassed Jonathan, and he stopped coming. Soon after, he stopped climbing altogether as his new home and his collection of paintings absorbed all his interest.

"Yeah," Ben shouted as they landed back in the seat after a bad bump, "I sure paid that old bitch back, didn't I?"

"You ever consider what would have happened if you had gotten local frostbite?"

Ben laughed. "Oh, my! There'd have been wailing and moaning on the reservation, and lots of Indian girls dripping tears, ol' buddy."

They broke over a little rise and started winding down into Ben's valley, leaving a rising trail of dust in their wake. Jonathan was surprised as he looked down on Ben's spread. It certainly had changed. Gone was the modest grouping of cabins around a cookhouse. There was a large swimming pool flashing emerald and surrounded on three sides by the body and wings of a pseudo-Indian lodge, and what appeared to be a patio lounge was dotted with the white blobs of people in swimming suits who looked nothing at all like climbers. There was no comparison between this and the Spartan training school he remembered.

"How long has all this been here?" he asked as they slithered down the steep road.

"About two years. Like it?"

"Impressive."

They sped across the gravel parking area and banged into a retaining log before rocking to a stop. Jonathan climbed out slowly and stretched his back to regroup his bones. The unmoving earth underfoot was a pleasure.

It was not until they were sitting in the shadowy cool of the bar, concentrating on much appreciated glasses of beer, that Jonathan had leisure to look at his host. Robust virility was projected through every detail of Ben's face, from the thick, close-cropped silver hair to the broad leathery face that looked as though it had been designed by Hormel and shaped with a dull saber. Two deep creases folded in his

134

heavily tanned cheeks, and the corners of his eyes crinkled into patterns like aerial photographs of the Nile Delta.

The first beers drained off, Ben signaled the Indian bartender for two more. Jonathan recalled Ben's epic fondness for beer that had been an object of comment and admiration among the climbing community.

"Very posh," Jonathan complimented, scanning his surroundings.

"Yeah, it begins to look like I'll make it through the winter."

The bar was separated by a low wall of local stone from the lounge, through which an artificial stream wound its way among the tables, each of which was on a little rock island connected to the walkways by an arched stone bridge. A few couples in sports clothes talked quietly over ice-and-foliage drinks, enjoying the air conditioning and ignoring the insipid music from ubiquitous but discreet speakers. One end of the lounge had a glass wall through which could be seen the pool and bathers. There was a scattering of prosperous-looking men with horizontal suntans who sat in drinking groups around white iron tables, or sat on the edges of gaudy padded sun chairs, concentrating on stock journals, their stomachs depending between their legs. Some waddled aimlessly along the sides of the pool.

Young ladies lolled hopefully on beach chairs, most of them with one knee up, revealing a beacon of inner thigh. Sunglasses were directed at books and magazines, but eyes above them scouted the action.

Ben regarded Jonathan for a moment, his drooping blue eyes crinkled up at the sides. He nodded. "Yeah, it's really good to see you, ol' buddy. My phony guests really make my ass weary. How you been doing? Keeping the world at arm's length?"

"I'm staying alive."

"How's that screwy church of yours?"

"It keeps the rain off my head."

"Good." He was pensive for a moment. "What's this all about, Jon? I got this telegram telling me to take care of you and get you into condition for a climb. They said they would pay all expenses. What does that mean, ol' buddy? 'All expenses' can cover a lot of ground. Are these people friends? Want me to take it easy on them?"

"By no means. They're not friends. Soak them. Give me the best accommodations you have, and put all your meals and drinks on my bill."

"Well now! Ain't that nice! Goddam my eyes if we don't have some kind of ball at this expense. Hey! Talking about climbing. I've been invited to be ground man for a bunch taking a shot at the Eiger. How about that?"

"It's great." Jonathan knew his next statement would cause comment, so he tried to drop it off-handedly. "Matter of fact, that's the climb I'm here to train for." He waited for the reaction.

Ben's smile faded frankly, and he stared at Jonathan for a second. "You're kidding."

"No."

"What happened to Scotty?"

"He had an auto accident."

"Poor bastard. He was really looking forward to it." Ben communicated with his beer for a moment. "How come they picked you?"

"I don't know. Wanted to add class to an altogether undistinguished team, I guess."

"Come on. Don't bullshit me, ol' buddy."

"I honestly don't know why they picked me."

"But you are going?"

"That's right."

A girl in an abbreviated bikini came up to the bar and squeaked her still-damp bottom onto a stool one away from Jonathan, who did not respond to her automatic smile of greeting.

"Beat it, Buns," Ben said, slapping her ass with a moist smack. She giggled and went back to the poolside.

"Getting much climbing in?" Jonathan asked.

"Oh, I gimp up some small stuff, just for the hell of it. Matter of fact, that part of the business is long gone. As you can see, my patrons come here to hunt, not climb." He reached over the bar and took an extra bottle of beer. "Come on, Jon. Let's go talk."

They threaded their way along the lounge walkway and over a bridge to the most secluded island.

After waving the waiter away, Ben sipped his beer slowly, trying to collect his thoughts. Then he carefully dusted the top of the table with his hand. "You're—ah—what now? Thirty-five?"

"Thirty-seven."

"Yeah." Ben looked out across his lounge toward the pool, feeling he had made his point.

"I know what you're thinking, Ben. But I have to go."

"You've been on the Eiger before. Twice, as I recall."

"Right."

"Then you know."

"Yes."

Ben sighed with resignation, then he changed the tone of his comments, as befitted a friend. "All right, it's your thing. The climb starts in six weeks. You'll want to get to Switzerland for some practice runs, and you'll need a little rest after I'm done with you. How long do you want to spend conditioning here?"

"Three, four weeks."

Ben nodded. "Well, at least you don't have any fat on you. But you're going to have to sweat, ol' buddy. How are the legs?"

"They reach from the crotch to the ground. That's about all you can say for them."

"Uh-huh. Enjoy that beer, Jon. It's your last for a week at least."

Jonathan finished it slowly.

ARIZONA:
June 16-27

The insistent grind of the door buzzer insinuated itself into the narrative structure of Jonathan's dream, then it shattered his heavy sleep, and local reality flowed in through the cracks. He stumbled to the door and clawed it open without ever getting both eyes open at the same time. As he leaned against the frame, his head hanging down, the Indian bellboy wished him a good morning cheerily and told him that Mr. Bowman had left instructions to be sure Dr. Hemlock was wide awake.

"Whadymizid?" Jonathan asked.

"Pardon me, sir?"

"What . . . time . . . is . . . it?"

"Three thirty, sir."

Jonathan turned back into the room and fell across the bed, muttering to himself, "This can't be happening."

No sooner had he slipped into a vertiginous sleep than the phone rang. "Go away," he mumbled without picking up the receiver, but it rang on without mercy. He pulled it onto the bed and pawed around with his eyes clamped shut until he had located the receiver.

"Rise and shine, ol' buddy!"

"Ben—argh—" He cleared his throat. "Why are you doing this to me?"

"Breakfast in ten minutes."

"No."

"You want me to send someone up there with a bucket of ice water?"

"He better be someone you're tired of having around."

Ben laughed and hung up. Jonathan rolled out and groped his way around until he lucked into the bathroom where he let a cold shower drum consciousness into him until he felt the danger of accident by falling was remote.

Ben pushed two more eggs onto Jonathan's plate. "Put them down, ol' buddy. And finish that steak."

They were alone in the lodge kitchen, surrounded by glowing, impersonal, stainless steel. Their voices had a cell-block bounce.

Jonathan looked at the eggs with nausea constricting his throat. "Ben, I've never lied to you, have I? Honest to God, I believe I'm dying. And I've always wanted to die in bed."

"Sit back down and get at that chow!"

It was one thing to push food into his mouth, but another to swallow it.

Ben chatted on, impervious to the stares of hate. "I've been up half the night working out details of the Eiger climb. I'm buying the heavy equipment for the team and bringing it over with me. I'll order your climbing kit with the rest. You can go with jeans and soft shoes for the first few days here. We ain't going to do anything hard right at first. Come on! Drink the milk!" Ben finished his beer and opened another can. The beer for breakfast was more than Jonathan could stand to look at. "You still get your climbing boots in Spain?"

Jonathan nodded heavily and found the lower part of the motion so appealing that he let his head hang there and tried to return to sleep.

"All right. Leave me their name and your account number and I'll get a cable off today. Come on! Time's a-wasting! Eat!"

The one-mile, two-minute drive across open grassland in inky predawn dark brought Jonathan fully awake.

For three hours without a rest they climbed a rough, switch-back trail up one of the faces that ringed around the flat-bottomed depression in which Ben had established his lodge. Morning came while they were trudging upward, but Jonathan took no joy in the russet mantle. When the path was wide enough, Ben walked alongside and chatted. The slight limp from the missing toes was all but imperceptible, save that he pushed off more strongly from one foot. Jonathan spoke little; he puffed along concentrating on the pains in his thighs and calves. He was carrying a thirty-five pound training pack because Ben did not want him to get used to going light. That would not be the way of things on the Eiger.

About eight, Ben looked up the trail and waved. There was a figure sitting in the deep shadow of a rock, obviously waiting for them.

"Well, I'm going to turn back, ol' buddy."

"Thank God."

"No, not you. You need the work. George Hotfort yonder will take you on up."

The figure was coming down to meet them.

Jonathan protested, "Hey, she's a girl!"

"Yeah, there's been a lot of people notice that. Now, George," Ben said to the young Indian girl who had joined them, "this here's Jonathan Hemlock, my old climbing buddy. Jon, meet George Hotfort. Now listen, George, you bring him up another couple of hours, then get him back to the place in time for dinner." The girl nodded and leveled a scornful and superior look at Jonathan.

141

"I'll see you, ol' buddy." And Ben turned back down the trail.

Jonathan watched him go with genuine hate in his soul, then he turned to the girl. "You don't have to do everything he tells you, you know. Here's your chance to strike back at the white man."

The girl gazed on him without the trace of an expression on her wide-cheekboned, oriental face.

"Georgette?" he ventured.

She made a curt motion with her head and started up the hill, her long strong legs effortlessly pulling the trail under her swinging bottom.

"How about Georgianna?" He huffed along after her.

Each time she got a distance ahead, she waited, her back against a rock, watching his exertions calmly. But as soon as he came close enough to appreciate the filled denim shirt, she would push off the rock and move on, her hips swinging metrically with the long regular strides. Even at the steep angle of the rise, her ankles were supple enough to allow her heels to touch the ground, as the heels of Alpine guides do. Jonathan's calves were tight and inelastic; he was walking mostly on his toes, and feeling every step.

The trail steepened, and his legs started to wobble, causing him to lose his footing occasionally. Whenever this happened, he would look up and find her gazing at him with distant disgust.

The sweat ran from his hair into his eyes, and he could feel the thump of his pulse against his eardrums. The web straps of his pack chafed his shoulders. He was breathing orally by now, and his lips were thick and coated.

He wiped the sweat out of his eyes and looked up after her. Directly in front of him was a vertical bank about thirty feet high with only little dents in the baked earth for foot and hand holds. She stood on top looking down at him. He shook his head definitely and sat down on the trail. "Oh, no. No-o, no, no."

But after a couple of minutes of silence broken only by the distant whip of a lark, he turned to discover that she had not moved and was still regarding him placidly. Her face was smooth and powdery, not a trace of perspiration on it, and he hated her for that.

"All right, George. You win."

With a catalogue of pain, he clawed his way up the bank. When he had scrambled to the top he grinned at her, expecting some kind of praise. Instead, she archly walked around him, getting no nearer than three feet, and started on the return trip to the lodge. He watched her glissade easily down the bank and take the downward trail.

"You are a savage, George Hotfort. I'm glad we took your land!"

Back in the rock garden lounge, he consumed an enormous dinner with the concentration of a Zen neophyte. He had showered and changed clothes, and he felt a little more human, although his legs and shoulders still protested with dull, persistent aches. Ben sat across from him, eating with his usual vigor and drawing off great gulps of beer to wash the food down. Jonathan envied him the beer. George had left him a few hundred yards from the lodge and had returned up the trail without a word.

"What do you think of George?" Ben asked, stabbing at his face with a napkin.

"Lovely person. Warm and human. And a conversationalist of considerable accomplishment."

"Yeah, but she's a climbing fool, ain't she?" Ben spoke with paternal pride.

Jonathan admitted that she was that.

"I use her to help break in the handful of climbers who still come for conditioning and training."

"No wonder your trade has fallen off. What's her real name, anyway?"

"George *is* her real name."

"How did that happen?"

"She was named after her mother."

"I see."

Ben studied Jonathan's face for a moment, hoping to discover the discouragement that would make him give up the idea of climbing the Eiger. "Feeling a little bashed?"

"A little. I'll remember that workout the rest of my life. But I'll be ready to get back to work tomorrow."

"Tomorrow's balls! That was just an appetizer. You go back up in an hour."

Jonathan started to object.

"Hush up and listen to your ol' buddy." Ben's broad face bunched up in folds around his eyes as he became serious for a moment. "Jon, you're no kid anymore. And the Eiger's one bitch-kitty of a face. Now, if I had my druthers, I'd have you give up this whole idea."

"Can't."

"Why not?"

"Just take my word for it."

"All right. I think you're out of your head, but if you're set on going, then goddam my eyes if I don't make sure you're in top condition. Because if you ain't, you're pretty likely to end up a grease spot on those rocks. And it's not just for you either. I'm ground man for the team. I'm responsible for all of them. And I'm not going to let them be dragged off by a headstrong old man, you, who ain't ready for the climb." Ben punctuated his uncommonly long tirade with a deep pull of beer. "Now you just take yourself a swim in the pool yonder and then lay around in the sun eye-balling the skin. I'll have them call you when it's time."

Jonathan did as he was told. He had begun to

enjoy the game of estimating the ballistic competence of the various young ladies around the pool when a waiter came to tell him his rest period was over.

Once again Ben took him partway up the trail, then he was turned over to George, who paced him even farther and faster than in the morning. Jonathan spoke to her several times, but he could not dent the expressionless facade, much less get a word from her. It was twilight when she left him as before, and he limped back to his suite. He showered and fell on the bed with a lust for sleep. But Ben arrived just in time to prevent him from finding that refuge.

"No you don't, ol' buddy. You still got a big meal to put away."

Although he nodded off repeatedly over his plate, Jonathan consumed a big plank steak and a salad. And that night he found sleep without the usual soporific assistance of the Lautrec article.

The next morning (if three-thirty has any right to that title) found his joints filled with cement and pain. But he and Ben were on the trail by four-thirty. It was a different path and noticeably steeper, and again he was turned over to George Hotfort about halfway up. Again the easily swinging hips drew him upward as he muttered curses against his pain, the heat, his trembling legs, and all Indians. Again at each pause George's mocking, disdainful eyes observed his struggles without comment.

Dinner and a swim, and up again in the afternoon. And the next day; and the next; and the next.

His climbing trim came back faster than he had dared to hope, and faster than Ben cared to admit. By the sixth day he was enjoying the training and keeping up with George all the way. They moved higher and steeper each day, always making more distance in the same amount of time, and sometimes now Jonathan led and George followed. On the seventh day he was scrambling up a shale drift when he looked back to see (oh, rewarding sight!) perspiration on George's brow. When she got to him she sat down and rested, breathing hard.

"Oh, come on George!" Jonathan pleaded. "We can't spend out lives sitting here. Upward, upward. Get thine swinging ass in gear." Because she never spoke, he had fallen into the habit of talking to her as though she could not understand. George evaluated the hang of scruffy rock above them and shook her head. Her denim shirt was dark with sweat under the arms and at each pocket where her breasts pressed against the cloth. She smiled at him for the first time, then she started back down the trail.

Never before had she accompanied him all the way back to the lodge, but this time, while Jonathan showered, she and Ben had a long talk. That evening a champagne cooler with half a dozen bottles of beer buried in ice appeared with dinner, and Ben told Jonathan that the first phase of his conditioning was over. They were through with the soft shoe work. His kit had been assembled, and the next morning they would go to work on the stone faces.

A second six-pack was consumed in Ben's rooms where he outlined the next few days. They would begin on easy faces, no more than ten or fifteen feet above the scree, where Jonathan would get the feel of the rock again. Once Ben was satisfied with his progress, they would move up and put a little void under themselves.

Their plans made, the two men chatted and drank beer for an hour. Ben took vicarious pleasure in watching his comrade's delight in the cold brew he had been denied throughout the first phase of conditioning, although he admitted mistrusting any man who could go without beer for that many days.

For some time Jonathan had been aware that his hardening body was growing eager to make love, not as an affectionate expression, but as a biological eruption. It was for this reason that he asked Ben, more or less offhand, "Do you have anything going with George?"

"What? Oh! No." He actually blushed. "For Christ's sake, I'm twenty-five years older than her. Why do you want to know?"

"Nothing really. I'm just feeling tough and full of sperm. She happens to be around and she looks capable."

"Well, she's a grown-up girl. I guess she can go with whoever she wants."

"That might present a difficulty. I can't say she's been pestering me with her attentions."

"Oh, she likes you all right. I can tell from the way she talks about you."

"Does she ever speak to anyone but you, Ben?"

"Not as I know of." Ben finished his bottle at one long pull and opened another. "Kind of funny," he commented.

"What is?"

"You wanting George. Considering the way she's been grinding you down, a body would think you'd have some kind of hate going for her."

"Who knows the devious working of the id? In the back of my mind I may be carrying the image of impaling her—stabbing her to death, or something."

Ben glanced at Jonathan with a hint of a wince in his eyes. "You know what, ol' buddy. Way down deep you've got the makings of a real bad ass. I don't know that I'd like to be alone on a desert island with you if there was a limited food supply."

"No worry. You're a friend."

"Ever have any enemies?"

"A few."

"Any of them still around and kicking?"

"One." Jonathan considered for a moment. "No, two."

There had been rather a lot of beer, and Jonathan was asleep quickly. The Jemima dream began, as it had each night, with deceptive gentleness—a rehearsal in sequence of their relations from the first meeting on the plane. The sudden images of Dragon's derisive face, like quick intercuts in a motion picture, never lasted long enough to force Jonathan awake. The flickering hurricane lamps dissolved into harlequin flecks. The arc of her cigarette glowed in the dark. He reached out for her, and she was so real he experienced a tactile tingle as he slid the flat of his hand over her hard-under-soft stomach. He felt it press up against his palm—and he was fully awake! Before he could sit up, George drew him tightly against her, gripping him with strong arms and wrapping supple legs around his. Her eyes too had a Mongol cast, and it was possible to make the substitution.

He did not wake until after five. Because of recent habit, the late hour seemed to accuse. But then he recalled that they would be working faces today, and you cannot work a face before light. George had gone. She had left as silently as she had come. A stiffness in his lower back, a feeling of tender emptiness in his groin, and a slightly alkaline smell from beneath the sheets reminded him of the night. He had been awake when she left, but he feigned sleep, fearful of being called on to perform again.

As he showered, he promised himself to use the girl sparingly. She would send a man to a sanatorium in a fortnight, if he let her. She climaxed quickly and often, but was never satisfied. Sex for her was not a gentle sequence of objectives and achievements; it was an unending chase from one exploding bubble of thrill to the next—a plateau of sensation to be maintained, not a series of crests to be climbed. And if the partner seemed to flag, she introduced a variation calculated to renew his interest and vigor.

Like those of swimming, the techniques of climbing are never forgotten, once properly learned. But Jonathan knew he would have to discover what new limitations the past few years of age and inactivity had placed on his skill and nerve.

The experienced climber can move up a face he cannot climb to. A regular, predicted set of moves from one point of imbalance to its counterpoise will keep him on the face, so long as he continues moving, rather in the way a bicycle rider has little trouble with balance, unless he goes too slowly. It is necessary to read the pitch accurately, to plot out and rehearse the moves kinesodically, then to make them with smooth conviction from hold to hold, ending in a predicted and reliable purchase. In the past, this constellation of abilities had been Jonathan's forte, but during his first day of free climbing he made several misjudgments that sent him slithering down ten or fifteen feet to the scree, banging a little skin off elbows and knees and doing greater damage to his self-esteem. It was some time before he diagnosed his problem. The intervening years since his last climb had had no effect on his analytical powers, but they had eroded the fine edge of his physical dexterity. This erosion was beyond repair, so it was necessary that he train himself to think within the limits of his new, inferior body.

At first, for safety, Ben insisted that they use many pitons, making the face look as though lady climbers or Germans had been there. But it was not long before they were making short grade five and six pitches with a more Anglo-Saxon economy of ironmongery. One problem, however, continued to plague Jonathan, making him furious with himself. In the midst of a skillful and businesslike series of moves, he would suddenly find himself fighting the rock, succumbing to the natural, but lethal, desire to press his body against it. This not only deprived him of leverage for tension footholds, but it made it difficult to scan the face above for cracks. Once a climber presses the face, a fearful cycle begins. It is an unnoticed welling up of animal fear that first makes him hug the rock; hugging weakens his footholds and blinds him to purchases that might be within grasp; and this, now real, danger feeds the original fear.

On one occasion, after Jonathan thought he had overcome this amateurish impulse, he suddenly found himself caught up in the cycle. His cleated boots could find no grab, and suddenly he was off.

He fell only three of the forty meters between him and the rock below before his line snapped up short and he was dangling and twisting from the rope. It was a sound piton.

"Hey!" Ben shouted from above. "What the fuck you doin'?"

"I'm just hanging from this piton, wise ass! What are you doing?"

"I'm just holding your weight in my powerful and experienced hands and watching you hang from that piton. You look real graceful. A little stupid, but real graceful."

Jonathan kicked angrily off the rock and swung out and back, but he missed his grab.

"For Christ's sake, ol' buddy! Wait a minute! Now, don't do anything. Just rest there for a minute."

Jonathan dangled from the line, feeling foolish.

"Now think about it." Ben gave it a moment. "You know what's wrong?"

"Yes!" Jonathan was impatient, both with himself and with Ben's condescending treatment.

"Tell me."

With the singsong of rote Jonathan said, "I'm crowding the rock."

"Right. Now get back on the face and we'll go down."

Jonathan took a mind-clearing breath, kicked out and swung back, and he was on the face. During the whole of the retreat he moved glibly and precisely, forgetting the vertical gravity of the valley and responding naturally to the diagonal gravity of weight-versus-rope that kept him leaning well away from the face.

On the valley floor they sat on a pile of scree, Jonathan coiling rope while Ben drank the bottle of beer he had stashed in the shade of a rock. They were dwarfed by the nine "needles" towering around them. It was on one of these that they had been working, a column of striated, reddish rock that rose from the earth like a decapitated trunk of a giant fossil tree.

"How would you like to climb Big Ben tomorrow?" Ben asked out of lengthy silence. He was referring to the tallest of the columns, a four-hundred-foot shaft that eons of wind had eroded until it was wider at the top than at the base. It was the proximity of these peculiar formations that had caused Ben to select this spot for his climbing school, and he had promptly named the grandest after himself.

Jonathan squinted at the needle, his eyes locating half a dozen dicey areas before it had swept halfway up. "You think I'm ready?"

"More than ready, ol' buddy. Matter of fact, I figure that's your problem. You're overtrained, or trained too fast. You're getting a little skitterish." Ben went on to say that he had noticed Jonathan pushing off too hard when he was in a tension stance, taking little open moves without being sure of the terminal purchase, and letting his mind wander from the rock when it seemed too easy. It was during these moments of inattention that Jonathan suddenly found himself hugging the face. The best cure for all this might be an endurance run—something to break down the overcoiled legs and to humble the dangerously confident animal in Jonathan.

His eyes picking their way up from possible stance to stance, Jonathan played with the climb for twenty minutes before he accomplished the optical ascent. "Looks hard, Ben. Especially the top flange."

"It ain't no bedpost." Ben stood up. "Goddam my eyes if I don't think I'll come along with you!"

Jonathan glanced at Ben's foot before he could help it. "You really want to go?"

"No sweat. I've stumped up it once before. What do you say?"

"I say we walk up it tomorrow."

"Great. Now why don't you take the rest of the day off, ol' buddy."

As they walked back to the lodge, Jonathan experienced a lightness of spirit and eagerness for the morrow that had, in the old days, been the core of his love for climbing. His whole being was focused on matters of rock, strength, and tactic, and the outside world with its Dragons and Jemimas could not force its way into his consciousness.

He had been eating well, sleeping perfectly, training hard, drinking much beer, and using George with gingerly discretion. This kind of elemental life would bore him beyond standing in a couple of weeks, but just then it was grand.

He leaned against the lodge's main desk, reading an effervescent postcard from Cherry sprinkled with *underlinings,* and ———, and !!!!, and . . . . . ., and (parenthesis), and ha! ha! ha! No one, evidently, had burned down his home. Mr. Monk was as angry and scatological as ever. And Cherry wanted to know if he could suggest some reading on the preparation of aphrodisiacs for a friend of hers (someone he had never met) for use on a man (whom he had also never met) and whom he would probably not like, inasmuch as this nameless party was such a heartless *turd!!!* as to allow lusty girls to go untapped.

Jonathan felt something touch his foot and looked down to see a nervous little Pomeranian with a rhinestone collar sniffing around. He ignored it and returned to his postcard, but the next moment the dog was mounting an amorous attack on his leg. He kicked it aside, but the dog interpreted this rejection as maidenly coyness and returned to the attack.

"Leave Dr. Hemlock alone, Faggot. I am sorry, Jonathan, but Faggot has not learned to recognize the straight, and he hasn't the patience to wait for an invitation."

Without looking up, Jonathan recognized the chocolate baritone of Miles Mellough.

ARIZONA:
June 27

Jonathan watched the lace-cuffed and perfectly mani-
cured hands descend to pick up the Pomeranian. He
followed the dog up to Miles's face, tanned and handsome as ever, the large blue eyes gazing languidly
from beneath long black lashes, the broad, lineless
forehead supporting a cluster of trained soft waves
that swept around to the sides in a seemingly artless
pattern that was the pride of Miles's hairdresser. The
dog kissed at Miles's cheek, which affection he accepted without taking his eyes from Jonathan.

"How have you been, Jonathan?" There was a
gentle mocking smile in his eyes, but their movements
were quick, ready to read and avoid a thrust.

"Miles." The word was not a greeting, it was a
nomination. Jonathan put his postcard into his pocket
and waited for Miles to get on with it.

"How long has it been?" Miles dropped his eyes
and shook his head. "A long time. Come to think
of it, the last time we met was in Arles. We had
just finished that Spanish thing—you and I and
Henri."

Jonathan's eyes flickered at the mention of Henri
Baq.

"No, Jonathan." Miles laid his hand on Jonathan's
sleeve. "Don't imagine I have made a verbal blunder.
It's about Henri that I want to chat. Do you have a

moment?" Feeling the forearm muscles tense, Miles patted Jonathan's arm and withdrew his hand.

"There's only one possibility, Miles. You have an incurable disease and lack the guts to kill yourself."

Miles smiled. "That's very good, Jonathan. But wrong. Shall we have a drink?"

"All right."

"Rather like old times."

"Not at all like old times."

The eyes of all the young ladies in the lounge followed Miles as he preceded Jonathan along the walkway and over an arched stone bridge to an isolated table. His uncommon good looks, the grace and strength of his dancer's walk, and the extreme styling of his clothes would have eclipsed a man of less panache, but Miles moved slowly among the girls, granting them the benediction of his easy smile, honestly pitying them because he was ultimately unavailable.

As soon as they were seated, Miles released the dog which vibrated with tense energy until its toenails clicked on the rock, scrambling in circles of frenzy, then scampered along to a nearby table where he was captured, whimpering, by three young ladies in bikinis who were clearly delighted to possess this entree to the handsomest man they had ever seen. One of them approached the table carrying the shivering, clawing animal in her arms.

Miles rested his eyes on her breast languidly, and she produced a nervous laugh. "What do you call him?" she asked.

"Faggot, my dear."

"Oh, that's cute! Why do you call him that?"

"Because he's a bundle of nerves."

She did not understand, so she said, "That's cute!"

Miles beckoned the girl to his side and placed his hand lightly on her buttock. "Would you do me a great favor, dear?"

She giggled at the unexpected contact, but did not withdraw. "Surely. Glad to."

"Take Faggot and go play with him for a while."

"All right," she said. Then, "Thank you.' '

"There's a good girl." He patted the buttock in dismissal and the girl left the lounge, followed by her companions who were just dying to know what had transpired.

"They're cute little tricks, aren't they, Jonathan. And not completely without their uses. Bees are attracted to the honey."

"And drones," Jonathan added.

A young Indian waiter stood by the table.

"A double Laphroaig for my friend, and a brandy Alexander for me," Miles ordered, looking deeply into the waiter's eyes.

Miles's gaze followed the waiter as he made his way along the walkway and over the artificial streams of bubbling water. "Good-looking boy, that." Then he turned his attention to Jonathan, touching his palms together and resting his forefingers against his lips, his thumbs under his chin. Over the tips of his fingers, his still eyes smiled with gentle frost, and Jonathan reminded himself how dangerous this ruthless man could be, despite appearances. For a minute neither of them spoke. Then Miles broke it with a rich laugh. "Oh, Jonathan. No one can best you at the game of cold silence. I should have known better than to try. Was my memory accurate about the Laphroaig?"

"Yes."

"A whole monosyllable! How gracious."

Jonathan supposed Miles would come to the subject in his own time, and he had no intention of helping him. Until the drinks came, Miles scanned the men and girls around the pool. He sat poised in his black velvet suit, high-rolled linen collar with a drooping velvet cravat, slim and expensive Italian boots. Obviously, he was doing well. It was rumored that, after leaving CII, Mellough had set himself up in San Francisco where he dealt in all kinds of merchandise, chiefly drugs.

In essential ways, Miles had not changed. Tall, brilliant in his physical trim, he pulled off his epic homosexuality with such style that plebeian men did not recognize it, and worldly men did not mind it. As always, girls were attracted to him in gaggles, and he treated them with amused condescension of a glamorous Parisian aunt visiting relatives in Nebraska. Jonathan had seen Miles in tight and dangerous spots during their time together in CII, but he had never seen a hair out of place or a rumpled cuff. Henri had frequently mentioned that he knew no equal to Miles for cold physical courage.

Neither Jonathan nor Henri had objected to their comrade's sexual preference; indeed, they had benefited upon occasion from the clusters of women he attracted but did not satisfy. Miles's divergence had been one of his most valuable assets to CII. It had put him in contact with people and sources not open to the straight, and had given him the power of blackmail over several highly placed American political figures.

As the waiter placed the drinks on the table, Miles spoke to him. "You're a very attractive young man. It's God's gift to you, and you should be grateful for it. I hope you are. Now run along and attend to your duties."

The waiter smiled and left. Once he was out of earshot, Miles sighed and said, "I would say he's made, wouldn't you?"

"If you have time."

Miles laughed and raised his glass. "Cheers." He sipped the frothy mixture thoughtfully. "You know, Jonathan, you and I have similar approaches to love, or to balling, if you prefer. Both of us have discovered that the confident cold turkey technique drops more of them than all the romantic mooning around our sexual inferiors bait their little traps with. After all, the targets *want* to be made. They simply ask to be protected from guilt by feeling they've been swept off their feet. And it is refreshing for them to have their paths to evil lubricated with urbanity. Don't you agree?"

"I assume you're covered?"

"Of course."

"Where is he?"

"Behind you. At the bar."

Jonathan turned and glanced along the bar until, at the end, he sighted a blond primate who must have weighed two hundred twenty pounds. Jonathan guessed him to be in his mid-forties, despite the heavy purplish sun lamp tan and the long bleached hair that fell over his collar. He was typical of the ex-wrestlers and beachboys Miles carried along, half as bodyguards, half as lovers, should nothing better turn up.

"And that's all the cover you have?" Jonathan asked, returning to his drink.

"Dewayne is very strong, Jonathan. He used to be a world's champion."

"Didn't they all."

"I'll send Dewayne away, if he makes you nervous."

"He doesn't look like much of a threat."

"Don't depend on that. He's very well paid, and he's totally devoted to me." Miles's movie smile displayed his perfect teeth as he pushed the mash of ice around in his glass with a swizzle stick. Then he began rather tentatively, "It must seem odd to you that I have sought you out, instead of waiting for you to step up to me someday and relieve me of the burden of existence."

"Your phrasing answered any questions I might have had."

"Yes, I've grown weary of ice in my stomach every time I see a man who resembles you." He smiled. "You have no idea how damaging it's been to my cool."

"It will soon be over."

"One way or another. And I think I'm in a good bargaining position."

"Forget it."

"Not even curious?"

"About one thing. How did you know I was here?"

"Oh, you remember what we used to say: CII secrets and common knowledge differ only in that common knowledge . . ."

". . . is harder to come by. Yes, I remember."

Miles rested his large, soft eyes on Jonathan. "I didn't actually kill Henri, you know."

"You set him up. You were his friend and you set him up."

"But I didn't actually kill him."

"I probably won't actually kill you."

"But I'd rather be dead than like the Greek you gave Datura to."

Jonathan smiled with the bland, gentle look he donned before combat. "I didn't actually prepare the Datura. I paid someone else to do it."

Miles sighed and looked down, his long lashes covering his eyes. "I see your point." Then he looked up and tried a new tact. "Did you know that Henri was a double agent?"

In fact, Jonathan had discovered this several months after Henri's death. But it did not matter. "He was your friend. And mine."

"It was only a matter of time, for God's sake, Jonathan! Both sides wanted him dead."

"You were his friend."

Miles's voice became crisp. "I hope you'll understand if I find this harping on ethics a little presumptuous in a killer!"

"I was holding him when he died."

Miles's tone softened instantly. "I know. And I'm truly sorry about that."

"You remember how he always joked about going out with a clever line? At the last minute he couldn't think of one, and he died feeling foolish." Jonathan's control was flaking off.

"I'm sorry, Jonathan."

"Oh, that's fine. You are really and truly sorry! That fixes everything!"

"I did what I could! I arranged a small income for Marie and the children. What did you do? You rammed your rod up her that very night!"

Jonathan's hand flashed over the table, and Miles was snapped sideways in his chair with a backhand across the face. Instantly, the blond wrestler left his barstool and started toward the table. Miles stared hate at Jonathan, tears smarting in his eyes, then, after a struggle with his self-control, he raised his hand, and the wrestler stopped where he was. Miles smiled sadly at Jonathan and gestured the bodyguard away with the backs of his fingers. Angry at being denied his prey, the wrestler glared for a moment before returning to the bar.

Jonathan realized at that moment the first thing he would have to do would be to discourage the blond bodyguard.

"My fault probably, Jonathan. Shouldn't have baited you. I imagine my cheek is red and unsightly?"

Jonathan was angry with himself for allowing Miles to taunt him into premature action. He finished his Laphroaig and gestured to the waiter.

Until the waiter left the table, neither Jonathan nor Miles spoke, nor did they look at each other until the cerebral toxic of adrenalin had drained off. Miles had turned away, not wanting the Indian waiter to see his glowing cheek.

161

Miles smiled forgiveness at Jonathan. He had not wiped the tears from his eyes, imagining they might help his case. "I tender you a bit of information as a propitiatory offering."

Jonathan did not respond.

"The man who made the fiscal arrangements with me for Henri's death was Clement Pope—Dragon's boy."

"That's good to know."

"Jonathan—tell me. What if Henri had set *me* up?"

"He would never have done that to a friend."

"But if he had. Would you have gone after him like you've come after me?"

"Yes."

Miles nodded. "I thought so." He smiled wanly "And that vitiates my case considerably. But I still don't intend to allow myself to die, a sacrifice to your peculiar reverence for the epic traditions of friendship. Neither heaven nor reincarnation attracts me. The one seems dull, the other undesirable. So I feel bound to protect this fleeting life of mine with all my energies. Even if it means killing you, dear Jonathan."

"What are your other choices?"

"I would hardly have come to the marketplace if I were not in a position to bargain."

Big Ben entered the lounge. With his habitual broad smile, he started to join Jonathan, then he saw Miles, and sat at the bar instead, eyeing the blond wrestler with flagrant disdain.

"You might at least give me your attention, Jonathan."

"A friend just walked in."

"Does he realize the possible cost of that privilege?"

"You're wasting my time, Miles."

"I may be saving your life."

Jonathan retreated into his gentle combat smile.

"When I left CII, Jonathan, I went into business in San Francisco. I'm in transportation. I move things from one point to another point and distribute them. All sorts of things. It's amazingly profitable. But life has not been comfortable for me, with the specter of you lurking in every shadow."

"Distressing."

"Then, early this month, I received an assignment to transport a bit of information from Montreal to . . . somewhere else. Gaining the information necessitated the killing of an agent. I didn't participate in the assassination because, unlike you, I am not a predator." He glanced to see the reaction. There was none. "But I know who did the killing. You got one of them shortly later. And now you're after the other. Dragon has told you that he will have the identity of this other person by the time of the sanction. Maybe. Maybe not. I know who it is, Jonathan. And until you have that information, you're in great danger."

"How so?"

"If I tell this person who and what you are, the hunted will become the hunter."

"But you're willing to sell this man out to me?"

"In return for your promise to stop stalking me. Don't let this bargain pass you by."

Jonathan looked out the window at a circle of girls near the pool laughing and screeching as they playfully teased the neurotic Pomeranian, which danced frantically in one spot, its claws clicking on the tile, urine dribbling from beneath it. Jonathan turned and looked at the wrestler still sitting at the bar, keeping him under observation. "I'll think about it, Miles."

Miles smiled with patient fatigue. "Please don't play me like an amateur. I can't remain inactive and unprotected while you 'think about it.' I believe it was you who first advised me never to con a con."

"You'll know my decision within five minutes.

How's that?" Then Jonathan's voice mellowed. "Whichever way it goes, Miles. We were once friends . . . so . . ." He held out his hand. Miles was surprised, but pleased. They shook hands firmly before Jonathan left for the bar where only Ben and the blond bodyguard sat. The latter leaned back on two legs of his stool, his back to the bar and his elbows hooked over it, eyeing Jonathan with a snide superior expression. Jonathan approached him, his whole bearing diffident and apologetic. "Well, as you saw, Miles and I have made up," Jonathan said with a weak, uncertain smile. "May I buy you a drink?"

The wrestler scratched his ear in disdainful silence and leaned further back on his stool to create more distance between himself and this fawning nobody who had dared to slap Mr. Mellough.

Jonathan ignored this rejection. "Boy, I'm glad it worked out all right. No man of my size looks forward to tangling with a guy built like you."

The wrestler nodded understandingly and pressed his shoulders down to set the pectorals.

"Well, just so you know," Jonathan said. He converted his motion of departure into a skimming kick that swept the tilted barstool from beneath the wrestler. First the edge of the bar, then the brass rail cracked the blond head as it thudded down. Dazed and hurt, his long hair tumbled into his face, the wrestler had no time to move before Jonathan had stepped on his face with his heel and pivoted. The nose crunched and flattened underfoot. The sound brought gall to the back of Jonathan's throat, and his cheeks drew back with nausea. But he knew what was necessary in situations like these: they must remember the hurt.

Jonathan knelt over the wrestler and snatched the face up by the hair until it was only inches from his own.

"Hear me. I don't want you out on my flank like

that. It scares me. I don't like being scared. So hear this. Come near me ever, and you're dead. Hey! Listen to me! Don't pass out while I'm talking to you!"

The wrestler's eyes were dulled by pain and confusion, and he did not respond.

Jonathan shook him by the hair until several strands came out between his fingers. "Did you understand what I said?"

"Yes." The reply was faint.

"Good boy." Jonathan set the head back gently on the floor. He stood up and faced Ben, who had watched the whole thing without moving. "Will you take care of him, Ben?"

"All right, ol' buddy. But goddam my ass if I understand what's going on."

"Talk about it later."

Two Indian busboys grunted under the task of conducting the toppling giant to his room, as Jonathan walked back to the entrance of the lounge. He stood there, looking across at Miles who, alone of the patrons, had been aware that a conflict had occurred. Their eyes, so similar in color and frost, intersected for a moment. Then Miles nodded slowly and turned his attention away, gracefully flicking a particle of dust from the sleeve of his velvet jacket. He had his answer.

ARIZONA:
That Evening

His back against a vertical pillow, his feet straight out before him, Jonathan sat up in his bed. He rolled and licked his second smoke, then forgot to light it as he stared, eyes defocused, into the deepening gloom.

He was working out, in rough, how he would put Miles away. There was no chance of getting to him before he could alert the sanction target to his identity. Everything in Switzerland would hinge on Search identifying the man early.

Jonathan's attention suddenly narrowed to the present as he heard a faint metallic click outside his door. He slowly rose from bed, keeping a rolling downward pressure with his hands to reduce the sound of the springs. There was a soft knock, one calculated not to awaken him if he were sleeping. He had not expected Miles to make his move this quickly. He regretted the absence of a gun. The tapping was repeated, and again he heard the click of metal. He crept to the wall on the hinge side of the door. A key turned in the lock, and the door opened a crack, a shaft of light bisecting the room. He tensed and waited. The door swung open deliberately, and someone without whispered. Two shadows spilled across the rug, one of a man, the other a monstrous figure with a huge disk poised over its head. As the shadows advanced, Jonathan kicked the door shut and threw his weight against it. There was a crash and clatter of metal and shattering glass, and he realized instantly what it must have been.

Sheepishly he opened the door and looked out. Big Ben was leaning against the wall across the corridor, and an Indian waiter sat stunned on the floor in the midst of a wreckage of dishes and silver, his white uniform jacket a visual menu.

"Now you wouldn't believe this, ol' buddy, but there are folks who just say so when they ain't hungry."

"I thought you were someone else."

"Yeah. Well, I hope!"

"Come on in."

"What you got up your sleeve this time? Going to clout me with a chest of drawers?" Ben gave orders for the mess to be cleaned up and another dinner to be served, then he went into Jonathan's room, making much of leaping through the doorway in a bound and turning on the lights before something else befell him.

Jonathan assumed a businesslike tone, partially because he wanted to work on a plan he had made while sitting in the dark, partially because he did not want to dwell on his recent *faux pas*.

"Ben, what information do you have on the three men I'll be climbing the Eiger with?"

"Not much. We've exchanged a few letters, all about the climb."

"Could I read them over?"

"Sure."

"Good. Now, another thing. Do you have a detailed map of the area around here?"

"Sure."

"Can I have it?"

"Sure."

"What lies to the west of us?"

"Nothing."

168

"That's what it looked like from the high country. What kind of nothing is it?"

"Real bad-ass country. Rock and sand and nothing else. Goes on forever. Makes Death Valley look like an oasis. You don't want to go out there, ol' buddy. A man can die out there in two days. This time of year it gets up to a hundred fifteen in the shade, and you'd play hell finding any shade."

Ben picked up the phone and asked that a map and a packet of correspondence be brought from his office, along with a six-pack of beer. Then he called out to Jonathan who had gone into the bedroom to empty his ashtray, "Goddam my eyes if I know what's going on around here! 'Course, you don't have to tell me, if you don't want to."

Jonathan took him at his word.

"No. You don't have to tell me about it. What the hell? Slap guys around in my lounge. Break heads at my bar. Bust up my dishes. None of my business."

Jonathan came into the room. "You keep a few guns around, don't you, Ben?"

"Oh-oh."

"Do you have a shotgun?"

"Now, wait a minute, ol' buddy . . ."

Jonathan sat in a chair across from Ben. "I'm in a tight spot. I need help." His tone suggested that he expected it from a friend.

"You know you got all the help I can give, Jon. But if people are going to get killed around here, maybe I should know something about what's going on."

There was a knock at the door. Ben opened it, and the waiter stood there with the beer, the file, and the map. He entered only after looking carefully around the door, and he left as quickly as he decently could.

"Want a beer?" Ben asked, tearing the top from a can.

"No, thanks."

"Just as good. There's only six."

"What do you know about this Miles Mellough, Ben?"

"The one you were talking to? Nothing much. He looks like he could give you change for a nine-dollar bill, all in threes. That's about all I know. He just checked in this morning. You want me to throw him out?"

"Oh, no. I want him right here."

Ben chuckled. "Boy, he's sure tickling the imaginations of a lot of girls. They're flocking around him as though he held the patent on the penis. I even saw George eyeing him."

"She'd be in for a letdown."

"Yeah, I figured."

"How about the other one? The big blond?"

"He checked in at the same time. They got adjoining rooms. I got the doctor up from town, and he fixed some on his nose, but I don't believe he's ever going to be a real close friend of yours." Ben crushed the empty beer can in his hands and opened another thoughtfully. "You know, Jon? That fight really bothered me some. You came at that man pretty slick for an aging college professor."

"You've gotten me into top shape."

"Uh-unh. No, that ain't it at all. You set him up like you were used to setting people up. He was so faked out, he never had a chance. You remember I told you how I'd hate to be with you on a desert island with no food? Well, that's the kind of thing I mean. Like stepping on that big guy's nose. You'd already made your point. A body could get the feeling you got a real mean streak in you somewheres."

It was obvious that Ben needed at least a limited explanation. "Ben, these people killed a friend of mine."

"Oh?" Ben considered that. "Does the law know about it?"

"There's nothing the law can do."

"How come?"

Jonathan shook his head. He did not intend to pursue the matter.

"Hey, wait a minute! I just got a real scary flash. I suddenly got the feeling that all this has something to do with the Eiger climb. Else why would they know you were here?"

"Stay out of it, Ben."

"Now, listen to me. You don't need any more trouble than that mountain's going to give you. I haven't told you this, but I better. You're training real good, and you're still a crafty climber. But I've been watching you close, Jon. And to be honest, you don't have more than a fifty-fifty chance on the Eiger at best. And that doesn't count your fooling around trying to kill people and them trying to kill you. I don't mean to dent your confidence, ol' buddy, but it's something you ought to know."

"Thanks, Ben."

A waiter knocked at the door and brought in a tray with a training meal for two, which they consumed in silence while Jonathan pored over the terrain map and Ben finished the cans of beer.

By the time the meal was a clutter of dirty dishes, Jonathan had folded up the map and put it into his pocket. He began questioning Ben about his forthcoming climbing partners. "How close has your correspondence with them been?"

"Nothing special. Just the usual stuff—hotel, rations, team rope and iron, how to handle the reporters —that sort of stuff. The German guy does most of the writing. He kind of thought the whole thing up in the first place, and he makes noise like a leader. That reminds me. Are you and I going to fly over together?"

"I don't think so. I'll meet you there. Listen, Ben, have any of them . . . ? Are they all in good physical shape?"

"At least as good as you."

"Have any of them been hurt lately? Or wounded?"

"*Wounded?* Not as I know of. One of them—the German—wrote that he had a fall early this month. But nothing serious."

"What kind of fall?"

"I don't know. Roughed up his leg some."

"Enough to make him limp?"

"Well, that's pretty hard to tell from a guy's handwriting. Hey, why you asking me all this shit?"

"Never mind. Will you leave this file of correspondence with me? I want to read it over—get to know these men a little better."

"No skin off my ass." Ben stretched and groaned like a sated bear. "You still planning to make that climb on the needle in the morning?"

"Of course. Why wouldn't I?"

"Well, it might be a little tough, climbing with a shotgun cradled over your arm."

Jonathan laughed. "Don't worry about it."

"Well, in that case, we better get some sleep. That needle ain't no tent pole, you know."

"You mean it ain't no bedpost."

"It ain't neither one."

Shortly after Big Ben had gone, Jonathan was propped up in bed studying the letters from the other climbers. In each case, the first letter was rather stiff and polite. Evidently, Ben's answers had been robust and earthy, because all succeeding letters cleaved to hard technical matters of climbing: weather reports, observations about conditions on the face, descriptions of recent training climbs, suggestions for equipment. It was in one of these letters that the German mentioned a short fall he had taken resulting in a gashed leg which, he assured Ben, would be in fine shape by the Eiger ascent.

Jonathan was deep in this correspondence, trying to read personality between the arid lines, when he recognized the scratching knock of George Hotfort wanting to be let in.

His recent encounter with Mellough made him cautious. He turned off his reading light before crossing to unlatch the door. George entered into the darkness uncertainly, but Jonathan latched the door behind her and conducted her to the bed. He was eager to use her as sexual aspirin, to relieve the tensions of the afternoon, although he knew he would only experience discharge and release without local sensation.

Throughout the event, George's eyes locked on his, expressionless in their Oriental mold, totally severed from her aggressive and demanding body.

Sometime later, while he slept, she slipped away without a word.

ARIZONA:
June 28

He sensed that he was going to be magnificent.

Immediately upon waking, he was eager for the climb on Big Ben Needle. Once or twice in his climbing career he had experienced this scent of victory—this visceral hunch. He had it just before he set a time record on Grand Teton, and again when he introduced a new route up the Dru into the mountaineering handbooks. His hands felt strong enough to punch holds into the rock, if need be, and his legs carried him with more than vigor and ease, with a sensation of moon gravity. He was so finely tuned to this climb that his hands, when he rubbed the palms together, felt like rough chamois gloves capable of adhering to flat, slimy rock.

After his shower, he neither shaved nor combed his hair. He preferred to be rough and burry when he met the rock.

When Ben knocked at his door, he was already tying off his boots and admiring their feel: broken in from his recent training climbs, but the cleats in excellent condition.

"You look mighty ready." Ben had just gotten out of bed and was still in his pajamas and robe, grizzled and carrying with him his first can of beer.

"I feel great, Ben. That needle of yours has had it."

"Oh, I wouldn't be surprised if it took some of the

shine off you before it's all over. It's near four hundred feet, mostly grade 6."

"Tell your cooks we'll be back in time for lunch."

"I doubt that. Especially considering you got to drag a tired old man along behind you. Come to my room and I'll get dressed."

He followed Ben down the hall and into his rooms where he declined the offer of a beer and sat watching dawn quicken, while Ben slowly found and donned the various elements of his climbing gear. The finding was not easy, and Ben grumbled and swore steadily as he shoveled clothes out of drawers onto the floor and emptied boxes of random paraphernalia onto his rumpled bed.

"You say I'm going to pull you along behind, Ben? I had imagined you would lead. After all, you know the route. You've been up before."

"Yeah, but I ain't one to hog all the fun. Goddam my eyes if I can find that other sock. Can't stand wearing socks that don't match. Puts me off balance. Hey! Maybe if I worked it out just right I could make up for these missing toes by wearing a lighter sock on that foot! 'Course I'd run the risk of ending up with the opposite of a limp. I might find myself up an inch or two off the ground, and that'd play hell with my traction. Hey, get off your ass and kick around in this stuff and see if you can find my climbing sweater. You know, the old green one."

"You're wearing it."

"Oh, yeah. So I am. But lookee here! I ain't got no shirt on under it!"

"Not my fault."

"Well, you ain't helping much."

"I'm afraid if I got out into the middle of the room they'd never find me again."

"Oh, George would come across you when she put all this mess away."

"George cleans up your room?"

"She's on my payroll, and she's got to do more to earn her keep than just be a spittoon for your sperm."

"You have a delicate sense of imagery, Ben."

"No shit? All right, I give up. Goddam my eyes if I can find them boots. Why don't you let me use yours?"

"And I go up barefoot?"

"Considering how sassy-assed and prime you're feeling, I didn't figure you'd notice the difference."

Jonathan leaned back in the chair and relaxed with the dawn view. "I really do feel good, Ben. I haven't felt like this for a long time."

Ben's characteristic gruffness fled for a moment. "That's good. I'm glad. I remember how it used to be for me."

"Do you miss climbing much, Ben?"

Ben sat on the edge of his bed. "Would you miss it if someone ran off with your pecker? Sure, I miss it. I'd been climbing since I was eighteen. At first, I didn't know what to do with myself. But then . . ." He slapped his knees and stood up. "Then, I got this place. And I'm living high on the hog now. Still . . ." Ben wandered over to the closet. "Here's my boots! I'll be goddamed!"

"Where were they?"

"In my shoe rack. George must have put them there, goddam her."

Over breakfast in the glittering, empty restaurant kitchen, Jonathan asked if Miles Mellough had done anything of interest after the fight.

"He worry you, Jon?"

"Right now I'm only worried about the climb. But I'll have to deal with him after I get back."

"If he don't deal with you first."

"Say it out."

"Well, one of my help heard this Mellough and his friend having a set-to in their rooms."

"Your help spends a lot of time with their ears to doors?"

"Not usually. But I figured you might want me to keep an eye on these guys. Anyway, the fancy one was some kind of pissed off at the way the other guy let you set him up. And the big fellow said that it would be different next time. Then later on they ordered a rental car from town. It's parked out front now."

"Maybe they want to take in the countryside."

"What's wrong with our guest cars? No, I figure they want to get somewhere in a hurry. Maybe after they've done something to be ashamed of. Like killing somebody."

"What makes you think they're going to kill somebody?"

Ben paused, hoping to make an effect, "The waiter told me the big fellow carries a gun." Jonathan concentrated on sipping his coffee and denied Ben the expected reaction. Ben tore off the top of a can of beer. "You don't seem much bothered about that guy carrying a gun."

"I knew he did, Ben. I saw it under his coat. That's why I stepped on his nose. So he wouldn't be able to see clearly. I needed walking away time."

"Here I was thinking you had a mean streak, and all the time you was just doing what you had to do."

"You should be ashamed of yourself."

"I could cut out the tongue that spoke evil of you, ol' buddy."

"I was just trying to stay alive."

"And that's why you want the shotgun?"

"No, not for protection. I need it for attack. Come on! That hill's eroding out there. There won't be much left of it by the time you get ready."

Jonathan's boots crunched over the loose fall rock around the base of the needle which beetled out overhead, still black on its western face in the early morning. A rock drill, a hammer, and fifteen pounds of pitons, snap rings, and expansion bolts clanged and dangled from the web belt around his waist.

"Right about here," he judged, guessing the position of a long vertical crack he had observed the day before. The crack, averaging four inches in width and running up from the base for a hundred feet, seemed to him to be the highway up the first quarter of the face. It was after the fissure petered out that the mushroom top began its outward lean, and then the going would be more challenging.

"Is this the way you started up, Ben?"

"It's one way, I guess," Ben said noncommittally.

They roped up. "You don't intend to be very helpful, do you?" Jonathan said, passing the loose coils of line to his partner.

"Hell, I don't need the practice. I'm just along for the ride."

Jonathan adjusted the straps on the light pack Ben had insisted he carry for training. Just before taking to the rock, they urinated into the arid ground, pressing out the last drops. Numberless beginners have overlooked, in their eagerness to start, this propitiatory libation to the gods of gravity, and have rued the oversight when they were later faced with the natural problem while on the face, both hands engaged in the more pressing matter of survival. The only solution available under such circumstances is not calculated to make the climber a social success during the press of congratulations following the climb.

"OK, let's go."

The move up the crack went quickly and uneventfully, save in places where the fissure was too wide for a snug foot jam. Jonathan drove no pitons for climbing, only one each thirty feet or so to shorten the fall, if there was one.

He enjoyed the feel of the rock. It had character.

It was well-toothed and abrasive to the grip. There were very few good piton cracks, however. Most of them tended to be too wide, requiring one or two additional pitons as wedges, and they did not drive home with the hard ring of the well-seated peg. This would matter more once they began the three hundred feet of outward-leaning climb. Jonathan realized he would have to use the drill and expansion bolt more than he cared to. He had always drawn a fine, but significant line between piton and expansion bolt. The conquest of a face by means of the piton had elements of seduction about it; the use of the drill and bolt smacked of rape.

They moved smoothly and with high coordination. Ben tied off and belayed from below, while Jonathan inched up as far as his rope would allow before finding an acceptable purchase from which to belay Ben up to him. Ben's passage was always faster. He had the psychological advantage of the line; he used the holds and grips Jonathan had worked out.

Even after the crack petered out and progress slowed, Jonathan's feeling of indomitability persisted. Each square meter of face was a gameboard of tactics, a combat against the unrelenting, mindless opposition of gravity in which the rock was a Turkish ally, ready to change sides if the going got rough.

They inched up, Ben's experienced and sympathetic pressure on the line lending it cooperative life, always slack when Jonathan was moving, always snug when it alone held him on the face. For some time there had not been a free purchase where either man could hold to the rock without rope or piton.

Jonathan began to tire; the drag of his pack and the knotting pressure on thighs and calves were constant mortal reminders. But his hands were still strong, and he felt fine. Particularly did he enjoy the touch of the rock, warm where the sun was upon it, cool and refreshing in the shade. The air was so clean it had a green flavor, and even the salt taste of his sweat was good. Nevertheless, he did not object when, after three hours and with two-thirds of the face under them, Ben called for a rest.

It was another quarter of an hour before they found a slim lip of rock into which they could plant their heels. Jonathan tapped in extra pitons, and they hung there side by side against the ropes, facing outward, squatting on their haunches to rest their legs. Their bodies leaned some twenty degrees away from the face, which itself inclined ten degrees from the vertical. Ben struggled with his pack and produced a loaf of hard-crusted bread and a thick disc of cheese which he had carried along out of Alpine tradition. They ate with slow satisfaction, leaning out against their ropes and looking down at the small knot of thrill-seekers who had gathered near the base of the needle once someone at the lodge had seen men on the face of this seemingly impossible pillar.

"How you feeling, ol' buddy?"

"Just . . . really great, Ben."

"You're climbing fine. Best I ever seen you climb."

"Yes. I know I am." Jonathan's admiration was frank, as though he stood outside himself. "It might just be a fluke—a coincidence of conditioning and temperament—but if I were on the Eigerwand right now . . ." His voice trailed off as his imagination overcame each of the Eiger's notorious obstacles.

Ben returned to an old theme. "Why go at all, Jon? What do you want to prove? This is a great climb. Let it go at this."

Jonathan laughed. "You certainly have it in for the Eiger."

"I just have this feeling. That isn't your mountain, ol' buddy. She's knocked you off twice before. Hell's bells! This whole thing is screwy-assed! That fairy down there waiting to shoot you up. Or you waiting to shoot him up. Whichever it is. And all this about checking up on the men you're going to climb with. I don't know what's going on, and I don't think I want to know. But I got a feeling that if you try to take the Eiger while your mind's on these other things, that hill's going to flick you off onto the rocks. And you *know* that's going to smart some!"

Jonathan leaned out, not caring to talk about these matters. "Look at them down there, Ben. Miniature people. Miniaturized by the Japanese technique of slowly decreasing their intake of courage and individuality until they're only fit to serve on committees and protest air pollution."

"Yeah, they ain't much, are they? They'd sure get their cookies if one of us was to fall off. Give them something to talk about for the better part of the afternoon." Ben waved his arm. "Hi, turds!"

Those below could not hear, and they waved back vigorously and grinned.

"How'd you like a beer, ol' buddy?"

"I'd love one. Why don't you shout down for room service. Of course, the boy would deserve a considerable tip."

"We got beer."

"I hope you're kidding."

"Never. I kid about love and life and overpopulation and atomic bombs and such shit, but I don't ever kid about beer."

Jonathan stared at him with disbelief. "You carried a six-pack of beer up this rock? You're insane, you know that."

"Maybe insane, but not stupid. I didn't carry it. You did. I put it in your pack."

Jonathan contorted his body and grappled a six-pack out of his backpack. "I'll be goddamned! I think I'm going to throw you down on those rubbernecks."

Wait until I finish this beer."

Jonathan ripped the top off a can and sucked at the foam. "It's warm."

"Sorry about that. But I thought you'd balk at carrying ice."

They ate and drank in silence, Jonathan occasionally feeling a ripple of butterflies in his stomach as he looked into the space below him. In all his years of climbing, he had never completely lost the fluttering in the stomach and the tingle in the groin that came over him when he was not concentrating on problems of the face. It was not an unpleasant sensation and one that he associated with the natural way of things on a mountain.

"How far up would you say we are, Ben?"

"About two-thirds in distance. About halfway in time."

Jonathan nodded agreement. They had observed the day before that the last quarter of the climb, where the mushroom top began its outward flange, would be the most difficult. Jonathan was eager to get at it. "Let's push on."

"I haven't finished my beer!" Ben said with genuine offense.

"You've had two."

"I was talking about this third one." He tugged the top off the can and tipped it up until it was empty, swallowing with great gulps, some beer trickling from the corners of his mouth.

The next three hours involved a sequence of tactical problems, one after the other, the last forgotten as the next was met. For Jonathan there was nothing in Creation but himself and the rock—the next move, the quality of the piton, the sweat in his hair. Total freedom purchased at the risk of a fall. The only way to fly, if you happen to be a wingless animal.

The last five feet were rather special.

The weather had worked its erosive will on the fragile flange around the flat top of the needle. The outward angle was thirty degrees, and the rock was rotten and crumbling. Jonathan moved laterally as far as he could, but the rock did not improve and he could find no valid seat for a piton. He traversed back to just above Ben.

"What's going on?" Ben called up.

"Can't find a way up! How did you make it?"

"Oh, guts, skill, determination, talent. That sort of stuff."

"Screw you."

"Hey, look ol' buddy. Don't do nothing hasty. This piton is mostly for show."

"If I go, the beer goes."

"Oh, my."

There was no safe way to make the curling lip. Jonathan swore under his breath as he clung to the face, considering the problem. An improbable solution presented itself.

"Give me some slack," he shouted down.

"Don't do nothing foolish, Jon. We've had a nice climb like it is."

"Ninety-nine percent of the way is called a failure. Give me the goddam slack!"

Crouched under the overhang, facing outward, Jonathan flattened his palms against the rock shelf above him. By maintaining constant pressure between his legs and the heels of his hands, he could ease out, one hand after the other. As the angle of his body increased, the force required to wedge himself in became greater until he could no longer lift a palm from the rock above lest he shoot out into space. He had to skid his hands along, inch by inch, grinding the skin off his palms and moistening the rock with blood. At last, his legs trembling with fatigue, his fingers found the edge of the flange and curled over it. He could not judge the soundness of the lip, and he knew that when he pulled up his knees his body might swing so far out that his hold would be lost.

But he was no longer facing a decision. He could neither return nor hold the stance much longer. His strength was almost gone.

He squeezed until the finger bones were in contact with the rock through the pads of his fingertips. Then he released and tuck-rolled up.

For an instant, only his legs from the hips down were over the flange; the heavier part of his body and his pack began to drag him, head downward, into the void. He scrambled and fought back, slithering on his stomach, without finesse or technique, in a desperate animal battle against gravity.

He lay face down, panting, his mouth ajar and saliva dripping onto the flat hot rock of the top. His heart thudded in his ears painfully, and the palms of his hands stung with the bits of grit embedded in the raw flesh. A slight breeze cooled his hair, matted and thick with sweat. When he could, he sat up and looked around at the barren slab of stone that had been the goal of all this effort. But he felt just fine. He grinned to himself with the elation of victory.

"Hey? Jon?" Ben's voice came from under the lip. "Anytime you're through admiring yourself, you might bring me up with you."

Jonathan passed the line around a small outcropping of rock and held it in a sitting belay as Ben scrambled up over the edge.

They did not talk for ten minutes, weary with their climb and awed by the prospect around them. They were the highest things in the basin. To the west the desert stretched out forever, shimmering and featureless. From one edge of the tabletop they could look down on Ben's lodge, compressed by distance, its swimming pool a fragment of broken mirror glinting in the sun. Occasional gusts of wind swept the heavy heat off the rock and chilled their sweat-dampened shirts.

They opened the two remaining beers.

"Congratulations, ol' buddy. You bagged yourself another first."

"What do you mean?" Jonathan sipped the tepid froth gratefully.

"I never thought anybody'd climb this needle."

"But you've climbed it yourself."

"Who told you a thing like that?"

"You did."

"You ain't going to get very far in life, listening to known liars like that."

Jonathan was silent for a time.

"All right. Tell me about it, Ben."

"Oh, just this plot of mine that backfired. Some pretty fair country climbers have taken shots at this needle. But it stayed cherry. It's that last little bit that stopped them all. You got to admit that it was a mite hairy. Matter of fact, no sane man would have tried it. Especially with a friend tied on to the other end of the rope."

"I'm sorry, Ben. I didn't think about that."

"You're not the type likely to. Anyway, I figured that if you couldn't make a climb you thought I had made, even with my game foot, you'd think twice about going after the Eiger."

"You're all that set against my going?"

"I am, and that's a fact. I'm scared of it, ol' buddy." Ben sighed and crushed his beer can. "But, like I said, my plot kind of backfired. Now that you've made this climb, I guess nothing in the world's going to keep you away from the Eiger."

"I have no choice, Ben. Everything's tied to the climb. My house. My paintings."

"From what I hear, dead people don't get much kick out of houses and paintings."

"Look. Maybe this will make you feel better about it. If everything goes well, I may not have to make the climb after all. There's a chance that I can finish my business before the climb starts."

Ben shook his head as though he felt something loose inside. "I don't get all this at all. It's too screwy-assed."

Jonathan touched his palms together to test for pain. They were tacky with the thick clear liquid of coagulation, but they did not hurt much. "Let's go back down."

Leaving their pitons for future climbers, and rapelling in great descending swoops, they reached the flat land in forty minutes, which seemed somehow unfair after the grueling six hours of the climb.

Immediately, they were surrounded by a throng of backslappers and congratulators who offered to buy drinks and gave suggestions on how they would have made the climb, if they had been climbers. Ben, one arm around each of two cute young things, led the crowd back to the lodge; and Jonathan, suddenly drained and leaden, now that nervous energy no longer sustained him, trudged along behind the convivial parade. He had been suprised to see Miles Mellough standing apart from the welcoming group, aloof and cool in a sky blue suit of raw silk, his well-combed Pomeranian squirming and whining in his arms. Miles fell in step with him.

"An impressive display. Do you know, Jonathan, that in all the time we were friends, I never saw you climb? It's rather graceful, in its way."

Jonathan walked on without answering.

"That last little part there was particularly tingling. It sent little thrills down my spine. But you made it after all. What's the matter? You seem rather done in."

"Don't count on it."

"Oh, I don't underrate you." He shifted the jittery dog from one arm to the other, and Jonathan noticed that it wore around its neck a ribbon of the same blue silk as Miles's suit. "It is you who insist on underrating me."

"Where's your boy?"

"Back in his room. Moping, I suspect. And looking forward to his next encounter with you."

"There better not be one. He's dog meat if I see him again on my side of the street."

Miles snuggled his nose into Faggot's fur and purred, "You mustn't take offense, little boy. Dr. Hemlock wasn't talking about you. He was using one of the little vulgarisms of his profession."

The dog whimpered and licked vigorously at Miles's nostrils.

"I hope you've reconsidered, Jonathan." The flat professionalism of Miles's tone contrasted sharply with the cooing purr he had used to the dog. Jonathan wondered how many men had been lulled into a lethal sense of security by Miles's feminine facade.

He stopped and turned to face Miles. "I don't think we have anything to talk about."

Miles adjusted his stance, putting the weight on one foot and pointing the toe of the other out in a relaxed variant of the fourth position in ballet, the better to show the line of his suit. "As a climber, Jonathan, your sense of brinksmanship is well developed. You're telling me now that you're willing to face an unknown target, rather than make your peace with me. All right. Allow me to raise the ante a little. Suppose I contact the target and identify *you*. That would put him in the shadow and you in the light. How would that feel? An interesting reversal of the normal pattern, isn't it?"

Jonathan had considered this uncomfortable possibility. "You don't have as good a bet as you think, Miles. Search is working on the identity of the man."

Mellough laughed richly. The sound startled Faggot. "That is lovely, Jonathan! You're willing to bet your life on the efficiency of CII? Does your barber perform operations on you?"

"How do I know you haven't already contacted the target?"

"And played away my last trump? Really, Jonathan!" He burrowed his nose into Faggot's fur and playfully nipped at his back.

Jonathan walked away toward the lodge.

Miles called after him. "You don't leave me much choice, Jonathan!" Then he nuzzled against Faggot's ear. "Your daddy doesn't have any choice, does he. He'll just have to tell on Dr. Hemlock." He looked after the retreating figure. "Or kill him."

Ben was grumpy and incommunicative throughout supper, but he manfully put away quantities of food and beer. Jonathan made no attempts at conversation, and often his attention strayed from the food and focused on an indeterminate point in space. At length he spoke without breaking his vacant stare. "Anything from your switchboard operator?"

Ben shook his head. "Neither of them has tried to call out, if that's what you mean. No telegrams. Nothing."

Jonathan nodded. "Good. Whatever you do, Ben, don't let them make contact with the outside."

"I'd sure give my front seat in hell to know what's going on around here."

Jonathan looked at him for a long moment, then asked, "Can I borrow your Land-Rover tomorrow?"

"Sure. Where you going?"

Jonathan ignored the question. "Do me a favor, will you? Have one of your people fill it up and put two extra jerry cans of gas and one of water in the back."

"This has something to do with this Mellough character?"

"Yes."

Ben was moodily silent for a time. "All right, Jon. Whatever you need."

"Thanks."

"You don't have to thank me for helping you put your ass in a sling."

"You know that shotgun we talked about yesterday? Will you load it and have it put in the Rover too?"

"Whatever you say." Ben's voice was grim.

Unable to sleep, Jonathan sat up in bed late into the night, working turgidly on the Lautrec article that had been the sponge of his free time for almost a month. George's scratching knock presented an excuse to abandon the arid labor. As usual, she was wearing jeans and a denim shirt, its collar turned up under her long black hair, the three top buttons undone, and her unbound breasts tugging the shirt up from the jeans in taut folds.

"How are you this evening, George?"

She sat on the edge of his bed and regarded him blandly with her large, dark eyes.

"Did you watch Ben and me make that climb today? Wasn't that something?" He paused, then responded for her. "Yes, that was something."

She slipped off her shoes then stood to unbutton and unzip her jeans with the brisk movements of a person with business to attend to.

"It looks as though I'll be leaving tomorrow or the day after. In some ways, George, I'll miss you."

With a clapper action of her bottom, she forced the jeans over her hips.

"No one can say that you've cluttered up our relationship with sticky sentiment or unnecessary chatter, and I appreciate that."

She stood for a second, the tails of her shirt brushing her olive thighs, then she began unbuttoning it, her placid eyes never leaving his.

"I have an idea, George. Why don't we give up this banal chatter and make love?" He barely had time to get his notes off the bed and turn off the light before she was tangled up amongst his limbs.

He lay on his stomach, his arms thrown limply across the bed, every muscle liquid with relaxation as George trickled her fingers from the small of his back to the nape of his neck. He hovered on the rim of sleep as long as he could, trying not to anticipate the eddies of thrill her fingernails churned up as they slid with barely perceptable contact around his waist, up his sides, and outward along his upper arms. By way of thanks, he hummed a couple of times with contentment, although he would rather not have put forth the effort.

She stopped stroking him, and he began to slip over the edge of consciousness.

"Ouch!"

He felt something like a wasp sting in his shoulder. George leaped out of bed and cowered in the darkest corner of the room. He fumbled the light on and looked around, squinting against the sudden glare. Quite nude, George pressed into her corner, the hypodermic needle still in her hands, both thumbs against the plunger and the point directed at him, as though it were a gun she could protect herself with.

"You little bitch." Jonathan, also nude, advanced on her.

Fear and hate flickering in her eyes, she made a lunge at him with the needle, and with one broad backhand blow he reeled her along the wall and into the opposite corner, where she crouched like a treed cougar, blood trickling from the corner of her mouth and one nostril, her lips drawn back in a frozen snarl that revealed her lower teeth. He was moving in to expand on her punishment when the buzzing in his ears settled toward his stomach and made him stagger. He turned back toward the door, now an undulating trapezoid, but he realized he would never make it. He stumbled toward the phone. His knees buckled under him, and he went down, knocking over the bedside table and plunging the room into darkness as the lamp burst with a loud implosion. The buzzing pulsed louder and in tempo with the dancing bursts of light behind his eyes.

"Desk," answered a thin, bored voice near him on the floor, somewhere in the rubble of broken glass. He pawed about blindly, trying to find the receiver. "Desk." He felt a volley of pains in the small of his back, and he knew the little bitch was kicking him with the relentless rhythm of frightened fury. "Desk." The voice was impatient. He could not ward off the kicks; all he could do was curl up around the receiver and take it. The pains became duller and duller until they were only pressures. "Desk." Jonathan's tongue was thick and alien. With his disobedient lips pressing against the mouthpiece, he struggled to form a word.

"Ben!" he blurted with a treble whimper, and the word chased him down into warm black water.

ARIZONA:
June 29

A light fluttered on the black water, and Jonathan, disembodied, rushed through miles of space toward it. He gained on the spark, and it grew larger, until it developed into a window with stripes of daylight glaring through a venetian blind. He was in his room. A great flesh-colored glob hung over him.

"How's it going, ol' buddy?"

He tried to sit up, but a thud of pain nailed him to the pillow.

"Relax. Doctor said you're going to be just fine. He says it may hurt for a few days when you piss. George sure gave your kidneys a going over."

"Give me something to drink."

"Beer?"

"Anything." Jonathan inched his way to a sitting position, moving up through strata of thickening headache.

Ben made a clumsy attempt to feed him the beer, but Jonathan relieved him of his heavy solicitude by snatching the can away after a third of it had spilled on his chest. "Where is she?" he asked once his thirst was slaked.

"I got her locked up, and a couple of my staff are watching her. Want me to call into town for the sheriff?"

"No, not yet. Tell me, Ben . . ."

"No, he hasn't. I figured you'd be wondering if this Mellough had checked out. The desk will call me if he tries."

"So it was Miles?"

"That's what George says."

"All right. He's had it. Let's get me into the shower."

"But the doctor said—"

Jonathan's suggestion as to what the doctor could do with his advice was beyond the routine of physiotherapy and, moreover, beyond ballistic probability.

Ben half carried him into the shower where Jonathan turned on the cold water and let it beat on him, clearing the moss from his mind. "Why, Ben? I'm really not that bad."

"The oldest reason in the world, ol' buddy," he shouted over the noise of the shower.

"Love?"

"Money."

The water was doing its work, but with the return of feeling came a pounding headache and pains in his kidneys. "Toss me in a bottle of aspirin. What did she shoot into me?"

"Here." Ben's big paw thrust the bottle through the shower curtain. "Doctor says it was some relative of morphine. He had a name for it. But it wasn't a lethal dose."

"So it would appear." The aspirin disintegrated in his hand with the splatter of water, so he tipped the bottle up to his mouth then washed the tablets down by gulping under the shower head. He gagged as bits of aspirin caught in his throat. "Morphine figures. Miles is in the drug business."

"Is that right? But how come he went that far and didn't put you away for good? George said he had promised her nothing serious would happen to you. Just wanted to scare you off."

"Her concern is touching."

"Maybe she just didn't want to die for murder."

"That sounds more like it." Jonathan turned off the water and began to towel himself down, but not too vigorously, because every sharp motion slopped pain around in his head. "My guess is that Miles intended to come in after George put me under and shoot me full of junk. The death would be attributed to an overdose. It's typical Mellough. Safe and oblique."

"He's a bad ass all right. What are you going to do about him?"

"Something massive."

After Jonathan dressed, they went down the hall to the room in which George was being kept. He felt a twinge of regret when he saw her swollen eye and the split lip he had given her, but this quickly faded when the bruises along his spine reminded him of how she had tried to help the morphine put him away.

She looked more Indian than ever, clutching a blanket around her shoulders, under which she was as naked as she had been when Ben broke in to save him.

"How much did he pay you, George?" he asked.

She almost spat back her response. "Goddam your eyes, you shit!"

These were the only words he ever heard her speak.

Ben could not help chuckling as they returned to Jonathan's room. "I guess she's been around me too much."

"It's not that, Ben. They always talk about my eyes afterwards. Look, I'm going to get a couple hours' sleep. Will you have your people at the desk make up my bill?"

"You leaving right away?"

"Soon. Is the Land-Rover ready?"

"Yeah."

"And the shotgun?"

"It'll be on the floorboards. I imagine you don't want Mellough to know you're checking out."

"On the contrary. But don't do anything special about it. He'll find out. Miles is a specialist in information."

He awoke refreshed three hours later. The effects of the morphine had worn off and his headache was gone, but his kidneys still felt a little soggy. He dressed with special care in one of his better suits, packed his suitcases, and telephoned to the desk to have them put in the Land-Rover.

As he entered the lounge he saw the blond wrestler sitting at the bar, a broad strip of tape over his swollen nose.

"Good afternoon, Dewayne." Ignoring the bodyguard's glare of hate, he passed through the lounge, along a walkway, and over a bridge to the table at which Miles sat, poised and impeccable in a suit of metallic gold.

"Join me, Jonathan?"

"I owe you a drink."

"So you do. And we all know what a stickler you are for old debts. You're looking very nice. Your tailor is accurate, if uninspired."

"I'm not feeling too well. I had a bad night."

"Oh? I'm sorry to hear that."

The young Indian waiter who had served them the first day approached the table, his glances at Miles filled with tender remembrance. Jonathan ordered, and the two of them watched the bathers around the pool until the drinks arrived and the waiter departed.

"Cheers, Jonathan?"

Jonathan drank off the Laphroaig and put the glass on the table. "I've decided to forget about you for now, Miles."

"Have you? Just like that?"

"I'm going to be staying here in training for a

couple more weeks, and I won't be able to concentrate on it with you on my mind. I have a big climb
in front of me." Jonathan was sure that Miles knew
he had checked out. The obvious lie was calculated
to make Miles think he had him on the run, and Miles
was the kind to press such an advantage.

"I sympathize with your problem, Jonathan. Truly
I do. But unless this means you are crossing me off
your list for good . . ." He lifted his shoulders in
helpless regret.

"I might do just that. Let's have dinner together
tonight and talk about it."

"A delightful idea."

Jonathan had to admire Miles's silky control.

Jonathan rose. "See you this evening."

"I'm looking forward to it." Miles raised his glass
in salute.

The Land-Rover was parked in the loading zone
in front of the lodge. As Jonathan climbed in, he
noticed on the floorboards next to the shotgun a
thoughtful gift from Ben: a six-pack of cold beer. He
opened a can and sipped at it while he glanced over
the area map on his lap. He had earlier located a
long dirt road running in thin broken lines deep into
the desert. Ben had told him it was a little-used rut
track that only government rangers drove on. For
more than a hundred fifty miles, the road pierced into
the core of the western desert, then it stopped
abruptly.

Tracing back with his finger, he found the place
where the dirt track began, branching west from a
north-south gravel access road. This gravel road
joined the main highway about a mile west of the
turnoff to Ben's place. Considering the difference in
speed between the Rover and the rental car at Miles's
disposal, that mile of good highway promised to be
the most dangerous stretch.

Fixing the map in his mind, Jonathan folded it

away and drove off, slowly winding up from the basin. On one of the cutbacks he glanced down to find that Miles's car was already in pursuit. He pressed down on the gas.

Seated beside Dewayne, Faggot in his arms, Miles saw Jonathan's sudden increase in speed. "He knows we're following him. Go get him, Dewayne. Here's your chance to reinstate yourself in my good graces." And he fondly scratched behind Faggot's ears as the car sprayed dust in a skidding turn.

The Rover's superior traction and suspension made up for its disadvantage in speed, and the distance between the two did not much alter throughout the race until the last flat hundred yards before the highway, during which Miles gained perceptibly on the Rover. Dewayne pulled an automatic from his shoulder holster.

"Don't," Miles ordered. "We'll pull along side on the highway where we can be sure of it." Miles knew the Rover had no chance of outdistancing him along the five miles of good road to town.

Jonathan approached the highway at full speed and quickly turned west, away from town.

For an instant Miles was troubled by the unexpected move. Then he decided that Jonathan realized the hopelessness of an open race and was seeking some back road on which the qualities of the Rover would give him a chance.

"I think this would be a good time to get him, Dewayne."

The car torqued low on its springs as it bounced onto the highway and screamed around the corner in pursuit.

Jonathan held the accelerator to the floor, but at seventy the Rover was flat out, and the automobile gained on him steadily. The gravel cutoff was only half a mile away, but the car behind was so close that he could distinguish Miles through the rearview mirror. In a moment they would swing out and pull up beside him. He saw Miles roll down his window and lean back to give Dewayne a clear field of fire.

When they were almost on his bumper, Jonathan reached down and switched on his lights.

Seeing the tail lights flash, and imagining Jonathan had hit his brakes, Dewayne jammed down on his own, and the wheels squealed and smoked, while the Rover roared on at its best speed.

By the time Dewayne had fumbled his foot back onto the gas, Jonathan had gained sufficient distance to reach the gravel road with fifty yards lead. Miles swore to himself. It had been Henri who had told them about the headlight ploy.

Several times on the gravel road, when his lead was threatened, Jonathan wagged the wheel and caused the Rover to zigzag slightly, raising clouds of blinding dust which forced the car to fall back. In this way he held his advantage until he came to the ranger trail that led out into the desert. Once he was on this meandering track of potholes, and unbanked turns, and ruts so deep the automobile repeatedly bottomed, he had no difficulty maintaining his lead. He was even able to open another can of beer, although it splashed over him when he bounced into an unexpected hole.

"Just keep him in sight, Dewayne." At the turnoff onto the dirt road Miles had seen a weathered sign warning drivers that there was no outlet. Sooner or later, Jonathan would have to turn back. The road, often winding between giant outcroppings of sandstone, was not wide enough for two cars to pass. He had Jonathan in a box.

For nearly an hour the vehicles sped over the flat, gray-tan country where nothing grew in the powdery, baked earth. Dewayne had returned his gun to its holster where its pressure made him sweat freely. Faggot whimpered and pranced with sharp claws in

Miles's lap. Sliding from side to side with each abrupt turn, Miles braced himself with pressure between feet and back. His lips were tight with chagrin at being unable to sit with poise. Even Faggot's frantic and moist gestures of affection irritated him.

The vehicles raced and jolted over the desert, lofting two high plumes of fine dust behind them.

Despite the stream of air gushing in through the open side of the Rover, Jonathan's back adhered with perspiration to the plastic seat. As he bounced over a rut, the jerry cans behind him clanged together, reminding him that it would not do for those chasing him to run out of fuel. He began to search for a site appropriate to his needs.

Dewayne hunched over the wheel and squinted into the dust rising before him. His jaw muscles flexed in anticipation of revenge.

About two miles farther on, Jonathan caught sight of an outcropping of rock, a single ragged sandstone boulder around which the track made an S-turn. It was ideal. He slowly eased off on the gas, allowing those behind to close to within a hundred yards. The instant he made the first turn, he hit his brakes, skidding to a stop and raising dense clouds of choking dust. He snatched the shotgun off the seat, leaped out of the Rover, and dashed for the boulder, knowing he had only seconds in which to scramble around the rock and come out from behind.

As Dewayne steered into the first turn, he was blinded by the swirl of dust. The Land-Rover loomed in front of him, and he jammed down on the brakes. Before the car had slid to a stop, Miles had his door open and had

Jonathan snapped back the hammers of the shotgun as he raced desperately around the boulder. He heard the squeal of brakes, and plunged through the dust at a full run. Dewayne's face emerged out of the billow-

rolled out onto the ground. Dewayne twisted the window handle, grappling desperately at his automatic. Hemlock! The barrels of the shotgun jabbed painfully into his left side.

He never heard the shot.

ing white fog. He was trying to get his window down. Jonathan rammed the gun in through the half opened window and snapped on both triggers. The blast was deafening.

Dewayne snorted like a hammered steer as the force of the impact slid him across the seat and halfway out the open door, where he dangled and twitched until his nerves discovered they were dead.

Jonathan stepped around in front of the car and reached in under the hanging arm to extract the automatic. He wiped his sticky fingers off on a fragment of Dewayne's jacket he found several feet away from the car.

Miles stood in the settling dust, straightening his cuffs and slapping dirt from his gold suit. The Pomeranian danced epileptically about his legs.

"Really, Jonathan! This suit cost me three hundred dollars and, what's more, five fittings."

"Get into my car."

Miles picked up the squirming dog and walked in front of Jonathan to the Rover, his casual dancer's stride betraying no effect of recent events.

They drove on westward, deeper into the desert. Their lips began to crack with the salt that prevented the most meager vegetation from growing. Jonathan held the automatic high in his left hand so he could fend off any attempt Miles might make for it.

For an hour and a half they pressed on through the shimmering heat of the desert. Jonathan knew that Miles was ready to make his try for the gun. Slight contractions of his hand on his lap, and minute tensings of his shoulders predicted Miles's move. Just as he threw himself after the gun, Jonathan hit the brakes, and Miles went face first into the steering wheel. Jonathan snapped back the emergency brake and jumped out, dragging Miles after him by the collar. He dumped him onto the crackled ground and sprang back into the Rover. By the time Miles had staggered to his feet, a rivulet of blood caked with dirt running from his nose, Jonathan had backed the Rover in a sharp arc. Miles stood in the road, blocking the path with his body.

"You're not going to leave me out here!" The recognition of Jonathan's plan for him grew and filled him with horror as no bullet in the head could have.

Jonathan tried to steer around him, but before he could get up any speed Miles jumped onto the hood. He lay over it, his face pressed against the glass.

"For Christ's sake, Jonathan," he screamed. "Shoot me!"

Jonathan raced forward. then hit the brakes, dumping Miles off the hood. He roared in reverse away from the crumpled body, then sped on, making a wide curve to avoid him.

By the time Jonathan could see his dancing image in the rearview mirror, Miles had reclaimed his characteristic composure and was standing, the dog in his arms, looking after the diminishing Land-Rover.

Jonathan never forgot his last image of Miles, the gold suit glinting in the sunlight. Miles had set the dog down and had taken a comb from his pocket. He ran it through his hair and patted the sides into place.

KLEINE SCHEIDEGG:
July 5

Jonathan sat at a round metal table on the terrace of the Kleine Scheidegg Hotel, sipping a glass of grassy Vaudois, enjoying the slight snap of its latent effervescence. He looked across the up-tilted meadow to the gloomy north face of the Eiger. The unstable warmth of the weightless mountain sunlight was puffed away time and again by wisps of crisp highland air.

Touched only once a day and briefly by the sun, the dark concave face hovered malignantly above him, looking as though it had been scooped out of the body of the mountain by some olympian shovel, its brittle gray-black crescent rim cutting into the glittering blue of the sky.

A breeze stirred, and he shivered involuntarily. He remembered his two previous attempts at the face, both beaten back by those brutal storms that roll in from the north and are collected and amplified in the natural amphitheatre of the Eigerwand. So common are those rages of wind and snow that the dour Bernese Oberland guides speak of them as "Eiger Weather." After the last nine-hour dicey retreat from the high ice field called the White Spider—that salient epitome of the mountain's treachery—he had promised himself never to try again.

And yet . . . It would be a fine mountain to take.

He adjusted his sunglasses and gazed with reluctant fascination at the awful sublimity of the Eiger. The view was uncommon; normally, heavy shrouds of mist hang from the crest, obscuring the storms that lash it, and muffling the crack and roar of avalanches that constitute the mountain's most potent defensive weapon. His eyes snagged on each of those features associated with the defeat and death of some mountaineer.

He was afraid of the mountain; his groin tingled with the fear. But at the same time, his hands itched for the touch of its cold rock, and he was exhilarated at the thought of trying that fine savage again. This perverse dialogue between the flinching mind and the boisterous body is one every climber has experienced at one time or another. It was a pity that his sanction target would be nominated before the climb started. Maybe after it was over . . .

A long-limbed blond with a mountain tan squeezed between the close-set tables (although there was no one else on the terrace) and nudged Jonathan with her hip, causing some wine to spill from his glass.

"I *am* sorry," she said, willing to allow this accident to open a conversation.

Jonathan nodded a curt acceptance of her apology, and she passed on to use the coin-operated telescope that was in a direct line between him and the mountain (although there were six others available to her). She bent over the instrument, directing her excellent bottom toward him, and he could not help noting that her suntan must have been acquired in those very shorts. Her accent had been British, and she had the general look of the horsey type, the long taut legs developed from gripping the animal between her knees. He noticed that her shoes, however, were not British. Since the advent of mini, English women had gotten away from those remarkable clogs that once identified them on sight. It used to be said that

British women's shoes were made by excellent craftsmen who had had shoes carefully described to them, but who had never actually seen a pair at first hand. They were, however, comfortable, and they wore well. And those were also the principal virtues of the women who wore them.

He followed the line of her telescope and rested his eyes again on the Eiger.

The Eiger. Appropriate name. When the early Christians came into these high meadows, they bestowed benign labels on the two higher mountains of the massif: Jungfrau, the Virgin; and Monch, the Monk. But this most malicious promontory was named for an evil pagan spirit. Eiger: the Ogre.

Before the turn of the century, all the faces of the Eiger had been climbed, except one, the north Eigerwand: the Ogre's Wall. Experienced mountaineers had listed it among the "impossible" faces, and so it was in the days of pure climbing, before sportsmen armed themselves with piton and snap ring.

Later, under the ring of the hammer, the "impossible" faces fell to the record books one by one, but the north face of the Eiger remained virgin. Then, in the mid-thirties, the Nazi cult of mountain and cloud sent wave after wave of young German boys, filled with a lust to accrue glory to their dishonored Fatherland, against the Eiger's defenses. Hitler offered a gold medal to whomever made the first ascent; and in neatly regimented sequence the flaxen-haired romantics died. But the mountain retained its hymen.

In mid-August of 1935 came Max Sedlmayer and Karl Mehringer, two lads with considerable experience in the more difficult climbs and a searing desire to chalk up the Eiger on the German scoreboard. Tourists watched their ascent through telescopes from this very terrace. These voyeurs of death were the ancestors of the modern "Eiger Birds," those carrion crows of the jet set who flock to te Kleine Scheidegg Hotel and pay exorbitant sums to titillate to the vicarious thrill of the climbers facing death, then return to their lives of musical beds refreshed and reinspired.

Sedlmayer and Mehringer moved up the first 800 feet which is not especially difficult, but totally exposed to falling rocks. To observers below it seemed that the climb was going well. Rope length after rope length, they skillfully belayed each other up. At the end of the first day they bivouaced at 9,500 feet, well above the windows of the Eigerwand tunnel of the Jungfrau Railway, a remarkable bit of engineering that cuts right through the massif, bringing trainsful of tourists to the Bernese highlands. These windows were originally designed to jettison rubble and to ventilate the tunnel, but they have figured dramatically in attempts to rescue climbers.

Throughout the next day, Sedlmayer and Mehringer enjoyed uncommonly benevolent weather, and they made the upper rim of the First Ice Field, but they were moving very slowly. The vultures at the telescopes could see that the climbers had to hold their knapsacks over their heads to get some protection from the falling rocks and ice with which the Ogre greeted them. Time and again they were forced to stop and take refuge under some scanty overhang to avoid the more determined salvoes from above. Just as they got to the rim of the Second Ice Field, a curtain of mist descended, and for a day and a half they were obscured from the view of the grumbling tourists. During that night a storm raged around the Eiger, crashing such huge boulders down the face that several of the hotel guests complained that their sleep had been interrupted. It is possible that Sedlmayer and Mehringer slept poorly too. The temperature in the valley sank to −8°. Who can guess how cold it was up there on the face? The fine weather with which the White Spider had lured the boys into its web was over. Eiger Weather had begun.

When the clouds lifted on Sunday, the climbers were sighted, still moving up. The hotel guests cheered and toasted one another, and bets were placed against the time the young Germans would reach the top. But experienced climbers and guides glanced embarrassedly at one another and walked away from the crowds. They knew the lads had no chance and climbed only because avalanches had cut off their retreat, and anything was better than simply hanging from their pitons awaiting death.

They moved up slowly toward the Flatiron (the highest point Jonathan's party had reached during his first attempt at the Ogre). The clouds descended again, and the tourists were cheated of the thrill of watching them die.

That night a gale lashed the face.

There was a half-hearted attempt to organize a rescue team, but more in response to the desire to do something than to any hope of reaching them alive. In manifestation of typical Swiss compassion, the Bernese Oberland guides haggled over wages until it was too late to bother with the rescue. An intrepid German flyer dared the treacherous air currents to fly close to the face and search. He spotted the boys, frozen to death, still hanging from their harnesses.

With this, the Eiger began its nomenclature of human tragedy. To this day that spot on the point of the Flatiron above the Third Ice Field is called Death Bivouac. The game between the Eiger and Man was begun.

Score: Ogre—2; Man—0

Early in 1936 two Germans came to reclaim the bodies of their countrymen from where they had stood frozen against the wall for a year, a target for the prying telescopes on clear days. If possible, they were also going to attempt the summit. They decided to take a training climb first. An avalanche caught one up and broke his neck against a rock.

Ogre—3; Man—0

In July of that same year German Youth challenged the Ogre again. This time it was a team of four: Rainer, Angerer, Kurtz, and Hinterstoisser. Again the tourists watched and placed bets. The young men, suffused with the *Zeitgeist* of Hitler's early days, made such melodramatic statements to the press as: "We must have the Wall, or it must have us!"

It had them.

The most experienced of the party, Hinterstoisser, discovered a tricky traverse across the face that turned out to be the key to subsequent climbs. But so confident were they of victory that they pulled in the rope after the last of the party had crossed. This gesture of cocky confidence killed them.

The party climbed well, although Angerer appeared to be injured, probably by falling rock, and the others had to slow down to help him along. Their first bivouac was just above the Rote Fluh, that red rock crag that is one of the more salient landmarks of the face. In one day they had gone more than halfway up the Eiger!

The next day, with the injured man becoming steadily weaker, they gained the Third Ice Field and tied off to camp just below Death Bivouac. When dawn allowed the rubbernecks at the coin-operated telescopes to enjoy the drama, the party had begun a descent. Obviously the condition of the injured man prevented them from continuing.

Smoothly and with remarkable speed, considering the incapacitated climber, they descended the first two ice fields. But night caught them, and they were forced to make a third bivouac. That night, with

Eiger Weather freezing their soaked clothes into clanging armor of ice, must have been brutal. Their reserves of strength were sapped by the cold, and through all of the next day they managed only 1,000 feet.

For a fourth time, and now out of food, they had to bivouac on the inhospitable face.

Some novices at the hotel opined that the team had a good chance. After all, they had only the Hinterstoisser Traverse and the Difficult Crack before them, then the going would be relatively easy.

But the team had overconfidently retrieved their rope from the traverse.

And the next morning it was completely iced over. Again and again, with a growing desperation that never overwhelmed his skill, the gifted Hinterstoisser attempted to make the verglas and slime of the traverse, and each time he was stopped by the hungry Ogre.

The mists descended, and the tourists could hear the roar of avalanches all through the night. Another name was attached to the Eiger: The Hinterstoisser Traverse.

Ogre—7; Man—0

Throughout 1937 team after team attacked the Eiger, only to be driven back. The mountain came close to claiming more victims during the remarkable retreat of Vorg and Rebitsch from Death Bivouac.

But the score remained the same.

In June of 1938 two Italians (there were national movements afoot in Italy too) fell to their deaths near Difficult Crack.

But rope and piton techniques were steadily perfected, while the natural defenses of the mountain remained as they had been since the memory of man, so in July of that year a German team finally removed the north face of the Eiger from the list of "impossibles."

Ogre—9; Man—1

Throughout the war years, the Eiger was free from incursions into its privacy. Governments provided young men with other ways to inscribe their names on the roles of glory—ways that converted suicide into murder, and soothed all with the balm of patriotism.

But directly these avenues to danger were sealed off by peace, the vertical snare of the Eiger beckoned again. In recent years, more than thirty men have slogged up the last snow slope, panting and crying and promising never to touch the stone of the Ogre again. But most of the attempts are still driven back by weather and avalanche, and the death toll continues to rise regularly. The critical ice field of the White Spider has played the antagonist role in most of the recent tragedies, like the one in 1957 in which three men died and a fourth was rescued only after hunger and thirst had driven him to splinter his teeth on glacier ice in an attempt to get something into his stomach.

Jonathan stared ahead, his mind unrolling the death record of the Eiger.

"Is there something wrong?" the English girl at the telescope asked.

He had forgotten her.

"Why are you staring at me like that?" She smiled, anticipating the reason.

"I wasn't staring at you, dear. I was staring through you."

"How disappointing. May I join you?" She interpreted his silence as invitation. "You've been looking at that mountain with such concentration

210

that I couldn't help noticing you. I do hope you're not thinking of climbing it."

"Oh, no. Never again."

"You've climbed it before?"

"I've tried."

"Is it awfully fierce?"

"Awfully."

"I have a theory about mountain climbers. By the way, my name's Randie—Randie Nickers."

"Jonathan Hemlock. What's your theory, Randie?"

"Well . . . may I have some wine? That's all right. I'll just use your glass, if you don't mind. Well, my theory is that men climb mountains out of some kind of frustration. I think it's a kind of sublimation of other desires."

"Sexual, of course."

Randie nodded earnestly as she swallowed a sip of wine. "Yes, probably. This wine's half fizzy, isn't it?"

He put his feet upon an empty chair and leaned back to receive the sun. "It has the giggling sparkle of Swiss maidens, blushed but pleased by the attention of rural swains, but these high spirits do not eclipse the underlying tartness of the petulant Oberland peasant that resides largely in the wine's malolactic fermentation."

Randie was silent for a moment. "I do hope you're teasing."

"Of course I am, Randie. Don't people usually tease you?"

"Not men. They typically try to make love to me."

"How do they do? Typically."

"Well, of late they've been doing very well indeed. I'm in Switzerland for a sort of holiday before I go home and settle down to a most proper married life."

"And you're spreading the blessings of your body around while there's still time."

211

"Something like that. Not that I don't love Rodney. He's the dearest person, really. But he *is* Rodney."

"And he's rich."

"Oh, I imagine so." Her brow clouded over for an instant. "I certainly *hope* he is. Oh, of course he is! What a fright you gave me. But the nicest thing about him is his name."

"Which is?"

"Smith. Rodney Smith."

"And that's the nicest thing about him?"

"It's not that Smith is all that grand of itself. I believe it's actually a fairly common name. But it will mean that I shall finally be rid of my name. It's been a plague to me all my life."

"Randie Nickers sounds all right to me."

"That's because you're an American. I could tell that from your accent. But 'knickers' is British slang for panties. And you can imagine what the girls at school did with that."

"I see." He took his glass back and poured himself some wine. He wondered what it was about him that attracted the nutty ones.

"You see what I mean?" Randie asked, forgetting that she had been thinking, rather than speaking.

"Not exactly."

"Oh, I have this theory that strangers gravitate immediately to the topics of their greatest mutual interest. And here we are talking about panties. It rather tells on us, doesn't it?"

"You ride horses, don't you," he said, succumbing to the rule of non sequitur Randie's mind demanded.

"Yes, as a matter of fact! I show for my uncle. How on earth did you know?"

"I didn't know, really. I more hoped. Do you have a theory about women who delight in having strong beasts between their legs?"

She frowned. "I hadn't really thought about it. But

212

I imagine you're right. It's something like your mountain climbing, isn't it? It's always delightful to have something in common." She looked at him narrowly. "Don't I know you from somewhere. The name's familiar." She mused, "Jonathan Hemlock . . . Ah! Aren't you an author?"

"Only a writer."

"Yes! I have it! You write books about art and everything. They're very keen on you at Slade."

"Yes, it's a good school. What would you rather we did, Randie? Take a walk through the village? Or shall we rush directly to bed."

"A stroll through the village would be grand. Romantic, actually. I'm glad we're going to make love. I have a theory about lovemaking. I view it as a first-rate icebreaker. You make love with a man, and the first thing you know you're holding hands and calling each other by first names. I prefer first names. Probably because of my own family name. Did I tell you what knickers are in England?"

"Yes."

"Well then, you can appreciate my attitude toward names. I have this theory about attitudes . . ."

Jonathan was not disconsolate when he discovered that Randie would be returning to London the following morning.

KLEINE SCHEIDEGG:
July 6-7

It had been necessary to dress twice that morning, and they nearly missed the train. The last Jonathan saw of Miss Nickers as the train began to move away from the platform, she tugged down her compartment window and called, "You really have smashing eyes, you know, Jonathan!" Then she settled into her seat next to a homeward-bound skier and began animatedly explaining one of her theories to him.

Jonathan smiled as he remembered her tactic of self-excitation which consisted of calling parts, places, and postures by their most earthy names.

He turned up the steep cobblestone road that connects the village to the hotel. He had arranged to take a training climb with a local guide up the west flank of the Eiger. Although a far cry from the North Face, this west route had been blooded often enough to demand respect.

Beyond the training and acclimatization, there was another reason prompting him to stay away from the hotel as much as possible. Somehow, as always, despite the greatest precautions, the management of the hotel had sensed there was an attempt at the Eigerwand pending. Discreet telegrams had been sent out; the best suites were being held vacant for rich "Eiger Birds" who would soon begin to descend on the hotel. Like all climbers, Jonathan resented and detested these excitement-hungry jet setters who seek to titillate their calloused nerve ends by vicarious thrill. He was glad that Ben and the other members of the climbing team had not yet arrived, because with them the carrion would descend in force.

Halfway up the cobblestone road, Jonathan stopped off at an outdoor café for a glass of Vaudois. The fragile mountain sun was pleasant on his cheek.

"Do you ever buy wine for girls you meet in bars?"

She had approached from behind, from the dark interior of the café. Her voice hit him like a palpable thing. Without turning around, and with fine command of his feelings, he reached over and pushed out a chair for her. She sat looking at him for a time, sadness balanced in her eyes.

The waiter came, received the order, returned with the wine, and departed. She slid her glass back and forth over a small puddle of water on the table, concentrating on it, rather than on his cool, uninviting eyes. "I had this whole speech worked out, you know. It was a good one. I could say it quickly, before you interrupted me or walked away."

"How did it go?"

She glanced up at him, then away. "I forget."

"No, come on. Let's hear it. I'm easily conned, as you know."

She shook her head and smiled faintly. "I surrender. I can't handle it on this level. I can't sit here and swap cool, mature words with you. I'm . . ." She looked up, desperate at the paucity of words in the face of human emotions. "I'm sorry. Really."

"Why did you do it?" He was not going to melt.

"Try to be a little fair, Jonathan. I did it because I believed—I *still* believe—you have to take this assignment."

"I've taken the assignment, Jemima. Things worked out just fine."

"Stop it! Don't you know what it would mean if the

other side had a major biological weapon before we did?"

"Oh, of course. We have to keep it out of their hands at all costs! They're the kind of heartless shits who might drop it on some unsuspecting Japanese city!"

She glanced down. "I know you don't think it makes any difference. We talked about it that night. Remember?"

"Remember? You're not a bad in-fighter."

She sipped her wine, the silence heavy on her. "At least they promised me that you wouldn't lose your painting."

"They kept their promise. Your conscience is clear."

"Yes." She sighed. "But there's still this problem I have."

"What's that?"

She said it matter-of-factly. "I love you."

After a pause, he smiled to himself and shook his head. "I've underrated you. You're a great in-fighter."

The silence grew denser, and she realized that she must abandon this heavy line of talk lest he simply walk away. "Say, I saw you walking around yesterday with a most un-Jemima type—blond and Anglo and all. Was she good?"

"Adequate."

"As good as—"

"No."

"I'm glad!"

Jonathan could not help smiling at her frankness. "How did you know I was here?"

"I studied your file in Mr. Dragon's office, remember? This assignment was detailed in it."

"I see." So Dragon had been so sure of him that he had included this sanction. Jonathan despised being predictable.

"Will I see you tonight, Jonathan?" There was bravery in her voice. She was willing to be hurt.

"I have a date to climb a hill today. We'll be up there overnight."

"What about tomorrow?"

"Please go away. I have no intention of punishing you. I don't want to hate you, or love you, or anything. I just want you to go away."

She folded her gloves in her lap. She had made up her mind. "I'll be here when you come down from the mountain."

Jonathan rose and dropped a bill on the table. "Please don't."

Her eyes brimmed suddenly with tears. "Why are you doing this, Jonathan? I know this isn't a one-way thing. I know you love me too."

"I'll get over it." He left the café and walked to the hotel with vigorous strides.

True to type, the Swiss guide grumbled and complained that they should have started with the first light of dawn. As it was, they would have to pass the night on the mountain. Jonathan explained that he had all along intended to pass the night there, for the conditioning. The guide classified himself: At first he did not understand (genus, Teutonic), then he refused to budge (species, Helvetic). But when Jonathan offered to double the fee, there was a sudden comprehension coupled with the assurance that the idea of spending a night on the mountain was a splendid one.

Jonathan had always found the Swiss to be a money-loving, dour, religious, money-loving, independent, well-organized, money-loving people. These men of the Bernese Oberland are fine mountaineers, always willing to face the rigors and risks of rescuing a climber trapped on the face of a mountain. But they never fail to send a carefully itemized bill to the man they have saved or, that failing, to his next of kin.

The climb was rigorous enough, but relatively uneventful. Jonathan would have resented the guide's interminable complaining about the cold during the overnight bivouac, had it not served to keep his mind from Jemima.

Back at the hotel the next day, he received his bill. It seemed that, despite the double fee there were many little items still to be paid for. Among these were medical supplies they had not used, food for the bivouac (Jonathan had brought his own to test the freeze-dried rations), and a charge for "1/4 pair of boots." This last was too much. He called the guide to his room and questioned him. The guide assumed an attitude of cooperation and weary patience as he explained the obvious. "Shoes wear out; you would not deny that. Surely one cannot climb a mountain barefooted. Agreed? For Matterhorn I usually charge half a pair of shoes. Eiger is more than half the altitude of Matterhorn, and yet I only charged you for a quarter pair. I did this because you were a pleasant companion."

"I'm surprised you didn't charge me for wear on the rope."

The guide's eyebrows lofted. "Oh?" He took up the bill and scanned it minutely. "You are perfectly right, sir. There has been an omission." He drew a pencil from his pocket, licked the point, and painstakingly wrote in the neglected item, then corrected and checked the total. "Can I be of further service?" he asked.

Jonathan pointed to the door, and with a curt bow the guide left.

Jonathan's undefined sense of tension and anticipation was exacerbated by the depression Switzerland always brought upon him. He considered the placement of the magnificent Alps in this soulless country to be one of nature's more malevolent caprices. As he wandered around the hotel aimlessly, he came upon a group of lower-class Eiger Birds playing the fondue-kirsch-kiss game and giggling stupidly. He turned back toward his room with disgust. No one really likes Switzerland, except those who prefer cleanliness to life, he thought. And anyone who would live in Switzerland would live in Scandinavia. And anyone who would live in Scandinavia would eat lutefisk. And anyone who would eat lutefisk would. . . .

He paced up and down in his room. Ben would not arrive until the next day, and Jonathan would be damned if he would spend an unnecessary day in this hotel, among these people, an object of curiosity for the early-arrived Eiger Birds.

His telephone rang.

"What!" he snapped into the receiver.

"How did you know it was me?" Jemima asked.

"What do you have planned for tonight?"

"Making love with you," she answered without hesitation.

"Dinner first at your café?"

"Great. Does this mean everything is all right between us?"

"No." He was surprised at her assumption.

"Oh." The line was silent for a moment. "See you in twenty minutes."

"Fifteen?"

Night had fallen quickly around the café terrace, as it does in the mountains, and they sipped in silence the last of their brandy. Jemima had been careful to make no allusions to their time together in Long Island. His mind was far away, and he failed to

220

notice the inset of cool air slipping down from the flanks of Eiger.

"Jonathan?"

"Hm-m?"

"Am I forgiven?"

He shook his head slowly. "That isn't the point. I would never again be able to trust you."

"And you would want to?"

"Sure."

"Then you're really saying we might have made something of it."

"I'm pretty sure we could have."

"And now no chance? Ever?"

He did not answer.

"You're a warped man. And you know something else? You haven't kissed me yet."

He corrected the oversight. As their faces drew slowly apart, Jemima sighed, "Corn in Egypt, man. I didn't know lips had a memory of their own."

They watched the last yellow light desert the ragged crests surrounding them.

"Jonathan? About that business at your home . . ."

"I don't want to talk about it."

"It wasn't really the money that hurt you, was it? I mean—we were so good together. All day long, I mean. Not just in bed. Hey, you want to know something?"

"Tell me."

She laughed at herself. "Even after taking your money, I had to overcome an impulse to go back and make love to you again before I left. That would really have made you angry when you found out, wouldn't it?"

"Yes. Really."

"Say, how's the crazy one? What's his name?"

"Mr. Monk? I don't know. I haven't been back for some time."

"Oh?" She knew that bode poorly for her.

"No." Jonathan stood up. "I assume your room has a bed."

"It's pretty narrow."

"We'll work it out."

She knew better than bring up the past again that night.

KLEINE SCHEIDEGG:
July 8

He took a late supper in the hotel dining room at a table somewhat apart from the thin scattering of patrons.

He was not pleased with himself. He felt he had handled the Jemima business badly. They had risen early, taken a walk through the tilted meadows, watched the dew make the tips of their shoes glisten, taken coffee on the terrace of her café, chatted nonsense, made jokes at the expense of passersby.

Then they shook hands, and he left for his hotel. The whole thing was unclean. Particles of emotion clung to their relationship. She was a presence down there in the village, waiting, and he was annoyed with himself for not making a clean break. He knew now that he would not punish her for her perfidy, but he also knew that he would never forgive her for it. He could not remember ever having forgiven anyone.

Several of the guests had dressed for dinner— early-arrived Eiger Birds. Jonathan noticed that half of the terrace telescopes had been roped off for the private—and costly—use of people nominated by the hotel management.

He pushed food around his plate without appetite. There were too many unsettled things churning at the back of his mind. There was Jemima, and the sanction assignment, and the knowledge that Mellough might have alerted his target, and the despised Eiger Birds. Twice he had noticed himself being pointed out by men in tuxedos to their young/pretty/dumb companions. One middle-aged ogler had waved him a tentative semaphore of greeting with her napkin.

It was with relief that he heard a familiar voice booming through the dining room from the lobby beyond.

"Goddam my ass if this ain't something! What the hell you mean you ain't got a room for me?"

Jonathan abandoned his coffee and brandy and crossed the dining room to the desk. The hotel manager, a tight little Swiss with the nervous propriety of his class, was attempting to calm Big Ben down.

"My dear Herr Bowman—"

"Dear Herr's ass! Just stick your nose back in that book and come up with my reservations. Hey, ol' buddy! You're looking good!"

Jonathan gripped Ben's paw. "What's the trouble?"

"Oh, this rinky-dink's screwed up my reservations. Says he can't find my telegram. From the looks of him, he couldn't find his tallywhacker with a six-man scouting party."

Jonathan realized what was going on. "The Eiger Birds are starting to fly in," he explained.

"Oh, I see."

"And our friend here is doing everything he can to create vacancies he can sell to them at inflated prices." Jonathan turned to the listening manager. "Isn't that it?"

"I didn't know this person was a friend of yours, Dr. Hemlock."

"He's in charge of the climb."

"Oh?" the manager asked with extravagant innocence. "Is someone going to climb our mountain?"

"Stop it."

"Perhaps Herr Bowman could find a place in the village? There are cafés that—"

"He's going to stay here."

"I am afraid that is impossible, Herr Doctor." The manager's lips pursed tightly.

"All right." Jonathan drew out his wallet. "Make up my bill."

"But, if you leave . . ."

"There will be no climb. That's correct. And your incoming guests will be very angry."

The manager was the essence of agonized indecision.

"Do you know what I think?" Jonathan said. "I think I saw one of your clerks sorting a batch of telegrams in your inner office. It's possible that Mr. Bowman's was among them. Why don't you go back and look them over."

The manager grasped at the offer to save face and left them with a perfunctory bow.

"You met the others yet?" Ben asked, looking around the lobby with the undisguised distaste of a competitor.

"They haven't arrived."

"No shit? Well, they'll be in tomorrow then. Personally, I can use the rest. My hoof's been acting up the last couple of days. Gave it too much workout while you were at the place."

"How's George Hotfort?"

"Quiet."

"Is she grateful that I didn't turn her over to the authorities?"

"I guess. She ain't the kind to burn candles."

The manager returned and performed a masque of surprised delight. He had found Ben's telegram after all, and everything was in order.

"You want to go directly to your room?" Jonathan asked as the uniformed bellhops collected Ben's luggage.

"No. Guide me to the bar and buy me some beer."

They talked late into the night, mostly about the technical problems of the Eigerwand. Twice Ben brought up the Mellough incident, but both times Jonathan turned him back, saying they could talk about it later, maybe after the climb. Since he had arrived in Switzerland, Jonathan had come more and more to believe that he would make the climb. For long periods of time, he forgot what his real mission was. But this fascination was too expensive a luxury, so before turning in for the night he asked to borrow again all the correspondence between Ben and the climbers who would arrive the next morning.

Jonathan sat up in his bed, the letters arranged in three stacks on the blankets, one for each man. His concentration circumscribed by the tight pool of his bedside lamp, sipping at a glass of Laphroaig, he tried to fashion personalities from the scant evidence of the correspondence.

Jean-Paul Bidet. Forty-two years old. A wealthy manufacturer who had by dint of unsparing work expanded his father's modest shop into France's foremost producer of aerosol containers. He had married rather late, and had discovered the sport of mountain climbing while on his honeymoon in the Alps. He had no climbing experience outside Europe, but his list of Alpine conquests was formidable. He had made most of his major climbs in the company of famous and expensive guides, and to a degree it was possible to accuse him of "buying" the peaks.

From the tone of his letters, written in a businessman's English, Bidet seemed congenial, energetic, and earthy. Jonathan was surprised to discover that he intended to bring his wife along to witness his attempt at the meanest mountain of them all.

Karl Freytag. Twenty-six years old. Sole heir to the Freytag industrial complex specializing in commercial chemicals, particularly insecticides and herbicides. He had begun climbing during college holidays, and before he was twenty he had formed an organization of German climbers over which he presided and which published a most respectable quarterly review of mountaineering. He was its editor-in-chief. There was a packet of offset reprints from the review that described his climbs (in the third person) and accented his capacities as a leader and route-finder.

His letters were written in a brittle, perfect English that did not admit of contractions. The underlying timbre suggested that Freytag was willing to cooperate with Herr Bowman and with the international committee that had sponsored the climb, but the reader was often reminded that he, Freytag, had conceived of the climb, and that it was his intention to lead the team on the face.

Anderl Meyer. Twenty-five years old. He had lacked the means to finish his medical studies in Vienna and had returned to earning his living as a carpenter with his father. During the climbing season he guided parties up his native Tyrolean Alps. This made him the only professional in the team. Immediately upon being forced to leave school, Meyer had become obsessed with climbing. By every means from scrimping to begging, he had managed to include himself in most of the major climbs of the last three years. Jonathan had read references to his activities in the Alps, New Zealand, the Himalayas, South America, and most recently in the Atlas Range. Every article had contained unreserved praise for his skill and strength (he was even referred to as a "young Hermann Buhl") but several writers had alluded to his tendency to be a loner and a poor team man, treating the less gifted members of his parties as anchors against his progress. He was what in gambling would be called a plunger. Turning back was, for him, the ultimate disgrace; and he would make moves on the face that would be suicide for men of more limited physical and psychic dispositions. Similar aspersions had been cast on Jonathan, during his years of active climbing.

Jonathan could form only the vaguest image of Meyer's personality from the letters. The veil of translation obscured the man; his English was stilted and imperfect, often comically obtuse because he translated directly from the German syntax, dictionary obviously in hand, and there were occasional medleys of compounded nouns that strung meaninglessly along until a sudden terminal verb tamped them into a kind of order. One quality, however, did emerge through the static of translation: a shy confidence.

Jonathan sat in bed, looking at the piles of letters and sipping his Scotch. Bidet, Freytag, Meyer. And whoever it was might have been alerted by Mellough.

KLEINE SCHEIDEGG:
July 9

He slept late. By the time he had dressed and shaved, the sun was high and the dew was off the meadow that tilts up toward the north face of Eiger. In the lobby he passed a chatting group of young people, their eyes cleansed, their faces tightened by the crisp thin air. They had been out frolicking in the hills, and their heavy sweaters still exuded a chill.

The hotel manager stepped around the desk and spoke confidentially. "They are here, Herr Doctor. They await you."

Jonathan nodded and continued to the dining room entrance. He scanned the room and discovered the group immediately. They sat near the floor-to-ceiling windows that gave onto the mountain; their table was flooded with brilliant sunlight, and their colorful pullovers were the only relief from the dim and sparsely populated room. It looked as though Ben had assumed, as the natural privilege of his experience and age, social command of the gathering.

The men rose as Jonathan approached. Ben made introductions.

"Jonathan Hemlock, this here's Gene-Paul Bidette." He clearly was not going to have anything to do with these phony foreign pronunciations.

Jonathan offered his hand. "Monsieur Bidet."

"I have looked forward to meeting you, Monsieur

Hemlock." Bidet's slanted peasant eyes were frankly evaluative.

"And this is Karl Freytag."

Amused, Jonathan matched the unnecessary force of Freytag's grip. "Herr Freytag?"

"Herr Doctor." He nodded curtly and sat down.

"And this here's Anderil Mayor."

Jonathan smiled professional approval into Meyer's wry, clear blue eyes. "I've read about you, Anderl," he said in German.

"I've read about you," Anderl answered in his soft Austrian accent.

"In which case," Jonathan said, "we have read about each other."

Anderl grinned.

"And this lady here is Missus Bidette." Ben sat down immediately his uncomfortable social duty was discharged.

Jonathan pressed the offered fingers and saw his reflection in her dark sunglasses. "Madame Bidet?"

She dipped her head slightly in a gesture that was, at one time, a greeting, a shrug at being Madame Bidet, and a favorable evaluation of Jonathan—a gesture altogether Parisienne.

"We just been small-talking and eyeballing the hill," Ben explained after Jonathan had sent the waiter after a fresh pot of coffee.

"I had no idea this mountain Jean-Paul has been talking about for a year now would be so beautiful," Madame Bidet said, taking off her sunglasses for the first time that morning and letting her calm eyes rest on Jonathan.

He glanced up at the Eiger's cold, shadowed face and the long wisps of captured cloud at the summit.

"I would not say beautiful," Bidet offered. "Sublime, perhaps. But not beautiful."

"It is the possibility of conflict and conquest that

is beautiful," Freytag clarified for all time and for all people.

Anderl peered at the mountain and shrugged. Obviously he had never thought of a mountain as beautiful or ugly: only as difficult or easy.

"Is that all you are having for breakfast, Herr Doctor?" Freytag asked as Jonathan's coffee was served.

"Yes."

"Food is an important part of conditioning," Freytag admonished.

"I'll bear that in mind."

"Meyer here shares your peculiar eating habits."

"Oh? I didn't know you were acquainted."

"Oh, yes," the German said. "I contacted him shortly after I organized this climb, and we have made several short climbs together to attune him to my rhythms."

"And you to his, I assume."

Bidet reacted to the cool tone of the exchange by inserting a hasty note of warmth and camaraderie. "We must all use first names. Don't you agree?"

"I'm afraid I don't know your wife's first name," Jonathan said.

"Anna," she offered.

Jonathan said the full name to himself and repressed a smile that only a native English speaker would understand.

"How are the weather reports?" Karl asked Ben officially.

"Not real good. Clear today; maybe tomorrow. But there's a bunch of weak fronts moving in on us that makes it pretty dicey after that."

"Well, that settles it," Karl announced.

"What does that settle?" Jonathan asked between sips of coffee.

"We must go now."

"Have I time to finish my coffee?"

231

"I mean, we must go as soon as possible."

Ben squinted at Karl incredulously. "With the possibility of a storm in three days?"

"It has been climbed in two." Karl was crisp and on the defensive.

"And if you don't make it in two? If you're pinned down up there in heavy weather?"

"Benjamin has a point there," Jean-Paul interposed. "We must not take childish risks."

The word "childish" rankled Karl. "One cannot climb without some risk. Perhaps the young face these risks more easily."

Jonathan glanced from the mountain to Ben, who turned down the corners of his mouth, closed his eyes, and shook his head heavily.

Anderl had not been a part of this discussion. Indeed, his attention was fixed on a group of attractive young girls out on the terrace. Jonathan asked his opinion on the advisability of climbing with a two-day weather limit. Anderl thrust out his lower lip and shrugged. He did not care whether they climbed in good weather or bad. Either would be interesting. But if they were not going to climb today or tomorrow, he had other things he might give his attention to.

Jonathan liked him.

"So we reach an impasse," Karl said. "Two in favor of climbing right now, and two opposed. The dilemma of the democratic process. What compromise do you suggest? That we climb halfway up?" His voice was heavy with Teutonic wit.

"It's *three* opposed," Jonathan corrected. "Ben has a vote."

"But he will not be climbing with us."

"He's our ground man. Until we touch rock, he has more than a vote; he has complete control."

"Oh? Has that been decided upon?"

Anderl spoke without taking his eyes from the

girls on the terrace. "It is always like that," he said with authority. "The ground man has the last word now, and the leader once we are on the face."

"Very well," Karl said to cut off discussion on a point he was losing. "That brings us to another issue. Who is to be leader?" Karl glanced around the table, ready to defend himself against any opposition.

Jonathan poured himself another cup and gestured with the pot; his offer of coffee was declined by Karl with a brusque shake of the head, by Jean-Paul who put his hand over his cup, by Anna with a movement of her fingertips, by Anderl who was paying no attention, and by Ben with a grimace, his beer mug still a quarter full. "I thought it was pretty much set that you would lead, Karl," Jonathan said quietly.

"And so it was. But that decision was reached before the American member of the team had his unfortunate accident and was replaced by a man of such international repute—up until a few years ago, at least."

Jonathan could not repress a smile.

"So that we start off with a firm understanding," Karl continued, "I want to make sure everyone is in agreement about who shall lead."

"You make a good point," Jean-Paul said. "It is true that Jonathan has climbed the mountain twice before."

Gallic reasonableness was countered with Teutonic exactitude. "A correction, if I may. The good doctor has *failed* to climb the mountain twice. I don't mean to offend you, Herr Doctor, but I am forced to say that I do not consider a record of failure automatically grants you the right to lead."

"I'm not offended. Is it all that important to you that you lead?"

"It is important to our group. I have spent months designing a new route that departs in significant ways from the classic ascent. I am sure that once I have gone over it with you, you will all agree it is well thought out and quite feasible. And taking the face by a new route will put us in the record books."

"And *that's* important to you?"

Karl glanced at him with surprise. "Of course."

Anderl had pushed his chair away from the table and was watching the power struggle with amusement in the folds of his thin, heavily tanned face.

Anna relieved her boredom by shifting her glance from Jonathan to Karl, the two natural leaders of the group. Jonathan sensed she was making a choice.

"Why don't we leave it at this," Jean-Paul said, moderating. "This afternoon we shall all go over the route you have planned, Karl. If it looks good to us, then you will be leader on the mountain. But until we are on the face, Benjamin will be in command."

Karl agreed, certain the appeal of his new route would convince them. Ben concurred with a glum glance at Karl. Jonathan agreed. And Anderl didn't care one way or the other.

"So!" Jean-Paul clapped his hands together to punctuate the end of what had been, for him, an unpleasant encounter. "Now we will take our coffee and become better acquainted with one another. Right?"

"Oh?" said Jonathan. "I had assumed that you and Karl were already acquainted."

"How so?" Jean-Paul asked, smiling.

"In a business way, I had imagined. Your company makes aeresol containers, his produces pesticides. It would seem natural that . . ." Jonathan shrugged.

Karl frowned at the mention of pesticides.

"Ah! I see," Jean-Paul said. "Yes, I can see that it would be a natural error. As a matter of fact, our meeting here is the first. It is sheerest coincidence that we are in related industries."

Anna glanced out the window and spoke to no one in particular. "In fact, I had assumed that every manufacturer of liquids in Europe had been to our house at one time or another."

Jean-Paul laughed and winked at Jonathan. "She finds some of my colleagues a little dull."

"Oh?" Jonathan asked, wide-eyed.

The conversation turned to social trivialities, and after fifteen minutes of this Ben rose and excused himself, saying he wanted to check over the equipment. Anderl decided to help him, and the two of them went off.

Jonathan watched Ben depart with his characteristic hyperenergetic hopping gait with which he compensated for his limp. A thought crossed his mind.

"I hear you were injured last month," he said conversationally to Karl.

"Yes. A fall. Nothing really."

"It was your leg, I believe."

"Yes. I cut it against a rock. I assure you it will not hamper my climbing in the least."

"Good."

Karl and Jean-Paul fell to chatting about mountains they had both climbed, comparing routes and events. Jonathan had an opportunity to sit back with his cup and examine the three of them at his leisure. There had been nothing in the behavior of any member of the team to suggest he knew what Jonathan was and why he was there.

Anna Bidet's thoughts had turned inward, hidden behind the long lashes which veiled her quick, intelligent eyes. For some time she had been withdrawn, quite content with the company of her own mind. From time to time she would focus out on the men around her and listen for a moment before deciding there was nothing to interest her in the conversation, then she would dissolve back into herself. Jonathan let his eyes rest on her. Her clothes, her rare comments, her glances occasionally flashing in question or amusement, then eclipsing with a sudden drop of the lashes—everything was studied and effective. She was at one time dignified and provocative, a combination that is the exclusive property of Parisian women of a certain class and age.

She emerged from her reverie with the feel of Jonathan's gaze upon her. She returned it frankly and with amusement.

"An interesting combination," she said quietly.

"What is?"

"Art critic, scholar, and mountain climber. And I'm sure there's more to you than that."

"What do you make of it?"

"Nothing."

Jonathan nodded and turned his attention to Jean-Paul, who obviously did not come from her world. His recent wealth fit him like his clothes, a little imperfectly because he lacked the panache to dominate them. He was over age for a major climb, but there was no fat on his sturdy agricultural body. One eye dropped down like a tragic clown's, but his expression was alive with intelligence and conviviality. His nose made a long, thin line starting rather too far up above the eyes and taking a capricious jog to one side about halfway down. The mouth was crooked and mobile enough to grant him that facial plasticity so intrinsic to a French peasant's communication. All in all, the face looked as though Nature had designed a perfectly nondescript mold, then had laid its palm against the muzzle while the clay was fresh and had given a slight twist to the left.

Jonathan appreciated his qualities. His dislike of conflict and his logical moderation made him the ideal lubricant among the dynamic and aggressive personalities common to climbing. It was a pity that he was a cuckold—at least an emotional cuckold. Jonathan pictured him with a nightcap, a candlestick in one hand, and a *pispot* in the other.

It was an unkind image, so he shifted his attention

to Karl Freytag who at that moment was carefully and significantly advancing an argument proving that the route Jean-Paul had taken up the Dru the season before had been poorly chosen. When Jean-Paul laughed and said, "All I know is that it got me to the summit and back!" Karl shrugged, unwilling to continue reasoning with a man who took the matter so lightly.

Karl's face was broad and regular, but too immobile to be interesting; he was handsome without being attractive. His blond—really colorless—hair was fine and lank, and he combed it back in a flat pompadour from his wide, aggressively intelligent forehead. He was the tallest man in the party by two inches, and his excellent body tone enabled him to maintain his rigid sitting posture without appearing foolish.

"Well!" Jean-Paul said, breaking off his chat with Karl and turning to Jonathan and Anna. "You two don't seem to have been chatting."

"We were comparing silences," Jonathan said, "and hers turned out more interesting than mine."

"She's a remarkable woman." Jean-Paul looked at his wife with undisguised pride.

"I believe that."

"She was in ballet before her unfortunate marriage, you know." Jean-Paul was in the habit of protecting himself by beating others to the assumption that the union had been socially and emotionally morganatic. It was not only that he was a manufacturer; his company made a comically common household article.

Anna laughed softly. "Jean-Paul likes to think he snatched me from the stage at the height of my career. Actually, age and declining popularity were working toward the same goal."

"Nonsense!" Jean-Paul asserted. "No one could ever guess your age. How old do you think she is, Jonathan?"

Jonathan was embarrassed for both of them.

"My husband admires frankness, Doctor Hemlock. He considers tact to be a kind of deviousness."

"No but. Come on, Jonathan. How old would you say Anna is?"

Jonathan lifted his hands palms up in a gesture of helplessness. "I—ah—imagine a man would only consider her age if he were trying to decide whether the praise should go to Nature or to the lady herself."

It had not been very good, but Anna applauded mockingly, soundlessly tapping the tips of three fingers into her palm.

Sensing that nothing of consequence was going to be talked about here, Karl rose and excused himself. Jean-Paul moved down one chair to tighten the party.

"It is certainly magnificent," he said, looking dreamily out to the Eiger. "It's a perfect choice for my last mountain."

"Your last?"

"I am no longer young, Jonathan. Think of it! At forty-two, I shall be the oldest man to climb it. These two young men are fantastic climbers. We shall have our work cut out, you and I. You are—forgive me but—you are . . .?"

"Thirty-seven."

"Ah! Just my wife's age!"

She closed her eyes and opened them tiredly.

To change the subject, Jonathan asked, "Are you interested in climbing, Anna?"

"Not especially."

"But she will be proud of me when I return, won't you, dearest?"

"Very proud."

"I don't know when I've felt so good," Jean-Paul said, stretching his arms athletically and allowing one to drop across Anna's shoulders. "I feel I have achieved the best conditioning possible at my age.

Each night for the past six months I have performed a complicated set of calisthenics. And I have been religious about them. I work so late that my poor wife is usually asleep when I join her." He laughed and patted her.

"By now she must be very eager," Jonathan said, "to see you make the climb."

Anna glanced at him, then looked away to the windows which were beginning to dapple with a light rain.

From habit Jean-Paul cursed the break in the weather, but his experience in these Bernese Alps told him that the preceding sunshine, not this rain, was the exception.

"This will bring fresh snow to the upper reaches," he said matter-of-factly.

"Yes, some," Jonathan agreed. He refilled his cup and excused himself to step out onto the terrace where he stood under an overhanging eave and enjoyed the smell of the rain.

The sky was zinc, and the color of the few gnarled evergreens that clung to the rocky soil of Kleine Scheidegg had been subtracted to olive drab by the loss of sunlight. There was no wind, and he sipped his coffee and listened to the rustle of rain in the meadow grass.

They were a cool lot. One of them, at least, was cool. He had met the possible sanction targets, but no gesture, no nervousness, no glance had given him a hint. Jonathan would be on dicey ground until Search contacted him with the target's identity.

Gray and listless mists concealed the upper third of the North Face. He recalled the ghoulish pun German sports writers resurrected each time a team attempted the Eiger. Instead of Nordwand, North Wall, they called it the Mordwand, Murder Wall. The days were past when German and Austrian youths threw their lives against the Eigerwand with reckless

Wagnerian *Todeslieb;* great names had mastered the face: Hermann Buhl, Lionel Terray, Gaston Rébuffat; and dozens of lesser men had climbed it, each eroding, with his success, a fragment of the glory accruing to the task; but nonetheless, as he stood in the half-shelter sipping his coffee and looking across the meadow, Jonathan experienced an expanding desire to try again the face that had twice driven him back.

On his way up to Ben's room, he passed Anderl in the corridor, and they exchanged nods of greeting. He had taken an instant liking to this short, sinewy lad with his mop of dark hair so obviously unused to the comb, and his long strong fingers designed by nature for finding and clinging to the smallest indentations in the rock. It would be too bad if Anderl turned out to be the sanction target.

His knock at Ben's door was answered by a booming, "Fuck off!"

Jonathan opened the door and peeked in.

"Oh, it's you, ol' buddy. Come on in. And lock the door behind you."

Jonathan moved a coil of nylon line off the spare bed and stretched out. "Why the fierce greeting?"

Ben had been packing the haversacks, evenly distributing the weight, but making sure each pair of kits contained every necessity for a good bivouac, should the team break into two climbing ropes. "Oh, I thought you were one of those reporters." He grumbled something to himself as he snatched tight a strap. Then, "Goddam my eyes if they ain't been pecking at my door every five minutes. There's even a newsreel team here. Did you know that?"

"No. But I'm not surprised. The Eiger Birds are here in force now. The hotel's filled up and they're spilling over into Alpiglen and Grindelwald."

"Fucking ghouls."

"But the fattest cats of all are right here in the hotel."

Ben tied off one of the haversacks with a grunt. "Like who?"

Jonathan mentioned the names of a Greek merchant and his recently-acquired American society wife. The management of the hotel had erected a large rectangular oriental tent that gave onto one of the telescopes on the terrace. The tent was hung in silk and equipped with heaters and a small refrigerator, and the telescope had been reserved for their personal use, after being scrubbed down carefully with disinfectant. Every social precaution had been taken to insulate them from the company of the lesser Eiger Birds, but the Greek's penchant for lavish waste and gross practical jokes had instantly attracted the attention of the press.

Jonathan noticed a powerful brass telescope in the corner of the room. "You bring that with you?"

"Sure. You figure I'm going to line up with a pocketful of coins to watch you on the face?"

"I'm afraid you're going to have to make your peace with the newsmen."

"Why?"

"It would be best if you kept them informed, once we're on the hill. Just basic statistics: how high we are, the weather, our route—things like that."

"Tell 'em nothing, that's my motto. Fuck 'em."

"No. I think you should cooperate a little. If you don't, they'll make copy out of their imaginations."

Ben tied off the last of the kits and opened a bottle of beer from his supply on the dresser. "Whew! I've been busier than a one-legged man in an ass-kicking contest. But I got you people ready to move out at a minute's notice. There's a report of a cone of high pressure moving in, and you *know* that bitch-kitty of a hill ain't going to give you more than two or three

241

days of weather." He tossed a ring of ice pitons off his bed and stretched out.

Jonathan asked for his evaluation of the climbers, and Ben screwed up his face. "I don't know. Too much of a mixed bag for my taste. That German kid's too cocky-assed."

"I have a feeling he's a good climber, though."

"Could be. But he ain't many grins in a bivouac. He's got all the makings of a first-class snot. Doesn't seem to realize that we were making major climbs when he was still shitting yellow. Now that Austrian boy—"

"Anderl."

"Yeah, Anderl. Now, he's a climber. He's got the right look. Kinda looks like you did." Ben leaned up on one elbow and added pointedly. "Thirteen years ago."

"All right. All right."

"Hey, ol' buddy? Toss your poor crippled friend another can of beer?"

Jonathan grunted up and did so, noticing for the first time that Ben was drinking American beer, an extravagance in Switzerland. But like most big American beer drinkers, Ben had no taste for the relatively thick German product. Jonathan leaned against the window and watched the rain. He saw Anderl out on the meadow, his arm around a girl who had his jacket over her head. They were returning to the hotel. "What do you think about Jean-Paul, Ben?"

"Not so good. The way I peg it, you are just a gnat's ass inside the age limit for this kind of go. And he's on the other side of the line."

Jonathan did not agree. "He looks to me like he has a lot of staying power. There's generations of peasant endurance in the man."

"If you say so, ol' buddy." Ben swung his legs down and sat up, his tone changing suddenly, like a man who is finally getting to the point. "Back at my place you said that maybe you wouldn't be making this climb after all. Is that still the way it is?"

Jonathan sat on the windowsill. "I don't know. There's a job I have to do here. The climbing's really only side action."

"Pretty big league, for side action."

"True."

"What kind of job?"

Jonathan looked into Ben's laugh-lined face. There was no way to tell him. Out beyond the window there were islets of snow on the meadow being grayed and decayed by the rain. "The skiers must be cursing this rain," he said for something to say.

"What kind of job?" Ben persisted. "Does it have something to do with that Mellough guy?"

"Only obliquely. Forget it, Ben."

"Kinda hard to forget. After you left, all hell broke loose at the lodge. There were government men all over the place, talking tough and generally making asses of themselves. They were scouting out in the desert and getting themselves lost and organizing patrols and cutting around with helicopters. They had the whole county in an uproar before they were through."

Jonathan smiled to himself at the image of a CII operation of this type: all the coordination of a joint Arab/Italian invasion. "They call it undercover work, Ben."

"Is that what they call it? What happened out there anyway? When you brought back the shotgun, it had been fired. And no one ever saw Mellough and his boyfriend again."

"I don't want to talk about it. I have to do what I do, Ben. Without it, I would lose my house and things I have spent years collecting."

"So? You lose your house. You could still teach. You like teaching, don't you?"

Jonathan looked at Ben. He had never really thought about whether or not he liked teaching. "No, I don't think so. I like being around good heads that appreciate my mind and taste, but as for simple teaching—no. It's just a job."

Ben was silent for a time. He finished the beer and crushed the can in his hand. "Let's call off the climb," he said firmly. "We'll tell 'em you're sick or something. Trouble with hemorrhoids, maybe."

"My Achilles anus? No way, Ben. Forget it." Jonathan wiped the haze from the window with the back of his hand and peered out at the misted mountain. "You know what's weird, Ben?"

"You."

"No. What's really weird is that I want another shot at the hill. Even forgetting the thing I have to do here, it's something I really want to do. You understand the feeling?"

Ben fiddled for a moment with a coil of nylon line. "Of course I understand it. But I'll tell you something, ol' buddy. The sweet smell of decay is heavy in the air."

Jonathan nodded.

Conversation among the team at luncheon centered on the weather, which had settled to a steady, plump rain which occasional gusts of wind rattled against the windows. They knew it would bring fresh snow to the Third Ice Field and, higher, to the White Spider. Much depended on the temperature on the face. If it was cold, and the snow dry and powdery, it would slip off in regular hissing slides, leaving the glaciated perennial ice and névé clean enough for a climb. If, on the other hand, the temperature should rise and make the snow moist and cohesive, it would build up, poising on the 60° inclines of the ice fields, ready to avalanche at the slightest disturbance.

Ben knew Jonathan had studied the surface of the

North Face during his conditioning climb up the west flank two days before.

"Could you see much?"

"Yes. The weather was clear."

"Well?" asked Karl.

"It looked fine, for Eiger. The snow was old and crusted. And the whole face was dryer than I've ever seen it." Jonathan was referring to the inexplicable "drying up" of the North Wall that had been in progress over the past thirty years. Pitches that had been expansive snowfields in the late thirties were wet and icy rock by the end of the fifties. "One good thing. The Hinterstoisser Traverse was almost clear of ice."

"That does not affect us," Karl announced. "My route does not include the Hinterstoisser Traverse."

Even the phlegmatic Anderl shared the general silence this statement generated. Jonathan's cup of chocolate hovered for an instant in its rise to his lips, but he recovered quickly and sipped without comment, denying Karl the pleasure of shocking him. That Traverse, to which a young German had given his name in death, had been the key to all successful ascents of the mountain. No team had ever bypassed that critical bridge and made the summit, and only one team that had dared returned alive.

"I shall detail my route after luncheon," Karl said, shunting away the negative silence.

With a gentle smile concealing his thoughts, Jonathan watched Karl over his cup for a moment, then he shifted his attention to the meadow and the mountain beyond.

The climbing team had reserved a table overlooking the meadow, and they generally sat with their backs to the restaurant, trying to ignore the presence of the Eiger Birds who, by now, had arrived en masse.

Several times during each meal, waiters had

arrived with notes from the more affluent or aggressive Eiger Birds inviting the climbers to supper or to some evening entertainment which, if accepted, would have elevated the host in the eyes of his peers. These notes were always passed to Ben who took pleasure in slowly tearing them up unread in full view of the smiling, waving sender.

The discerning ornithologist would have distinguished three species of Eiger Bird among the flittering gathering that babbled in half a dozen languages.

The *gratin* of the Eiger Bird society were internationally famous idlers who had flown in from midsummer *étapes* on their annual pleasure migrations to have their sensation-drained nerves tickled by the sexual stimulant of death. They had gathered from all parts of the world, but not one had come from those once-popular refuges that have been contaminated by middle-class imitators: the Riviera, Acapulco, the Bahamas, the Azores, and, most recently lost to upward social mobility, the Morocco coast. Their pecking order was rigid, and each new arrival stepped obediently into his place, more defined by who belonged beneath him than by who belonged above. The Greek merchant and his wife assumed as their fiscal right the apex of the social pyramid; fragile-blooded and thin-faced Italian nobility with limited means were at the bottom.

A lower subspecies of leisure necrophiles were much more numerous. They were easily distinguishable by the garishness of their plumage and the tense and temporary nature of their mating habits. There were paunchy men with purplish tans, cigars, thinning hair, and loud, awkward gestures designed to communicate youthful energy. They were to be seen during feeding time fumbling after their teatty, sponsored companions who giggled and went vacant in the face when touched.

The female of this subspecies were women of uncertain age, crisp of feature, monotonically dyed hair, skin tight at the temples from cosmetic surgery. Their alert and mistrusting eyes darted to follow the dark Greek and Sicilian boys they carried with them and used.

And on the fringes, virile lesbians protected and dominated their fluttering lace-and-mauve possessions. And male homosexuals bickered and made up.

The lowest order of Eiger Bird was the newspaper and television men who fed on the orts and droppings of the others. They were conspicuous by their clannishness and their inexpensive clothes, often rumpled as a badge of their romantic migratory lives. For the most part they were a glib and overdrinking lot who took cynical advantage of the reduced rates offered them by the hotel in return for the advertisement value of the Kleine Scheidegg dateline.

Film actors formed an interconnecting subculture of their own. Lacking the fiscal credentials to associate with the elite, they carried with them a communicable visibility that made them valuable to all who would be seen and read about. Actors were not treated as people, but as social possessions. In this way, they resembled Grand Prix drivers.

One exception to this general status of film personalities was a husband and wife team who, because of their accumulated wealth and personal brass, were a kind of *gratin* in their own right. Since their arrival at the hotel that morning, an arrival attended by great flutter and flap, loud greetings of casual acquaintances, and histrionic overtipping, they had made two overtures to the climbers, both of which had been parried. The actor had responded to the rejection with heroic resignation; the actress had been loudly miffed, but had recovered her aplomb when she heard that the Greek merchant's wife had done no better.

Different from the Eiger Birds, and alien to them, were a small group of young men who had been attracted to Kleine Scheidegg by the rumor of the ascent. These were the only people with whom the team had intercourse or sympathy. In shy twos and threes, young climbers had arrived by train and motorcycle from Austria, Germany, and Chamonix to set up their red or yellow tents on the meadow, or to rent rooms in the cheaper cafés of Alpiglen and Grindelwald. Feeling out of place among the rich hotel guests, they quietly sought out Ben to mumble good wishes and shake hands. Many of them slipped bits of paper into Ben's palm containing their addresses or the locations of their tents, then they departed quickly, always refusing offered refreshment. The scribbled notes were for Ben's use if it became necessary to form a rescue party. All these climbers knew the reputation of the Bernese guides, and they knew that a man on the face could freeze to death before necessary financial arrangements could be worked out. The more forward of these young men ventured to shake hands with Jonathan or Anderl, the two members of the party of whom they had read in mountain journals. This did not please Karl.

Throughout the meal, Anderl amused himself by eye-fencing with two little twits who had arrived with a merchant type with a loud voice and a penchant for prehensile attention. The merchant made clear his annoyance at the flirtation, and this amused Anderl the more.

Ben's eyes twinkled with paternal teasing as he said to Anderl, "Now you watch it, boy. You're going to need all your energy on the hill."

Anderl answered without looking away from the girls. "I climb only with my hands and feet."

Jonathan finished his coffee and rose, promising to meet the others in Ben's room in half an hour to go over Karl's proposed route. Anna got up too; she had no intention of boring herself with the forthcoming planning session. Together they walked to the lobby where Jonathan picked up his mail. One envelope had neither stamp nor postmark, so he tore it open first and glanced at the note. It was an invitation to an intimate supper with the Greek merchant and his American wife. Mentioned also (in the wife's round, plump hand) was the fact that they had recently purchased a lot of paintings through Sotheby's. She would be delighted to have Jonathan glance them over and make an evaluation. She reminded him that he had once performed a similar service for her first husband.

Jonathan stepped to the desk and hastily wrote a note. He mentioned that evaluation was a professional, not social, activity for him. He added that he had to decline the offer of supper as he would be involved in preparations for the climb and, anyway, he was suffering from a debilitating hangnail.

Anna looked at him quizzically from the other side of the elevator car, her habitual expression of defensive amusement crinkling her eyes.

"That must have given you pleasure."

"You read over my shoulder?"

"Of course. You're very like my husband, you know."

"Would he have declined an invitation from those people?"

"Never! His self-image would have driven him to accept."

"Then how am I similar?"

"You also acted without choice. Your self-image forced you to decline." She paused at the door to her suite. "Would you care to come in for a moment?"

"I think not, thank you."

She shrugged. "As you wish. Opportunities to decline seem to abound for you today."

"If I read the signs correctly, I am not the one you've selected anyway."

She arched her eyebrows, but did not respond.

"I assume it's Karl," he continued.

"And you also assume it is any concern of yours?"

"I have to climb with both of them. Be discreet."

"I thought you were usually paid for your evaluations." She entered her room and closed the door behind her.

Jonathan sat in a deep chair beside the window. He had just finished a smoke and was in full relax. On his lap was a small bundle of mail that had, from the evidence of superimposed postal hieroglyphics, been chasing him for some time. The rain, mixed now with dancing pebbles of hail, drilled against the window in treble timpani, and the light filling the room was greenish-gray and chill.

He went through his mail listlessly.

From the chairman of his department: ". . . and I'm pleased to be able to announce a considerable salary increase for the next academic year. Of course, it is impossible to reflect in dollars the value . . ."

Yeah, Yeah. Flip. Into the wastepaper basket.

A bill on the house. Flip.

"The administration has granted a mandate to form a special committee on student unrest, with particular emphasis on the task of channeling this social energy into productive and. . . ."

Flip. He missed the basket. It was his practice never to serve on committees.

A bill on the house. Flip.

The journal was in dire need of his article on Lautrec. Flip.

The last was a postage-free official envelope from the American Embassy in Bern. It contained a photocopy of a cryptogram from Dragon.

"Message starts . . . Hemlock . . . break . . . Search

has had no success in designating your objective . . . break . . . Alternate plan now in operation . . . break . . . Have placed details in the hands of Clement Pope . . . break . . . Plan will crystalize for you tomorrow . . . break . . . Can anything be done to decrease the attention the news media have given to your proposed climb . . . question mark . . . break . . . Miss Brown remains outside our cognizance . . . break . . . best regards . . . break, break . . . Message ends."

Flip.

Jonathan relaxed into the depths of his chair and watched the hail pebbles ricochet up from the windowsill. Two basso rolls of thunder caused his attention to strain through the clatter of rain and hail. He wanted very much to hear the heavy rumble of an avalanche on the face, because if avalanches did not scrub the face clean of amassed snow and poised rubble . . .

He would have to do something definite about Jemima.

It was all piling up on him.

He rolled another smoke.

What was Dragon's purpose in putting Pope in charge of designating the target? Despite his mannerisms of the B-movie detective, Pope had had no very distinguished record with Search before Dragon had elevated him to number two position in SS Division.

This sudden infliction of Pope upon the scene was disturbing, but there was no unraveling the serpentine patterns of check and double check, of distrust and redundancy that substituted for security in CII, so Jonathan put it out of his mind for the moment.

He slumped down in his chair and closed his eyes while the smoke loosened him up. It was the first time he had had to himself since meeting the other climbers, and he took the opportunity to recall how each had reacted. Nothing had indicated the least suspicion or fear. Good. He was fairly sure that Miles Mellough had not had a chance to contact the target before the affair in the desert, but he was relieved to have the added evidence of their behavior.

Th jangle of his telephone intersected his thoughts.

"Guess where I'm calling from?"

"I don't know, Gem." He was surprised at the fatigued sound of his own voice.

"From Bern. How about that?"

"What are you doing in Bern?" He was both relieved and oddly distressed.

"I'm not in Bern. That's just it. I'm in my café, just a pleasant fifteen-minute walk from your hotel. Which you may take as an invitation, if you have a mind to."

Jonathan waited, assuming she would explain.

"They routed my call through Bern. Isn't that weird?"

"Not really." Jonathan had experience with Swiss telephone systems, which rival only the French for efficiency. "The whole thing is based on the assumption that the shortest distance between two points is a cube."

"Well, *I* thought it was weird."

He suspected she had no real reason for calling him, and he could sense a tone of helpless embarrassment in her voice.

"I'll try to see you tomorrow, Gem."

"OK. But if you feel an irresistible urge to drop in on me tonight, I'll try to arrange my schedule to make . . ." She gave up on it. Then, after a pause, "I love you, Jonathan." The ensuing silence begged for a response. When none came, she laughed without foundation. "I don't mean to drip all over you."

"I know you don't."

Her pickup was artificially gay. "Right then! Until tomorrow?"

"Until then." He held the line for a moment, hoping she would hang up first. When she did not, he placed the receiver gently onto its cradle, as though to soften the end of the conversation.

The sun glinted through a rift in the clouds, and hail and rain fell in silver diagonals through shafts of sunlight.

Two hours later the five men sat around a table in the middle of Ben's room. They leaned over a large photographic blowup of the Eigerwand, the corners of which were held down by rings of pitons. Karl traced with his finger a white line he had inked on the glossy surface.

Jonathan saw at a glance that the proposed route was a blend of the Sedlmayer/Mehringer approach and the classic path. It constituted a direct climb of the face, a linear attack that met the obstacles as they came with a minimum of traversing. It was almost the line a rock would take if it fell from the summit.

"We take the face here," Karl said, pointing to a spot three hundred meters left of the First Pillar, "and we go straight up to the Eigerwand Station. The climb is difficult—grade five, occasionally grade six—but it is possible."

"That first eight hundred feet will be wide open," Ben said in objection. And it was true that the first pitch offered no protection from the rock and ice that rattles down the face each morning when the touch of the sun melts the frost that has glued the loose rubble to the mountain through the night.

"I am aware of that," Karl responded. "I have weighed all the dangers. It will be vital that we cover that pitch in the early morning."

"Continue," Jean-Paul urged, already seduced by the prospect of being one of the first to take the face on a direct line.

"If all goes well, our first bivouac should be here." Karl's finger brushed a dark spot on the snow-crusted face just above the Eigerwand Station. There was a long gallery cut through the mountain during the building of the Jungfrau railroad tunnel. The gallery had been drilled through for ventilation and for jettisoning rubble from the main tunnel, and it was a favorite stopping-off place for tourists who walked to its well-protected edge and gaped down over the breath-catching void.

"In fact, we might get as high as Death Bivouac on the first day." Karl's finger traced a rippled shadow of mixed ice and rock. "And from then on, it's a matter of following the classic route." Freytag was aware that he had elided past the hitherto un-climbed part of the face, so he looked around the circle of men, ready to face objections.

Anderl leaned over the enlarged photograph and squinted for several minutes at a narrow diagonal band below the Eigerwand Station window. He nodded very slowly. "That might go. But we would have to stay out of the ice—hold to the rock as much as possible. It's a chute, Karl. I'll bet water rushes through it all day long. And it's a natural alley for avalanche. I would not care to be standing in it directing traffic like a policeman when the avalanche comes roaring through."

The laughter that greeted the image petered out hollowly. Jonathan turned from the table and looked down at the hazy meadow below the window.

Ben spoke slowly. "No one's ever been on that part of the face. We have no idea what it's like. What if the rock doesn't go? What if you're forced down into the gut of the chute?"

"I have no interest in suicide, Herr Bowman. If the edges are not a go, we shall retreat and follow the Sedlmayer/Mehringer route."

"The route that brought them to the Death Bivouac," Ben clarified.

"The weather killed them, Herr Bowman! Not the route!"

"You got some deal with God on weather?"

"Please, please," Jean-Paul interposed. "When Benjamin questions your route, Karl, he is not attacking you personally. For myself, I find the route intriguing." He turned to Jonathan at the window. "You have said nothing, Jonathan. What do you think?"

The mist had lifted from the face, and Jonathan was able to address his statements to the mountain. "Let me make sure of a couple of things, Karl. Assuming we make the Third Ice Field as you plan, the rest of the ascent will be classic, am I right? Up the Ramp, across the Traverse of the Gods, into the Spider, and up the Exit Cracks to the Summit Ice Field?"

"Exactly."

Jonathan nodded and ticked off each of the salient features on the face with his eyes. Then his glance returned to Karl's diagonal chute. "Certainly you realize that your route would not do for a retreat, if we were blocked higher up."

"I consider it self-defeating to plan in terms of retreat."

"I consider it stupid not to."

"Stupid!" Karl struggled with his control. Then he shrugged in peevish accord. "Very well. I shall leave the planning of a retreat route to Doctor Hemlock. After all, he has had more experience in retreating than I."

Ben glanced at Jonathan, surprised that he allowed this to pass with only a smile.

"I may take it then that my plan is accepted?" Karl asked.

Jonathan nodded. "Under the condition that the weather clears and freezes the new snow on. Without that, no route would go for a few days."

Jean-Paul was pleased with the agreement and went back over the route step by step with Karl, while Jonathan drew Anderl aside and asked him how he felt about the climb.

"It will be fun to try that diagonal pitch," was Anderl's only comment.

Ben was clearly unhappy with the route, with the team, with the whole idea of the climb. Jonathan crossed to him.

"Buy you a beer?"

"No thanks."

"What?"

"I dont feel like a beer. I feel like getting out of this whole business."

"We need you."

"I don't like it."

"What's the weather report like?"

Ben admitted reluctantly that the three-day prediction looked very good indeed: a strong high and a drop in temperature. Jonathan shared this good news with the party, and in a general mood of confidence they broke up, promising to take supper together.

By supper the weather in the valley had healed up with a palpable drop in temperature and a sudden clearing of the air. There was moonlight on the snow, and the stars could be counted. This fortuitous change and certain orthographic errors in the menu constituted the common small talk at the beginning of dinner, but before long the six of them had divided into four islands of concentration.

Jean-Paul and Karl chatted in French, limiting themselves to the climb and its problems. Karl enjoyed displaying the thoroughness with which he had considered every facet of the problem, and Jean-Paul enjoyed understanding.

Anna focused her attention on Anderl, converting his native wry humor into wit, as women of experience can, by minute gestures of appreciation and attention, until he was performing at his social maximum. Jonathan recognized that she was using Anderl as an extramarital red herring, but he was pleased that the normally reticent Austrian was enjoying himself, whatever the reason.

Ben was in an undisguised funk. He pushed food around on his plate with neither hunger nor interest. Emotionally, he was through with the climb; he was no longer a part of the team, although he would perform his duties responsibly.

For a time, Jonathan was tangent to the rims of the two conversations, making comments only when a pause or a glance seemed to call for it. But soon he was able to withdraw into himself, unheeded and unlamented. He had been troubled by the tone of Dragon's communication. Search had not yet settled on the name of his target. What if they failed to nominate him until immediately before the climb? Could he do it on the face?

And which one? It would be hardest to kill Anderl, easiest to kill Karl. But not really easy. Always before, the sanction had been a name, a catalogue of habits and routines described in the arid Search tout. He had never seen the man's face until minutes before the sanction.

". . . disinterest you so much?" Anna was speaking to him, amusement in her eyes.

"I beg your pardon." Jonathan focused out of his reverie.

"You have not said twenty words all night. Do we disinterest you so much?"

"Not at all. I simply haven't had anything pertinent or amusing to say."

"And that prevented you from speaking?" Karl laughed heartily. "How un-American!"

Jonathan smiled at him, thinking how terribly in

need of a spanking he was. A trait of the Germans—
a nation in need of a spanking.

Ben rose and mumbled his excuses. If the weather
held—and they wouldn't know for sure until tomorrow—the climb would begin in twenty-nine hours, so
he suggested that everyone get as much sleep as possible and run a final check of personal equipment. He
left the table brusquely, and in his handling of the
newsmen who spoke to him in the lobby he was
especially curt and scatological.

Karl rose. "What Herr Bowman says is true. If
the weather holds, we shall have to be away from
here by three in the morning, day after tomorrow."

"So tonight is our last night?" Anna looked calmly
at him, then bestowed her eyes on each of the company in turn for exactly equal time.

"Not necessarily our last night," Jonathan said.
"We may get down again, you know."

"Bad joke," Karl pronounced.

Jonathan bade the departing party good-night, then
sat down again to his coffee and brandy alone. He
slipped again into umber thoughts. Dragon had only
twenty-four hours in which to designate the target.

The mountain, and the target, and Jemima. And
behind it all, his house and paintings—they were
what mattered.

He found himself tightening up, so he sent little
calming messages along his nerve system to sap and
control the tension. But still his shoulders were stiff
and it required muscular contraction to flatten the
frown from his forehead.

"May I join you?" The phrasing was interrogative,
but not the tone. Karl sat before Jonathan responded.

There was a short silence during which Jonathan
sipped off the last of his brandy. Freytag was ill at
ease, his normally rigid posture tightened to brittle.
"I came to have a word with you."

"I assumed that, yes."

"I want to thank you for this afternoon."

"Thank me?"

"I had expected that you would oppose my route—my leadership. If you had, the others would have joined you. Herr Bowman is really your man, after all. And Bidet blows with the wind." Karl glanced down without altering his angular posture. "It is important to me, you know. Leading this party is important to me."

"So it would seem."

Freytag picked up a spoon and carefully replaced it where it belonged. "Herr Doctor?" he said without looking up. "You don't like me very much, do you?"

"No. Not much."

Karl nodded. "I thought not. You find me—unpleasant?" He looked at Jonathan, a faint smile bravely in place.

"Unpleasant, yes. Also socially inept and terribly unsure of yourself."

Karl laughed hoarsely. "Me? Unsure of myself?"

"Uh-huh. With the usual overcompensation for altogether justified feelings of inferiority that marks the typical German."

"Do you always find people to be typically this or that?"

"Only the typical ones."

"How simple life must be for you."

"No, life isn't simple. Most of the people I meet are."

Freytag adjusted the position of the spoon slightly with his forefinger. "You have been good enough to be frank with me, Herr Doctor. Now I shall be frank with you. I want you to understand why it is so important to me to lead this climb."

"That isn't necessary."

"My father—"

"Really, Karl. I don't care."

"My father is not sympathetic with my interest in

climbing. I am the last of the family line, and it is his wish that I follow him in the business. Do you know what our corporation makes?"

Jonathan did not answer; he was surprised and uncomfortable at the fragile tone of Karl's voice, and he did not want to be a receptacle for this boy's troubles.

"We make insecticides, our family." Karl looked out the window toward patches of snow fluorescent with moonlight. "And that is rather amusing when you realize that during the war we made . . . we made . . ." Karl pressed his upper lip against his teeth and blinked the shine from his eyes.

"You were only five years old when the war ended, Karl."

"Meaning it wasn't my fault?"

"Meaning you have no right to the artificial tragedy you enjoy playing."

Karl looked at him bitterly, then turned aside. "My father thinks I am incapable—not serious-minded enough to assume my responsibilities. But he will have to admire me soon. You said that you find me unpleasant—socially inept. Well, let me tell you something. I do not have to depend on social niceties to achieve—what I want to achieve. I am a great climber. Both by natural gift and intensive training, I am a great climber. Better than you. Better than Anderl. When you are behind me on the rope, you will see." His eyes were intense. "Someday everyone will say that I am a great climber. Yes." He nodded curtly. "Yes. And my father will boast to his business friends about me."

Jonathan was angry with the boy at that moment. Now the sanction would be difficult, no matter which one it was. "Is that all you wanted to say to me, Karl?"

"Yes."

"Then you'd better get along. I assume Madame Bidet is awaiting you."

"She told you . . ."

"No." Jonathan turned away and looked out through the window to where the mountain's presence was a bulky starlessness in the night sky.

After a minute, he heard the young man rise and walk out of the dining room.

KLEINE SCHEIDEGG:
July 10

Jonathan awoke late, the sun already flaring through his window and pooling warmly on his blankets. He was not eager to face the day. He had sat up late in the dining room, staring at the black rectangle of the window beyond which was the invisible Eiger. His thoughts had wandered from the climb, to the sanction, to Jemima. When at last he had forced himself to go up to his room for sleep, he had met Anna in the hall; she was just closing the door to Karl's room.

Not a hair out of place, not a wrinkle in her dress, she stood looking at him calmly, almost contemptuously, sure of his discretion.

"May I offer you a nightcap?" he asked, pushing open his door.

"That would be nice." She passed before him into his room.

They sipped Laphroaig in silence, an odd bond of comradeship between them based on their mutual realization that they constituted no threat to each other. They would never make love; the qualities of emotional reserve and human exploitation they shared and admired insulated them from each other.

"Blessed are the meek," Anna mused, "for we shall inherit them."

Jonathan was smiling in agreement when suddenly

he stopped and listened attentively to a distant rumbling.

"Thunder?" Anna asked.

Jonathan shook his head. "Avalanche."

The sound pulsed twice to higher volumes, then subsided. Jonathan finished his Scotch.

"They must be very frightening when you are up there," Anna said.

"They are."

"I cannot understand why Jean-Paul insists on making this climb at his age."

"Can't you?"

She looked at him dubiously. "For *me?*"

"As you well know."

She dropped her lavish lashes and looked into her whiskey glass. *"Pauvre être,"* she said quietly.

There were noticeable changes in emotional disposition around the breakfast table. Ben's funk had worn away and his more typical hardy humor had returned. The crisp weather and a strong high pressure cone that had moved in from the north inflated his hopes for the success of the climb. The recent snow on the higher ice fields had not had time to glaciate and bind to the perennial névé, but so long as the weather held, a major avalanche was not likely.

"Unless a foehn comes in," Karl corrected morosely.

The possibility of a foehn had been in the back of each climber's mind, but there was nothing to be gained by mentioning it. One could neither predict nor protect himself from these vagrant eddies of warm air that slip into the Bernese Oberland infrequently. A foehn would bring raging storms to the face, and the warmer air would make the snow unreliable and avalanche-prone.

Karl's mood had changed also since the evening before. A kind of self-indulgent petulance had replaced the typical nervous aggression. This was due partly, Jonathan imagined, to regret over having spilled his emotional garbage at Jonathan's feet. It was also due in part to his having made love to Anna, a burden his sin-sodden Protestant morality could not face glibly the next morning in the presence of the husband.

And indeed Jean-Paul was dour that morning. He was tense and irritable and their waiter—never a model of skill and intelligence—received the brunt of his displeasure. It was Jonathan's belief that Jean-Paul was struggling with inner doubts about age and ability now that the moment of the climb was approaching inexorably.

Anderl, with his face creased in a bland smile, was in an almost yoga calm. His eyes were defocused and his attention turned inward. Jonathan could tell that he was tuning himself emotionally for the climb, now only eighteen hours away.

So it was by social default that Jonathan and Anna carried the burden of small talk. Anna suddenly stopped midphrase, her eye caught by something at the entrance to the dining room. "Good God," she said softly, laying her hand on Jonathan's arm.

He turned to see the internationally known husband and wife team of film actors who had arrived the day before to join the Eiger Birds. They stood at the entrance, slowly scanning about for a free table in the half-empty room until they were satisfied that no one of importance had missed their presence. A waiter, a-quiver with servility, hastened to their side and conducted them to a table near the climbers. The actor was dressed in a white Nehru jacket and beads that conflicted with his puffy, pock-marked, middle-aged face. His hair was tousled to a precise degree of tonsorial insouciance. The wife was aggressively visible in floppy pants of oriental print with a gathered blouse of bravely clashing color, the looseness of which did much to mute her bread-and-butter dumpiness, the plunging neckline designed to direct the eye to more acceptable amplitudes. Banging about between the breasts was a diamond of vulgar size. Her eyes, however, were still good.

After the woman had been seated with a flurry of small adjustments and sounds, the man stepped to Jonathan's table and leaned over it, one hand on Anderl's shoulder, the other on Ben's.

"I want to wish you fellows the best kind of luck in the whole wide world," he said with ultimate sincerity and careful attention to the music of his vowels. "In many ways, I envy you." His clear blue eyes clouded with unspoken personal grief. "It's the kind of thing I might have done . . . once." Then a brave smile pressed back the sadness. "Ah, well." He squeezed the shoulders in his hands. "Once again, good luck." He returned to his wife, who had been waving an unlit cigarette in a holder impatiently, and who accepted her husband's tardy light without thanks.

"What happened?" Ben asked the company in a hushed voice.

"Benediction, I believe," Jonathan said.

"At all events," Karl said, "they will keep the reporters' attention away from us for a while."

"Where the devil is that waiter!" Jean-Paul demanded grumpily. "This coffee was cold when it arrived!"

Karl winked broadly to the company. "Anderl. Threaten the waiter with your knife. That will make him come hopping."

Anderl blushed and looked away, and Jonathan recognized that Freytag, in his attempt at humor, had blundered into an awkward subject. Embarrassed at the instant chill his *faux pas* had brought to the table, Karl pressed on with a German instinct for making things right by making them bigger. "Didn't you know, Herr Doctor? Meyer always carries a knife. I'll bet it's there under his jacket right now. Let us see it, Anderl."

Anderl shook his head and looked away. Jean-Paul attempted to soften Freytag's brutishness by explaining quickly to Jonathan and Ben. "The fact is, Anderl climbs in many parts of the world. Usually alone. And the village folk he uses as porters are not the most reliable men you could want, especially in South America, as your own experience has doubtless taught you. Well, in a word, last year poor Anderl was climbing alone in the Andes, and something happened with a porter who was stealing food and—anyway—the porter died."

"Self-defense isn't really killing," Ben said, for something to say.

"He wasn't attacking me," Anderl admitted. "He was stealing supplies."

Freytag entered the conversation again. "And you consider the death penalty appropriate for theft?"

Anderl looked at him with innocent confusion. "You don't understand. We were six days into the hills. Without the supplies, I would not have been able to make the climb. It was not pleasant. It made me ill, in fact. But I would have lost my chance at the mountain otherwise." Clearly, he considered this to be a satisfactory justification.

Jonathan found himself wondering about how Anderl, poor as he was, had collected the money for his share in the Eiger climb.

"Well, Jonathan," Jean-Paul said, evidently to change the subject, "did you have a good night?"

"I slept very well, thank you. And you?"

"Not at all well."

"I'm sorry. Perhaps you should get some rest this afternoon. I have sleeping pills, if you want them."

"I never use them," Bidet said curtly.

Karl spoke. "Do you use pills to sleep in bivouac, Herr Doctor?"

"Usually."

"Why? Discomfort? Fear?"

"Both."

Karl laughed. "An interesting tactic! By quietly admitting to fear, you give the impression of being a very wise and brave man. I shall have to remember that one."

"Oh. Are you going to need it?"

"Probably not. I also never sleep well in bivouac. But with me it is not a matter of fear. I am too charged with the excitement of the climb. Now Anderl here! He is amazing. He tacks himself to a sheer face and falls asleep as though he were bundled up in a feather bed at home."

"Why not?" Anderl asked. "Supposing the worst, what is the value in being awake during a fall? A last glimpse at the scenery?"

"Ah!" Jean-Paul ejaculated. "At last our waiter finds a moment for us in his busy schedule!"

But the waiter was coming with a note for Jonathan on a small silver tray.

"It is from the gentleman over there," the waiter said.

Jonathan glanced in the indicated direction, and he experienced a stomach shock.

It was Clement Pope. He sat at a nearby table, wearing a checked sport coat and a yellow ascot. He waved sassily at Jonathan, fully realizing that he was blowing Jonathan's cover. The defensive, gentle smile came slowly to Jonathan's eyes as he controlled the flutter in his stomach. He glanced at the other members of the party, trying to read the smallest trace of recognition or apprehension in their faces. He could distinguish none. He opened the note, scanned it, then nodded and thanked the waiter. "You might also bring M. Bidet a fresh pot of coffee."

"No, never mind," Jean-Paul said. "I no longer have a taste for it. I think I shall return to my room and rest, if you will excuse me." With this he left, his stride strong and angry.

"What's wrong with Jean-Paul?" Jonathan asked Anna quietly.

She shrugged, not caring particularly at that moment. "Do you know that man who sent you the note?" she asked.

"I may have met him somewhere. I don't recognize him. Why?"

"If you ever see him again, you really should drop a hint about his clothing. Unless, of course, he wants to be taken for a music hall singer or an American."

"I'll do that. If I ever see him again."

Anderl's attention was snagged by the two young twits of the day before who passed the window and waved at him. With a shrug of fatalistic inevitability, he excused himself and stepped out to join them.

Immediately afterward, Karl invited Anna to join him in a stroll to the village.

And within three minutes of Pope's appearance, the company was reduced to Jonathan and Ben. For a time they sat sipping their cool coffee in silence. When he looked casually around, Jonathan saw that Pope had left.

"Hey, ol' buddy? What's got into John-Paul?" Ben had changed from the mispronunciation based on print to one based on ear.

"Just jumpy, I guess."

"Now, jumpy's a fine quality in a climber. But he's more than jumpy. He's pissed off about something. You been drilling his wife?"

Jonathan had to laugh at the directness of the question. "No, Ben. I haven't."

"You're sure?"

"It's a thing I'd know."

"Yeah, I guess. About the last thing you guys need

is bad blood. I can just see you on the face, thumping on each other with ice axes."

The image was not alien to Jonathan's imagination.

Ben was pensive for a while before he said, "You know, if I was going up that hill with anybody—excepting you, of course—I'd want to be roped to Anderl."

"Makes sense. But you better keep your hands out of the larder."

"Yeah! How about that? When he decides to climb a mountain, he don't fool around none."

"Evidently not." Jonathan rose. "I'm going to my room. See you at supper."

"What about lunch?"

"No. I'll be down in the village."

"Got a little something waiting for you down there?"

"Yes."

Jonathan sat by the window in his room, staring out toward the mountain and bringing his thoughts into order. The bold appearance of Pope had been a surprise; for an instant he had been off balance. There had been no time to consider Dragon's reasons for so blatantly rupturing his cover. Because Dragon was chained immobile to his dark, antiseptic cell in New York, it was the face and person of Clement Pope that were universally recognized as SS Division leadership. There could be only one reason for his making so flagrantly open a contact. Jonathan became tight with anger at the recognition of it.

The anticipated knock came, and Jonathan crossed to the door and opened it.

"How's it been going, Hemlock?" Pope extended his broad businessman's hand which Jonathan ignored, closing the door behind them. Pope lowered himself with a grunt into the chair Jonathan had been occupying. "Nice place you got here. Going to offer me a drink?"

"Get on with it, Pope."

Pope's laugh lacked joy. "OK, pal, if that's the game you want to play, we'll use your ball park. Dismiss formalities and get to the nitty and the gritty. Right?"

As Pope tugged a small packet of note cards from his inside coat pocket, Jonathan noticed he was starting to run to fat. An athlete in his college days, Pope was still strong in a slow, massive way, but Jonathan estimated that he could be put away fairly easily. And he had every intention of putting him away—but not until he had drained him of useful information.

"Let's get the little fish out of the pond first, Hemlock, so we can clear the field of fire."

Jonathan crossed his arms and leaned against the wall by the door. "Let's mix any metaphors you want."

Pope glanced at his first note card. "You wouldn't have any news about the whereabouts of active 365/55—a certain Jemima Brown, would you?"

"I would not."

"You better be telling it like it is, pal. Mr. Dragon would be mucho pissed off to discover that you'd harmed her. She was just following our orders. And now she's disappeared."

Jonathan reflected on the fact that Jemima was in the village and that he would be meeting her within the hour. "I doubt that you'll ever find her."

"Don't make book on it, baby. SS has a long arm."

"Next card?"

Pope slipped the top card to the bottom of the pack and glanced at the next. "Oh, yeah. You really left us with a mess, baby."

Jonathan smiled, a gentle calm in his eyes. "That's twice you've called me 'baby.'"

"That's kind of a burr under your blanket, isn't it?"

"Yes. Yes, it is," Jonathan admitted with quiet honesty.

"Well, that's just tough titty, pal. The days are long gone when we had to worry about your feelings."

Jonathan took a long breath to contain his feelings, and he asked, "You were saying something about a mess?"

"Yeah. We had teams all over that desert trying to find out what happened."

"And did you?"

"The second day we came across the car and that guy you blew out of it."

"What about the other one?"

"Miles Mellough? I had to leave before we found him. But I got word just before I left New York that one of our teams had located him."

"Dead, I presume."

"Plenty dead. Exposure, hunger, thirst. They don't know which he died of first. But he was beaucoup dead. They buried him out on the desert." Pope snickered. "Weird thing."

"Weird?"

"He must have been real hard up for chow there toward the last."

"Oh?"

"Yeah. He ate a dog."

Jonathan glanced down.

Pope went on. "You know how much it cost us? That search? And keeping the whole thing quiet?"

"No. But I assume you'll tell me."

"No, I won't. That information's classified. But we get a little tired of the way you irregulars burn money like it was going out of style."

"That's always been a burr under your blanket, hasn't it, Pope? The fact that men like me earn more for one job than you get in three years."

Pope sneered, an expression his face seemed particularly designed for.

"I admit that it would be more economical," Jonathan said, "if you SS regulars did your own sanctioning. But the work requires skill and some physical courage. And those qualities are not available on government requisition forms."

"I'm not pissed about the money you're making on this particular job. This time you're going to earn it, baby."

"I was hoping you'd get around to that."

"You've already guessed—a big university professor like you must have guessed by now."

"I'd enjoy hearing it from you."

"Whatever turns you on. It's different strokes for different folks, I guess." He flicked to the next card. "Search has drawn a blank on your target. We know he's here. And he's on this climb with you. But we don't know which one for sure."

"Miles Mellough knew."

"Did he tell you?"

"He offered to. The price was too high."

"What did he want?"

"To live."

Pope looked up from the note card. He did his best to appear coldly professional as he nodded in sober understanding. But the cards fell from his knee, and he had to paw around to collect them.

Jonathan watched him with distaste. "So you've set me up to make the target commit himself, right?"

"No other way, buddy-boy. We figured the target would recognize me on sight. And now he has you spotted as a Sanction man. He's got to take a crack at you before you get him. And when he does, I have him identified."

"And who would do the sanction, if he got me?" Jonathan looked Pope over leisurely. "You?"

"You don't think I could handle it?"

273

Jonathan smiled. "In a locked closet, maybe. With a grenade."

"Don't bet on that, buddy. As it happens, we're going to bring in another Sanction man to do the job."

"I assume this was your idea?"

"Dragon OK'd it, but it came from me."

Jonathan's face was set in his gentle combat smile. "And it really doesn't matter that you've blown my cover, now that I have decided to stop working for you."

"That is exactly the way it crumbles." Pope was enjoying his moment of victory after so many years of smarting under Jonathan's open disdain.

"What if I just walk away and forget the whole thing?"

"No way, pal. You wouldn't get your hundred thousand; you'd lose your house; we'd confiscate your paintings; and you'd probably do a little time for smuggling them into the country. How does it feel to be in a box, pal?"

Jonathan crossed to pour himself a Laphroaig. Then he laughed aloud. "You've done well, Pope. Really very well! Want a drink?"

Pope was not sure how to handle this sudden cordiality. "Well, that's mighty white of you, Hemlock." He laughed as he received his glass. "Hey, I just said that was mighty white of you. I'll bet this Jemima Brown never said that to you. Right?"

Jonathan smiled beautifully. "No. As a matter of fact, she never did."

"Hey, tell me. How is that black stuff? Good, eh?"

Jonathan drank off half his glass and sat in a chair opposite Pope's, leaning toward him confidentially. "You know, Pope, I really ought to tell you in advance that I intend to waste you a little." He winked playfully. "You would understand that, in a case like this, wouldn't you?"

"Waste me? What do you mean?"

"Oh, Just West Side slang. Look, if Dragon would rather I did the sanction myself—and I assume he would—I'm going to need a little information. Go over the Montreal thing with me. There were two men involved in the hit on whatshisname, right?"

"His name was Wormwood. He was a good man. A regular." Pope flipped through several cards and scanned one rapidly. "That's right. Two men."

"Now, you're sure of that? Not a man and a woman?"

"It says two men."

"All right. Are you sure Wormwood wounded one of the men?"

"That's what the report said. One of the two men was limping when he left the hotel."

"But are you sure he was wounded? Could he have been hurt earlier? Maybe in a mountain accident?"

"The report said he limped. Why are you asking? Was one of your people hurt in some kind of accident?"

"Karl Freytag says he hurt his leg in a short fall last month."

"Then Freytag could be your man."

"Possibly. What else have the Search people dragged up about our man?"

"Almost nothing. Couldn't have been a professional. We'd have gotten a line on him by now, if he were a professional."

"Could he have been the one who cut Wormwood open?"

"Maybe. We always assumed Kruger did the actual cutting. It's his kind of thing. But it could have been the other way, I suppose. Why?"

"One of the climbers had the capacity to kill a man with a knife. Very few people can do that."

"Maybe he's your man. Whoever it was, he has a weak stomach."

"The vomit on the floor?"

"Right."

"A woman might do that."

"There's a woman in this?"

"Bidet's wife. She could have worn male clothing. And that limp might have been anything—a twisted ankle coming down the stairs."

"You got yourself quite a can of worms there, baby."

For some perverse reason, Jonathan enjoyed drawing Pope along the mental maze he had wandered through for the last two nights. "Oh, it's more a can of worms than you think. Considering that this whole affair centers on a formula for germ warfare, it's kind of interesting that one of these men owns a company that makes aerosol containers."

"Which one?"

"Bidet."

Pope leaned forward, his eyes squeezed up in concentration. "You might be onto something there."

Jonathan smiled to himself. "I might be. But then, another of them is in the business of making insecticides—and there is reason to believe that they made nastier things during the war."

"One of the two of them, right? Is that the way you figure it?" Pope looked up suddenly, the light of an idea in his eyes. "or maybe *both* of them!"

"That's a possibility, Pope. But then—why? Neither of them needs the money. They could have hired the thing done. Now the third climber—Meyer—he's poor. And he needed money to make this climb."

Pope nodded significantly. "Meyer could be your man." Then he looked into Jonathan's eyes and blushed with the angry realization that he was being put on. He tossed off the rest of his drink. "When are you going to make your hit?"

"Oh, I thought I would wait until I knew which one was the target."

"I'll hang around the hotel until it's done."

"No, you won't. You're going to go right back to the States."

"No way pal."

"We'll see. One more thing before you go. Mellough told me that you were the one who paid him for Henri Baq's sanction. Is that right?"

"We found out he was playing switchy-changey with the other side."

"But it was you who set him up?"

"That's my job, pal."

Jonathan nodded, a distant look in his eyes. "Well, I guess that's about it." He rose to see Pope to the door. "You should be pleased with yourself, you know. Even though I'm the man in the box, I can't help admiring the skill with which you've set me up."

Pope stopped in the middle of the room and looked at Jonathan narrowly, trying to decide whether he was being put on again. He decided he was not. "You know, pal? Maybe if we had given each other a chance, we might have become friends."

"Who knows, Pope?"

"Oh. About your gun. I've got one waiting for you at the desk. A CII standard with no serial number and a silencer. It's gift wrapped in a candy box."

Jonathan opened the door for Pope, who stepped out then turned back, bracing his weight against the frame, one hand on either side of the opening. "What was all that about 'wasting' me?"

Jonathan noticed that Pope's fingers had curled into the crack of the door. That was going to hurt. "You really want to know?"

Sensing a put-on again, Pope set his face into its toughest expression. "One thing you'd better keep in mind, baby. So far as I'm concerned, you irregulars are the most expendable things since paper contraceptives."

"Right."

Two of Pope's fingers broke as Jonathan slammed the door on them. When he jerked it open again, the scream of pain was in Pope's eyes, but it did not have time to get to his throat. Jonathan grabbed him by his belt and snatched him forward into an ascending knee. It was a luck shot. Jonathan felt the squish of the testicles. Pope doubled over with a nasal grunt that spurted snot onto his chin. Jonathan grasped the collar of his coat and propelled him into the room, driving his head against the wall. Pope's knees crumpled, but Jonathan dragged him to his feet and snapped the checked sports coat down over his arms before he could pass out. Jonathan guided Pope's fall so that he toppled face down across the bed, where he lay with his face in the mattress and his arms pinned to his sides by the jacket. Jonathan's thumbs stiffened as he sighted the spot just below the ribs where the kidneys could be devastated.

But he did not drive the thumbs in.

He paused, confused and suddenly empty. He was going to let Pope go. He knew he was going to, although he could hardly believe it. Pope had arranged Henri Baq's death! Pope had set him up as a decoy! Pope had even said something about Jemima.

And he was going to let Pope go. He looked down at the crumpled form, at the silly sports coat, at the toed-in flop of the unconscious legs, but he felt none of the cold hate that usually sustained him in combat. For the moment, something was missing in him.

He rolled Pope over and went into the bathroom, where he dipped a towel into the toilet, holding it by one end until it was sodden. Back in the room, he dropped the towel over Pope's face, the shock of the cold water producing an automatic convulsion in the unconscious body. Then Jonathan poured himself a small Laphroaig and sat in the chair again, waiting for Pope to come around.

With an unmanly amount of strangled groaning,

278

Pope eventually regained consciousness. He tried twice to sit up before succeeding. The total of his pain—the fingers, the groin, the throbbing head—was so great that he could not tug his jacket back up. He slid off the bed and sat on the floor, bewildered.

Jonathan spoke quietly. "You're going to be all right, Pope. For a few days, you may walk a little oddly, but with proper medical attention you'll be just fine. But you won't be of any use here. So you're going to go back to the States as soon as possible. Do you understand that?"

Pope stared at him with bulbous, confused eyes. He still did not know what had happened to him.

Jonathan enunciated slowly. "You are going back to the States. Right now. And I am never going to see you again. That's right, isn't it?"

Pope nodded heavily.

Jonathan helped him to his feet and, bearing most of his weight, to the door. Pope clung to the frame for support. The teacher in Jonathan exerted itself. "To waste: to tear up, to harm, to inflict or cause to be inflicted physical punishment upon."

Pope clawed his way out, and Jonathan closed the door.

Jonathan opened the back of his portable typewriter and got out makings for a smoke. He sat deep in the chair, holding the smoke as long as he could on the top of his lungs before letting it out. Henri Baq had been a friend. And he had let Pope go.

Jemima had sat across from him in the dim interior of the café for a silent quarter of an hour, her eyes investigating his face and its distant, involute expression. "It's not the silence that bothers me," she said at last. "It's the politeness."

Jonathan tugged his mind back to the present. "Pardon me?"

She smiled sadly. "That's what I mean."

Jonathan drew a deep breath and focused himself on her. "I'm sorry. My mind is on tomorrow."

"You keep saying things like that—I'm sorry, and pardon me, and please pass the salt. And you know what really bothers me?"

"What?"

"I don't even have the salt."

Jonathan laughed. "You're fantastic, madame."

"Yeah, but what does it get me? Excuses. Pardons. Sorrys."

He smiled. "You're right. I've been miserable company. I'm—"

"Say it and I'll kick your shin!"

He touched her fingers. The tone of banter evaporated instantly.

Under the table, she squeezed his foot between hers. "What are you going to do about me, Jonathan?"

"What do you mean?"

"I'm yours to do with, man. You could kiss me, or press my hand, or make love to me, or marry me, or talk to me, or hit me, or . . . you are shaking your head slowly from side to side, which means that you do not intend to hit me, or make love to me, or anything at all, right?"

"I want you to go home, Gem."

She stared at him, her eyes shining with hurt and pride. "Goddam you, Jonathan Hemlock. Are you God or something? You make up your set of rules, and if somebody hurts you or tricks you, then you come down on him like a machine of fate!" She was angry because unwanted tears were standing in her eyes. She pushed them away with the back of her hand. "You don't make any distinction between a person like Miles Mellough and somebody like me— somebody who loves you." She had not raised her voice, but there was anger in the crisp consonants.

Jonathan counterpunched with the same hard tone.

"Come on now! I wouldn't be in this thing if you hadn't stolen from me. I brought you to my house. I showed you my paintings. And briefly I loved you. And you know what you did? You gave Dragon the leverage to force me into this situation. A situation I have goddamned little chance of surviving. Tell me about love!"

"But—I had never met you when I took on the assignment!"

"You took the money in the morning. *Afterwards.*"

Her silence admitted the significance of the sequence. After a time, she tried to explain, but gave it up after a few words.

The waiter arrived with a carafe of coffee, and his presence froze them in an awkward hiatus. They cooled during the pause. When the waiter left, Jemima settled her emotions with a deep breath and smiled. "I'm sorry, Jonathan."

"Say 'I'm sorry' again and I'll kick your shin."

The sting of the conflict was gone.

She sipped her coffee. "Is it going to be bad? This thing on the mountain?"

"I hope it doesn't get to the mountain."

"But it's going to be bad?"

"It's going to be wet."

She shuddered. "I've always hated that phrase: wet work. Is there anything I can do?"

"Nothing at all, Jemima. Just keep out of it. Go home."

When next she spoke, her voice was dry, and she was examining the situation fairly and with distance. "I think we're going to blow it, Jonathan. People like us hardly ever fall in love. It's even funny to think of people like us in *luv*. But it happened, and we did. And it would be a shame . . . it would be a goddam shame . . ." She shrugged and looked down.

"Gem, some things are happening to me. I, ah—"

He was almost ashamed to say it. "I let Pope go today. I don't know why. I just . . . didn't care."

"What do you mean? You let Pope go?"

"The particulars don't matter. But something funny . . . uncomfortable . . . is happening. Maybe in a few years—"

"No!"

The immediate rejection surprised him.

"No, Jonathan. I am a grown-up, desirable woman. And I don't see myself sitting around waiting for you to get mature enough, or tired enough to come knocking at my door."

He thought about it before answering. "That makes good sense, Gem."

They sipped their coffee without speaking. Then she looked up at him with growing realization in her harlequin eyes. "Jesus Christ," she whispered in wonder. "It's really happening. We're going to blow it. We're going to say goodbye. And that will be that."

Jonathan spoke gently. "Can you get a flight to the States today?"

She concentrated on the napkin in her lap, pressing it flat again and again with her hands. "I don't know. I guess so."

Jonathan rose, touched her cheek with the backs of his fingers, and left the café.

The climbers' last meal together was strained; no one ate much except Anderl, who lacked the nerve of fear, and Ben who after all did not have to make the climb. Jonathan watched each of his companions in turn for signs of reaction to Clement Pope's arrival, but, although there were ample manifestations of perturbation, the natural pressures of the impending climb made it impossible to disentangle causes. Bidet's ill humor of the morning had ripened into cool formality; and Anna did not choose to emerge from behind her habitual defense of amused poise.

Karl took his self-imposed responsibilities too seriously to indulge in social trivia. Despite the bottle of champagne sent to the table by the Greek merchant, the meal was charged with silences that descended unnoticed, until their weight became suddenly apparent to all, and they would drive them away with overly gay small talk that deteriorated into flotsam of half sentences and meaningless verbal involutions.

Although the room was crowded with Eiger Birds in garish informal plumage, there was a palpable change in the sound of their conversation. It lacked real energy. There was a sprinkling of girlish laughter allegro vivace sforzando over the usual drone of middle-aged male ponderoso. But underlying all was a basso ostinato of impatience. When was this climb going to start? They had been there two days. There was business to conclude and pleasure to pursue. When could one expect these falls—God forbid they should happen?

The actor and his florid mate entered the dining room late, as was their practice, and waved broadly to the climbers, hoping to create the impression that they were privileged with acceptance.

The meal closed on a businesslike note with Karl's unnecessary instructions that everyone get to sleep as soon as possible. He told the climbers that he himself would make the rounds of the rooms two hours before dawn, waking each man so that they could steal out before the guests and reporters knew they were gone.

The lights were off in Jonathan's room. Filtered moonlight from the snow beyond the window made the starched linen of the bed glow with its own phosphorescence. He sat in the dark; in his lap lay the gun Pope had left for him, heavy and clumsy with the silencer that gave it the look of an iron-monger's mutant. When he had picked it up at the desk (the gift of candy from one man to another arching the

283

desk clerk's eyebrows) he had learned that Pope had departed for the States after receiving first aid for what he had creatively described as a series of slips in his bathtub.

Despite his need for sleep before the climb, Jonathan dared not take a pill. This night was the target's last chance to make his defensive move, unless he had decided to wait until they were on the face. Although a hit on that precarious mountain would endanger the whole rope, it would certainly leave no evidence. Jonathan wondered how desperate the target was; and how smart.

But no use sitting there worrying about it! He pushed himself out of the armchair and unrolled his sleeping bag on the floor opposite the door where anyone entering would be silhouetted against the hall light. After sliding into the sleeping bag, he clicked the revolver off safety and cocked the hammer—two sounds he would not have to make later when sound might count. He placed the gun on the floor beside him, then he tried to sleep.

He had no great faith in these kinds of preparations. They were the kinds his sanction targets always made, and to no avail. His mistrust was well founded. In the course of turning and adjusting his body in search of a little sleep, he rolled over on the gun, making it quite inaccessible under his sleeping bag.

He must have slept, because he experienced a plunging sensation when, without opening his eyes, he became aware of light and motion within the room.

He opened his eyes. The door was swinging ajar and a man—Bidet—was framed in the yellow rectangle. The gun in his hand was outlined in silver against the edge of the black door as he stealthily pressed it closed behind him. Jonathan did not move. He felt the pressure of his own gun under the small of his back, and he cursed the malignant fate that had put it there. The shaded bulk of Bidet approached his bed.

Although he spoke softly, Jonathan's voice seemed to fill the dark room. "Do not move, Jean-Paul."

Bidet froze, confused by the direction of the sound.

Jonathan realized how he had to play this. He must maintain the soft, authoritative drone of his voice. "I can see you perfectly, Jean-Jaul. I shall certainly kill you if you make the slightest undirected movement. Do you understand?"

"Yes." Bidet's voice was husky with fright and long silence.

"Just to your right there is a bedside lamp. Reach out for it, but don't turn it on until I tell you."

There was a rustle of movement, then Jean-Paul said, "I am touching it."

Jonathan did not alter the mesmeric monotone of his voice, but he felt instinctively that the bluff was not going to hold up. "Turn on the lamp. But don't face me. Keep your eyes on the light. Do you understand?" Jonathan did not dare the excessive motion required to get his arms out of the sleeping bag and scramble about under it for his gun. Do you understand, Jean-Paul?"

"Yes."

"Then do it slowly. Now." Jonathan knew it was not going to work!

He was right. Bidet did it, but not slowly. The instant the room flooded with eye-blinking light, he whirled toward Jonathan and brought his gun to bear on him where he lay incongruously in the eiderdown cocoon. But he did not fire. He stared at Jonathan with fear and anger balanced in his eyes.

Very slowly, Jonathan lifted his hand within the sleeping bag and pointed his finger at Bidet, who realized with a dry swallow that the protuberance within the bag was directed at the pit of his stomach.

Neither moved for several seconds. Jonathan resented the painful lump of his gun under his shoulder. But he smiled. "In my country, this is called a Mexican standoff. No matter which of us shoots first, we both die."

Jonathan admired Bidet's control. "How does one normally resolve the situation? In your country."

"Convention has it that both men put their guns away and talk the thing out. Any number of sleeping bags have been preserved from damage that way."

Bidet laughed. "I had no intention of shooting you, Jonathan."

"I guess it's your gun that confused me, Jean-Paul."

"I only wanted to impress you. Frighten you, perhaps. I don't know. It was a stupid gesture. The gun isn't even loaded."

"In which case, you would have no objection to tossing it onto the bed."

Bidet did not move for a moment, then his shoulders slumped and he dropped the gun onto the bed. Jonathan rose slowly to one elbow, keeping his finger pointed at Jean-Paul, as he slipped his other hand under the sleeping bag and retrieved his gun. When Bidet saw it emerge from beneath the waterproof fabric, he shrugged with a Gallic gesture of fatalistic acceptance.

"You are very brave, Jonathan."

"I really had no other choice."

"At all events, you are most resourceful. But it wasn't necessary. As I told you, I did not even load the gun."

Jonathan struggled out of the bag and crossed to his armchair where he sat without taking his gun off Bidet. "It's a good thing you decided not to shoot. I'd have felt silly wiggling my thumb and saying bang, bang."

"Aren't *both* men supposed to put their guns away after a Mexican—whatever?"

"Never trust a Gringo." Jonathan was relaxed and confident. One thing was certain: Jean-Paul was an amateur. "You had some purpose in coming here, I imagine."

Jean-Paul examined the palm of one hand, rubbing over the lines with his thumb. "I think I shall return to my room, if you don't mind. I have made an ass of myself in your eyes already. Nothing can be gained by deepening that impression."

"I think I have a right to some kind of explanation. Your entrance into my room was—irregular?"

Bidet sat heavily on the bed, his body slumping, his eyes averted, and there was something so deflated in his manner that Jonathan had no qualms about the fact that his gun was now within reach. "There is no more ridiculous image in the world, Jonathan, than the outraged cuckold." He smiled sadly. "I never thought I would find myself playing the Pantaloon."

Jonathan experienced that uncomfortable combination of pity and disgust he always felt toward the emotionally soft, particularly those who lacked control over their romantic lives.

"But I cannot become much more ludicrous in your eyes," Bidet continued. "I imagine you already know about my physical limitations. Anna usually tells her studs. For some reason, it inspires them to greater effort on her behalf."

"You are putting me in the awkward position of having to declare my innocence, Jean-Paul."

Jean-Paul looked at Jonathan with hollow nausea in his eyes. "You needn't bother."

"I'd rather. We have to climb together. Let me say it simply: I have not slept with Anna, nor have I any reason to believe that advances would be greeted with anything but scorn."

"But last night . . ."

287

"What about last night?"

"She was here."

"How do you know that?"

"I missed her . . . I looked for her . . . I listened at your door." He looked away. "That is despicable, isn't it?"

"Yes, it is. Anna was here last night. I met her in the hall, and I offered her a drink. We did not make love."

Jean-Paul picked up his gun absently and toyed with it as he spoke. Jonathan felt no danger; he had dismissed Bidet as a potential killer. "No. She made love last night. I touched her later. I could tell from—"

"I don't want to hear about it. I have no clinical curiosity, and this is not a confessional."

Jean-Paul toyed with the small Italian automatic. "I shouldn't have come here. I have behaved in poor taste; and that is worse than Anna, who had only behaved immorally. Let me ascribe it to the stress of the climb. I had had great hopes for this climb. I thought if Anna were here to see me climb a mountain that very few men would dare to even touch— that might—somehow. I don't know. Whatever it was, it was a senseless hope." He looked over at Jonathan with beaten eyes. "Do you despise me?"

"My admiration for you has found new limits."

"You phrase well. But then, you have the intellectual advantage of being emotionless."

"Do you believe me about Anna?"

Jean-Paul smiled sadly. "No, Jonathan. I don't believe you. I am a cuckold, but not a fool. If you had nothing to fear from me, why were you lying there on the floor, anticipating my revenge?"

Jonathan could not explain and did not try.

Jean-Paul sighed. "Well, I shall return to my room to blush in private, and you will be freed from the duty of having to pity and detest me." In a gesture of dramatic finality, he snapped back the slide of the automatic, and a cartridge arced from the chamber, struck against the wall, and bounced onto the rug. Both men looked at the shiny brass with surprise. Jean-Paul laughed without mirth. "I guess I am deceived more easily than I thought. I could have sworn this gun was empty."

He left without saying good-night.

Jonathan smoked and took a sleeping pill before attempting sleep again, this time in his bed, considering it now safe with the same kind of superstitious faith in antichance that prompts bomber pilots to fly into ack-ack puffs, or woodsmen to seek shelter from storms under lightning-cleft trees.

EIGER:
July 11

The only sounds they made as they walked singlefile toward the base of the mountain were the soft trudge of their footfalls and the hiss of Alpiglen grass against their gaitered boots, wet and glistening with dew. Bringing up the rear, Jonathan looked up at the mountain stars, still crisp and cold despite the threat of dawn to mute their brilliance. The climbers walked without the burden of pack, rope, and climbing iron. Ben and three of the young climbers who camped on the meadow had preceded them carrying the heavy gear as far as the foot of the scree slope.

The team responded to the silence, the earliness of the hour, and the weight of their objective with that sense of unreality and emotional imbalance common to the verge of a major climb. As he always did just before a climb, Jonathan attended hungrily to all physical stimuli. Within his body he followed the tingle and ripple of anticipation. His legs, tuned high for hard climbing, pulled the flat land under him with giddying ease. The chill brush of predawn wind on the nape of his neck, the smell of the grass, the organic viscosity of the dark around him—Jonathan focused on each of these in turn, savoring the sensations, gripping them with his tactile, rather than mental, memory. He had always wondered at this odd significance of common experience just before a hard climb. He realized that this particularization of the mundane was a product of the sudden mutability of the world of the senses. And he knew that it was not the wind, the grass, the night that was threatened with mortality; it was the sensing animal. But he never dwelt on that.

Jean-Paul slackened his pace and dropped back to Jonathan, who resented this intrusion on his sacramental relations with simple sensation.

"About last night, Jonathan—"

"Forget it."

"Will you?"

"Certainly."

"I doubt it."

Jonathan lengthened his stride and let Jean-Paul fall behind.

They approached the fireflies of light that had directed them across the lea and came upon Ben and his group of volunteers laying out and checking the gear with the aid of flashlights. Karl considered it necessary to his posture as leader to issue a couple of superfluous instructions while the team quickly geared up. Ben groused heavily about the cold and the earliness of the hour, but his words were designed only to combat the silence. He felt empty and useless. His part in the climb was over, and he would return to Kleine Scheidegg to handle the reporters and watch the progress of the climbers through the telescope he had brought for the purpose. He would become an active member again only if something happened and he had to organize a rescue.

Standing next to Jonathan, but looking away up toward the mountain that was a deeper black within a blackness, Ben pulled his ample nose and sniffed, "Now you listen to me, ol' buddy. You come off that hill in one piece, or I'm going to kick your ass."

"You're a sloppy sentimentalist, Ben."

"Yeah, I guess." Ben walked away and gruffly

ordered his young volunteers to accompany him back to the hotel. When they were younger and more dramatic, he might have shaken hands with Jonathan.

The climbers moved out in the dark, scrambling up the scree and onto the rock rubble at the base. By the time they touched the face proper, the first light had begun to press form into the black mass. In that cringing light, the rock and the snow patches appeared to be a common, dirty gray. But Eiger rock is an organic tonic gray, produced by the fusion of color complements in balance, not the muddy gray that is a mixture of black and white. And the snow was in reality crisp white, unsooted and unpitted by thaw. It was the light that was dirty and that soiled the objects it illuminated.

They roped up, following their plan to make the lower portion of the face in two separate, parallel lines of attack. Freytag and Bidet constituted one rope, and Karl had most of their pitons clanging about his middle. He intended to lead all the way, with Bidet retrieving such iron as had to be planted. Jonathan and Anderl had shared their iron because, by common unspoken assent, they preferred to leapfrog, alternating the sport of route-finding and leading. Naturally, they moved much faster this way.

It was nine in the morning, and the sun was touching, as it did briefly twice each day, the concave face of the Eigerwand. The principal topic of conversation among the Eiger Birds in the dining room was a prank the Greek merchant had played on his guests during a party the night before. He had soaked all the rolls of toilet paper in water. His American society wife had considered the prank to be in poor taste and, what is more, unnecessarily wasteful of money.

Ben's breakfast was interrupted by a shout from

the terrace followed by an excited rush of Eiger Birds toward the telescopes. The climbers had been spotted. The economic machinery of the hotel went into operation with the lubrication of careful preparation. Uniformed attendants appeared at each telescope (except the one that had been reserved at great cost by the Greek merchant). With typical Swiss efficiency and monetary foresight, the attendants were equipped with tickets—a different color for each instrument—on which three-minute time allocations were printed. These were sold to the Eiger Birds at ten times the normal cost of the coin-operated machines, and milling queues immediately began to form around each telescope. The tickets were sold with the understanding that the management would not return money in the case of heavy weather or clouds obscuring the climbers.

Ben felt the bitter gorge of disgust rise in the back of his throat at the sight of these chattering necrophiles, but he was also relieved that the climbers had been discovered. Now he could set up his own telescope in the open meadow away from the hotel and keep a guardian eye on the team.

He was just rising from his coffee when a half dozen reporters breasted upstream against the current of the excited exodus and pushed into the dining room to surround Ben and ask him questions about the climb and the climbers. Following earlier plans, Ben distributed brief typewritten biographies of each man. These had been prepared to prevent the newspeople from resorting to their florid imaginations. But the personal accounts, containing only the birthplaces and dates, occupations, and mountaineering careers of the team members, were barren resources for those newsmen who sought human interest and sensationalism, so they continued to assail Ben with a babble of aggressive questions. Taking his breakfast beer along with him, his jaw set in grim silence,

Ben pushed through them, but one American reporter grasped his sleeve to stop him.

"Now, you're real sure you have no further use for that hand?" Ben asked, and he was instantly released.

They followed him tenaciously as he crossed the lobby with his energetic, hopping stride, but before he could get to the elevator door a tweeded English woman columnist—tough, stringy, and sexless, with precise clipped diction—interposed herself between him and the elevator door.

"Tell me, Mr. Bowman, in your opinion do these men climb out of a need to prove their manhood, or is it more a matter of compensating for inferiority feelings?" Her pencil poised over her notebook as Ben responded.

"Why don't you go get yourself screwed? Do you a lot of good."

She had copied down the first words before the gist of the message arrested her pencil, and Ben escaped into the elevator.

Jonathan and Anderl found a shallow shelf just to the west of the mouth of the chute that Karl had estimated would be the key to the new route. They banged in a piton and tied themselves on while they awaited the arrival of Karl and Jean-Paul. Although the beetling cliff above them flowed with icy melt water, it protected them from the rock fall that had been plaguing their climb for the last half hour. Even as they arranged coils of rope under them to keep out the wet, chunks of rock and ice broke over the crest of the cliff and whined past, three or four feet out in front of them, to burst on the rocks below with loud reports and a spray of mountain shrapnel.

Their ledge was so narrow that they had to sit hip to hip, their legs dangling out over the void. The climb had been fast and magnificent, and the view was breathtaking, so, when Anderl produced a bar of hard chocolate from his coat pocket and shared it with Jonathan, they felt exhilarated and contented, munching away wordlessly.

Jonathan could not ignore the sound that surrounded them as totally as silence. For the last hour, as they approached the mouth of the chute on a line a little to the right of it, the roar of rushing water had increased in volume. He imagined, although he could not see from his perch, that the chute was a cataract of melt water. He had climbed up through waterfalls like this before (the Ice Hose over on the normal route was no mean example) but his experience had not decreased his respect for the objective danger.

He glanced over at Anderl to see if his worry was shared, but the blissful, almost vacant smile on the Austrian's face was evidence that he was in his element, full of contentment. Some men are native to the mountain and, while they are on rock, the valley does not exist, save as the focus point for that patient and persistent gravity against which they hold out. Jonathan did not share Anderl's contented insouciance. So long as he had been climbing, the world had narrowed to the rope, the rock, the purchase, and body rhythms. But now, with a safe stance and time to reflect, lowland troubles returned to him.

For instance, it could be Anderl. Anderl could be the target. And a hunter in his own right now. At least half a dozen times in the past three hours, Anderl had only to cut the rope and give a slight tug, and Jonathan would no longer be a threat. The fact that he had not done so in no way excluded him as a possibility. They were too close to the base; there would be evidence, and a cut rope looks very different from a frayed rope. And too, they were probably being watched at every moment. From far down there, from the toy terrace of the miniature hotel there were probably half a score of eyes empowered by convex glass to observe them.

Jonathan decided he could rest easy. If it happened, it would be higher up, up where the distance made them little dots, barely distinguishable to the most powerful glass. Perhaps when cloud and mist descended to conceal them altogether. Up where the body and the severed rope would not be found for months, even years.

"What are you frowning about?" Anderl asked.

Jonathan laughed. "Morbid thoughts. About falling."

"I never think about falling. What's the use? If a fall wants to happen, it will happen without my thinking about it. I think about climbing. That requires thinking." He punctuated this simple philosophy by pushing the last of the chocolate into his mouth.

This was the longest speech Jonathan had ever heard Anderl make. Clearly, here was a man who came to full life only on the mountain.

First Karl's hand, then his head came into view over the outcropping of rock below, and soon he was in a stance just under theirs, steadily taking in the line that led down to Jean-Paul until he too had hoisted himself over the ridge, red-faced but triumphant. The new arrivals found a slim ledge for themselves, banged in protecting iron, and rested.

"What do you think of my route now, Herr Doctor?" Karl shouted up.

"So far so good." Jonathan thought of the roaring melt water above them.

"I knew it would be!"

Jean-Paul drew lustily at his water bottle, then rested out against the rope that was connected to his piton by a snap ring. "I had no idea that you gentlemen intended to *run* up the hill! Have pity on my age!" He laughed hastily, lest anyone imagine he was not joking.

"You will have time to rest now," Karl said. "We shall be here for at least an hour."

"An hour!" Jean-Paul protested. "We have to sit here for an hour?"

"We shall rest and have a little breakfast. It's too early to climb up through the chute."

Jonathan agreed with Karl. Although a climber on the Eiger must expect to be the target for fairly regular sniping by rock and ice fall, there is no sense in facing the veritable fusillade with which the mountain covers its flanks in midmorning. Stones and mountain rubble that are frozen into place through the night are released by the melting touch of morning sun and come arcing, bouncing, and crashing down from the vast collection trough of the White Spider, directly, although distantly, above them. The normal line of ascent is well to the west of this natural line of fire.

"We shall allow the mountain to dump out her morning garbage before we try the chute," Karl announced. "Meanwhile, let us enjoy the scenery and have a bite to eat. Yes?"

Jonathan read in Karl's artificial cheer that he, too, was affected by the roar of water rushing down the chute, but it was equally obvious that he would not be receptive to criticism or advice.

Nevertheless: "Sounds like we have a wet time ahead of us, Karl."

"Surely, Herr Doctor, you have no objection to a morning shower."

"It's going to take a lot out of us, even if it is a go."

"Yes. Mountain climbing is demanding."

"Snot."

"What?"

"Nothing."

Jean-Paul took another drink of water then passed the plastic canteen over to Karl, who returned it, declining to drink. After he had struggled the bottle into his pack, Jean-Paul looked out over the valley with awe and appreciation. "Beautiful, isn't it. Really beautiful. Anna is probably watching us through a telescope at this very moment."

"Probably," Jonathan said, doubting it.

"We'll take the chute in a rope of four," Karl said. "I shall lead: Anderl will bring up the rear."

Jonathan attended again to the sound of the water. "This route would be easier in winter when there is less melt."

Anderl laughed. "Do you suggest we wait?"

Ben heard a bustle of excited talk on the terrace beneath his window, and a distinctly Texan voice epitomized the multilingual dirge of complaint.

"Shee-it! How about that? I use my tickets up watching them sit on the rock, then as soon as my time's over, they start doing something. Hey, Floyd? How much was that in real money?"

Ben ran down from his room and into the meadow, well away from the hotel and the Eiger Birds. It took him ten minutes to set up his telescope. From the first, this long diagonal chute of Karl's had worried him more than any other pitch on the climb. The distant face sharpened into focus, then blurred past it, then emerged clear in the eyepiece again. He began at the bottom of the chute and panned up and right, following the dark scar up the face. There was a fuzz of spray at the outlet of the chute that told him it must be a veritable river of rushing melt water, and he knew the climbers would have to fight their way upstream through it, the flow tugging them away from their holds, all the while exposed to the hazards of rock fall that rattled through this natural channel. His palms were clammy by the time he picked up the lowest climber. Yellow jacket: that would be Anderl. And up the thin spider thread of rope to a white jacket: Jean-Paul. Above him was the pale blue windbreaker of Jonathan. Karl was out of sight behind a fold of rock. They were moving erratically and very slowly. That gush of water and ice fragments must be hell, Ben thought. Why don't they break off? Then he realized that they could not retreat. Once committed in a string of four to pressing up through the weight of rushing water they had to go on. The slightest easing off, the slightest cooperation with the downward flow, and they stood a good chance of tumbling down through the channel and arcing out through the fuzz of spray into the void.

At least they were moving up; that was something. They climbed one at a time, while the others found what purchase they could to protect the vulnerable climber. Perhaps Karl had found a secure stance up there out of sight, Ben told himself. Perhaps they were safer than they seemed.

There was a sudden tension in the string of colored dots.

They were no longer moving. Ben's experience told him something had happened.

He cursed at not being able to see better. A slight, impatient movement of the telescope, and he lost them. He swore aloud and located them again in the eyepiece. The thread above Anderl was slack. White jacket—Bidet—was hanging upside down. He had fallen. The rope above him was taut and led up to blue jacket—Jonathan, who was stretched out spreadeagle on the rock. That meant he had been pulled off his stance and was holding his own weight and Bidet's with his hands.

"Where the hell's Karl!" Ben shouted. "Goddam his ass!"

Jonathan clenched his teeth and concentrated his whole being on keeping his fingers curled into the crack above him. He was alone in an agony of effort, isolated by the deafening roar of water just to his left. A steady, numbing stream flowed down his sleeves and froze his armpits and chest. He did not waste breath shouting. He knew that Anderl below would do what he could, and he hoped that Karl above and out of sight had found a crack for a piton and was holding them in a strong stance. The dead weight of Jean-Paul on the rope around his waist was squeezing the air out of him, and he did not know how long he could hold on. A quick look over his shoulder revealed that Anderl was already scrambling, open and unprotected, up through the roaring trough toward Bidet, who had not stirred since the rock that had sung past Jonathan's ear had struck him on the shoulder and knocked him out of his stance. Jean-Paul lay head downward in the middle of the torrent, and the thought flashed through Jonathan's mind that it would be ridiculous to die of drowning on a mountain.

His hands no longer ached; there was no feeling at all. He could not tell if he was gripping hard enough to hold so he squeezed until the muscles in his forearms throbbed. If water or rock knocked Anderl off, he would never be able to hold them both. What in hell was Karl up to!

Then the rope slackened around his middle, and a surge of expanding pain replaced the pressure. Anderl had reached Jean-Paul and had jammed his body crosswise in the chute, holding Bidet in his lap to give Jonathan the slack he needed to recover his stance.

Jonathan pulled upward until his arms vibrated with the effort, and after interminable seconds, one boot found a toehold and the weight was off his hands. They were cut, but not too deeply, and the flow of icy water prevented them from throbbing. As quickly as he dared, he uncoiled enough rope to allow him to climb up, and he followed the arcing line of rope up and around a fold of rock where he found Karl.

"Help me!"

"What's the matter?" Karl had found a niche and was braced in it to belay the climbers below. He had been totally unaware of the crisis beneath him.

"Pull!" Jonathan shouted, and by main strength they dragged Bidet up away from Anderl's wedged body. Not a moment too soon. The strong Austrian's legs had begun to quiver with the task of holding Bidet up.

Anderl bypassed Jean-Paul's inert body and climbed up to the stance recently occupied by Jonathan. Bidet was safe now, held from two points of purchase. From their position, neither Jonathan nor Karl could see what was occurring below, but Anderl told them later that Jean-Paul had a comically quizzical expression on his face as he returned to consciousness and found himself dangling in a vertical river. The falling rock had done him no real damage, but he had struck his head hard against the face when he fell. With the automatic responses of the climber prevailing over his dizziness, he began to scramble up. And before long the four of them were crowded into Karl's small, secure niche.

When the last jacket disappeared behind the fold of rock at the top of the chute, Ben stood up from his telescope and drew the first full breath he had taken in ten minutes. He looked around for deep grass, and he vomited.

Two of the young climbers who had been standing by, concerned and helpless, turned away to give Ben privacy. They grinned at each other out of embarrassment.

"Wet and cold, but not much the worse for wear," Karl diagnosed. "And the worst of it is behind us. You really needn't be so glum, Herr Doctor."

"We can't get back through that chute," Jonathan said with finality.

"Fortunately, we shall not have to."

"If it comes to a reatreat—"

"You have a Maginot mentality, Herr Doctor. We shall not retreat. We shall simply climb up out of this face."

Jonathan felt a hot resentment at Karl's bravado, but he said nothing more. Instead, he turned to Anderl who shivered on the ledge beside him. "Thank you, Anderl. You were fine."

Anderl nodded, not egotistically, but in genuine appreciation of the sureness and correctness of his actions. He received his own critical approval. Then he looked up at Karl. "You didn't know we were in trouble?"

"No."

"You didn't feel it on the line?"

"No."

"That is not good."

Anderl's simple evaluation stung Karl more than recriminations could have.

Jonathan envied Anderl his composure, sitting there on the lip of rock, looking out over the abyss, musing into space. Jonathan was in no way composed. He shivered, wet through and cold, and he was still nauseated with the sudden spurt of adrenalin.

Bidet, for his part, sat next to Jonathan, gingerly touching the bump on the side of his head. He suddenly laughed aloud. "It's strange, isn't it? I remember nothing after the stone knocked me off my stance. It must have been quite an event. Pity I slept through it."

"That's the spirit!" Karl said, slightly accenting the first word to differentiate between Jean-Paul's attitude and Jonathan's. "Now, we shall rest here for a moment and collect our senses, then up we go! From my study of the route, the next four hundred meters should be child's play."

Every fiber of Ben's body was weary, drained by the sympathetic tensions and physical stresses with which he had tried to help the climbers, conducting their movements, as it were, by kinesthetic telepathy. His eyes burned with strain, and the muscles of his face were set in grooves of concern. He had to give a grudging credit to Karl who, once the torrent of the chute was behind, had led the party up in a clean, rapid ascent of the virgin rock; up past the windows of the Eigerwand Station and through a long gully packed with snow and ice that brought them to a prominent pillar standing out from the rock pitch separating the First and Second Ice Fields. Making that pillar had consumed two hours of desperate climbing. After two unsuccessful attempts, Karl had disemburdened himself of his pack and had attacked it with such acrobatic abandon that he had received an unheard flutter of applause from the hotel terrace when he topped it. Belayed from above, the other climbers had made the pillar with relative ease.

Following its diurnal custom, Eiger's cloudcap descended and concealed the climbers for two hours in the afternoon, during which time Ben relaxed his cramped back and responded to insistent reporters with grunts and monosyllabic profanity. Those Eiger Birds who had been cheated of their turns to ogle and thrill complained bitterly, but the hotel management was adamant in its refusal to refund money, explaining with uncharacteristic humility that it could not control acts of God.

Moving rapidly to conserve what daylight they had, the team climbed up through the mist, ascending the ice couloir that bridges the Second and Third Ice

Fields. When the clouds lifted, Ben could see them making what appeared to be a safe, if uncomfortable bivouac a little to the left of the Flatiron and below Death Bivouac. Sure the day's climbing was done, Ben allowed himself to break the invisible thread of observation that had bound him to the climbers. He was satisfied with the day's work. More than half the face was beneath them. Others had climbed higher the first day (indeed, Waschak and Forstenlachner had climbed the face in a single stretch of eighteen hours through ideal weather conditions), but none had done better over an unexplored path. From this point on, they would be following the classic route, and Ben felt more confident of their chances—providing the weather held.

Drained of energy and a little sick with the acid lump in his stomach, Ben folded up the legs of his telescope and walked heavily across the terrace. He had not eaten since breakfast, although he had fortified himself with six bottles of German beer. He paid no attention to the Eiger Birds still clustered around the telescopes. And indeed, the Birds' attention was wandering away from the climbers who, it seemed, would be running no further risks that day and providing no further excitement.

"Isn't that precious!" one of the rigorously made-up older women gushed to her paid companion, who dutifully squeezed her hand and pointed his Italian profile in the required direction. "Those little flecks of cloud!" the woman rhapsodized, "all pink and golden in the last light of day! They're really very, very pretty."

Ben looked up and froze. Ripples of buttermilk cloud were scudding in rapidly from the southeast. A *foehn*.

Attacking the reluctant Swiss telephone system with desperate tenacity, and crippled by his lack of

German, Ben finally contacted the meteorological center. He discovered that the foehn had run into the Bernese Oberland without warning. It would hold through the night, bringing fierce storms to the Eiger face and melting out much of the snow and ice with its eerie press of warm air, but they assured Ben that a strong high descending from the north would drive the foehn out by midday. With the high, however, was expected record cold.

Ben replaced the phone in its cradle and stared sightlessly at the mnemonic graffiti on the wall of the telephone *cabine*.

A storm and a melt, followed by record cold. The entire face would be glazed with a crust of ice. Ascent would be impossible; retreat would be extremely difficult and, if the Hinterstossier Traverse were heavily iced over, equally impossible. He wondered if the climbers in their precarious bivouac knew what Eiger Weather had done for them.

The two slight lips of rock they had found were scarcely adequate for bivouac, but they had decided against climbing on through the last half hour of light and running the risk of night finding them with no shelter at all. They had perched in their order on the rope; Karl and Jonathan occupying the higher ledge, Anderl and Jean-Paul taking the lower, slightly wider site. Scooping out snow with their ice axes and driving in a pattern of pitons on which to secure themselves and their gear, they nested as well as the stingy face would allow. By the time bivouac was made, the first bold stars had penetrated the darkening sky. Night descended quickly, and the sky was seeded with bright, cold, indifferent stars. From that north face, they had no hint of the foehn storm closing in on them from the southeast.

A collapsible spirit burner balanced tentatively on the slim ledge between him and Jean-Paul, Anderl brewed cup after cup of tepid tea made from water that boiled before it was really hot. They were close enough to pass the cups around, and they drank with silent relish. Although each man forced himself to swallow a few morsels of solid food, glutinous and tasteless in their desiccated mouths, it was the tea that satisfied their cold and thirst. The brewing went on for an hour, the tea relieved occasionally by a cup of bouillon.

Jonathan struggled into his eider-filled sleeping bag and found that, by forcing himself to relax, he could control the chattering of his teeth. Save when he had actually been climbing, the cold that followed their drenching in the frigid water of the chute had made him shudder convulsively, wasting his energy and eroding his nerves. The ledge was so narrow that he had to sit astride his pack to cling without continuous effort, and even then his position was almost vertical. His rope harness was connected to the pitons behind by two separate ropes, just in case Karl should attempt to cut one while he dozed. Although Jonathan took this sensible precaution, he considered himself to be fairly safe. The men below could not reach him easily, and his position directly above them meant that if Karl knocked or cut him off, his fall would carry the other two with him, and he doubted Karl would care to be on the face alone.

After his own safety, Jonathan was most concerned about Jean-Paul, who had made only the most minimal arrangements for comfort. Now he slumped his weight against the restraining pitons and stared down into the black valley, receiving the proffered cups of tea dumbly. Jonathan knew there was something very wrong.

The rope connecting two men on a mountain is more than nylon protection; it is an organic thing that transmits subtle messages of intent and disposition from man to man; it is an extension of the tactile senses, a psychological bond, a wire along which currents of communication flow. Jonathan had felt the energy and desperate determination of Karl above him, and he had sensed the vague and desultory movements of Jean-Paul below—odd manic pulses of strength alternating with the almost subliminal drag of uncertainty and confusion.

As the fall of night combined with their physical inactivity to give the cold a penetrating edge, Anderl shook Jean-Paul out of his funk and helped him struggle into his sleeping bag. Jonathan recognized from Anderl's solicitude that he, too, had sensed something defocused and queer through the rope that had connected his nervous system to Jean-Paul's.

Jonathan broke the silence by calling down, "How's it going, Jean-Paul?"

Jean-Paul twisted in his harness and looked up with an optimistic grin. Blood was oozing from his nostrils and ears, and the irises of his eyes were contracted. Major concussion.

"I feel wonderful, Jonathan. But it's strange, isn't it? I remember nothing after the stone knocked me off my stance. It must have been quite an event. Pity I slept through it."

Karl and Jonathan exchanged glances. Karl was going to say something when he was interrupted by Anderl.

"Look! The stars!"

Wisps of cloud were racing between them and the stars, alternately revealing and concealing their twinkle in a strange undulating pattern. Then, suddenly, the stars were gone.

The eeriness of the effect was compounded by the fact that there was no wind on the face. For the first time in Jonathan's memory, the air on Eiger was still. And, more ominous yet, it was warm.

No one spoke to break the hush. The thick plasticity of the night reminded Jonathan of typhoons in the South China Sea.

Then, low at first but increasing in volume, came a hum like the sound of a large dynamo. The drone seemed to come from the depths of the rock itself. There was the bitter-sweet smell of ozone. And Jonathan found himself staring at the head of his ice axe, only two feet from him. It was surrounded by a greenish halo of St. Elmo's fire that flickered and pulsed before it arced with a cracking flash into the rock.

Faithful to the last to his Teutonic penchant for underlining the obvious, Karl's lips formed the word, *"foehn!"* just as the first rock-shaking explosion of thunder obliterated the sound of the word.

EIGER:
July 12

Ben snapped up from a shallow doze with the gasp of a man drowning in his own unconsciousness. The distant roar of avalanche bridged between his chaotic sleep and the bright, unreal hotel lobby. He blinked and looked around, trying to set himself in time and space. Three in the morning. Two rumpled reporters slept in chairs, sprawled loose-hinged like discarded mannikins. The night clerk transferred information from a list to file cards, his movements somnolent and automatic. The scratch of his pen carried across the room. When Ben rose from his chair, sweat adhered his buttocks and back to the plastic upholstery. The room was cool enough; it was the dreams that had sweated him.

He stretched the kinks out of his back. Thunder rumbled distantly, and the noise was trebled by the crisper sound of snowslide. He crossed the lobby and looked onto the deserted terrace, lifeless in the slanting light through the window, like a stage setting stored in the wings. It was no longer raining in the valley. All the storm had collected up in the concave amphitheatre of the Eigerwand. And even there it was losing its crescendo as a frigid high from the north drove it out. It would be clear by dawn and the face would be visible—if there were anything to be seen.

The elevator doors clattered open, the noise uncommonly loud because it was not buried in the ambient sound of the day. Ben turned and watched Anna walk toward him, her poise and posture betrayed by makeup that was thirty hours old.

She stood close to him, looking out the window. There had been no greetings. "The weather is clearing a little, it seems," she said.

"Yes." Ben did not feel like talking.

"I just heard that Jean-Paul had an accident."

"You *just* heard?"

She turned toward him and spoke with odd angry intensity. "Yes, I just heard it. From a young man I was with. Does that shock you?" She was bitter and punishing herself.

Ben continued to stare dully into the night. "I don't care who you fuck, lady."

She lowered her lashes and sighed on a tired intake of breath that fluttered. "Was Jean-Paul hurt badly?"

Ben inadvertently paused half a beat before answering. "No."

Anna examined his broad, heavily lined face. "You are lying, of course."

Another, more distant roll of thunder echoed from the mountain. Ben slapped the back of his neck and turned away from the window to cross the lobby. Anna followed.

Ben asked the desk clerk if he could get him a couple of bottles of beer. The clerk was effusive in his regrets, but at that hour there was no way within the rigid boundaries of his printed instructions that he could accommodate.

"I have brandy in my room," Anna offered.

"No thanks." Ben cocked his head and looked at her. "All right. Fine."

In the elevator Anna said, "You didn't answer when I said you were lying. Does that mean Jean-Paul's fall was serious?"

Fatigue from his long watch was seeping in and saturating his body. "I don't know," he admitted. "He moved funny after his fall. Not like something was broken, but—funny. I got the feeling he was hurt."

Anna unlocked the door to her room and walked in ahead of Ben, turning on the lights as she passed through. Ben paused for a moment before entering.

"Come in, Mr. Bowman. What is wrong?" She laughed dryly. "Oh, I see. You half expected to see the young man I mentioned." She poured out a liberal portion of brandy and returned to him with it. "No, Mr. Bowman. Never in the bed I share with my husband."

"You draw the line in funny places. Thanks." He downed the drink.

"I love Jean-Paul."

"Uh-huh."

"I did not say I was true to him physically; I said I love him. Some women have needs beyond the capacities of their men. Like alcoholics, they are to be pitied."

"I'm tired, lady."

"Do you think I am trying to seduce you?"

"I have testicles. There don't seem to be any other requirements."

Anna retreated into laughter. Then instantly she was serious. "They will get down alive, won't they?"

The brandy worked quickly up the dry wick of Ben's worn body. He had to struggle against relaxation. "I don't know. They may be. . . ." He set down the glass. "Thanks. I'll see you around." He started for the door.

She finished the thought with atonic calm. "They may be dead already."

"It's possible."

After Ben left, Anna sat at her dressing table, idly

lifting and dropping the cut glass stopper of a perfume bottle. She was at least forty.

The four figures were as motionless as the mountain they huddled against. Their clothing was stiff with a brittle crust of ice, just as the rock was glazed over with a shell of frozen rain and melt water. It was not yet dawn, but the saturation of night was diluting in the east. Jonathan could dimly make out the ice-scabbed folds of his waterproof trousers. He had been crouched over for hours, staring sightlessly into his lap, ever since the force of the storm had abated sufficiently to allow him to open his eyes. Despite the penetrating cold that followed the storm, he had not moved a muscle. His cringing posture was exactly what it had been when the *foehn* struck, tucked up in as tight a ball as his stance permitted, offering the elements the smallest possible target.

It had broken upon them without warning, and it was not possible to reckon the time it had lasted— one interminable moment of terror and chaos compounded of driving rain and stinging hail, of tearing wind that lashed around them and wedged itself between man and rock, trying to drive them apart. There were blinding flashes and blind darkness, pain from clinging and numbness from the cold. But most of all there had been sound: the deafening crack of thunder close at hand, the persistent scream of the wind, the roar and clatter of the avalanche spilling to the right and left and bouncing in eccentric patterns over the outcropping of rock that protected them.

It was quiet now. The storm was gone.

The torrent of sensation had washed Jonathan's mind clean, and thought returned slowly and in rudimentary forms. He told himself in simple words that he was looking at his pants. Then he reasoned that they were covered with a crust of ice. Eventually, he interpreted the pain as cold. And only then, with doubt and wonder, but no excitement, he knew that he was alive. He must be.

The storm was over, but the dark and the cold only slowly retreated from his consciousness, and the transition from pain and storm to calm and cold was an imperceptible blend. His body and nerves remembered the fury, and his senses told him it had passed, but he could recall neither the end of the storm nor the beginning of the calm.

He moved his arm, and there was a noise, a tinkling clatter as his movement broke the crust of ice on his sleeve. He clenched and unclenched his fists and pressed his toes against the soles of his boots, forcing his thickened blood out to his extremities. The numbness phased into electric tingle, then into throbbing pain, but these were not unpleasant sensations because they were proofs of life. The dark had retreated enough for him to make out Karl's bowed and unmoving back a few feet from him, but he wasted no thought on Karl's condition; all his attention was focused on the returning sense of life within himself.

There was a sound just beneath him.

"Anderl?" Jonathan's voice was clogged and dry.

Anderl stirred tentatively, like a man checking to see if things were still working. His coating of ice shattered with his movement and tinkled down the face. "There was a storm last night." His voice was gruffly gay. "I imagine you noticed."

With the advance of dawn came a wind, persistent, dry, and very cold. Anderl squinted at his wrist altimeter. "It reads forty meters low," he announced matter-of-factly. Jonathan nodded. Forty meters low. That meant the barometric pressure was two points higher than normal. They were in a strong, cold high that might last any amount of time.

He saw Anderl move cautiously along his ledge to attend to Jean-Paul, who had not yet stirred. A little later Anderl set to the task of brewing tea on the spirit stove, which he placed for balance against Jean-Paul's leg.

Jonathan looked around. The warmth of the foehn had melted the surface snow, and it had frozen again with the arrival of the cold front. An inch of ice crusted the snow, slippery and sharp, but not strong enough to bear a man's weight. The rocks were glazed with a coat of frozen melt water, impossible to cling to, but the crust was too thin to take an ice piton. In the growing light, he asssessed the surface conditions. They were the most treacherous possible.

Karl moved. He had not slept, but like Anderl and Jonathan he had been deep in a protective cocoon of semiconsciousness. Pulling himself out of it, he went smoothly and professionally through the task of checking the pitons that supported him and Jonathan, then he exercised isometrically to return circulation to his hands and feet, after which he began the simple but laborious job of getting food from his kit— frozen chocolate and dried meat. All through this he did not speak. He was humbled and visibly shaken by the experiences of the night. He was no longer a leader.

Anderl twisted against the rope holding him into his nook and stretched up to offer Jonathan a cup of tepid tea. "Jean-Paul . . ."

Jonathan drank it down in one avaricous draught. "What about him?" He passed the metal cup back down and licked the place where his lip had adhered to it and torn.

"He is dead." Anderl refilled the cup and offered it up to Karl. "Must have gone during the storm," he added quietly.

Karl received the tea and held it between his palms

as he stared down at the rumpley and ice-caked form that had been Jean-Paul.

"Drink it," Jonathan ordered, but Karl did not move. He breathed orally in short, shallow breaths over the top of the cup, and the puffs of vapor mixed with the steam rising off the tea.

"How do you know he is dead?" Karl asked in an unnaturally loud, monotonic voice.

"I looked at him," Anderl said as he refilled the small pot with ice chips.

"You saw he was dead! And you set about making a cup of tea!"

Anderl shrugged. He did not bother to look up from his work.

"Drink the tea," Jonathan repeated. "Or pass it over here and let me have it before it gets cold."

Karl gave him a look saturated with disgust, but he drank the tea.

"He had a concussion," Anderl said. "The storm was too much. The man inside could not keep the man outside from dying."

For the next hour, they swallowed what food they could, exercised isometrically to fight the cold, and placated their endless thirsts with cup after cup of tea and bouillon. It was impossible to drink enough to satisfy themselves, but there came a time when they must move on, so Anderl drank off the last of the melted ice and replaced the pot and collapsible stove in his pack.

When Jonathan outlined his proposal for action, Karl did not resist the change in leadership. He had lost the desire to make decisions. Again and again his attention strayed and his eyes fixed on the dead man beneath him. His mountain experience had not included death.

Jonathan surveyed their situation in a few words. Both the rock and the snow were coated over with a crust of ice that made climbing up out of the question.

A frigid high, such as the one then punishing them with cold could last for days, even weeks. They could not hole up where they were. They must retreat.

To return down Karl's chute was out of the question. It would be iced over. Jonathan proposed that they try to get down to a point just above the Eigerwand Station Window. It was just possible that they might be able to rope down from there, despite the beetling overhang. Ben, waiting and watching them from the ground, would realize their intention, and he would be waiting with help at the Window.

As he spoke, Jonathan read in Anderl's face that he had no great faith in their chances of roping down from above the Station Window, but he did not object, realizing that for reasons of morale, if nothing else, they had to move out. They must not stay there and face the risk of freezing to death in bivouac as, years before, Sedlmayer and Mehringer had done not a hundred meters above them.

Jonathan organized the rope. He would lead, slowly cutting big, tublike steps in the crusted snow. Karl would be next on the rope. A second, independent line would suspend Jean-Paul's body between them. In this way Karl could belay and protect Jonathan without the additional drag of Jean-Paul, then, when they were both in established stances, they could maneuver the load down, Jonathan guiding it away from snags, Karl holding back against gravity. As the strongest in the party, Anderl would be last on the rope, always seeking a protected stance in case a slip suddenly gave him the weight of all three.

Although the dangers of the descent were multiplied by bringing Jean-Paul with them, no one thought of leaving him behind. It was mountain tradition to bring your dead with you. And no one wanted to please the Eiger Birds by leaving a grisly memento on the face that would tingle and delight them at their telescopes for weeks or months until a rescue team could retrieve it.

As they packed up and tied Jean-Paul into the sleeping bag that would act as a canvas sled, Karl grumbled halfheartedly against the bad luck that had kept them from bagging the mountain. Anderl did not mind retreating. With surface conditions like these, it was equally difficult to move in either direction, and for him the challenge of climbing was the point of it all.

Watching the two men at their preparations, Jonathan knew he had nothing to fear from his sanction target, whoever it was. If they were to get down alive, they would have to cooperate with every fiber of their combined skill and strength. The matter would be settled in the valley, if they reached the flat land intact. In fact, the whole matter of his SS assignment had the unreal qualities of a fantastic operetta, viewed in terms of the grim presence of the mountain.

The descent was torturously slow. The frozen crust of the snow was such that at one step the surface was so hard the crampons would take no bite, but at the next the leg would break through to the softer snow below and balance would be lost. The snow-field clung to the face at an angle of 50°, and Jonathan had to lean out and down from the edge of each big step to chop out the next with his ice axe. He could not be content with those stylish toe steps that can be formed with two skillful swings of the axe; he had to hack out vast tubs, big enough to hold him as he leaned out for the next, and big enough to allow Anderl to take a belaying stance at each step.

The routine was complicated and expensive of energy. Jonathan moved down alone for one rope length, belayed from above by Karl who, in turn, was held by Anderl. Then he cut out an especially broad stance from the protection of which he carefully guided Jean-Paul's body down to him as Karl let the burden slip bit by bit, always fighting its tendency to tear itself from his grip and fly down the face carrying all of them with it. When the canvas bundle reached Jonathan, he secured it as best he could, driving Jean-Paul's ice axe into the crust and using it as a tie-off. Then Karl came down to join him, moving much more quickly down the big steps. The third phase of the pattern was the most dangerous. Anderl had to move down half the distance to them, where he could jam himself into one of the better steps and set his body to protect them through the next repetition of the cycle. Anderl moved essentially without protection, save for the "psychological rope" that regularly slackened between him and Karl. Any slip might knock his fellow climbers out of their step or, even should his line of fall miss them, they would have very little chance of withstanding the shock of a fall twice the length of the rope. Anderl knew his responsibiilty and moved with great care, although he continually called down to them cheerfully, grousing about the pace or the weather or any other trivial matter that came to mind.

Slow though their progress was, for Jonathan, who had to cut each of the steps and who could rest only while the others closed up from above, it was desperately tiring.

Three hours; two hundred and fifty meters.

He panted with exertion; the cold air seared his lungs; his arm was leaden with swinging the axe. And when he stopped to receive Jean-Paul and let the others close up, one torture was exchanged for another. At each rest, the frigid wind attacked him, freezing the perspiration to his body and racking him with convulsions of shivering. He wept with the pain of fatigue and cold, and the tears froze on his stubbled cheeks.

The goal of the cliffs above the Eigerwand Station

was too demoralizingly distant to consider. He concentrated on objectives within human scope: one more swing of the axe, one more step to hack out. Then move on.

Five hours; three hundred twenty-five meters.

Progress diminishing. Must rest.

Jonathan conned his body, lured it into action. One more step then you can rest. It's all right. It's all right. Now, just one more step.

The jagged edges of the ice crust around each deep step cut through his waterproof pants as he leaned out. It cut through his ski pants. It cut into his flesh, but the cold dulled the hurt.

One more step, then you can rest.

Since the first light of dawn Ben had been in the meadow, scanning the face with his telescope. The young climbers who had volunteered for the rescue grouped themselves around him, their faces tight with concern. No one could recall weather this cold so late in the season, and they estimated in low voices what it must be like up on the face.

Ben had prepared himself psychologically to find nothing on the face. In his mind he had rehearsed the calm way he would stroll back to the hotel and send off telegrams to the Alpine Clubs sponsoring the climbers. Then he would wait in his room, perhaps for days, until the weather softened and he could organize a team to recover the bodies. He promised himself one petcock for his emotions. He was going to hit somebody: a reporter, or better yet an Eiger Bird.

He swept the telescope back and forth over the dark crease beside the Flatiron where, just before nightfall, he had seen them making bivouac. Nothing. Their clothing iced over, the climbers blended invisibly into the glazed rock.

On the hotel terrace Eiger Birds were already

queued up at the telescopes, stamping about to warm themselves, and receiving great bowls of steaming coffee from scuttling waiters. The first rumors that there was nothing to be seen on the face had galvanized the tourists. Hungry for sensation and eager to display depths of human sympathy, Eiger Hens told one another how terrible it all was, and how they had had premonitions during the night. One of the twits Anderl had used burst suddenly into tears and ran back into the hotel, refusing to be consoled by her friends. When they took her at her word and left her alone in the empty lobby for twenty full minutes, she found the inner resources to return to the terrace, red-eyed but brave.

The Eiger Cocks nodded to one another significantly and said that they had known it all along. If anyone had had the sense to ask their advice, they would have told them that the weather looked ugly and changeable.

Muffled up securely against the cold, and convoyed by a solicitous entourage, the Greek merchant and his American wife walked through the crowd which grew silent and pressed back to make way for them. Nodding to the left and right, they assumed their roles as major mourners, and everyone said how especially hard this must be on them. Their tent had been kept warm through the night by two portable gas stoves, but still they had to endure the rigors of chill wind as they took turns rising from breakfast to scan the mountain with the telescope that had been reserved for their private use.

Ben stood in the meadow, sipping absently at the tin cup of coffee one of the young climbers had pressed anonymously into his hand. A murmur, then a squealing cheer came from the terrace. Someone had spied a trace of movement.

He dropped the cup on the rimed grass and was at the eyepiece in an instant. There were three of them moving slowly downward. Three—and something else. A bundle. Once they were well out onto the snow, Ben could make out the colors of their windbreakers. Blue (Jonathan) was in the lead. He was moving down very slowly, evidently cutting out wide steps of the kind that cost time and energy. He inched down almost a rope's length before the second man—red (Karl)—began to lower a gray-green something—lump—down to him. Then Karl descended relatively quickly to join Jonathan. The last —yellow (Anderl)—climbed carefully down, stopping halfway and setting a deep belay. There was no one behind Anderl.

The bundle must be Jean-Paul. Injured . . . or dead.

Ben could imagine what the surface must be like after the melting foehn and the hard freeze. A treacherous scab of ice that might pull away from the under snow at any time.

For twenty minutes Ben remained at the telescope, his tightly reined body aching to do something helpful, but uncertain of the intentions of the climbers. Finally, he forced himself to straighten up and stop the torment of guessing and hoping. At their terribly slow pace, it would be hours before he could be certain of how they would try to execute their retreat. He preferred to wait in his room where no one could observe his vicarious fear. They might attempt the long traverse over the classic route. Or they might retrace their line of ascent, forgetting that Karl's chute was iced over now. There was a third possibility, one Ben prayed Jonathan would have vision enough to elect. They might try for the cliffs above the Eigerwand Station Window. It was remotely possible that a man might rope down to the safety of that lateral gallery. No one had ever attempted it, but it seemed the best of a bad lot of alternatives.

"Morning! Are you going to be using your telescope?"

Ben turned to see the confident, boyish smile of the actor beaming at him. The stiffly made-up actress wife stood beside her husband, her sagging throat bound up in a bright silk neckerchief, shivering in the stylish ski clothes that had been specifically designed to make her appear taller and less dumpy.

The actor modulated richly, "The lady would hate to go home without having seen anything, but we really can't have her standing around in line with those other people. I know you understand that."

"You want to use *my* telescope?" Ben asked, unbelieving.

"Tell him we'll pay for it, love," the wife inserted, then she blessed the young climbers with her handsome eyes.

The actor smiled and used his most chocolate voice. "Of course we'll pay for it." He reached out for the instrument, smiling all the while his effective, disarming grin.

Contrary to subsequent news reports, Ben never really hit him.

The actor reacted to the flash of Ben's hand and winced away with surprising celerity. The movement cost him his balance, and he fell on his back on the frozen ground. Instantly, the wife screamed and threw herself over her fallen mate to protect him from further brutality. Ben snatched her up by the hair and bent over them, speaking in rapid, hushed tones. "I'm going up to my room, and I'm leaving this telescope right where it is. If either of you fucking ghouls touches it, your doctor's going to have one hell of a time getting it out."

He walked away to the sound of laughter from the young climbers and a spate of scatological vitriol from the actress that revealed her familiarity with most of the sexual variants.

Ben bore across the terrace with his energetic, hopping stride, not swerving an inch from his course through the milling crowd, and taking a retributive pleasure in each jolting impact that left one of the Eiger Birds dazed and startled in his wake. In the deserted bar he ordered three bottles of beer and a sandwich. While he waited, Anna approached, pressing through the terrace throng to join him. He did not want to talk to her, but the barman was slow.

"Is Jean-Paul all right?" She asked as she neared him.

"No!" He took up the clinking bottles between the ingers of one hand and the sandwich in the other, and he left the bar for his room.

He ate and drank sitting morosely on the edge of his bed. Then he lay down, his fingers locked behind nis head, staring at the ceiling. Then he got up and walked around the room, pausing at the window at each circuit. Then he lay down again. And got up again. Two hours dragged on in this way before he gave up the attempt to rest.

At the telescope in the meadow again, Ben was nearly certain that the climbers were making for the cliffs above the station window. They were near the edge of a rock pitch that separates the ice field from the small shelf of snow above the window. The distance between them and safety could be covered by a thumb at arm's length, but Ben knew there were hours of labor and risk in that stretch. And the sun was slipping down. He had made arrangements for a special train to carry the rescue team up the cogwheel railroad that bore through the heart of the mountain. They would depart when the time was right and be at the window to receive the climbers.

He hunched over his telescope, pouring sympathetic energy up the line of visual contact.

His whole body jolted convulsively when he saw Anderl slip.

There was a grating sound, and Anderl realized the surface was moving beneath him. A vast scab of crusted snow had loosened from the face and was slipping down, slowly at first, and he was in the middle of the doomed island. It was no use digging in; that would be like clinging to a falling boulder. Reacting automatically, he scrambled upward, seeking firm snow. Then he was tumbling sideward. He spread his limbs to stop the deadly roll and plunged his axe into the surface, covering it with his body. And still he slipped down and sideward, a deep furrow above him from the dig of his axe.

Jonathan had been huddled with Karl and Jean-Paul in the deep step he had just cut out. His eyes were fixed on the snow before him, his mind empty, and he shivered convulsively as he had at each *étape*. At Karl's shout, a sudden squirt of adrenalin stopped the shivering instantly and, his eyes glazed with fatigue, he watched with a stupid calm the snowslide come at him.

Karl pushed Jonathan down upon the encased corpse and covered both with his body, locking his fingers around the ice axe that was their belay point. The avalanche roared over them, deafening and suffocating, clutching at them, piling up under them and trying to tug them away from their step.

And with a sudden ringing silence, it was over.

Jonathan clawed his way up past Karl's limp body and scooped the fresh snow out of the step. Then Karl scrambled up, panting, his hands bleeding, skin still stuck to the cold axe. Jean-Paul was half covered with snow, but he was still there.

"I can't move!" The voice was not far from them.

Anderl was spread-eagled on the surface of the snow, his feet not three meters from the edge of the rock cliff. The snowslide had carried him down, then had capriciously veered aside, over the others, and left him face down, his body still covering the axe that had broken his slide. He was unhurt, but each attempt to move caused him to slip downward a few inches. He tried twice, then had the good judgment to remain still.

He was just out of reach, and the freshly uncovered snow was too unstable to be crossed. The rope from Karl to Anderl lay in a hairpin loop up toward his earlier stance and back sharply, but only the two ends of it emerged from the snow that had buried it.

Anderl slipped down several inches, this time without attempting to move.

Jonathan and Karl tugged and whipped the rope, trying desperately to unbury it. They dared not pull with all their strength lest it suddenly come free and precipitate them off the face.

"I feel foolish," Anderl called. And he slipped farther down.

"Shut up!" Jonathan croaked. There was nothing for an ice piton to hold onto, so he hurriedly slapped his axe and Karl's deep into the soft snow, then he laced the slack they had tugged in from Anderl's line back and forth between the two axe handles. "Lie down on that," he ordered, and Karl mutely obeyed.

Jonathan unroped himself and started up Anderl's buried line, alternately clinging to it and ripping it out of the snow. Each time he gained a little slack he lay still on the steeply inclined surface as Karl whipped the loose rope around the axes. It was all-important that there be as little slack as possible when the line came free. Once he reached the point at which the rope began to curve down toward Anderl, he had to move quickly, knowing that he must be very close to Anderl when the line came free. Movement now was most awkward, and the adrenalin that had fed Jonathan's body was burning off, leaving heavy-limbed nausea in its stead. He wrapped his legs around the rope and tugged it loose with one hand, expecting at any moment to come sliding down on top of Anderl as they both snapped to the end of their slack.

It happened when they were only ten feet apart, and fate was in a humorous mood. The line slipped slowly out of the snow and they skidded gently sideward, Jonathan atop Anderl, until they were directly below Karl and the protection of the big step, their feet overhanging the lip of the rock cliff. They scrambled up with little difficulty.

The instant he fell into the almost vertical snow cave, Jonathan collapsed from within. He crouched near Jean-Paul's body, shivering uncontrollably, limp with fatigue.

Anderl was cheerful and talkative, and Karl was obedient. Between them they widened the step, and Anderl set about making tea. The first cup he gave to Jonathan with two small red pills, heart stimulants.

"I certainly felt ridiculous out there. I wanted to laugh, but I knew that the motion would make me slip, so I bit my lip. It was wonderful the way you came out to get me, Jonathan. But in the future I wish you would not use me to ride around on like a sled. I know what you were doing. Showing off for the people down on the terrace. Right?" He babbled on, brewing tea and passing it around like a solicitous Austrian aunt.

The heart stimulant and the tea began to make inroads on Jonathan's fatigue. He practiced controlling his shivering as he stared at the maroon ooze of blood around the rips in his pants. He knew he would not be able to stand another night in open bivouac. They had to move on. His exhalations were whimpers: for him, the last stages of fatigue. He was not certain how long he could continue to wield the ice axe. The muscles of his forearms were knotted and stiff, and his grip was a thing of rusted metal. He

could clamp his fist shut or release it totally, but he
had no control over the middle pressures.

He knew perfectly well that, in this condition, he
should not be leading. But he did not dare turn the
rope over to either of the younger men. Karl had
retreated into automaton depression, and Anderl's
brassy chatter had a disturbing note of hysteria about
it.

They collected themselves to move out. As he took
the metal cup back, Anderl examined Jonathan's
gray-green eyes as though seeing him for the first
time. "You're very good, you know, Jonathan. I've
enjoyed climbing with you."

Jonathan forced a smile. "We'll make it."

Anderl grinned and shook his head. "No, I don't
think so. But we shall continue with style."

They took the cliff quickly, rappelling on a doubled
rope. That which looked most daring to Eiger Birds
below was in reality much less demanding than slog-
ging down through the snowfields. Evening was
setting in, so they did not waste time retrieving
Anderl's rope.

Months later it could still be seen dangling there,
half rotten.

One more snowfield to cross and they would be
perched above the station windows. The brutal cycle
began again. It was colder now with the sun going.
Jonathan set his jaw and turned off his mind. He
cut step after step, the shocks against the axe head
traveling up his throbbing arm directly to the nape
of his neck. Chop. Step down. Lean out. Chop. And
shiver convulsively as the others close up. The minutes were painfully long, the hours beyond the
compass of human time.

Time had been viscous for Ben too; there would
have been consolation in action, but he controlled his
impulse to move until he was sure of their line of

descent. When he had seen the last man rappel from the cliff and move out onto the final relatively narrow snowfield, he stood up from the telescope. "All right," he said quietly, "let's go."

The rescue team trudged to the train depot, making a wide arc around the hotel to avoid arousing the interest of reporters and rubbernecks. However, several newsmen had received reports from the PR-minded railroad authorities and were waiting at the platform. Ben was sick of dealing with them, so he did not argue about taking them along, but he made it most clear what would happen to the first man who got in the way.

Despite the arrangements made earlier, time was wasted convincing the Swiss officials that the costs of the special train would indeed be met by the organizations sponsoring the climb, but at last they were on their way, the young men sitting silently side by side in the car as it jolted and swayed up to plunge into the black of the tunnel. They reached their destination within thirty minutes.

The clatter of climbing gear and the scrape of boots echoed down the artificially lit tunnel as they walked from the Eigerwand Station platform along the slightly down-sloping lateral gallery that gave onto the observation windows. The mood of the group was such that even the reporters gave up asking stupid questions and offered to carry extra coils of rope.

With great economy of communication, the team went to work. The wooden partitions at the end of the gallery were wrenched out with ice axes (while railroad officials reminded Ben that this would have to be paid for) and the first young man stepped out onto the face to plant an anchoring set of pitons. The blast of freezing air they encountered humbled them all. They knew how that cold must be sapping the strength of the men on the face.

Ben would have given anything to lead the group making the rescue, but his experience told him that these young men with all their toes intact and youthful reserves of energy could do the job better than he. Still, he had to fight the desire to make many small corrective suggestions because it seemed to him that they were doing everything just a little bit wrongly.

When the young leader had reconnoitered the face, he crawled back into the gallery. His report was not reassuring. The rock was plastered with a coating of ice half an inch thick—too thin and friable to take an ice piton, but thick enough to cover and hide such viable piton cracks as the rock beneath might have. They would have to peck away at the ice with their axes to bare the rock for each piton. And that would be slow.

But the most disturbing information was that they would not be able to move upward toward the climbers more than ten meters. Above that, the rock face beetled out in an impassable overhang. It looked as though a skillful man could move out as much as a hundred feet to the right or left from the window ledge, but not up.

As the young man gave his report, he slapped his hands against his knees to restore circulation. He had been out on the face for only twenty minutes, but the cold had stiffened and numbed his fingers. With the setting of the sun, the gallery tunnel seemed to grow palpably colder. Low-temperature records would be set that night.

Having established an anchoring base just outside the window, there was nothing to do but wait. The likelihood of the climbers chancing to rope down directly above the window was remote. Even assuming the direct line would go, they had no way to know from above exactly where the window was. Because of the overhang, the first man would be dangling out several yards from the face. They would have to inch over to him, somehow get a line out to him, and pull him in. Once that line was tied down, the retrieval of the others would be easier . . . if they had the strength left to make it down . . . if they had enough rope to pass the overhang . . . if the cold had not stupefied them . . . if their running line did not jam . . . if their anchor point above on the lip of the cliff held.

Every few minutes, one of the young men went out on the face and yodeled up. But there was no answer. Ben paced up and down the gallery, the newsmen sagely pressing against the rock walls to stay out of his way. On one return walk, he cursed and stepped out on the face himself, unroped, holding one of the anchoring pitons with one hand and leaning out with something of his former insouciant daring. "Come on, Jon!" he shouted up. "Get your ass off that hill!"

No answer.

But something else struck Ben as odd. His voice had carried with abnormal crisp resonance. There was no wind on the Eiger. It was strangely still, and the cold was settling down like a silent, malignant presence. He listened to the eerie silence, broken only occasionally by the artillery crack of a random chunk of rock arcing off from somewhere above and exploding against the base far below.

When he scrambled back in through the gallery window, he slid his back down the tunnel wall and sat crouching among the waiting rescuers, hugging his knees until the shivering stopped, and licking his hand where he had left palm skin on the steel piton.

Someone lit a portable stove, and the inevitable, life-giving tea began to be passed around.

The temperature fell as the daylight at the end of the gallery grew dimmer and bluer.

One of the young men at the mouth of the tunnel yodeled, paused, and yodeled again.

And an answering call came from above!

There was a mumble of excitement in the gallery, then a sudden hush as the young climber yodeled again. And again he received a clear response. A newsman glanced at his watch and scribbled in a notepad, as Ben stepped out on the lip of the window with the three men selected to make contact with the climbers. An exchange of calls was made again. In the windless hush, it was impossible to tell how far from above the calls were coming. The yodeler tried again, and Anderl's voice replied with peculiar clarity. "What is this? A contest?"

A young Austrian in the rescue team grinned and nudged the man next to him. That was Anderl Meyer for you! But Ben detected in the sound of Anderl's voice the last desperate gesture of a proud, spent man. He lifted his hand, and those on the ledge with him were silent. There was a scuffling sound above and to the left. Someone was being lowered over the bulge of rock, far to the left, a hundred and twenty feet from safety. From the clink of snap rings, Ben knew he was coming down in an improvised harness. Then the boots appeared, and Jonathan slipped down slowly, twisting under his line, dangling some ten feet away from the face. Twilight was setting in quickly. While Jonathan continued his slow, twirling descent, the three rescuers began to traverse toward him, chipping away at the treacherous coating of ice, and rapping in pitons each time they uncovered a possible crack. Ben stayed on the ledge by the window, directing the activities of the three. There was no room out there for others who were eager to help.

Ben did not call out encouragement to Jonathan. He knew from the slump of the body in the harness that he was at the very rim of endurance after having broken the way for all three since dawn, and he had no breath to waste on talk. Ben prayed that Jonathan would not succumb to that emotional collapse so common to climbers once the end was almost within grasp.

The three young men could not move quickly. The face was almost vertical with only an iced-over ledge three inches wide for toehold. If they had not been experienced at executing tension traverses against the line, they would not have been able to move at all.

Then Jonathan stopped in mid-descent. He looked up, but could not see over the lip of the overhang.

"What's wrong up there?" Ben called.

"Rope . . .!" Anderl's voice had the gritting of teeth in it. ". . . Jammed!"

"Can you handle it?"

"No! Can Jonathan get on the face and give us a little slack?"

"No!"

There was nothing Jonathan could do to help himself. He turned slowly around on the line, six hundred feet of void below him. What he wanted most of all was to sleep.

Although he was far below them, Ben could hear the voices of Karl and Anderl through the still frigid air. He could not make out the words, but they had the sound of an angry conference.

The three young men continued to move out, now halfway to Jonathan and starting to take chances, knocking in fewer pitons to increase their speed.

"All right!" Anderl's voice called down. "I'll do what I can."

"No!' Karl screamed. "Dont move!"

"Just hold me!"

"I can't!" There was a whimper in the sound. "Anderl, I can't!"

Ben saw the snow come first, shooting over the edge of the overhang, a beautiful golden spray in the last beam of the setting sun. Automatically, he pressed back against the face. In a flash, like one alien frame cut into a movie, he saw the two dark figures rush past him, veiled in a mist of falling snow and ice. One of them struck the lip of the window with an ugly splat. And they were gone.

Snow continued to hiss past; then it stopped.

And it was silent on the face.

The three young men were safe, but frozen in their stances by what they had witnessed.

"Keep moving!" Ben barked, and they collected their emotions and obeyed.

The first shock knocked Jonathan over in his harness, and he hung upside down, swinging violently, his mind swirling in an eddy of semiconsciousness. The thing hit him again, and blood gushed from his nose. He wanted to sleep, and he did not want the thing to hit him again. That was the extent of his demands on life. But for a third time they collided. It was a glancing blow, and their ropes intertwined. Instinctively, Jonathan grasped at it and held it to him. It was Jean-Paul, hanging half out of his bedroll shroud, stiff with death and cold. But Jonathan clung to it.

When Anderl and Karl fell, their weight snapped the line between them and the corpse, and it tumbled over the edge and crashed down on Jonathan. It saved him from falling, counterbalancing his weight on the line that connected them and passed through a snap link and piton high above. They swung side by side in the silent cold.

"Sit up!"

Jonathan heard Ben's voice from a distance, soft and unreal.

"Sit up!"

Jonathan did not mind hanging upside down. He was through. He had had it. *Let me sleep. Why sit up.*

"Pull yourself up, goddamit!"

They won't leave me alone unless I do what they want. What does it matter? He tried to haul himself on Jean-Paul's line, but his fingers would not close. They had no feeling. *What does it matter?*

"Jon! For Christ's sake!"

"Leave me alone," he muttered. "Go away." The valley below was dark, and he did not feel cold any longer. He felt nothing at all. He was going to sleep.

No, that isn't sleep. It's something else. All right, try to sit up. Maybe then they'll leave me alone. Can't breathe. Nose stopped up with blood. Sleep.

Jonathan tried again, but his fingers throbbed, fat and useless. He reached high and wound his arm around the rope. He struggled halfway up, but his grip was slipping. Wildly, he kicked at Jean-Paul's body until he got his legs around it and managed to press himself up until his rope hit him in the forehead.

There. Sitting upright. Now leave me alone. Stupid game. Doesn't matter.

"Try to catch this!"

Jonathan squeezed his eyes shut to break the film from them. There were three men out there. Quite close. Tacked on the wall. *What the hell do they want now? Why don't they leave me alone?*

"Catch this and slip it around you!"

"Go away," he mumbled.

Ben's voice roared from a distance. "Put it around you, goddamit!"

Mustn't piss Ben off. He's mean when he's pissed off. Groggily, Jonathan struggled into the noose of the lasso. *Now that's it. Don't ask any more. Let me sleep. Stop squeezing the goddamned breath out of me!*

Jonathan heard the young men call anxiously back to Ben. "We can't pull him in! Not enough slack!"

Good. Leave me alone, then.

"Jon?" Ben's voice was not angry. He was coaxing some child. "Jon, your axe is still around your wrist."

So what?

"Cut the line above you, Jon."

Ben's gone crazy. He must need sleep.

"Cut the line, ol' buddy. It'll only be a short fall. We've got you."

Go ahead, do it. They'll keep at you until you do. He hacked blindly at the nylon line above him. Again and again with mushy strokes that seldom struck the same place twice. Then a thought slipped into his numb mind, and he stopped.

"What did he say?" Ben called to the rescuers.

"He said that Jean-Paul will fall if he cuts the line."

"Jon? Listen to me. It's all right. Jean-Paul's dead."

Dead? Oh, I remember. He's here and he's dead. Where's Anderl? Where's Karl? They're somewhere else, because they're not dead like Jean-Paul. Is that right? I don't understand it. It doesn't matter anyway. What was I doing? Oh, yes. Cut the fucking rope.

He hacked again and again.

And suddenly it snapped. For an instant the two bodies fell together, then Jean-Paul dropped away alone. Jonathan passed out with the pain of his ribs cracking as the lasso jerked tight. And that was merciful, because he did not feel the impact of his collision with the rock.

ZURICH:
August 6

Jonathan lay in bed in his sterile cubicle within the labyrinthine complex of Zurich's ultramodern hospital. He was terribly bored.

". . . Seventeen, eighteen, nineteen down; by one, two, three, four, five . . . "

With patience and application, he discovered the mean number of holes in each square of acoustic tile in the ceiling. Balancing this figure on his memory, he undertook to count the tiles across and down, then to multiply for the total number of tiles. This total he intended to multiply by the number of holes in each tile to arrive at the grand total of holes in his entire ceiling!

He was terribly bored. But his boredom had lasted only a few days. For the greater part of his hospitalization, his attention had been occupied with fear, pain, and gratitude at being alive. Once during the trip down from the Gallery Window he had risen foggily to the surface of consciousness and experienced the Dantesque confusion of light and motion as the train swayed and clattered through a tunnel. Ben's face rippled into focus, and Jonathan complained thickly, "I can't feel anything from the waist down."

Ben mumbled some reassuring sounds and dissolved.

When Jonathan next contacted the world, Dante had given way to Kafka. A brilliant ceiling was flying past above him, and a mechanized voice was paging doctors by name. A starched white upside-down female torso bent over him and shook its dumpling head, and they wheeled him on more quickly. The ceiling stopped its giddy rush, and male voices somewhere nearby spoke with grave rapidity. He wanted to tell them that he could feel nothing from the waist down, but no one seemed interested. They had cut away the laces of his boots and were taking off his pants. A nurse clicked her tongue and said with a mixture of sympathy and eagerness, "That may have to be amputated."

No! The word rushed to Jonathan's mind, but he passed out before he could tell them that he would rather die.

Ultimately, they saved the toe in question, but not before Jonathan had endured days of pain, strapped to his bed under a plastic tent that bathed his exposure-burnt extremities in a pure oxygen atmosphere. The only relief he got from the bone-eroding immobility was a daily sponging down with alcohol and cotton. Even this respite carried its calculated indignities, for the mannish nurse who did the job always handled his genitals like cheap bric-a-brac that had to be dusted under.

His injuries were widespread, but not serious. In addition to the exposure and frostbite, his nose had been broken by the impact of Jean-Paul's corpse; two of his ribs had cracked when the lasso snapped tight; and his collision with the face had resulted in a mild concussion. Of all of these, the nose bothered him longest. Even after the physical restrictions of the oxygen atmosphere tent had been lifted and the ribs had mended sufficiently to make the adhesive tape more troublesome than the pain, the broad bandage across the bridge of his nose continued to torment him. He could not even read, because the visual distraction of the white pad tempted him to stare strabismically.

But boredom was the greatest plague of all. He received no visitors. Ben had not accompanied him to Zurich. He stayed at the hotel, paying off bills and attending to the retrieval and transportation of the dead. Anna remained too, and they made love a few times.

So great was the boredom that Jonathan was driven to finishing the Lautrec article. But when he read it over the next morning, he growled and tossed it into the wastebasket beside his bed.

The climb was over. The Eiger Birds flew south to their padded nests, sated with sensation for the moment. Newsmen waited around for a couple of days, but when it became apparent that Jonathan would survive, they left the city in a noisy flutter, like carrion disturbed at their cadaver.

By the end of the week the climb was no longer news, and soon the attention of the press was siphoned off to the most publicized event of the decade. The United States had deposited two grinning farm boys on the moon, by which achievement the nation aspired to infuse into the community of man a New Humility in the face of cosmic distance and American technology.

The only letter he received was a postcard from Cherry, one side of which was covered with stamps and postal marks that showed it had gone from Long Island to Arizona to Long Island to Kleine Scheidegg to Sicily to Kleine Scheidegg to Zurich. Sicily? The handwriting was oval and large at first, then regularly smaller and more cramped as she had run out of space.

"Wonderful news!!! I have been released from that burden (hem, hem) I carried for so long! Released and released! Fantastic man! Quiet, gentle, calm, witty—and a lover of *me*. Happened like that (imagine snap of fingers)!Met. Married. Mated. And in that order, too! What's this world coming to? You've lost your chance. Cry your eyes out. God, he's wonderful, Jonathan! We're living at my place. Come and see us when you get home. Which reminds me, I drop over to your place once in a while to make sure no one's stolen it. No one has. But some bad news. Mr. Monk quit. Got a steady job working for the National Park Service. How's Arizona? Released, I say! Tell you all about it when you get back.

"All right, how's Switzerland?"

Flip.

Jonathan lay looking up at the ceiling.

The first day after restrictions against visitors were lifted, he had the company of a man from the American Consulate. Short, plump, with long hair crisscrossed over the naked pate, raven eyes blinking behind steel-rimmed glasses, he was of that undramatic type CII recruits specifically because they do not fit the popular image of the spy. So consistently does CII use such men that they have long ago become stereotypes that any foreign agent can pick from a crowd at a glance.

The visitor left a small tape recorder of a new CII design that had the "play" and "erase" heads reversed, both operative in the "play" mode, so that the message was destroyed as it was played. The model was considered a marked improvement over its more secretive predecessor, which erased before playing.

As soon as he was alone, Jonathan opened the lid of the recorder and found an envelope taped to the underside. It was a confirmation from his bank of the deposit of one hundred thousand dollars to his account. Confused, he pushed the "play" button, and Dragon's voice spoke to him, even thinner and more

metallic than usual through the small speaker. He
had only to close his eyes to see the iridescent ivory
face emerging through the gloom, and the pink eyes
under tufted cotton eyebrows.

My dear Hemlock . . . You have by now opened
the envelope and have discovered—with surprise and
pleasure, I hope—that we have decided to pay the
full sum, despite our earlier threat to deduct your
more outrageous extravagances. . . . I consider this
only fair in light of the discomfort and expense your
injuries have cost you. . . . It seems obvious to us that
you were unable to make the sanction target reveal
himself, and so you took the sure, if grimly un-
economical, path of sanctioning all three men. . . .
But you always were extravagant. . . . We assume
the killing of M. Bidet was accomplished during your
first night on the mountain, under cover of dark. . . .
How you contrived to precipitate the other two men
to their deaths is not clear to us, nor does it interest
us particularly. . . . Results concern us more than
methods, as you may recall.

Now, Hemlock, I really ought to rebuke you for
the shopworn condition in which you returned
Clement Pope. . . . You escape my wrath only
because I had all along planned to bestow some
deserved punishment on him. . . . And why not at
your hands? . . . Pope had been assigned to the
Search task of locating your target, and he failed to
identify his man. . . . As an eleventh-hour expedient,
he came up with the notion of setting you up a decoy.
. . . It was certainly second-rate thinking and the
product of a frightened and incompetent man, but
there were no viable alternatives open to us. . . . I
had faith that you would survive the admittedly tense
situation, and, as you see, I was correct. . . . Pope
has been removed from SS and has been assigned to
the less demanding task of writing vice-presidential
addresses. . . . After the beating you gave him, he is

quite useless to us. . . . He suffers from what in a good hunting dog would be called gun-shyness.

It is with great reluctance that I place your file among the "inactives," although I will confide in you that Mrs. Cerberus does not share my melancholy. . . . To tell the truth, I suspect in my heart of hearts that we shall be working together before long. . . . Considering your tastes, this money will last no more than four years, after which—who can say?

Congratulations on your ingenious solution to the crisis, and good luck to you in your Long Island shrine to your self-image.

The end of the tape flap-flap-flapped as the take-up reel spun. Jonathan turned the machine off and set it aside. He shook his head slowly and said to himself helplessly, "Oh, God."

"Let me see now. It was forty-two down by—one, two, three, four . . ."

Ben had difficulty getting in the door. He swore and kicked at it viciously as he stumbled in, a huge cellophane-wrapped basket of fruit in his arms.

"Here!" he said gruffly, and he thrust the crinkling burden toward Jonathan, who had been laughing uncontrollably since first Ben burst in.

"What is this wonderful thing you bring me?" Jonathan asked between racks of laughter.

"I don't know. Fruit and such shit. They hustle them down in the lobby. What's so goddam funny?"

"Nothing." Jonathan was limp with laughing. "It's just about the sweetest thing anyone's ever done for me, Ben."

"Oh, fuck off."

The bed shook with a fresh attack of laughter. While it was true that Ben looked silly grasping a beribboned basket in his ample paw, Jonathan's laughter carried notes of hysteria born of boredom and cabin fever.

Ben set the basket on the floor and slouched down in a bedside chair, his arms folded across his chest, the image of grumpy patience. "I'm real glad I cheer you up like this."

"I'm sorry. Look. All right." He sniffed back the last dry, silent laugh. "I got your postcard. You and Anna?"

Ben waved his hand. "Funny things happen."

Jonathan nodded. "Did you find . . ."

"Yeah, we found them at the base. Anderl's father decided to have him buried in the meadow within sight of the face."

"Good."

"Yes. Good."

And there was nothing more to say. This was the first time Ben had visited Jonathan in the hospital, but Jonathan understood. There is nothing to say to a sick man.

After a pause, Ben asked if they were treating him all right. And Jonathan said yes. And Ben said good.

Ben mentioned the Valparaiso hospital after Aconcagua where their roles had been reversed while Ben recuperated from toe amputations. Jonathan remembered and even managed to dredge up a couple of names and places that they could both nod over energetically, then let slip away.

Ben walked around the room and looked out the window.

"How are the nurses?"

"Starched."

"Have you invited any aboard?"

"No. They're a pretty rank lot."

"That's too bad."

"Yes, it is."

Ben sat down again and flicked lint off his pants for a while. Then he told Jonathan that he intended to catch a plane back to the States that afternoon. "I should be in Arizona by tomorrow morning."

"Give my love to George."

"I'll do that."

Ben sighed, then stretched vigorously, then said something about taking care of yourself, then rose to go. When he picked up the fruit basket and put it near the bed, Jonathan began to laugh afresh. This time Ben stood there taking it. It was better than the long silences. But after a while he began to feel stupid, so he put the basket down and made for the door.

"Oh, Ben?"

"What?"

Jonathan brushed away the tears of laughter. "How did you get mixed up in the Montreal business in the first place?"

. . . Ben had stood for many minutes at the window, his forehead resting against the frame, looking down on the traffic that crawled along the colorless street lined with optimistic saplings. When at last he spoke, his voice was husky and subdued. "You really took me off balance."

"That's the way I had rehearsed it while I lay here counting holes in the ceiling."

"Well, it worked just fine, ol' buddy. How long have you known?"

"Just a couple of days. At first it was just bits and pieces. I kept trying to picture the man with the limp in Montreal, and none of the men on the mountain quite fit. You were the only other person coming for the climb. Then all sorts of things fell into place. Like the coincidence of meeting Mellough at your lodge. And why would George Hotfort stick me with a half dose? Miles wouldn't do that. He already had my answer. And why would George do that for Miles? So far as I know, there was only one thing that really interested her, and Miles couldn't offer that. But she might do something like that for you.

And you might want her to do it because you wanted me to kill Miles quickly, before he could tell me who the man in Montreal was."

Ben nodded fatalistically. "I used to wake up in a sweat, imagining that Mellough had told you out there on the desert, and you were playing cat and mouse with me."

"I never gave Miles a chance to tell me anything."

It was Jonathan who broke the ensuing silence. "How did you get mixed up with him?"

Ben continued to stare out the window at the traffic. Evening was setting in, and the first streetlamps had come on. "You know how I tried to make a go of it with that little climbing school after I couldn't climb anymore. Well, it never did pay for itself. Not many people came, and those who did—like you—were mostly old climbing buddies what I hated to charge. There's not a whole lot of ads in the help-wanted pages for gimpy ex-climbers. I suppose I could have found some nine-to-five sort of thing, but that isn't my style. I guess you know what I mean, considering what you do to make your money."

"I don't do it anymore. I've quit."

Ben looked at him seriously. "That's good, Jon." Then he returned to watching the traffic crawl through the darkening streets. His voice was dry when he spoke. "One day this Miles Mellough shows up out of nowhere and says he has a proposition for me. He'd set me up with a posh resort and a little climbing school on the side, and all I have to do is let his people come and go with no questions. I knew it was some kind of illegal. Matter of fact, Mellough never pretended it wasn't. But I was pretty far in debt and . . ." His voice trailed off.

Jonathan broke through the nicotine-colored cellophane and took an apple out of the basket. "Miles was big-leaguing dope. I imagine your place doubled

347

as a rest camp for his wholesale hustlers and a depot for east-west traffic."

"That's about it. It went on for a couple of years. And all that time I never knew that you and Mellough were enemies. I didn't even know you knew each other."

"All right, that ties you to Mellough. It doesn't explain why you went to Montreal."

"I don't get much kick out of talking about it."

"I think you owe me an explanation. I would never have gone on the mountain if you'd told me before."

Ben snorted. "No! You'd have shot me and collected your pay."

"I don't think so."

"You're telling me you'd have given up your house and paintings and everything?"

Jonathan was silent.

"You're not sure, are you, Jon?"

"No. I'm not sure."

"Honesty isn't enough, Jon. Anyway, for what it's worth, I tried many times to talk you out of going on the hill. I didn't want to die, but I didn't want you to die on the mountain because of me."

Jonathan was not going to be side-tracked. "Tell me how you got to Montreal."

Ben sighed stertorously. "Oh, I did some stupid things, ol' buddy. Things an experienced hand like you would never do. I signed for some shipments— things like that. Then, my . . ." He squeezed his eyes closed and pressed his thumb and forefinger into the sockets. "Then, my daughter got messed up with drugs and . . . Mellough took care of her. He brought her to a place where they cleaned her up. After that, he had me. And I owed him."

Jonathan frowned. "Your daughter, Ben?"

Ben's eyes chilled over. "Yes. Something you didn't know, Doctor. George Hotfort is my little girl."

348

Jonathan remembered making love to her and later slapping her around. He lowered his eyes to the unbitten apple and began polishing it slowly on the sheet. "You're right. It's something I didn't know."

Ben did not choose to linger on the subject of George. "All this time, Mellough knew, of course, that you and I were friends. He was angling for a way to set me up in big trouble so he could swap me in return for your taking him off your list and letting him breathe easy for a change."

"It's his kind of con. He always did things obliquely."

"And this Montreal business gave him the chance to set me up. He told me I had to come along. I had to go with some turd named Kruger while he received a paper or something. I didn't know anyone was going to get killed. Even if I had, I didn't have a whole lot of choice."

"But you didn't have anything to do with the killing, did you?"

"I guess you can't say that. I didn't stop it, did I? I just stood there and watched it happen." His voice was bitter with self-disgust. "And when Kruger started to cut him open, I . . ."

"You threw up."

"Yeah, that's right! I guess I'm not the killer type." He turned back to the window. "Not like you, ol' buddy."

"Spare me that crap. You don't have anything against killing in the abstract. You were perfectly willing to have me kill Mellough for you. It's just that you can't do it yourself."

"I suppose."

Jonathan dropped the apple back into the basket. It had been a gift from Ben. "Tell me. Why did you come up and get me off the face? If I had died with the others, you would have been home free."

Ben smiled and shook his head. "Don't imagine for a minute I didn't consider it, ol' buddy."

"But you're not the killer type?"

"That, and I owed you one for the time you walked me down off the Aconcagua." Ben turned squarely to Jonathan. "What happens now?"

"Nothing."

"You wouldn't bullshit an old buddy, would you?"

"The CII people are satisfied that they have their man. And I don't see any reason to disabuse them. Especially since I've already been paid."

"What about you? I know how you are about friends who let you down."

"I don't have any friends who have let me down."

Ben thought that over. "I see. Tell me, ol' buddy. Do you have any friends at all?"

"Your solicitude is touching, Ben. When do you catch your plane?"

"I've got to get going right now."

"Fine."

Ben paused at the door. "Take care of yourself, ol' buddy."

"Thanks for the fruit."

Jonathan stared at the door for several minutes after it closed behind Ben. He felt hollow inside. For several days he had known that he would never climb again. He had lost his nerve. And Ben was gone. And Jemima was gone. And he was tired of counting holes in the ceiling.

He turned the light off and the blue of late evening filled the room. He closed his eyes and tried to sleep.

What the hell. He didn't need them. He didn't need any of it. When he got back to the States, he was going to sell the goddam church.

But not the paintings!